Tyranny's Bloody Standard

J. D. Davies is the prolific author of historical naval adventures. He is also one of the foremost authorities on the seventeenth-century navy, which brings a high level of historical detail to his fiction, namely his Matthew Quinton series. He has written widely on the subject, most recently *Kings of the Sea: Charles II, James II and the Royal Navy*, and won the Samuel Pepys Award in 2009 with *Pepys's Navy: Ships, Men and Warfare, 1649-1689*.

Also by J. D. Davies

The Matthew Quinton Journals

Gentleman Captain
The Mountain of Gold
The Blast that Tears the Skies
The Lion of Midnight
The Battle of All The Ages
The Rage of Fortune
Death's Bright Angel
The Devil Upon the Wave
Ensign Royal

Jack Stannard of the Navy Royal

Destiny's Tide
Battle's Flood
Armada's Wake

The Philippe Kermorvant Thrillers

Sailor of Liberty
Tyranny's Bloody Standard

J. D. DAVIES

Tyranny's BLOODY STANDARD

CANELO

First published in the United Kingdom in 2023 by

Canelo
Unit 9, 5th Floor
Cargo Works, 1–2 Hatfields
London SE1 9PG
United Kingdom

Print ISBN 978 1 80436 091 0
Ebook ISBN 978 1 80436 090 3

Cover design by Patrick Knowles

Look for more great books at www.canelo.co

Printed and bound in Great Britain by Clays Ltd, Elcograf S.p.A.

1

For Aurelia

Pe far lato vendetta,
Sta sigur, vasta anche ella

From the old Corsican song 'Vocero du Niolo', quoted as the
epigraph to *Colomba*
by Prosper Mérimée (1803–70)

AUTHOR'S NOTE

For two years at the end of the eighteenth century, Great Britain and Corsica had the same king.

To all intents and purposes this was the same relationship as that which then existed between Britain and Ireland, and which existed between England and Scotland from 1603 to 1714. During these two years, the viceroy and effective ruler of the island was a Scot. British troops garrisoned Corsica's fortresses, British warships used its harbours. All of this was despite the fact that Corsica was the homeland of a rising but then little-known young general in the army of the infant French Republic named Napoleon Bonaparte. The brief and now almost entirely forgotten story of the Anglo-Corsican kingdom impacted on the history of Britain in other ways, too. The assault on an obscure but stubborn fortress on the Corsican coast led to its name being adopted for a geographical feature of the British Isles, Martello Towers, many of which survive to this day, while the campaigns on Corsica also contributed a defining physical characteristic to one of Britain's greatest heroes, namely the loss of Horatio Nelson's right eye.

Corsica has always possessed a fiercely independent streak, as well as being a land of many myths and mysteries. For centuries, one manifestation of this was a unique attitude to death and the dead, who were regarded as remaining close by and ever present. It was commonly believed that there were those who could foretell or even trigger death, and that the dead literally came to take the living. Another manifestation of this, which persists to the present day, is the unshakeable conviction of many Corsicans that Christopher Columbus was one of their own, a Genoese citizen in the days when Genoa ruled the island, but not a native of the city of Genoa itself. Another is the deadly tradition of vendetta, of blood feuds passed down for generations or even centuries (a major theme in the story that follows). Unlike many other societies, the Corsicans never accepted the principle of blood money, that is, payment to compensate for the murder of a family member. As a famous Corsican saying put it, 'blood is not for sale'.

Throughout this book, the French, Corsican and Russian characters use the words 'English' and 'British' interchangeably, as French people (and, of course, many other nationalities) often do to this day. Some of the names and words used by characters to describe different nationalities and races reflect the common, and in some cases universal, attitudes of both educated and uneducated people in the Western world in the 1790s.

PROLOGUE

Private Oswald Tebbutt of the second battalion, the Thirty-First (Huntingdonshire) Regiment of Foot, levelled his musket at the dozen or so drunken men rolling their unsteady way down from the direction of the Garrison Church toward his post at the Spur Gate.

'Halt and be recognised!'

The command seemed to have no effect on the party. Seamen, of course, by their dress and gait – what else would they be in Portsmouth? Not Frenchies, for the two men at the head of them, staggering arm in arm toward Tebbutt's position, were singing a bawdy drinking song very loudly in English.

> '...Voice, fiddle, and flute,
> No longer be mute,
> I'll lend you my name and inspire you to boot,
> And, besides I'll instruct you, like me, to intwine
> The Myrtle of Venus with Bacchus's vine!'

There had been a heightened state of alert through the entire garrison for the last two weeks, since a gang of prisoners escaping from one of the hulks up harbour stole a boat from the Camber docks. They did not get past the picket boats out of Fort Blockhouse, but both the civilians of the town and the troops assigned to guard duty felt an acute sense of nervousness.

'Halt and be recognised this moment, or I fire!'

Tebbutt should not have been on his own, but the men who should have been on duty with him, Mills and Corporal Matthews, both considerably senior to him, had decided one man was sufficient at Spur Gate. They were probably still asleep in the barracks, damn them. The February morning was cold, if not quite cold enough for snow, and the relentless drizzle coming off the strong north-westerly wind left Tebbutt soaked, chilled and miserable within a quarter hour of going on duty. There was little shelter and hardly any activity. In truth, Spur Gate was only a postern, opening onto the featureless marsh that formed the southern end of Portsea Island.

So why were these drunken seamen making for a gate that led nowhere?

His second order caused the oncoming men to halt. One of the fellows at the front, the one who was a little better dressed than the others, stopped singing and took a step toward Tebbutt, staring at him as though he was seeing the guard for the first time.

'We're friends, not foes,' said the fellow, slurring his words.

Tebbutt thought he sounded American. Even in Hunting-donshire whence the sentry hailed, there were several loyalist families who had been forced out of their homeland by the colonial rebellion, so even on the isolated farm where Tebbutt had grown up they knew what Americans sounded like. This one was of a little above medium height, sturdily built, with the weather-beaten look of a man who had been at sea for most of his life.

'State your name and business!' cried Tebbutt. Why in the name of God would a well-spoken Yank be approaching the Spur Gate with a gaggle of drunken rogues at his back? A gaggle that was still inching toward Oswald Tebbutt, despite his challenge and his gun?

'Name and business. Well, my fine English friend, my brave soldier of the king, I could tell you that. But these boys behind me, they've been away from their homes a long time and they're damn keen to put that right.'

What sort of answer was that? Where was Matthews? He would have known how to deal with this.

One of the men behind the American staggered and fell to the ground, much to the amusement of his companions. Tebbutt's attention switched momentarily to the fallen man, but a moment was all it took. The American sprang forward, grabbed the musket with his left hand and punched Tebbutt hard in the gut with his right. As the sentry doubled up, several pairs of hands grabbed hold of him. He saw rope and a cloth gag being produced.

Just before the rope was knotted tight around his wrists and the gag tightened over his mouth, the man who was not American smiled.

'*Je suis désolé, soldat*,' he said. *Sorry, soldier.*

–

In the same moment, one hundred and thirty miles away by the English reckoning, a man walked toward the guillotine that would shortly take his head from his shoulders.

Somehow, he had expected more people to be present to witness his execution. But this was Rouen, far from his home, far from Paris where he had spent the last few months in prison. He was unknown here, and if his name had ever meant anything to anybody in these parts it was probably long forgotten now. Besides, it was a bitter winter's day with snow on the ground. A brutal north-west wind brought fresh falls sweeping through the narrow streets, swirling around the towering facade of the great structure once known as the cathedral. Of choice, he would not have been out in such a day as this. He would have been in his favourite chair in front of the fire in the chateau, swigging *lambig* with his hunting dogs at his feet.

One of the National Guardsmen who formed the escort prodded him with the butt of his musket. Alexandre turned and scowled at the man. It was difficult to keep his footing and make progress toward his fate. But he walked as determinedly as he could, for he was set on dying well. For sure, he had not lived well these last few years. Most of those convicted by the revolutionary justice of the Republic went to the guillotine a day or two after their sentence was handed down, but disputes over jurisdictions and procedure had seen him taken from Brittany to Paris, left to languish for months in a pestilential, overcrowded cell, then ordered to be taken back to Brittany for execution. For reasons that were unclear to him, the journey was abruptly terminated in Rouen, and it was here that he would face the blade that had already taken away the lives of many men and women far more distinguished than Alexandre Kermorvant.

Onward, up the steps and onto the scaffold.

He had regrets, but now they would die with him, unsaid for eternity. He regretted drunkenly assenting to ride out on the hunt that ended with his near-fatal goring and emasculation by a boar. He regretted relying so much on *lambig* to make his long recovery and his new state as a eunuch bearable. He regretted how the fiery brandy had made him treat *her*. But it was now many weeks since he had drunk anything other than foul prison water. *Lambig*'s hold on him had long been released, and his tormented thoughts were now clearer than they had been for many years.

A face glimpsed as he wiped snow from his eyes…

She was here.

Despite his treatment of her, she had remained loyal to the end. She had come to be close to him when he died.

The ruffians assisting the executioner pushed him toward the bascule, but he continued to stare at her. Was she a ghost, appearing and disappearing at will? It was surely only the snow obscuring her momentarily. He called out, shouted his defiant last words to her and the few others, all strangers, who had gathered to witness his death. It was impossible to know whether she or any of the others had heard him over the fierce and unremitting snowstorm.

He was tied down and the bascule was pushed forward into position beneath the blade.

He loved her, despite all he had done to her. All might still be well if only *he*, Alexandre's damnable legitimate half-brother, had not suddenly come to France and the chateau. If only this man who shunned the title of Vicomte de Saint-Victor that Alexandre had craved all his life had never been born.

Did she love the half-brother, not him, Alexandre, her husband? Had she come to see him die because she still had a shred of love for him, or to witness for certain that she was newly made a widow, free to whore with *him*? Free to become his vicomtesse—

Alexandre heard the blade fall, then all his regrets and suspicions were carried away upon the wind and the snow.

Ten minutes after Alexandre's head bloodied the snow settling in the basket placed before the Rouen guillotine, Hervé Boullart hauled on an oar and thanked God for the strange captain who sat at the helm of the stolen boat, conning them out into the choppy waters of the anchorage the English called the Solent. Of course, the man at the helm was not actually Hervé's captain. That had been Duval of *Magicienne*, but Duval was killed by canister shot in the losing battle against HMS *Astute* on what the English still called New Year's Day, 1794, or as the new French republican calendar named it, 12 Nivôse II. Like the rest of *Magicienne*'s crew, Boullart found himself on the prison hulk *Agincourt* in Portsmouth harbour, and that was where he encountered the captain. His own ship, *Zephyr*, had been taken a few weeks earlier, and the captain was, it seemed, one of very few imprisoned French officers who had not given their parole and been sent to comfortable billets in obscure English country towns. The captain immediately gained the respect of the Magiciennes for that alone, but he went out of his way to cultivate them, giving an encouraging word here, ensuring a fair distribution of rations there.

The weeks after that had passed in a blur.

It was the captain's ship's carpenter who discovered the section of rotten wood adjacent to one of the gunports in the larboard quarter of the hulk and began the task of chipping and sawing through it using stolen tools, the prisoners adopting various stratagems to prevent the noise coming to the attention of the guards. Never had imprisoned Frenchmen sung so lustily, the movements of the makeshift saws and adzes matching the rhythm of each song, or played deck games so loudly. And all the time the oakum was slowly prised away from the timbers, the timber chippings spirited away into a thousand hiding places, until that glorious day when one of the carpenter's mates broke through and the watery light of an English winter dawn breaking could be glimpsed through the opening.

It was the captain who assiduously gathered intelligence from all the small boats that regularly crowded around the hulks, their crews trying to sell wares of various sorts to the prisoners. Amid all the hostile English faces were occasional neutrals whose ships had come into the great anchorage beyond the narrow mouth of the harbour. From them it was possible to get a sense of what was happening in France and in the great war France was fighting, but such tantalising fragments of intelligence only strengthened the resolve of every man on the hulk, the captain above all, to escape the squalor and degradation of *Agincourt* and return to France.

It was the captain who learned the identity of one particular ship that had come into the Solent for repairs after being damaged by a violent winter storm in the Soundings of La Manche.

It was the captain who knew Portsmouth, who had sailed there before, when he was younger.

It was the captain who formed the plan and who had been quick-witted enough to modify it when the poor fools trying to escape from the hulk *Bulwark*, recently moored astern of *Agincourt* to accommodate the ever-growing number of French prisoners from ships defeated by the English, stole a boat, tried to sail right through the only channel in or out of Portsmouth harbour, and died under a volley of fire from muskets and swivel guns. It was the middle of the night, so the men of *Agincourt* were locked below decks, but Hervé was quartered for'ard, heard the gunfire plainly and knew what it signified.

Above all, it was the captain who discovered that Boullart, a mere *matelot* third class from Dieppe, spoke a little English thanks to a merchant father who had been much involved in the cross-Channel trades, or to be more precise, smuggling. So the captain, who spoke English like a native, and Boullart played the part of two drunken English sailors, swigging and singing their way from the spit of land at the mouth of the harbour, where they landed after escaping the *Agincourt* in the middle of the night, past the guards at the first gate through the ramparts, then all through the sleeping town of Portsmouth until they approached the small postern gate just after dawn. Beyond it, the captain said, was a marsh and a beach where fishing boats would be hauled up. All they had to do was reach the beach before the alarm was raised properly in the town and dockyard, then sail or more likely row out to the distant hull in the Solent.

It all seemed too good to be true, too reliant on outrageous luck. If one of the men who had drawn a losing lot to be part of the escape party had been disgruntled enough to betray the attempt to the enemy... if the weather had been too bad on the moonless night chosen for the escape... if one of them had fallen from the strake along the ship's side or stern mooring cable securing *Agincourt* as they inched their way to freedom... if the longboat customarily moored to the buoy securing the stern cable had not been there... if the English had taken one of their occasional random midnight musters and thus discovered the escape from *Agincourt* sooner... if one of the drunken revellers ashore had been suspicious enough of their landing to raise the alarm... if the guards on what the captain said was called King James's Gate, which opened into the town of Portsmouth itself, had been more alert... if those guards had not been as inclined as they were to assume that any party of apparently drunken men coming their way at that time of night could only have spilled out of one of the many taverns and stews on the seemingly lawless spit of land that reached out into the harbour... if there had been more than one guard on the postern leading out of the other side of the town walls...

But somehow their luck had held.

Hervé Boullart knew as well as any man alive that luck could change, though. The morning muster would have been taken on *Agincourt* by now, and the alarm would surely have been raised behind the vast ramparts of Portsmouth. Boullart's chest felt tight from anxiety as well as exertion, and he could see the fretful looks on his crewmates' faces. Every man on the boat had their eyes peeled for any sight of a pursuit. From the helm, the captain scanned the anchorage methodically, looking not just at the beach and shore astern of them, the sight that the rowers like Boullart could see, but also at the ominous shapes that lay throughout the broad waterway before them. Intermingled with two score or more of merchant hulls were a dozen men-of-war in the familiar colour scheme of King George's Royal Navy, mainly frigates, but one that looked to be an Eighty, another a Seventy-Four. Perhaps one of them, with particularly alert lookouts and especially suspicious officers of the watch, was already preparing to issue a challenge or launch a pinnace to intercept them.

The boys from *Le Zephyr* said they were not surprised by their captain's fortune. He came from the old Breton lands of King Arthur and Merlin the sorcerer, they said. He had grown up in America and learned the ways of the Indians there. He had served in the navy of the legendary Empress Catherine of Russia. He had fought the Turks, and the Swedes, and the English. But most of all, he was said to be the son of Verité,

8

the famous writer who had been exiled from France for the viciousness of his attacks on the government and person of King Louis XV. Hervé's father admired the works of Verité, even though he did not agree with all the man's opinions. Still, being the son of a man who developed some of the ideas that inspired the revolution and the Republic surely explained why for all the peculiarity of his background the captain had gained a commission in the Marine Nationale. Otherwise, desperate as France was for good officers after all the resignations and denunciations and guillotinings, such a strange bird as the captain would surely never have been let near a man-of-war flying the new *Tricolore*.

The stolen boat turned in to the teeth of the flooding tide and the strong wind. Boullart's arms hurt, and he could see that his crewmates were beginning to struggle. But there was still no sign of a pursuit. A couple of broad-hulled, lumbering tenders were coming out of the harbour mouth, but no fast schooners or anything else that might signify the enemy had spotted them and was giving chase. Instead, they were closing on their target, a black-hulled, slovenly looking merchantman flying a torn and tattered version of the flag that was still relatively unfamiliar on the world's oceans: the red stripes and white stars on blue ground of the infant United States of America.

The captain gave the order to ship oars, then turned the boat deftly into the leeward quarter of a ship whose name at the stern proclaimed her to be the *General Gates*.

Willing hands helped the captain, Hervé and the rest of the men up onto the deck of the American vessel, a neutral in the great war between revolutionary France on the one side and Britain, together with most of the great kingdoms of Europe, on the other. The captain of the merchantman lounged against the binnacle, seemingly taking more interest in the state of his fingernails than in the escaping Frenchmen who sought sanctuary aboard his ship. He was nearly bald but also unshaven and fulsomely bearded, his appearance reminiscent of one of the prophets in the once-ubiquitous book found in the now closed churches.

Hervé Boullart was the only man from the boat who understood the exchange in English that followed.

Without looking up, the merchant skipper said, 'You took your damn time, Phil.'

The captain shrugged.

'Didn't think you'd wait, Jerry.'

'Damn near didn't. If my da knew I'd wasted days – weeks – pretending to be making repairs in this goddamn hole when I could have been earning him money... waiting for you to get your French ass out of Portsmouth harbour... You owe me, Phil. You owe me *again*.'

'Just get us safe to France, Jerry, then you can name your price. *Again*.'

The man called Jerry considered the matter.

'I've grown partial to that Whore Brian wine you Frenchies make. You can get me enough of that for two or three voyages?'

'Done. You're an easy man to please, Jerry. So now, Captain Gask, d'you reckon the wind stands fair?'

Jerry Gask studied the wind in his flags and rigging, looked out at the movement of the waves and the set of the other ships in the anchorage, then nodded his large, ponderous head.

'Reckon it does, Captain Kermorvant. Reckon it does.'

PART ONE

CHAPTER ONE

The British fleet was less than two leagues astern and closing.

Philippe studied the distant sails, spread like the wings of malevolent albatrosses. The winds were very light so that even with studdingsails set, the progress of both fleets was painfully slow. But there was no doubt that little by little the enemy ships were gaining as both fleets edged north-west. Through his telescope he could clearly make out the flagship at the heart of the British fleet, a huge Union standard hanging nearly limp from her maintop. That would be HMS *Victory*, which meant it was Admiral Lord Hood, the commander-in-chief of the fleet Britain had sent to the Mediterranean. Shamefully, in a sea that France had always regarded as its lake, that fleet was far larger than France's own, the fleet in which Philippe now served, and Hood was pursuing Admiral Martin's ships with a view to utterly destroying them. The enemy had five ships of around one hundred guns apiece, *Victory* being the most illustrious of them, the equally powerful vice-admiral's flagship, *Britannia*, sailing on her port beam like some terrible mirror image. The French had only one ship of the same rank, the flagship *Sans-Culotte*, formerly named *Dauphin Royal* in the time of the Bourbon tyrants. She carried far more guns than any individual Englishman – one hundred and twenty, no less – but on her own she stood no chance against King George's massed and menacing leviathans. Martin had in company with him only two Eighties, four Seventy-Fours and four frigates, one of which was Philippe's own. Hood had a total of two Hundreds, three Ninety-Eights, eight Seventy-Fours and four frigates. His superiority was so vast that he had been able to leave several other large men-of-war off Corsica, supporting the operations there, while he sailed in pursuit of the French.

Then again, it was a miracle that France had a Mediterranean fleet at sea at all. Six months earlier, around the time that Philippe Kermorvant was plotting his escape from Portsmouth, several of the ships under Martin's command had been lying beneath the waters of Toulon harbour, deliberately sunk by the British and their French royalist allies as they evacuated the port following a lengthy and successful siege by the republican army. They were the fortunate ones, for many of the other ships were burned by the enemy. It took a superhuman effort to raise the salvageable ships and repair them so that now, in June 1794, and reinforced by other ships sent from the Atlantic, the fleet was able to venture out toward Corsica, hoping to perform a miracle and prevent Calvi, the last remaining French republican stronghold on the island, from falling to the enemy. It was a token and utterly futile gesture. It was as though the enemy knew they were coming, their fleet holding exactly the right station to intercept them as they approached Corsica. At the first sight of Lord Hood's sails, the entire French fleet, including Philippe's command, had turned tail and was running for its own coast, pursued by the overwhelming strength of the British Royal Navy. Philippe could not blame his admiral. If the enemy caught Pierre Martin's fleet, it would be a massacre.

Philippe's command was named *Le Torrington*. Of course, it was not a French name and not, originally, a French ship. Named after a British admiral who had, naturally, fought against France in the days of the old Marine Royale, it had been launched nearly twenty years earlier. The French did not believe in renaming prizes they captured and then brought into their navy, leading to such oddities as one of their finest Seventy-Fours being named *Le Northumberland*. As for Philippe's command, she was somewhat broader in the beam, rather deeper in the water, and had a more commodious hold than most French frigates, while the captain's cabin, it seemed to Philippe, was so spacious it would not have been out of place at Versailles. She was powerfully armed with thirty-eight guns, most of them eighteen-pounders. She had a good crew too, many of them committed patriots who had come down to Toulon to resurrect the sunken fleet and take revenge on the enemies who thought to lord it over republican France. Many were experienced, battle-hardened *gabiers* or topmen who had served on privateers or else in the old Marine Royale, the helmsmen and their mates forming a particularly impressive cohort. They largely obeyed orders, a marked contrast to many of the crew aboard his last command, *Le Zephyr*, in the previous year. Then, during the white-hot frenzy of the Terror, sailors had brazenly defied their officers and disobeyed any commands they did not like, namely the great majority of them. Strangely, those who proved most inclined to do so were also those who cheered loudest and longest for *la République*, *la patrie*, and *liberté*, *égalité*, *fraternité*. The new rulers of France from Citizen Robespierre downward finally realised that such unre-volutionary notions as authority and hierarchy had existed for a reason, that in this one respect, at least, the Bourbon tyrants and their lickspittles might have known what they were talking about. A strict new disciplinary code was introduced, a few recalcitrants were flogged or in some cases even hanged as examples, and the Marine Nationale began to return to some semblance of a proper fighting force.

For all that, though, *Le Torrington* was a relatively old ship, built in the early years of the American war. This and the time her hull had spent underwater, followed by the haste with which she had been repaired and fitted for sea, meant that she was intolerably slow. Philippe's previous command, *Le Zephyr*, had been new, sleek and fast, but every time Philippe exhorted his crew with assurances that they served on the best frigate in the Marine Nationale the lie nearly caught in his throat. *Le Torrington* was a slug, an ancient, ungainly slug, and the freshest *matelots d'eau douce*, the so-called freshwater sailors, knew it. Even ignorant lubbers in Toulon could see it. Her nickname in the taverns of the port was *La Tortue Anglaise* – the English Tortoise.

Most of Philippe's *équipage*, his principal officers, stood close to him, albeit on the leeward side to allow him the captain's privileged position to windward. Not that windward and leeward mattered much in such a feeble breeze, with the sea gently lapping against the barely moving hulls. Not for the first time Philippe wondered what these men would be like if the English caught them and they had to give battle. Antoine Malhuret, the first lieutenant, was a gangling youth who looked barely old enough to shave, let alone occupy such a senior position on a warship, but he had been one of the last graduates from the naval college at Vannes before the revolutionary government decreed its closure on the grounds that the creation of a warrior elite was unegalitarian and potentially counter-revolutionary. Like so many young officers in the armed forces of the French Republic, Malhuret owed his advancement to fortunate connections, in his case an uncle who was an eminent judge, but he was efficient and, as far as Philippe could gauge, perfectly competent. Malhuret, who hailed from an obscure town in Burgundy, was an enthusiastic fellow, too wedded to the regulations for Philippe's liking, but he seemed well liked by the men. What he would be like if he had to wield a cutlass in a boarding battle was another matter. By contrast, the next most senior lieutenant, Enseigne de Vaisseau Marcel Grignon, short, broad and grey-haired despite being barely thirty, undoubtedly knew how to fight and hated the English with every breath in his body, blaming them for the death of his brother at the siege of Dunkirk. He came from an aristocratic family in Languedoc but had somehow survived the Terror of the last few months, despite spending a few weeks in gaol with the threat of the guillotine hanging over him. Philippe, who had also been imprisoned by the Republic and experienced the tingling in a neck that might leave its shoulders at any time, had made several attempts to engage Grignon in friendly conversation, but the lieutenant was a surly fellow who seemed to walk around with a black cloud of bitterness above his head. Like so many of his class, though – like Philippe himself, in fact – Grignon was born to command. If only the same had been true of the third lieutenant, Florent Bertin, a former skipper from the merchant service. Philippe had a lieutenant from such a background in his previous command, but Juan Ugarte was a lion of a man, or perhaps more accurately a raging elephant. Bertin, who hailed from Bordeaux and had greasy, unkempt black hair, was a mouse, diffident in his manner, uncomfortable in his uniform and his duty, lax and uncertain in his commands, despised by the men. Even before they first sailed from Toulon, Philippe realised that it was best if he was on deck as often as possible during Bertin's turns as officer of the watch.

It was Grignon who articulated the thought Philippe had barely formed.

'That fellow's marking us. The most weatherly frigate, sir. A Twenty-Eight, I'd say.'

Philippe switched his focus from HMS *Victory* to the ship in question.

'He's a brave captain if he is,' said Philippe. 'A Twenty-Eight venturing to engage a Thirty-Eight. Good odds for us, I'd say.'

Malhuret and Bertin smiled, but Grignon's face remained as implacable as a gravestone. No matter. Even if the enemy frigate really was intent on engaging *Le Torrington*, it would be hours at least before even their respective chase guns could exchange fire, let alone their broadsides. Philippe maintained a confident demeanour, but he knew, as did his officers, that any victory by *Le Torrington* over her distant adversary would be Pyrrhic. The British superiority in numbers was so overwhelming that they could to all intents and purposes assign two of their ships of the line to every one of those in the French fleet. That being so, whatever the two frigates did to each other would be of no importance whatsoever.

'Flagship's signalling, sir,' said Grignon. Signal lieutenant was one of his roles, and he was rapidly thumbing through the signal book assisted by Rampillon, the young *aspirant* assigned to the duty. But Philippe could already interpret Admiral Martin's order.

'We're making for Gourjean Bay,' he said.

'Why, Citizen Captain?' said the puzzled Bertin.

For the benefit of Bertin and the three *aspirants* (or, as the English called the rank, midshipmen), Rampillon, de la Porte and Vidos, Philippe gestured toward the enemy fleet.

'Whatever the strength of the wind, the English can cut us off from Toulon. But if we can get into Gourjean, we should be safe and can sit it out until they withdraw. Then, citizens, once we add the ships still under repair at Toulon and have the numbers to match theirs, we can go in search of a victory to surpass Villaret's, eh?'

Two of the three *aspirants* grinned. News had come to the fleet only a couple of days earlier of the great battle fought on 13 Prairial, or as the British called it, the first of June. Admiral Villaret de' Joyeuse and the Brest fleet, in which Philippe had served during the previous year, had ventured out to escort home a vast grain convoy from the neutral United States, its cargoes essential to stave off potential famine in France. Although Villaret lost seven ships, the fleet fought well, the convoy made it to safe harbours and the proud, confident English were denied the complete victory they always arrogantly anticipated when they fought the French.

The exception to the good humour was Rampillon, a bright young man and a fellow Breton, who asked the unspoken question that was also in Philippe's mind.

'But what if they don't withdraw, Citizen Captain?'

Philippe smiled.

'If they don't withdraw, *aspirant*, then we can all sit out the rest of the war in Cannes. I'm told it's pleasant there at this time of year.'

The *aspirants* laughed dutifully, Malhuret smiled, Bertin looked puzzled, and Grignon scowled at such levity from his captain.

CHAPTER TWO

A little more than four months had passed since Philippe's escape from the *Agincourt* hulk and Portsmouth. Jerry Gask had been true to his word, taking the escapees across to France and landing them at Le Havre. The Gasks were the family of Philippe's mother's first husband, an avaricious shipowner who had made enough money to buy a fine plantation on the Virginia tidewater. Philippe served on the family's ships after the American war ended and before he went to Russia with John Paul Jones. Jerry Gask had been like a cousin, unimpressed by Philippe's title, education and Frenchness. On a frozen January morning a boat had drawn up alongside the *Agincourt* prison hulk, its rough-and-ready crew shouting up to the prisoners that they were selling the best Virginia tobacco, special discount for the men who had helped the United States to win their independence, and so forth.

'What's your ship?' shouted Philippe in American-accented English that startled the men in the boat.

'*General Gates* out of Norfolk, Virginia, Captain Jeremiah Gask! Who asks?'

A hastily written letter smuggled down to the boat and then taken out to the ship at anchor in the Solent – this was the origin of the escape plan. Philippe never believed it would work. The old hands on the *Agincourt* swore that nobody had ever escaped from the prison hulks, and the fate of the men held on *Bulwark* seemed to bear them out. But Philippe persevered. He had lost the Catholic faith of his ancestors when he was a child, but it was surely impossible to ignore so manifest a miracle as Jerry Gask, of all men, fetching up in the Solent in a neutral ship.

Prisoners who successfully escaped from England were greeted as heroes in France. After going ashore from the *General Gates* Philippe and his men were dined by the mayor and leading citizens of Le Havre, who provided them all with the funds for new clothes and transport to wherever they wished to go within the Republic. Philippe considered going west, back to Brittany and his ancestral estate, to Leonore, but swiftly realised there was only one destination he could contemplate. For the first time in his life, he went to Paris. He took a small, damp room in a tenement on the Rive Gauche, then for two days did nothing but walk around in a daze, staring up at the towering buildings, visiting Notre Dame and the Louvre, drinking in the sights, smells and sounds of the enormous city like the most gauche country peasant. He went to taverns and listened to the gossip, to the frightened, whispered conversations about Robespierre and the Committee of Public Safety, to the rumours about what the enemy powers ranged against the French Republic might or might not be planning to do next. He watched a few guillotinings, the crowds at which were small and seemingly jaded. He wrote letters, including one to the Chateau de Brechelean, his family home far in the west of Brittany. He did not even know whether his older half-brother, Alexandre, who had attempted to denounce him as a traitor the year before only to be denounced in turn by his own wife, Leonore, and sentenced to death by a revolutionary tribunal, still lived or whether he had finally perished upon the guillotine. He did not really expect a reply and needed to concentrate on the most important task before him, so he went out, bought a new if modest suit, and went to the Ministry of the Marine to petition for a new command in the Marine Nationale.

It took weeks of daily attendance, weeks full of boredom and disappointment. Men younger and much less experienced than him were going into the offices of the Minister of Marine and his subordinates and coming out with the command of Seventy-Fours. It was as though his escape from Portsmouth had been in vain. In his bleaker moments, he judged that the whole of the last year of his life was a mistake. He could have stayed in comfortable employment in Russia, a respected captain in the navy of the Empress Catherine. But Russia held too many memories of Tasha and Ivan, his butchered wife and son. Russia still contained their murderer, Count Bulgakov, who had his freedom. Philippe could no longer bear to breathe the same air or stand on the same soil as the man who snuffed out the two lives most precious to him. So he came to France, the land that had nurtured his father and generations of Kermorvants before him, although the new and militant French Republic was a desperately dangerous place for any man with an aristocratic title and a landed estate. Somehow Philippe had escaped the guillotine and gained a command, only to lose it in battle against a larger British man-of-war. He had been through all that and escaped from captivity, but for what?

Then the letters came from Brittany.

There were two. The post-boy brought them to Philippe's rooms just as he was about to set out for another day of trying vainly to obtain an interview with the Minister of Marine or some other dignitary with influence. He paid the postage due, then went back indoors. Two letters, but he recognised the handwriting on one of them. He took a knife, broke open the wax seal, and began to read her words.

> Monsieur le Vicomte, Captain, Philippe,
>   I acknowledge receipt of your letter from Paris, informing me of your escape from England and the address of your lodgings. I rejoice that you are safe and once again breathe the air of France. I wish you well in

your endeavours to procure a new command. I understand when you say that regardless of their outcome, these efforts will prevent your return to Brittany and the chateau for the foreseeable future.

Duty demands that I should give you, the owner of the estate, an account of its condition. I am glad to say that we have thus far avoided the depredations of both sides in the continuing campaign of the Chouans against the Republic. The rebels are in arms in the Pays de Saint-Brieuc but there is little fighting in any of the lands adjoining Finisterre. We had an alarm when a column of Blue troops came to Brechelean and demanded to be billeted. Their captain was an impertinent fellow who seemed intent on conscripting the few remaining men of the estate for the service of the Republic, especially Roman and Olivier, the two boys that you took up from the streets of Brest and who are fast becoming sturdy men and good workers. (It transpires that Olivier can read and write conspicuously well, apparently a consequence of the efforts of an enlightened priest at the orphanage he once attended. I employ him as my clerk, and have entrusted him with sending you summaries of the estate accounts. You should receive his letter in the same post as this.)

To return to the Blue captain; I gave him short shrift, even though he seemed unimpressed to learn that the chateau's owner is the son of the renowned Verité and a heroic sea-captain captured and imprisoned in the service of the Republic. He reacted rather differently to the intelligence that I am a cousin of General Carnot, who remains a member of the Committee of Public Safety and talks daily with Citizen Robespierre. These names had a strangely sobering effect on the captain. He and his men moved on without spending so much as one night upon your land or purloining one loaf from your kitchen.

You ask about the fate of your brother, my husband. In truth, sir, it is a matter that still pains me greatly, and I trust you will forgive me if I do not elaborate. The delay in deciding his fate was a disgrace to all justice. He rotted in prison in Paris for months before it was decided that he should not have been brought there in the first place. I was informed that there was some sort of mistake in the judgement brought against him as well as serious clerical errors in the papers relating to his case, which then seem to have been lost for many weeks. In the end it was decided that he should be returned to Brittany for the execution of the sentence, but he got no further than Rouen before alarms of Chouan ambushes further west led to an arbitrary decision to execute him there. I have an uncle in Rouen who got word to me in time for me to go there and witness his beheading. I will not dwell on the matter, sir, other than to say that for all the evil he tried to inflict on you and the other kinds of evil he had inflicted on me, your brother of the half-blood died well.

With that, sir, my duty to you is done for now. I hope that you prosper and that your endeavours to obtain a new command are successful. Rest assured that I do my womanly best to manage your lands in a way that meets your approval.

I am, Captain Kermorvant, your most humble sister and servant in all things,
    Leonore Kermorvant
    Widow

There it was. That was all. The letter that he had dreamed of every waking moment on the English prison hulk and during his time back in France. Yet there was not a featherweight of feeling in it, not the slightest hint of any emotion other than duty. *Duty demands. Your most humble sister and servant in all things, Leonore Kermorvant, widow. Vous* rather than *tu.* To be fair, his letter to her had been even shorter and only a little less formal, but he had written *tu* without a thought.

Philippe sat on the edge of his uncomfortable bed and sighed. The idea that he could have a future with Leonore, the wife of a half-brother who had tried to send him to the guillotine and conspired against the Republic, was exposed for the fantasy it had always been.

He did not know how many minutes passed, but he finally took up and opened the second letter.

It was a revelation.

He had found the writer, a scrawny boy called Olivier, and his friend, Roman, begging on the streets of Brest. He saw a spark in them and took them into the service of the Chateau de Brechelean. He did not even know their surnames, and he certainly did not know that Olivier at least could read and write. But before he left to command the frigate *Le Zephyr* he ordered the two youths to watch over to Leonore, and to send him intelligence of her and the estate when they could. He should have paused to wonder how they could possibly do that if they could not read or write, but the letter in his hand astonished him, and not only for the proof it provided of the literacy of its writer.

> *Citizen Captain,*
>
> *Your sister-in-law, my mistress, Citizeness Kermor-vant, has instructed me to send you summary accounts for the estate. I enclose these and trust you will find them in good order. I am sure I do not need to give as educated and enlightened a gentleman as yourself a commentary upon them, as you will know better than I what the sums presented there mean. Instead, and if I may crave your forgiveness for the presumption, I will give you an account of the execution of her late husband, your brother,*
>
> *Citizen Alexandre Kermorvant.*

Philippe boggled at the letter, his mouth agape. He knew Olivier possessed a rough intelligence that had kept him and his friend alive and safe on the streets of Brest for several years, but he had never imagined the lively young thieving beggar to be a wordsmith. His kind usually struggled even to form the cross required to mark documents.

> *I accompanied Citizeness Kermorvant to Rouen in the first week of February. I procured rooms in a lodging house near the sometime cathedral, now a Temple of Reason. The citizeness spent two whole days trying to gain access to her husband, entirely without avail. I trust you will forgive me, Citizen Captain, but not even my best efforts to bribe the appropriate city officials on her behalf had any success. Throughout those days, I witnessed how troubled Madame Kermorvant was. When lost in his cups, Citizen Penhouet – the ancient steward of the Chateau de Brechelean, barely able to fulfil the demands of the office as Philippe recalled – told Roman and I of her treatment by her husband and of how at the last she had denounced him as a traitor to the Republic, yet she seemed racked with remorse over what was to befall him.*

Leonore's letter had contained none of this, but Philippe could well believe it. He had seen the pain in her eyes whenever she looked at him in the days between her denunciation of her husband and his departure for his command. Alexandre Kermorvant was a drunk, a wife-beater and a traitor who had tried to send his legitimate brother to the guillotine in a fit of jealous rage. Yet Leonore still held some feelings for him. Whether she had any for Philippe—

No. Such thoughts were not fitting.

> *His execution occurred on the third day of our being in Rouen. A street hawker told me that the guillotine was set up nearly on the very spot where Jeanne d'Arc, she who was once called a saint and said to have saved France, was burned by the English. I do not know if*

this was true or not, sir, but I can only conceive that a larger crowd witnessed the fate of the Maid of Orleans than that which attended your brother's. It was a bitter morning with a blizzard sweeping across the city, but even so I imagined more than a dozen citizens would stir themselves from their hearths to witness revolutionary justice being enacted. An old crone told me that it was a shame there was only one guillotining that day and that a better number would have drawn a larger audience. But it meant we were only a few paces from your brother as he was led to the scaffold, so I witnessed what transpired. At the sight of him, Madame Kermorvant shuddered and wept. She reached out but then withdrew her arm at once. I do not think he saw this. But when he was upon the scaffold, he turned and must have seen her then, for he looked directly at her before he was strapped to the device. The bell of the sometime cathedral struck nine times for the hour. As it tolled a sudden flurry of snow almost blotted out our sight of the guillotine. The howling of the wind ensured Citizen Kermorvant's last words were inaudible to all, I think, but Madame and myself. I hesitate to record your brother's last words, sir, but I would willingly swear an oath to state that they were 'Je t'aime, Leonore! Vive le roi!'. Then he was strapped to the device and the blade fell.

Citizeness Kermorvant fainted into my arms. Upon recovering herself she wept for hours, and to this day she remains withdrawn and quiet. She mourns, but I do not understand this, Monsieur le Vicomte. How can a woman mourn a man who treated her so, from what the Penhouets have told us? Roman says she mourns the man he once was, the man she married, not the man who died in Rouen, but this seems a strange notion to me. Perhaps she mourns the loss of something or someone else, but it is not my place to speculate upon such things.

No, it was not, thought Philippe, but for all the efforts to turn him and his friend into steady, dependable men fit to serve in the chateau of a nobleman, the untamed, impertinent, indiscreet wild boys from the streets of Brest still lurked beneath the well-dressed and respectful servants. When – *if?* – he returned to the chateau he would have to take them in hand.

There was more to the letter, but it was all concerned with the estate. The words barely registered on Philippe. Instead his thoughts remained fixed on the image of Leonore, standing in Rouen in the midst of a blizzard, watching the head come off the man she had once loved and called husband. What did Leonore feel about Alexandre's death? It was impossible to tell from Olivier's letter. Alexandre Kermorvant had been a brute of a husband, a man who compensated for the loss of his manhood in a hunting accident by turning to the bottle and mistreating his wife, but it was to his credit that with his last breaths he proclaimed his love for her and for the cause for which he died.

And what, if anything, did Leonore think about him, Philippe Kermorvant, Vicomte de Saint-Victor, the man whose life she had saved by destroying that of her husband, his brother? There was no understanding between them, no promises. How could there be? For an hour or more he thought of setting out at once for Brittany and abandoning the hopeless quest for another command. There might be even more troops passing the chateau in the coming weeks and months, men with less respect for a chatelaine alone but for a skeleton household staff of a few old men and women and two resourceful but outmatched youths who might be conscripted at any moment. Surely that was where his duty lay?

The thoughts were still consuming him when he set out from his lodgings the following morning after a sleepless night. Yes, he yearned to be with her, to protect her, but he was one man with no influence beyond his long-dead father's name. Would Leonore be any safer if he was with her?

He had no recollection of the route he followed, or of all the competing thoughts that raced and battled through his head. But when Philippe next looked around and registered his surroundings, he realised he was on the steps of the Ministry of the Marine.

CHAPTER THREE

'Damn me, Phil, you've got a face like a cuckolded gravedigger this morning.'

The large, cheerful northerner squeezed himself onto the chair next to Philippe, immediately dragging him away from his turbulent thoughts.

'You know many cuckolded gravediggers then, Frank?'

'Knew one in Montreuil once. Good fellow, pleasant company. Shame I fell out with him, really, but I was the one doing the cuckolding, y'see.'

The only redeeming feature of all the dire weeks of hopeful but increasingly dispiriting attendance at the Ministry of the Marine had been this growing friendship, the first he had made since he came to France for the very first time in his life during the spring of 1793, the first he had known since the good days in Russia. Day after day he sat across the anteroom in the Ministry from a square-shouldered, crop-headed fellow with a rough northern accent, and after a week or two, they chanced to sit next to each other. The northerner was much given to arm-waving and shoulder-shrugging, but he was amiable with a caustic sense of humour, forever inventing wicked quips about the sloth of the clerks or the ugliness of a certain lieutenant of Marines. He reminded Philippe a little of Kharabadze, his old and often outrageously witty friend in the naval service of the Empress Catherine.

'Francois Parmentier,' said the good-natured northerner on the morning when he finally introduced himself. '*Lieutenant de vaisseau*, formerly commander of the corvette *Valeur*. Wrecked

30

in the mouth of the Garonne, myself acquitted of any blame, as was only right and proper. Found by the court to be entirely the fault of a drunken Gascon pilot. You're Kermorvant, the Vicomte de Saint-Victor.'

'I'm honoured to make your acquaintance, Citizen Parmentier. I commiserate with you for the loss of your command and congratulate you upon your acquittal. But how do you know who I am?'

Parmentier grinned.

'Don't you read the news-sheets? You're famous, Captain. Quite the celebrity. The first captain to escape from England during this war, and so forth.'

Philippe shrugged off the compliment.

'The first of many, I hope. Tell me, though, have you been seeking a new command for long, Citizen Parmentier?'

'Since October. In January I thought of throwing it all in, going home to Dunkirk, getting myself a berth on a privateer. Good money to be had on 'em these days.'

Philippe nodded, recalling the successful prize-taking of the privateer that carried him from Gothenburg to Saint-Malo in the previous year. A successful cruise indeed until Caradec, her brave and estimable captain, was killed in a fight with an enemy ship almost within spitting distance of his home port.

'But then,' said Parmentier, 'but then, well, y'see, Madame Serron got a new girl in, a dusky wench fresh over from Haiti...'

Several hours of conversation felt to Philippe like the blinking of an eye, and that evening he and Parmentier dined in one of the new restaurants, a small, cheap place near the Porte Saint-Denis which served decent beef and drinkable wine. Parmentier was an open, perceptive fellow who had been no more than a master's mate before the revolution. But the decimation of the officer corps of the old Marine Royale – resigned, exiled or guillotined, with only a few fortunate exceptions – opened up sudden and unexpected routes to promotion for men from all sorts of backgrounds who would never have had the sniff of a quarterdeck under the *ancient regime*. Men like Bertin of *Le Torrington* and Ugarte of *Le Zephyr* came in from merchantmen, warrant officers like Parmentier rose to lieutenancies and commands. The Republic was even desperate enough to commission a man raised in a different country who had gained his experience under foreign flags. A man who bore an aristocratic name, the guaranteed high road to the guillotine for so many of similar social rank to Philippe. Yet there they were, the *vicomte* and a cooper's son who had worked his way up from cabin boy on Dunkirkers, trading jokes and anecdotes, discussing the relative merits of different frigate designs, enjoying good food, good wine and good company.

Even so, Philippe felt deeply aggrieved one morning in what would once have been the middle of April and was now the end of Germinal. Parmentier emerged from the office of the Minister of the Marine brandishing several sealed documents and grinning like a circus clown.

'*Forbin*!' he cried. 'Frigate of Twelve, thirty-two guns, at Toulon under the command of Admiral Martin! Damn me, Philippe, I'm for the sunshine and a tussle with Lord Hood!'

His friend's joy was irresistible, despite the glowering stares of the other dozen officers in the anteroom.

'I give you joy of your command, Capitaine Parmentier!'

They now addressed each other with the familiar *tu* instead of the formal *vous*.

'And I'll wait for you, Capitaine Kermorvant, so I can give you joy in your turn!'

'There might be nothing for me, Frank.'

'The way your luck held at the faro table last night, Phil, I'd be ready to wager you're going to be the new admiral of the Brest fleet!'

It was not the Brest fleet. Of course it was not. But the command offered by Minister Dalbarade, *Le Torrington* out of Toulon, was better than he expected. It was a bigger ship than either of the two he had previously commanded, *Le Zephyr* and, some years before her, the small Russian frigate *Strela*. It was considerably bigger than Frank's new command. There were new waters to sail and a real prospect of action. Even so, Philippe had a nagging sense of regret. Toulon was a very long way from Brittany, from the Brest fleet, from the Chateau de Brechelean, from Leonore. But that evening, as he and Frank toasted each other's success in a better class of restaurant just off Rue Honore, then laid their plans to travel together on one of the Turgotine stagecoaches to Toulon, Philippe felt a growing sense of acceptance and contentment. It was time to put both the impossible dreams of Leonore and the nightmares about Tasha behind him, and he would begin by ending the evening with Frank Parmentier at Madame Sarron's.

–

Philippe could see Frank's command, the sleek modern frigate *Forbin*, off to the north-east seconding Rear-Admiral Fidelin's flagship, *Ville de Poitiers*. His friend would be relishing that place of honour, even if the situation was so desperate. Frank had been so excited by the prospect of his new ship, displaying almost child-like glee throughout their interminable journey on one of the remarkably uncomfortable Turgotine coaches from Paris to Toulon by way of Courtenay, Toucy, Clamecy, Corbigny, Luzy, Lyon, Valence, Orange, Avignon and Aix-le-Provence. They secured rooms in a lodging house in the Saint-Roch quarter of Toulon, close to the custom house, the arsenal and the Hotel de la Marine, then ventured out to explore a town that was previously unknown to both of them. It was a sobering experience. Toulon had been regained for the Republic only in the previous December, following a siege of nearly four months' duration. The town still showed the scars of bombardment, fire and evacuation, with several large buildings reduced to blackened shells. The hills that surrounded Toulon on the landward side still bore the remains of the now deserted republican siege batteries. Most of the ships sunk when the

British, the Spanish and their French royalist allies evacuated the port, had been recovered, but the upper works of a couple of hulls were still visible, protruding above the waterline. Otherwise, the dockyard was busy with the sounds of hammering, sawing and loading as previously submerged or partially burned ships were repaired while others were fitted out for sea. The skeleton frames of new ships were being fashioned on the slipways, proof of the Republic's determination to restore its naval power in the Mediterranean. The Committee of Public Safety proclaimed that Toulon, so recently a nest of traitors and reactionaries, was now 'a workshop of national vengeance'.

'There's talk that hundreds of civilians were killed by our men as they entered the town,' said Philippe thoughtfully as they walked past the shot-scarred Hotel de Ville, which fronted the Old Harbour. Before it stood a newly planted Tree of Liberty, the obligatory symbol of the Republic that could be found in every town and city in France. 'Thousands, maybe. They say that many were trampled underfoot on the beach. Even more were drowned in overcrowded boats trying to reach the enemy ships.'

'What if they were?' said Frank Parmentier contemptuously. 'They were royalists. And they say many more thousands got away on the English and Spanish fleets. Traitors to France, the lot of them.'

Philippe, whose faith in the Republic had been shaken by the events of the previous year, merely nodded. He wanted the Republic to triumph, of course, but was bombarding a French town and slaughtering its citizens truly an act of fraternity?

The next morning, Captains Kermorvant and Parmentier boarded their respective commands, at anchor in the Inner Road of the commodious harbour. They met their officers, inspected their ships and crews, and awaited the order to proceed to sea under the command of Vice-Admiral Pierre Martin.

The French fleet's laggard progress in the desperately light winds still resembled that of *Le Torrington*'s jocular namesake, the tortoise, with the British making little if any headway to close the gap. Only the twenty-eight-gun frigate seemed to be inching closer, still seemingly intent on engaging Philippe's ship. He could sense the tension in his crew, the men aloft and on deck glancing silently at the enemy ship and the vast, ominous consorts astern of her. The lieutenants, *aspirants* and petty officers moved among the men, murmuring words of encouragement. There was no need for silence, but for once the notoriously garrulous French seamen were struck dumb by the precariousness of their situation.

Philippe had barely looked ahead at all during the last two or three hours, his attention fixed entirely on the enemy fleet astern of them, but finally he went up to the fo'c'sle, acknowledging the salutes of the men as he passed through them and exchanging a word with those he recognised. In all the posts he had held at sea in three navies, he prided himself on memorising the names and faces of every man in the crew. His greatest test had come in his first command as a captain, on the Russian frigate *Strela*, where the Cyrillic script, the spellings that were impenetrable in any language or alphabet, and the inexplicable insistence on referring to men by their patronymics as well as their surnames, tested him to his limit. The men of *Le Torrington* presented fewer difficulties, even strangely named Basques like the old man who saluted him at the foot of the mainmast.

'Ready for another bout with the English, Matelot Zabala?' said Philippe.

Fabien Zabala was an ancient *loup de mer*, at sea for well over thirty years, who as a boy had fought in the battles of the Seven Years War. The men around him grinned, but Zabala's expression remained entirely serious:

'Always, Citizen Captain. Time to avenge my old messmates.'

35

'Perhaps not today, Matelot, unless you can somehow conjure up a better wind.'

'Conjuring ain't republican, Citizen Captain. But if Reason judges today's the day for a fight, then that's what it'll be.'

The men nearby laughed or nodded. It was strange yet telling, Philippe thought, how quickly Reason had superseded, and taken on many of the attributes of, the old superstitions of the Catholic faith.

From the fo'c'sle, he looked due north and raised his telescope. Ahead, the landmarks of the Côte d'Azur were clearly visible. The nearest of the Lerin islands, the Île Saint-Honorat, was a small low-lying place dominated by the towering, ruinous buildings of a fortified monastery. To the north of it lay the longer, larger but equally flat Île Sainte-Marguerite, which had a substantial fort on its north coast and smaller batteries on the south, facing the oncoming fleets. Behind the islands, on the mainland, lay the small fishing town of Cannes, with the cape of Antibes to the east forming the other arm of the Bay of Gourjean, Admiral Martin's destination. The town of Antibes, heavily fortified with ramparts characteristic of the great Marshal Vauban, had long marked the extreme south-eastern limit of France, standing guard over the border with the County of Savoy and the nation that now possessed it, the Kingdom of Sardinia. But like so many of his brother European monarchs, Victor Amadeus III, King of Sardinia, had declared war on the regicidal French Republic. The front line was now well to the east of Antibes, following success after success for the republican armies, so no doubt Admiral Martin had calculated that the bay would be a safe refuge from the pursuing British fleet.

As he leaned on a swivel gun and studied the scene, though, Philippe felt a growing sense of doubt. The mouth of the Bay of Gourjean was broad, the bay itself shallow. If the French fleet got into the bay and anchored, would the batteries on the islands and around Antibes itself be sufficient to deter the enemy from making an attack? Had the Mediterranean fleet been resurrected from its watery grave in Toulon harbour only to be destroyed in Gourjean instead? The next few hours would tell.

CHAPTER FOUR

Edward, Lord Wilden, detested his home.

His relatives and neighbours – he had no friends – found this unaccountable. His lands formed a fair-sized and respectable landed estate in pleasant country on the borders of Shropshire and Worcestershire, if one liked that area, but he did not. It was fine hunting country, but he did not hunt. It brought in a good income, but he cared little for money. It contained a substantial mansion built by his grandfather only half a century before in the Palladian style, but in his one significant extravagance of taste, he preferred the utterly unfashionable Gothic. It had spacious rooms, ample for a family, but he had never married. It contained too many reminders. Reminders of the father who had died before he was born, of the mother who might as well have done, of the interminable procession of remote and severe governesses. Were it not for the responsibilities that devolved on the owner of such an estate, and which demanded his presence there from time to time, he would not have set foot in Alveley Hall from one year to the next. It was too far from London, from his sparsely furnished but perfectly adequate rooms in Hill Street, and above all from his office at the Admiralty in Whitehall, where he was nominally the most junior Civil Lord. All important correspondence was forwarded to him in the country, of course, but it all took so *much longer*. One never knew when a packet from France might bring vital intelligence from either the official or his own, invariably more reliable, sources. Intelligence that demanded more immediate action than any that could be ordered from Shropshire.

Still, needs must, and that Sunday morning, as the bells summoned the congregation to the local parish church where his family pew would stand empty yet again, Lord Wilden sat down at his desk in the library and began to work through his correspondence. Following the recent capture of Martinique, the home secretary, Henry Dundas, had hatched yet another scheme for an operation in the West Indies. Of course he had. The intolerable man seemed unable to think of anything or anywhere else. But then, thought Wilden, acquiring more French territory in that sphere meant plantations, and plantations meant money, and Dundas was a Scot.

As for the war in France and the Low Countries, that proceeded in its interminable, Treasury-draining way. The allies won a battle or two, the French won a battle or two, a few miles were lost or won, and so it went on. The heady optimism of the early months of the previous year, when Wilden and so many others confidently believed that the allied armies and their French royalist confederates would brush aside the raw republican levies, march into Paris and restore the divinely ordained monarchy, had long evaporated. Somehow the enemy had survived and even turned the tide. Even so, rebellion still continued in parts of France. The once-promising revolt in the Vendée was largely suppressed, but the royalist Chouans in Brittany were still in arms and Wilden and his superiors, notably Pitt himself, were looking at new ways of encouraging and supporting them. Perhaps, though, further expensive warfare on mainland Europe would not be needed after all. The republican leaders in Paris warred between themselves. For instance, Danton, once the great driving force of the revolution, as well as being Robespierre's friend and closest ally, had been executed a few weeks earlier. Robespierre himself, increasingly isolated and seemingly delusional, had instituted a new religion named 'the cult of the Supreme Being'. Wags in the Pall Mall clubs jested that the Supreme Being he wished people to bow down and worship was himself. Perhaps their brethren in the salons of

Paris made the same quips too, albeit rather more quietly. At any rate, on those rare occasions when Lord Wilden deigned to occupy his family pew, he prayed fervently for the leaders of the monstrous French Republic to continue to denounce and slaughter each other. In other words, to do his job for him.

An elderly footman entered, bowed, and placed on the side of Wilden's desk a glass of claret and one of the confections of bread and beef that bore the name of a previous lord of the Admiralty, the Earl of Sandwich. Before Wilden's time, of course, but in due course he hoped to leave a better legacy than to have his name remembered only for inventing a remarkably feeble substitute for a proper dinner.

Wilden took a sip of wine, nibbled a small corner of bread and beef, then turned to the intelligence from the Mediterranean. Since the loss of Toulon to the murderous republican gang in December, all of Britain's focus – and thus all of Wilden's – had been on Corsica, where the anti-French insurgent leader General Pasquale Paoli was eager to secure independence under British protection. Bastia had fallen after a lengthy siege and now only Calvi, also in the north, was left in French hands. Soon, God willing, the entire island would be free of the demented Jacobins, and the government's envoy Sir Gilbert Elliot was working night and day to persuade Paoli and the Corsicans to place themselves under British rule. If that happened, Corsica could take the place of Toulon as a base for British operations against the south coast of France and in Italy. Elliot was a Scottish Whig and thus a devil with two heads as far as the staunchly Tory Wilden was concerned, but for some reason Paoli trusted him. If nothing upset the applecart, King George would soon be proclaimed King of Corsica, a new dominion to add to England, Scotland, Ireland, Hanover and the lesser territories like Jamaica, Jersey, Canada and Wales. Leandri, another Corsican rebel leader who styled himself 'general', might be a problem if he took the French side, and there was that other family whose name he could never remember, several young brothers who proclaimed themselves loyal to the cause of Corsican union with France. As far as Wilden could see, the Corsicans were all peasants and bandits, their allegiances determined more by ancient family vendettas than by political principle. Well, it would all be academic if Elliot did his job, Paoli stayed true to his word and Admiral Hood captured Calvi. France dished and Corsica united with Britain: now there was a prospect. Lord Wilden hated travel, and especially foreign travel – his Grand Tour was remarkably brief by the standards of his contemporaries and had been looked upon by the participant as an ordeal to be suffered rather than a character-forming delight – but even he might be tempted to venture out one day to inspect King George's new kingdom. Perhaps he might even ask Pitt to make him the viceroy. After all, one of his neighbours (whom he had never met and who had, indeed, never set foot on his estate) was the prime minister of Naples. A Mediterranean climate would surely be better for Lord Wilden's health than that of Shropshire. When all was said and done, it could not be worse.

Wilden took another mouthful of the sandwich and washed it down with wine. The church bells were ringing, signifying the end of the morning service. Perhaps they had been ringing for some time and he had not been aware of them. As sure as night followed day, the vicar would call at Alveley Hall in the afternoon to pay his respects to the patron of his living and to enquire as to what invisible indisposition might have kept His Lordship from divine service once again. Perhaps this week Wilden would even allow the servants to admit him.

Finally, Lord Wilden turned to miscellaneous correspondence from various informants across Europe and the Americas. Nothing of note from the latter, of course – who cared a jot what the so-called President Washington thought and did? – but there, in a digest of items culled from various Parisian news-sheets by a clerk in the Alien Office who copied all of that department's correspondence to him, was something of interest.

It was nothing more than an innocuous list of the captains who had received commissions to command warships of the French Republic during the last few weeks, but one name stood out. Philippe Kermorvant, *capitaine de frégate*, to command *Le Torrington*, frigate of thirty-eight guns, in the fleet of Admiral Pierre Martin at Toulon.

Well, well, so cousin Philippe was prospering after his daring escape from captivity in England. He had rejected Wilden's offer to serve the French royalists and thus, by extension, Great Britain, his mother's homeland. He had even rejected the easy bondage of parole in some comfortable market town inland in favour of a return to a pestilential prison hulk at Portsmouth, whence he had somehow contrived to escape. Even so, the lord of the Admiralty felt a brief and unaccustomed surge of familial pride. Command of a frigate serving in the Mediterranean, though? That intelligence might prove very useful to Edward, Lord Wilden. Very useful indeed.

He took a fresh sheet of paper, placed it in front of him, and dipped his pen in the ink. He would compose a note to his senior clerk in Whitehall, instructing him to send a coded message by the usual channels to his agent in the French Toulon fleet. The time it would take his simple instruction to get from Alveley Hall to the Admiralty meant delay, the thing that Lord Wilden hated most in the world. It would all be so much easier if he never left London.

42

CHAPTER FIVE

The Bay of Gourjean and the little fishing harbours around it – Théoule, Cannes, Antibes – were alive with shipping now. Small craft of all sorts were coming out, many of them being rowed like the galleys of old. Others with sleek hulls and lateen rig managed better in the light winds than did the lumbering square-rigged men-of-war. Several of the oncoming vessels flew Tricolours. The seamen and fisherfolk of the Côte d'Azur, many of them wearing the red caps beloved of the fervent revolutionaries, were coming out en masse to help the warships of the Republic to a safe anchorage.

The headmost ships of the fleet were launching their own boats. Tow ropes were secured to these and to some of the boats that had come out from the shore, lines went taut, and the great ships of the French fleet began to gain momentum as they were towed slowly but inexorably into the Bay of Gourjean. *Bonnet-Rouge, Duquesne, Heureux*, Rear-Admiral Fidelin's *Ville de Poitiers…* Frank Parmentier's *Forbin* was under tow now, in the wake of the colossal fleet flagship *Sans-Culotte*. It was a splendid spectacle, but also, Philippe thought, a deeply shaming one. France's entire naval force in the Mediterranean was being driven into a burrow in the earth like a rabbit being chased by a cat.

Philippe turned his attention astern once again. *Le Torrington*, slow in the best of winds, was the rearmost ship of the fleet by some distance, while the English Twenty-Eight was equally well ahead of the towering hulls of Hood's *Victory* and all the rest of them. She looked to be fairly new, a taut and well-run ship, as so

43

many of the enemy frigates were. Their crews were generally much more experienced than their French adversaries. Their seamanship was superior to most, the exceptions being many of France's Breton, Basque and Provençal mariners who could often equal them. Consequently, the enemy gun crews, often better drilled and battle-hardened, could usually manage a faster rate of fire than the French. That had all been true during his one experience thus far of combat with a British man-of-war, the battle that ended with him giving the order to strike the *Tricolore* and surrendering his sword to Captain Prentice of HMS *Chester*. He had no desire or intention of repeating that experience, nor that of the squalid English prison hulks. This time his own command was bigger, the enemy ship smaller, but size mattered little in such engagements, which were usually determined by the skill of two crews, or sheer blind luck, or a combination of both. As he continued to watch the British frigate, his instincts told him that even in such poor wind, the two ships would engage well before *Le Torrington* came under the covering fire of the batteries on Saint-Honorat and Sainte-Marguerite.

Philippe turned to his officers and gave the command they were all expecting.

'All hands to quarters! Clear for action!'

'*Commande!*' cried Malhuret and Doucet, the *maitre d'équipage* or sailing master, a tough old Gascon who looked so ancient that some in the crew whispered he had been the helmsman on Noah's Ark.

The latter's sharp call on the *sifflet*, the whistle, was echoed by those of his master's mates. The ship's two boy drummers took their positions and began a rapid, insistent beat. Blue-tunicked Marines followed the orders of their lieutenant, Lauray, with some going up into the tops to act as sharpshooters if it came to close combat. Men emerged from below and ran to their stations, loading and hauling out the guns on both sides of the ship. It was unlikely that it would come to broadsides, but all it would take would be one lucky shot from the Englishman such as the one that had brought down the mizzen of his previous command, *Le Zephyr*, and compelled him to surrender to his opponent. If history repeated itself then *Le Torrington* might be swallowed up by the entire British fleet and bombarded by each successive leviathan as it came up. If that happened, Admirals Martin and Fidelin, the men on the French ships and the spectators on the islands and the Côte d'Azur would at least see Philippe's command perish with all its guns blazing.

Tremoulet, the one-eyed sergeant of Marines who served as master gunner, stepped before Philippe and saluted.

'Your order, Citizen Captain?'

'Wait another five minutes, Sergeant Tremoulet, then try the stern chasers. It'll still be too far, but it might make them think twice about closing any further.'

'*Commande! Oui, mon capitaine.*'

As the gunner withdrew, Philippe saw the three *aspirants* gathered together at the rail, fascinated by the sight of the oncoming enemy frigate.

'Any of you seen guns fired in anger before?' he asked.

Vidos and Rampillon shook their heads hesitantly. No surprise there, for this was the first voyage for Rampillon, the son of a Nantes merchant who had grown rich from the slave trade, while Vidos, the only child of a Parisian lawyer's widow, came to *Le Torrington* from one of the submerged and partially burned Seventy-Fours at Toulon that had been condemned for further service before she could put to sea. Only the always intense de la Porte responded to Philippe's question with a slight and reluctant nod.

'And where was that, *aspirant*?'

'Flanders, sir, in the spring of last year, when I had no ship and my father thought he could still persuade me to change my mind and follow him into the army. So he took me with him on the Neerwinden campaign to act as his aide-de-camp.'

Philippe knew the young man's father was exceptionally well-connected for a mere colonel, but taking a boy who was little more than a child onto a battlefield was surely inexplicable. It was also inexplicable that even the makeshift military regulations of the new republic permitted an *aspirant* of the navy to serve an unofficial attachment with an army officer. Inexplicable, at any rate, unless your name was de la Porte, one of France's most illustrious military dynasties and one of the few to adopt the republican cause. An ancestor of this serious, softly spoken and innocuous youth had commanded part of the French army that defeated the English at Castillon in 1453, another had been a marshal of France in Mazarin's time. The boy's grandfather had commanded a division at the battle of Hastenbeck in 1757 and would undoubtedly have known Philippe's father, who fought in that campaign. Philippe guessed that none of the previous de la Portes were disfigured by the large and livid birthmark on the right side of the young man's face, but such a fiery countenance seemed appropriate for a scion of a race of distinguished warriors.

'Well, Citizen de la Porte, what did you learn about war at Neerwinden?'

The *aspirant* frowned and seemed to think very hard about his answer. Philippe expected a response conditioned by the lad's upbringing, by all the ancestors whose legends must have been related to him since he was in his cradle. It would be a platitude, something to do with honour and glory and patriotism. But that was not at all what Thibaud de la Porte said.

'The only glory in it is to come out alive, Citizen Captain.'

The reply took Philippe aback, and it took him a moment to think of a response.

'Isn't death in battle glorious, then? A valiant death in the service of our country. Isn't that what we all dream of?'

'Others decide if you died gloriously or not, sir. It doesn't matter to you one jot, you're just dead.'

The other two *aspirants* stared at de la Porte with disbelief, but their captain nodded. Not even Philippe's father, the renowned philosopher Verité, could have formed a better precept.

The captain of *Le Torrington* looked back to the bows of the British frigate.

'Well, Citizen de la Porte, let's see if your battle-virgin friends, Aspirants Rampillon and Vidos here, come to agree with your opinion. To your stations, *aspirants! Vive la République! Vive la France!*'

He turned, saw Tremoulet's intent gaze, and nodded.

'Fire stern chasers!'

CHAPTER SIX

The quarterdeck of *Le Torrington* shook as the stern chase guns, both twelve-pounders, fired at the British frigate almost directly astern and perhaps a third of a league away. Both shots fell short, throwing up small spouts of water perhaps twenty *toises* ahead of the enemy's cutwater. It took a couple of minutes before the Englishman replied with his bow guns, but his fire got no closer to Philippe's ship. Once the gun crews finished reloading, Philippe ordered a second volley, but the fall of shot was not discernibly closer. The already feeble wind was easing further, the sails of both frigates almost limp, and the sea was beginning to resemble a vast carpet of glass. He turned his telescope to look toward the shore. The first of the great ships were already coming to an anchor off the village of Golfe-Juan, Admiral Martin's orders being to anchor in line, parallel to the shore, presenting the full weight of their broadsides to their enemies.

The British frigate fired again, the shots seeming to strike the water almost exactly where they had before. Philippe did not order a response. The exchange was futile and would only waste valuable powder and shot that would be needed when a proper engagement occurred.

'Flagship signalling, sir,' said Grignon. 'Each frigate to unship six guns and their crews.'

'Acknowledge,' said Philippe.

'Taking out some of our guns?' said de la Porte, his young face frowning. 'Why, Citizen Captain?'

'Look yonder, Aspirant, they're already getting ready to haul guns off some of the great ships. The admiral intends to

48

reinforce the shore batteries. Looks like they're making ready some of the local coasting craft to serve as floating batteries, too. A wall of heavy ordnance to bombard the English if they dare attempt to venture into the bay.'

The proximity of the existing batteries was sufficient to deter the enemy frigate with which they had exchanged fire, but which now abandoned any pretence at pursuit. As *Le Torrington* was towed slowly toward its anchorage in the lee of the Île Sainte-Marguerite, though, Philippe could see all too clearly the perilous position of the French fleet. If the batteries failed to deter the English, once the wind strengthened again Lord Hood and his ships would be able to sail straight into the bay. There would be sufficient water between the French fleet and the shore, as well as more than sufficient superiority in numbers, for the enemy to double Martin's ships, sailing down both sides at the same time and hammering the Mediterranean fleet to destruction. In the ignorant epochs before the revolution, sailors would have prayed to God, the Virgin and all the saints that the flat calm lasted long enough to prevent the British from making the attempt, and that when the wind got up again the hastily formed batteries would prove a sufficient deterrent. Philippe would not pray to Robespierre's Supreme Being, so he mouthed a silent prayer to the god his ancestors had worshipped and to the souls of his beloved wife, Tasha, and infant son, Ivan, whose slaughtered bodies lay buried beneath the soil of their Russian motherland.

'*Jeter l'ancre!*'

On Philippe's command, *Le Torrington* dropped anchor off the Pointe de Vengeur on the north coast of the Île Sainte-Marguerite, making her the westernmost of the moored French ships. A battery stood upon the headland but the guns from *Le Torrington* were intended for the Batterie de la Convention, on the eastern extremity of the island, which would undoubtedly take the brunt of the enemy's fire if Lord Hood decided to force the anchorage.

Tremoulet came before Philippe and saluted.

'We'll take out numbers three and four on the fo'c's'le, sir, as well as three, four, nine and ten on the main deck. Shouldn't affect the trim too much, so no need to shift any ballast.'

Tremoulet had the mournful tone of one reporting on the death of a lover. No gunner cheerfully accepted the loss of any of his charges. One ship's gunner Philippe had served with in Russia called the guns his children and wept for a day when one of them blew up.

'I'll take your word for it, master gunner, but I trust we'll have our full complement back by the time we next put to sea.'

The loss of six large guns and over forty men would significantly weaken *Le Torrington*'s strength if she returned to sea without re-embarking them, but the situation was dire and for the time being the guns were far more important to France than the ship or her men. The next hour saw a flotilla of small local craft come alongside, and in brisk fashion the ship's *matelots* and the rough local hands, many of them shouting excitedly in the unintelligible Occitan language, hauled the six guns outboard, then down onto the decks of the lighters and pinnaces. Tremoulet watched over his precious guns like an anxious swan fussing over her cygnets, snapping frequently at the local crews for their clumsiness and ineptitude. All the while, Philippe studied the dispositions of the two admirals, Hood and Martin. For the time being, the English remained stymied by the complete lack of wind. Their wooden titans sat no more than a league away, their sails entirely limp, the Union flag on HMS *Victory* no more than a flaccid rag. Hood and his officers would be watching the activity in the bay and would know exactly what Martin was doing. The English admiral would be calculating the risk, weighing the chances of being able to get past the French land defences and the new floating batteries once the wind strengthened again. Hood was an old man, nearly seventy, and Philippe had sailed against the fleet under his command in the American war. Hood was not known as an impetuous man. If God, or the Supreme Being, or the ancient gods of the Gauls and Bretons, favoured Admiral Martin, then perhaps the French fleet would not be destroyed in the Bay of Gourjean.

—

The British did not attack that day, nor in the week that followed. The calm weather endured, the wind never strengthening beyond light airs. The enemy ships paraded off the coast, occasionally making painfully slow tacks, but they made no attempt to attack the French fleet as it lay at anchor. Admiral Martin took full advantage of the fortunate calm, further strengthening the defences of the anchorage. The immediate alarm soon gave way to a profound ennui as, day after day, the ships swung at anchor. Frank Parmentier invited Philippe to dine aboard his ship and a few days later, Philippe returned the compliment. The following night they both dined on *Duquesne* with several other officers. The morning after, though, Philippe received an order to attend Admiral Martin aboard the flagship *Sans-Culotte*. *Le Torrington*'s longboat took him through the anchorage, the oars cutting through water that remained as placid as a pond in the gardens of Versailles.

Seated behind the table in his capacious admiral's cabin with his second-in-command, the slight, pale and sickly looking Rear-Admiral Sebastien Fidelin, beside him, the bovine, beetle-browed Pierre Martin was evidently not in a good humour.

'Madness,' he said as soon as Philippe was seated before him. 'What can be more urgent than preserving France's fleet in the Mediterranean, eh? What can justify plucking a captain in that fleet off his ship to go who knows where and do who knows what? Sheer madness.'

'Sir?'

Martin shook his head and smiled weakly at Philippe. The admiral was not known as a good-humoured man, and smiling was not his natural condition.

'My apologies, Captain. Not your fault, of course, and we must do whatever our masters in Paris decree. The best interests of the Republic, and all the rest of it.'

'I don't follow, Citizen Admiral.'

'Your name is known, it seems. Well of course it is, you are your father's son so your name marks you out as much as it would if you were called Bourbon or Marat. I don't know what they have in mind, but they could have sent for any captain in the fleet. Any lieutenant, come to that. Any *aspirant*. But no, I hold here an order from the Minister of the Marine for Citizen Captain Kermorvant of *Le Torrington* to proceed directly to a tavern in Le Muy, which is some little place up in the hills, or so I'm told, and follow the orders of some general or other who will meet him there tomorrow evening. The name's a blank so the minister meant for it to be filled in later, but the clerk must have omitted to do so. I don't envy you, Kermorvant. The orders of an army officer... I'll wager he'll want you to sail contrary to wind and tide, to sail to America and be back in a week, to fly to the moon. Whatever he demands, you must gently nudge him in the direction of the possible, Captain.'

Fidelin, a serious, quiet man from the Pas-de-Calais known for his brilliance as a frigate captain and his devotion to the republican cause, raised an eyebrow at his admiral's levity, but said nothing.

'As you say, sir,' said Philippe. 'But what of my ship? What if an opportunity presents itself for the fleet to leave the bay?'

Pierre Martin stood and went to his stern window, from which the distant enemy ships were clearly visible.

'I doubt very much if Lord Hood will oblige us with such an opportunity, Captain. But if he does, if there is an easterly storm that drives him off the coast and allows us to come out, well, then, that will be a different case, of course. You have faith in your first officer?'

'Lieutenant Malhuret is a capable officer, Citizen Admiral.'

'Capable enough for the acting command?'

'I believe so, sir.'

'I, too, know Lieutenant Malhuret,' said Fidelin. 'He was an *aspirant* under me on *Terpsichore* in the Indies. I concur with Captain Kermorvant's opinion of him. He is ready for command.'

'Good,' said Admiral Martin. 'Very good. Then I am content, although I don't envy you whatever lunacy this general and his friends in Paris may have concocted, Kermorvant.' Fidelin looked sharply at his superior. A few months before such a remark would probably have led Pierre Martin directly to the guillotine, but as Philippe had seen for himself in Paris, the fury of the Terror had abated somewhat. 'In the old days, of course, I'd have wished you God speed, Captain. Nowadays, my hand will have to suffice.'

They shook and exchanged *la bise*, although Rear-Admiral Fidelin did not make a similar gesture, merely giving Philippe the curtest of nods. Philippe left the admiral's cabin and went to his longboat to return to *Le Torrington*.

–

Admiral Martin watched the boat's crew propel it across the mirror-like waters of the bay, threading its way through the anchored frigates and ships-of-the-line, then turned to Fidelin.

'Fortunate timing for Captain Kermorvant, I'd say.'

'Fortunate, sir? How so? Surely his mission is nothing but *une fausse piste*, a wild goose chase.'

'Undoubtedly, Fidelin, undoubtedly. But it will remove him from the attentions of the honourable representative of the Committee of Public Safety, as and when that high dignitary finally arrives. Paris remains convinced that there is an English spy somewhere among the commanders of the fleet – it's said they've discovered letters in unbreakable cyphers in the homes of suspected royalists in Toulon, awaiting transmission to their ultimate recipient. Our masters seem to have settled on our friend Kermorvant as the likeliest candidate.'

Fidelin pondered this, then responded slowly and thoughtfully.

'His mother is English, after all, Admiral. His cousin is one of their Admiralty lords, said to be one of their principal spymasters. I cannot conceive of the reasons why a command in the Marine Nationale was bestowed on a man with such suspect credentials.'

'And I was born in Canada, which the English now rule. I expect that puts a query against my name in one or other of Citizen Robespierre's lists.'

Fidelin shrugged.

'I suppose his father's name still carries much weight in Paris and has tipped the scales in his favour. But if not Kermorvant for the enemy spy in the fleet, then who?'

Martin looked out at the distant mastheads of the enemy fleet, still massed outside the Bay of Gourjean, awaiting their moment.

'Whoever it is, Fidelin, I don't think their intelligence will be worth much for some time to come. *The French fleet remains at anchor. The French fleet has not moved. The French fleet shows no prospect of moving.* I can't imagine any of that heating the blood of King George and William Pitt, can you?'

'Even so, Citizen Admiral, is it good sense to send a suspected English agent on a confidential mission, whatever it may be?'

Martin smiled.

'My dear Fidelin,' he said, 'when has the question of who the army chooses to employ about any of its business ever concerned the navy in the slightest?'

—

Aboard *Le Torrington*, Philippe relayed Martin's orders to Malhuret and the other officers. The first lieutenant showed no excitement at the prospect of his first command, albeit in an acting capacity. He made no visible reaction at all. They dined together with the other officers, but it was a subdued business. Philippe's imminent departure brought home the likelihood that the rest of them, officers and men alike, would be blockaded in the Bay of Gourjean for weeks, rather than days or even hours. Grignon, who was courting a young lady of good family in Toulon, was particularly and uncharacteristically silent.

Philippe slept aboard that night. He rose before dawn to find the officers' *commis aux vivres* or steward, Courtois, completing the packing of a large kitbag.

'Five shirts, sir,' said the young man. 'Same of undergarments. Beyond those, I'm afraid you'll have to fend for yourself.'

The young man was eager, if overly fussy about the care of his captain, who had no valet or *maître d'hôtel* dedicated solely to his service. In a way that Philippe could not explain, Courtois reminded him of one of the slaves on the plantation in Virginia that his parents called home. This despite the fact that Courtois was very French, slight, white and above all male, whereas Arethusa had been a vast black woman.

'I shall do my best, Courtois.'

'But you don't know how long you'll be away, my lord.'

Despite being as staunch a republican as any man in the crew, Courtois had a weakness for noble birth and an exaggerated sense of deference.

'Don't worry about me, Courtois. Lieutenant Malhuret is the acting captain now, so he has become your principal concern. And at least you won't "my lord" him.'

'As you say, Citizen Captain.'

Philippe was piped off the ship and rowed ashore to Cannes, where a member of the admiral's retinue had already procured a horse for him. Mounted on what proved to be a lively but biddable grey and with the kitbag transformed into a makeshift saddlebag, he began the long ride up into the hills. The lush coastal plain gave way to a rugged land of hills, forests and deep valleys that reminded him of inland Virginia. The road was busy, above all with military traffic. France had captured Nice and its region early in the war, but the coalition arrayed against her sought to recapture the area before driving further into France. An offensive in the spring secured French control for the time being, but it was certain the coalition powers would seek to counter-attack. So the road was busy with infantry regiments marching east, toward the front, accompanied by artillery trains and the occasional detachment of cavalry. A naval uniform was a rarity, even something of a spectacle, and Philippe was aware of the eyes of countless soldiers on him as he rode past. A few of the older sergeants were aware enough to salute as he went by, but most of the men under their command simply gawped. A few officers stopped to engage him in conversation, but they, too, seemed to regard him as a creature from another planet.

On the rare stretches where the road was empty, Philippe was able to think about the strange mission he had been given. As Admiral Martin said, whatever task the nameless general had in mind for him could surely have been undertaken by many better qualified officers in the fleet. There were men of commissioned rank who had been sailing the Mediterranean for twenty or thirty years. Several of the captains and lieutenants of the fleet were Provençal, men born and raised on this coast, men who had been out in these waters as soon as they were able to walk. But none of them were the son of Verité, and for that reason whatever mission was in hand could seemingly be entrusted to him and him alone. Perhaps the man meant to be awaiting him in the inn at Le Muy would provide him with the answers.

CHAPTER SEVEN

Most esteemed, worthy and gallant father,

I trust you will forgive my unwarrantably long silence since my last letter to you from Toulon. The truth, sir, is that all of my time has been taken up by my change of circumstances since last I wrote. I refer to my appointment to a seagoing ship, the frigate Le Torrington of thirty-eight guns, and my consequent haste to leave Paris and join her at Toulon before she put to sea. So let me tell you something of my ship, if you can take a minute or two from your infinitely more important duties in the service of the Republic. Her name will tell you she is an English prize from the last war with them, but she is sturdy and well founded. I trust she will be the means by which I can prove myself to you and to France. I have many responsibilities, if a minute fraction of yours. I have the charge of men, and I find them as steadfast a body of patriots and sans-culottes as any to be in any part of France. You will be glad to hear that they seem aware of the name I bear and pay me the respect due to my rank and lineage. I have charge of them during the exercise of our armament, which takes place frequently at the insistence of the captain. In yesterday's drill my gun crews won the accolade for the fastest and most accurate fire! I have no doubt that the artillery companies of the Army of the North can perform better, and I remain aware of your thoughts on the deficiencies of those who pursue the sea for a career, but I trust you will allow that in this, the world I have chosen, I may allow myself a little pride upon the distinction.

My fellow aspirants and messmates are named Vidos and Rampillon. They are both good fellows. Enseigne de Vaisseau Grignon is a firm and serious officer but I like him best of the équipage. The first lieutenant, Citizen Malhuret, is always kind to me but he seems to prefer Rampillon, whose father you may perhaps have heard of as he is a famously rich merchant trading from Nantes to Africa and the Indies. Our captain is Kermorvant, the Vicomte de Saint-Victor. You may also have heard of him as his escape from the English prison hulks in Portsmouth harbour was widely reported. You will also know the name for he is the son of Verité, of whom I need say no more. Thus far I have had few real dealings with him. He takes we three aspirants through our lessons in navigation and mathematics, as is his duty, and teaches us competently as far as I am able to judge. He is said to be a good seaman, a competent navigator and a fierce and gallant fighter, but I have had no opportunity to make my own judgement of any of these matters. The captain has an unusual history for a man entrusted with one of the Republic's warships. Some of the men say he rode with the Cossacks, others that he was brought up by the savage Indian tribes of the Americas. I have wondered, respected father, how such a man has obtained a command in the Marine Nationale, but as you always say, we must always trust that those entrusted with power in Paris have good cause for their actions and the choices they make. All I will say is that he treats me fairly.

By the same post as this I send letters to my dear mother and sisters, presenting my compliments to them. I will hope to write to you again by means of the next merchantman we encounter or the next tender going back to Toulon for supplies. In the meantime, sir, I hope to

hear of the Army of the North's decisive victory over the
terrible alliance of enemy powers ranged against it. Vive
la patrie! Vive la France!
  I am well. Vive la République!
  Your dutiful and obedient son,
  T de la Porte

—

Le Muy was a large, prosperous-looking village sitting on something of a plateau among heavily forested foothills, with higher
peaks rising a league or two to the north and south of it. A plain
and clearly ancient round tower stood guard over its eastern
entrance. Its place on one of the principal routes between
France and Italy gave it a certain importance, and that was
very much in evidence as Philippe rode into the village. Several
regiments were plainly billeted in and around Le Muy, the
number of checkpoints suggesting that even here, a long way
behind the front line of the war with the Kingdom of Sardinia,
the Republic's soldiers were taking every precaution against
attack. Philippe had no difficulty finding an ostler to tend to
his horse, the army's presence acting as a magnet for those men
and women who ever profited from soldiers and their needs. He
found the tavern specified for his meeting with no difficulty,
got a table just outside the door to himself, and settled down to
wait. He was several hours early, so he had ample time to take a
meal of thin lamb broth, bread, cheese and olives washed down
by the rough local wine.

He spent the time watching the endless activity in the
village. Officers argued with householders and each other about
billeting, commissaries haggled with shopkeepers, exhausted
men soaked in sweat fell out from marching columns to take
water from the fountain or even the horse troughs, the older
menfolk of the village sat in the shade smoking their pipes and
sometimes breaking off for impromptu throws of dice against

men they must have known all their lives. Here, too, he was aware of many eyeing his naval uniform and either frowning or turning away, puzzled. After a while his thoughts began to wander. He hoped Malhuret was taking good care of his ship, that the crew's discipline was holding, and that they would not venture out without him against the might of Admiral Hood's blockade. Most of the officers in the *équipage* would undoubtedly acquit themselves well, Bertin being the only one whose ability he doubted. The Marines were mostly experienced men with Launay a good commander, while the *matelots* were largely capable enough. Of the *aspirants*, he had few concerns about Rampillon and Vidos, but de la Porte was an enigma. Philippe knew well the burden that came with bearing a famous name, and it clearly took some sort of courage for de la Porte to chart his own course into the Marine Nationale rather than follow in the family footsteps of dozens of soldier de la Portes. No, young Thibaud de la Porte would surely acquit himself well when the time came.

A shepherd drove his flock through the centre of the village, attracting curses and incredulous looks from the soldiers who were forced to get off the road. There was a war not too far away, and France was now a republic rather than a kingdom, but in places like Le Muy life went on essentially as it always had.

The interruption caused Philippe to chide himself for thinking of his command and imagining how well he thought her men would perform in battle. For as long as this mission lasted, none of it was his concern. This mission of which he knew nothing, other than the assumption that his name somehow qualified him for it and meant that he, of all the officers in all the ships and regiments of France, had been selected for it.

As the afternoon turned into evening Philippe thought more of the events that had brought him here, to this obscure village, and tried to deduce why he had been ordered to leave his command to meet this mysterious general who had some unknown purpose in mind for him. Philippe knew his name alone set him apart from all of his fellow officers of the Marine Nationale, even without taking into consideration his unique career. He reckoned that none other in Le Muy could tell a tale like his, the childhood in America where his father, the renowned philosopher Verité, had found both a safe refuge from political persecution and an English wife, his impetuosity in going to sea to fight against his mother's homeland, his perverse decision to follow John Paul Jones into the naval service of the fabled but fickle Russian Empress Catherine, fighting her wars against the Swedes and the Turks, his discovery of true love and, for the first time in his life, a brief glimpse of a life centred upon a settled home and a stable, loving family.

What was there in all of this that meant he, and he alone, was qualified for this unknown mission?

Surely it could be nothing to do with the sight of blood upon snow, the blood spilled from the bodies of his wife, Tasha, and little son, Ivan, onto the soil of Russia, their lives taken by Tasha's brother, Count Bulgakov, in a fit of drunken rage fuelled by Bulgakov's wrath against her marriage to a foreigner. That drove Philippe out of Russia and took him perversely to France, the homeland he had never known, where the threat of the guillotine was ever present for a man like him, a man of his name and lineage, the Vicomte de Saint-Victor. Somehow he had survived and become captain of a frigate of the new French Republic. He had also gone for the first time to his ancestral estate in Brittany, where he encountered his half-brother, Alexandre, and Alexandre's wife, Leonore—

'Captain Kermorvant?'

Deep in thought, he had been unaware of the approach of the young *sous-lieutenant* of infantry.

'I am he.'

'The general has arrived. I ask that you accompany me to him, sir.'

Philippe had been unaware of the arrival of any senior officer. The general must have entered the tavern incognito by a side or rear door. That was surprising, for in Philippe's experience generals and admirals alike invariably insisted on their presence being advertised as loudly and widely as possible. He followed the young officer into the building and into a back room where the shutters were already closed, the only light coming from a few candles. The general, a slight figure in a grey greatcoat that seemed too large for him, stood with his back to Philippe and his hands behind his back, facing the unlit fire.

'Thank you, Nordin, that will be all.'

The *sous-lieutenant* bowed his head and left. The general remained still for a few moments, then turned to face Philippe. He was impossibly young, certainly younger than Philippe, and surely very little older than the youth who had just left the room. He had a prominent chin, a mouth that seemed to be creased into a permanent frown, and long straight black hair.

'So, you are Philippe Kermorvant, the Vicomte de Saint-Victor. The son of the illustrious Verité. You'll want to know why I summoned you here, of course.'

There was no introduction of himself, no offer to sit. The general seemed impatient to be elsewhere as quickly as possible, and began pacing the room with barely a glance at Philippe.

'I am at your command, General,' said Philippe, unsure how to deal with the specimen before him. To the general's unsettling youth and obvious impatience, Philippe could add the man's accent. The French found Philippe's own voice, with its peculiar inflections absorbed in America and Russia, strange enough, but there were oddities in the general's speech, too. He was no Parisian, that was certain.

'Corsica,' said the general. 'What do you know of it?'

Philippe had not known what to expect from the strange rendezvous. He had certainly not expected the absence of any form of preamble. Instead, this was the sort of direct question a schoolmaster might ask a pupil he suspected of shirking. But it did not do to appear ignorant or nonplussed before a senior officer, so Philippe made some sort of an answer.

'That for centuries it was a satellite of the Republic of Genoa. Then, nearly forty years ago, it declared its independence—'

'Paoli,' said the general, seemingly dissatisfied with the speed and nature of Philippe's answer. 'Pasquale Paoli. He was the man who led the revolt against Genoa, then led the independent Corsica. A great man, Paoli, but his vision was impossible. Corsica can never be independent, it must be part of France. As it became a quarter-century ago, of course, despite all Paoli's efforts to hold back the inevitable march of destiny.'

That, then, was the general's accent, his identity. He, like Paoli, was a Corsican.

'I understood it was trying to declare independence again, to separate from France.'

'France is distracted. Foreign wars, domestic revolts, all that has happened in the last few years. So, yes, Paoli has returned to try his old game once again. This time, though, he has secured a powerful and dangerous ally. As we speak, Captain, Paoli is on the point of offering the crown of Corsica to England's king. After Corsica became a part of France he spent all his years of exile there, in England, cultivating all the great men, trying to convince them of his cause. He needed only the opportunity, and now he thinks he has it. We cannot let it happen. Corsica is part of France, and it cannot be an English puppet kingdom. It cannot be a base for Lord Hood and his damn ships. You see all this, Captain?'

'I see, Citizen General, but I do not see how I can play a part.'

The general was pacing with his back to Philippe, his hands clasped behind him, and seemed not to hear him.

'Our situation in Corsica is dire. Bastia has fallen to the English. They and Paoli control the rest of the island except for Calvi, our last garrison, which they have under siege. We cannot send a relief army because all of France's troops are required on other fronts to save the Republic. Besides, Admiral Martin assures me that even if he gets out of that damn bay where he now sits, he won't have the force to get past Lord Hood. We cannot deploy French arms to save Corsica, Captain, so we must employ French wit and cunning instead.'

The general took a watch from his pocket, considered it, and frowned.

'You see, there is another player on Corsica,' he continued. 'Ercule Leandri, who calls himself general, like Paoli. They fought together in the fifties and sixties, but there has always been suspicion and bad blood between their families. Leandri has remained aloof from Paoli's new rebellion and has not declared for either France or England. If he can be persuaded to take our side, then Corsica could still be saved from Paoli's damn English alliance and take its rightful place in our republic.'

'With respect, Citizen General, I still do not see what you think I can do to bring all this about.'

'There are two things, Captain. We are sending an emissary to Leandri, an emissary to whom he will certainly listen. That emissary is to convince Leandri that we can give him something that he has always wanted above anything else in the world, something with which he is obsessed, something the English cannot give him. I know him, Captain, I have met him often and he has talked about this nearly every time we have ever spoken. I believe that if we offer him this one thing, it will persuade him to declare for France, to turn his army against Paoli and the English.'

'This is a thing of great value, then.'

'To him, undoubtedly. To you and I, a mere triviality, a thing of as little consequence as dust. For that is it, you see, Captain, that is what it is. General Leandri wants dust, the dust of the dead. He wants the bones of Christopher Columbus.'

Philippe had surely misheard. He and this impossibly youthful general were discussing the highest matters of state, nothing less than France's entire strategy in the Mediterranean and the fate of the island of Corsica. The general surely could not be connecting that to the corpse of a man who had been dead for nearly three centuries.

'Of course, it is incredible to us, as men of reason,' said the general. 'And Leandri proclaims himself a man of reason too. That is why he insisted on you and no other as the escort for our emissary to him – he is a great admirer of the works of Verité, you see. He told me once that he met your father, some thirty years ago now. I expect he will tell you of it, too. He is not a reticent man. But for all his talk of reason, Captain, he is still a slave to the old Corsican superstitions, the obsession with death and the otherworld, all of it. My late lamented father, my brothers and I have spent our lives raging against it and trying to drag Corsica into the modern world. But for now, alas, the pull of the old ways is still too strong, in part thanks to Ercule Leandri and those who think like him.'

'But the body of Columbus, Citizen General? What does Columbus have to do with Corsica?'

For the first time, Philippe detected a slight smile on the general's lips.

'It's an old story that I learned in my childhood. Columbus was Genoese, of course, but at the time, Genoa ruled Corsica. The legend has it that Columbus was born in Calvi. To this day, the people there will show you the house where he is meant to have been born. Leandri believes it with all his heart. He has spent years searching old documents, looking for the proof. His dearest dream is to see the body of Columbus brought back to Calvi, to be given a last resting place in the cathedral there. He seeks a shrine, as much to his life's obsession as to the man who will be buried there.'

'Some of the Americans I knew in my youth made much of Columbus, Citizen General. He was a great man who did a great thing, there's no doubt of that. But surely he was buried on one of the islands in the West Indies?'

The general nodded.

'Hispaniola, in the cathedral of Santo Domingo. Spanish territory, but there is a campaign afoot on the island. For all we know, Captain, the city might already be under our control. If not, it undoubtedly soon will be. So our emissary will work to convince Leandri that we will repatriate the remains of Columbus to Calvi once Hispaniola is ours, as long as he acts against Paoli to prevent English rule over Corsica. As a sign of our good faith we are sending him both this emissary, who has been in France for years and whose return he has long sought, and you, the son of Verité. Together, the two of you will convince General Leandri of France's good intentions and our ability to fulfil his life's ambition.'

'With respect, General, I am no diplomat. I am no politician.'

The general's expression was contemptuous.

'A soldier is but a diplomat with a sword, a politician with a gun. You have held rank in three navies, Captain, so you'll know what it means to be under orders. You are now under mine. Paris knows of this strategy and approves it. I can secure written orders from there if you wish me to, but our rulers won't thank you for wasting days in which you could simply complete this mission, earn their, my and France's sincere gratitude, and return to your ship. Your decision, Captain Kermorvant?'

The general could be bluffing, but Philippe could not take the chance. He could risk a court-martial and a firing squad, or he could follow this confident young general's orders, escort his emissary safely to Corsica, meet this General Leandri whose allegiance could apparently be bought by nothing more than a box of old bones, and then return to the command of *Le Torrington*. In truth, he knew it was no choice at all.

'I am your servant, Citizen General,' said Philippe.

The general looked at his watch once again.

'Of course you are. I must be elsewhere, but one thing remains – you must meet your charge, Captain.'

The general knocked twice on the table, and the junior officer, Nordin, appeared so quickly it was as if he had been eavesdropping at the door.

'General?'

'Nordin, bring my other guest, then make the preparations for their safe passage to the coast. I'll expect to rendezvous with you again in Toulon.'

'As you say, Citizen General.'

The young man inclined his head to both Philippe and the general before leaving the room.

Philippe thought the general would speak to him again, but the man turned his back, clasping his hands behind him and seemingly intently studying something in the grate. The bell in the village clocktower tolled. Somewhere downstairs, a party of soldiers, obviously well gone in their cups, began a rollicking song about a baker's daughter from Amiens. Finally, there was a sound on the stairs and Nordin entered the room again.

Behind him stood the general's emissary.

A little older than Nordin and the general, Philippe reckoned, but a little younger than himself. Eyes cast downward demurely, avoiding his gaze. He knew he was staring, but he could not prevent it.

The emissary was a woman.

CHAPTER EIGHT

Her name was Carla Leandri, and she was the Corsican general's daughter.

The young general at Le Muy had introduced them, but told Philippe nothing about her or why she, of all people, should be undertaking a mission to her father on behalf of the French Republic. Her dress, a cotton jacket and skirt in restrained shades of green, and the dainty bonnet that she wore over curling auburn hair, provided no clues. Nor did her fixed, shy expression and quiet voice. For several hours after dawn the next day, when they began their journey to the coast through wild hill country escorted by Nordin and a dozen bored infantrymen, Philippe's occasional attempts to ride beside her carriage and engage her in conversation produced barely audible replies of one syllable, if she deigned to reply at all. Despite the obvious discomfort she was in from carriage wheels that coped badly with the rutted road through the foothills, Carla Leandri seemed lost in her thoughts. But as the country around them became more open as it descended toward the sea, the implausible emissary seemed to become more interested in both her surroundings and the men around her, especially in the man who, uniquely in that company, was wearing naval uniform.

After six hours or so, the party stopped to take refreshment in the shade of a ruined monastery built on the lower slopes of a jagged mountain. Apart from a few distant shepherds and their flocks, they were alone in the landscape. Nordin went to attend to his troops, leaving Carla Leandri alone in Philippe's company. The two of them sat facing each other on large lumps of fallen masonry, chewing greedily on the sausages and cheese that Nordin had requisitioned in Le Muy.

'You have been away from Corsica for some time, mademoiselle?' said Philippe, making an effort to initiate at least some cursory conversation.

The old bourgeois form of address for an unmarried woman, officially frowned upon in the brave egalitarian republic, seemed somehow more appropriate for the delicate, elegantly dressed creature before him than the state-sanctioned but austere word citizeness.

'Nearly four years, Citizen Captain,' she said, again so quietly that Philippe barely heard her. He expected that to be the sum total of her answer, but after a few moments' silence, she spoke again and with a little more confidence. 'I was sent to Paris to complete my education. In that time, so much has happened there, and in France. I saw the guillotining of the king – of Louis Capet, that is.' She was guarded in her speech, uncertain of how fanatical a republican Philippe might be. 'My father wanted me to come home, but...'

For so many families throughout France, there had been a 'but'. The revolution had destroyed ambitions and careers, families and lives, just as it had made others. Yet with Carla Leandri, it was clear that her 'but' had a multitude of meanings.

'And now you serve as France's envoy to your father, Mademoiselle Leandri.'

'Unofficially, in N— in the general's mind. It suits his purpose. His family and our family have known each other for countless generations, you see. I knew him as a child. Our fathers, they were for Paoli, then against him, then for him, then against him once more. That is the way of things in Corsica, Captain.'

'And is it part of the way of things in Corsica that your father might be persuaded to declare for France simply by an offer of the remains of Christopher Columbus? Not wealth or power, but a box full of dust and bones?'

She did not answer immediately, and when she did, she repeated herself.

'That is also the way of things in Corsica. We Corsicans see things differently to the rest of the world, Captain Kermorvant.'

Philippe had more questions for her, not least the pressing one being why her father, General Leandri, was so keen that he, Philippe, and no one else, should escort his daughter home to Corsica. But Nordin came over to inform them it was time to move out, so Carla Leandri returned to her carriage and Philippe mounted his horse for the final leg of the journey.

The road gradually sloped down to the sea and met it at Fréjus, a small port on the Mediterranean. It was evident to Philippe that this had once been a larger and far grander place. Towering ruins, obviously Roman, proclaimed that Fréjus was once a major seat of the empire of the Caesars. Now it was a sleepy backwater, a cenotaph of lost glories, well off the main routes between Marseilles, Toulon and the Italian front, its harbour too silted to serve any French warships that were not blockaded in the Bay of Gourjean or to accommodate large trading vessels. The streets and taverns were largely empty save for a few of those familiar, rough-hewn creatures who haunted every small, easily overlooked harbour in every coastal country in the world; swarthy, well-muscled men of indeterminate age and nationality who might have been fishermen, smugglers, pirates, or all three in one. Several of them made themselves scarce as soon as they saw the blue uniforms of Philippe, Nordin and the men with them. Those who remained watched curiously, then lustfully, as Carla Leandri emerged from her carriage, visibly relieved that the discomfort of the road was over.

'Your ship should be here, citizeness,' said Nordin. 'I will make enquiries.'

Carla Leandri inclined her head very slightly, and Nordin, after giving orders to his corporal, went off. Carla walked slowly along the quayside, gazing out to sea as though hoping for a glimpse of her native land. Philippe followed a few paces behind her. A few of the old fishermen mending nets and some of the children running around the harbourside stared at them, unaccustomed to the sight of an elegantly dressed young lady and a naval captain promenading in such a backwater as Fréjus.

Carla Leandri turned and gave him the thinnest of smiles.

'You need to remove your clothes, Captain.'

'Mademoiselle?'

'Your clothes,' she said with unexpected confidence and apparent seriousness. 'You need to change them. Apart from Calvi and my father's heartland, Corsica is ruled by the English and Paoli. Their troops will be everywhere. I'd advise against wearing that uniform when we land. Truth be told, Captain, you need to have something more of the peasant about you.'

The sense of her comment was obvious, especially as Courtois had omitted to pack any civilian clothing that made Philippe appear as anything other than a man of some status. So Philippe crossed to the stalls of the slopsellers, whose kind were present in every port in the world: widows and crippled seamen, earning a living by selling the clothes of dead men. A few minutes of haggling bought him an outfit that approximately fitted him but made him look like a clerk who had fallen on hard times, as, perhaps, had the original owner of the garments. The meticulous Courtois would probably faint if he saw the spectacle. Philippe vowed not to change into the costume until he was in sight either of Corsica or a British warship.

He returned to see that Nordin had with him a remarkably tall, bronzed, unfashionably bearded man dressed predominantly in black, who was speaking animatedly to Carla Leandri. At the sight of Philippe, he broke off, eyeing Philippe's uniform and sword with unconcealed contempt.

'Kermorvant,' he said. 'The one who escaped from England.'

'You have the advantage of me, sir.'

'In so many ways, Captain, in so many ways.'

Nordin intervened. 'Captain Giordano owns and commands the vessel that will take you and Citizeness Leandri to Corsica.'

'I do and will once I've seen sight of the Republic's gold. Luc Giordano doesn't hold with credit, citizens.'

The fellow was brazen, and his speech, very like that of the general at Le Muy, marked him as another Corsican. But he was clearly cast from the same mould as the other men who haunted the harbour in Fréjus, and Philippe wondered how much, if any, of Captain Luc Giordano's income derived from entirely legal sources.

'The payment's in hand,' said Nordin, 'just as I assured you. You'll sail on the morning ebb, as agreed?'

'A soldier who's heard of ebbs. Will you believe that, Captain Kermorvant? But yes, the morning ebb it'll be. Luc Giordano's given his word on it, y'see, and all men know my word's good from Alicante to Aleppo. So come along, my fine passengers, let's get you aboard and find you berths for the night. My cabin for you, Citizeness Leandri. Propriety is all, so I'll lay my head in the fo'c's'le. That'll do for you too, Captain Kermorvant. Not as grand as you're used to on frigates, I expect, but better than an English prison hulk, eh?'

Giordano led them along the quayside, past a number of yawls and skiffs under repair. Philippe did not like the man but could not explain why. He seemed perfectly respectful toward Carla Leandri, and he could not be blamed for insisting so forcefully on his payment. The Republic was notorious for late settlement of its debts, and all too often for a failure to pay at all, so Giordano's attitude was simple good sense. But there was still something about the man—

They were in the shadow of another ruinous, towering piece of Roman masonry when it came to Philippe.

With his long black beard and black clothing, Luc Giordano had a very slight resemblance to the young Orthodox priest who recited the prayers over the slaughtered bodies of Tasha and Ivan as they were laid to rest in the frozen soil of Kronstadt, then spent hours lecturing Philippe on the necessity of forgiveness. But no priest, no patriarch, no power in heaven or earth would ever persuade Philippe to forgive Count Vladimir Kyrilovich Bulgakov.

'There she is,' said Giordano, pointing to a vessel lying at single anchor in the main channel. '*Lucrezia*.'

'A schooner,' said Philippe appreciatively. 'I've seen plenty in American waters, but none before in this sea.'

'Faster than anything the English have got out there, for sure. Better than any xebec, even. You'll see tomorrow, Captain. Maybe I can teach the Marine Nationale a thing or two about sailing.'

–

Luc Giordano's opinion of his vessel's qualities was no exaggeration. After a few hours' uncomfortable sleep in a hammock in the cramped, crowded fo'c'sle of *Lucrezia*, Philippe was woken by the raising of the anchor. He went up on deck, dressed in his newly purchased slops, and as dawn broke, he watched Luc Giordano con the schooner out of the harbour of Fréjus. Philippe spent the entire day observing Giordano and his crew expertly work the schooner's rig to best advantage on the starboard tack in a helpful south-westerly breeze. The few coasters lumbering along the coast were slugs in comparison. A distant sail, proclaimed by Giordano to be an English frigate, made a desultory attempt to close the schooner but quickly abandoned its hopeless effort. Being a passenger on another man's ship always felt strange to Philippe. The wish to take the wheel and issue commands was almost overwhelming. If it were his command, Philippe would have ordered the deck clutter to be tidied, sometimes sailed more to windward and sometimes less, done a hundred little things differently. But he kept his mouth firmly closed. Luc Giordano may have acted like a pirate and looked like a man who had tried and failed to bring comfort to the bereaved and tortured Philippe Kermorvant, but he knew his business and he knew his vessel. Above all, Giordano had been right. *Lucrezia* was fast, and nothing that came within sight

73

throughout the voyage came remotely close to closing her or outrunning her.

After five or six hours the distant coast of Corsica began to come into sight, and Philippe had his first view of Carla Leandri's homeland. As *Lucrezia* drew nearer, the island appeared to Philippe to be simply a solid mountain range rising directly from the sea, successive peaks rearing up beside and behind each other. Low clouds and intermittent drizzle made the land appear and disappear, like some ghost island from the old stories. Corsica presented a far starker landscape than the coasts of Virginia where he had grown up and learned to sail, a less threatening landfall than the coast of Brittany that he had come to know in the previous year, but there was a unique air of mystery about the land ahead. Philippe began to believe it was the sort of place that might spawn men whose ambition was not for gold or power, but for the dust that had once been Christopher Columbus.

The unlikely emissary of the young general at Le Muy did not appear for the entire voyage, not even to get her first glimpse in years of the land of her birth. *Mal de mer*, Philippe assumed, for she had not seemed to have a particularly strong constitution during their journey down to Fréjus. Once again he wondered at the general's conviction that this retiring, insipid girl could somehow persuade her father to change the course of the war in Corsica, and change it by such a patently risible ploy as a promise to repatriate the bones of a long-dead navigator. All things taken into account, though, none of it was his concern. He would escort Carla Leandri to her father, satisfy the old man's odd but apparently sincere compulsion to meet the son of Verité, then return to France and the command of *Le Torrington*, even if that meant many more weeks of frustrating inactivity in the Bay of Gourjean.

'Ever been on a faster sailer than the old *Lucrezia*, Captain?'

Giordano had barely glanced at him since they left Fréjus, let alone spoken to him. But all captains take inordinate pride in their ships, and even the surliest enjoy nothing better than to show off their vessel's qualities to another mariner.

'I served briefly on a small schooner in the American war,' said Philippe. 'Coastal waters, though. No opportunity for such a run as this. But schooners are surely rare in this sea, are they not?'

'And that's *Lucrezia*'s advantage,' said Giordano, grinning. 'Nobody's encountered her like, and they don't know how fast she is until they see us shaking our bare arses their way as our stern vanishes far ahead of 'em. I won her at a bullfight in Alicante, betting on the outcomes with her owner. He claimed to be a Portugee but I reckon he was half-Moor and had sailed with the corsairs. Any rate, he made no objection to taking drink. That was how he lost *Lucrezia*. No objection to taking more drink, and more again, until his senses were washed away.'

Giordano raised his telescope to scan the horizon, then offered the instrument to Philippe, who accepted it gratefully. Habit dictated that he should first seek anything that might be a sail, but with nothing worthy of attention at any point of the compass, he focused finally on the land ahead, which was now close enough for him to make out individual features. The mountains ran to the sea in places, forming colossal cliffs, but elsewhere a coastal plain dotted with small settlements gradually rose to heavily forested foothills and then the mountains themselves. Rugged lands produced hard, independent-minded people, and Corsica was one of the most rugged terrains he had ever seen.

He was aware of movement behind him, and turned to see Carla Leandri finally emerge from below decks. The sight coincided with a sudden gust, and Philippe nearly lost his balance. He blamed the wind, but it might have been the unexpected spectacle before him. It was as though a different woman stood on the deck of *Lucrezia*. The jacket and skirt of a respectable young woman were gone, their place taken by a seaman's shirt and tunic, culottes, boots and a broad-brimmed hat. From her belt hung a dagger and a pistol. Gone, too, was the retiring Parisian maiden. Carla Leandri's face exuded confidence and joy. She gazed out toward the mountains of her homeland and smiled.

Giordano turned to face her, grinned at the sight and bowed his head respectfully.

'You've returned to us, *Generalissima*,' he said.

PART TWO

CHAPTER NINE

'The river, my lord? The Severn? Really?'

'Really, Jenkins. I'll find a trow or a sailing barge to take me upstream. Don't you consider that a fitting mode of conveyance for a Lord of the Admiralty?'

Lord Wilden smiled at his ancient coachman, to whom he gave far greater licence than any of his other servants. But none of the others had been there for literally as long as he could remember, from the very day of his birth and through the entirety of his fatherless childhood. Jenkins, a burly, powerful man in his younger days who had no children of his own, taught the young Ned Pardew, Lord Wilden, brought up in a household full of women, what it was to grow into a man.

'I hear,' Wilden continued, 'that the bargemen and rivermen of the Severn are proving most reluctant to volunteer for the navy and that the Press finds the inhabitants of those parts strangely elusive, despite such men being entirely eligible for service at sea. It's really the business of individual captains and the Navy Board, not the Admiralty, but it strikes me, Jenkins, that news of an Admiralty lord interesting himself directly in the backsliding of those who make their livings on the Severn might serve a salutary purpose.'

'Yes, my lord.'

The long-serving-retainer's face was inscrutable, as it always was. It was impossible to tell if he thought the scheme inspired or an act of the utmost lunacy.

'Besides, Jenkins, the road beyond Kidderminster is barely worthy of the name. Our journey down to Croome nearly did for my arse. The smug gentlemen who sit on the Turnpike Trust are utterly venal, pocketing all the money from tolls and spending none of it on repair and maintenance.'

'As you say, my lord. Utterly venal. Stourport for the river, then?'

'Stourport indeed, Jenkins. You may bring the coach back to Alveley in your own time, I shall not be needing it until I go back to London, and that will not be for several days now that I have the business of the cavalry to attend to.'

'My lord.'

They stood in the yard of an old black-and-white timbered inn in Ombersley, where they had stopped to rest and water the horses. Wilden had been at Croome Court near Pershore, the home of the Earl of Coventry, lord-lieutenant of Worcestershire. Coventry was a man in his seventies, as was one of the other attendees at the hastily convened meeting, Lord Bateman, Coventry's equivalent in Herefordshire. The third lord-lieutenant in attendance, Lord Clive from Wilden's own county of Shropshire, was a much younger man, not yet forty, but despite being the son of the man who had won India for Britain at the Battle of Plassey he was merely an Irish peer, so he was able to serve as an MP in the House of Commons. But Clive was a member of the Duke of Portland's faction of the Whig Party and thus a member of the opposition to the government of Prime Minister William Pitt, in which Wilden was proud to serve in a humble capacity. It was true that the Portland Whigs were loyal to Church and State, unlike their Foxite Whig so-called brethren, a gaggle of would-be revolutionary Robespierres and Oliver Cromwells led by Charles James Fox, that whoremongering card-sharp, that inciter of popular hysteria, that veritable English Satan. Lord Clive could not be tarred with that brush, but his Whiggism and Indian antecedents made him a little too exotic for Pitt's liking. Consequently, the prime minister, mindful of the advanced age of the other two lords-lieutenant in that middle part of the Welsh border country, had asked Wilden to attend their meeting to give it a backbone of loyalty, of relatively vigorous youth, and, it had to be said even if immodestly, of intelligence too.

The horses, his four splendid Cleveland Bays, were back in harness and Jenkins indicated that it was time to set off. Wilden nodded, finished his tankard of cider – a most unlordly but satisfyingly refreshing drink to which the coachman had introduced him when he was perhaps seven or eight – and climbed back into his coach-and-four, acknowledging the deferential bow from the landlord of the inn.

As he looked out across the verdant fields of Worcestershire, it was hard to imagine these peaceful acres ravaged by war. But the young Ned Pardew, encouraged by Jenkins, always had a vivid imagination, and in his mind's eye even now, as a grown man, he could see the crops trampled by arrogant French regiments, barns burned by their English Jacobin sympathisers, the cheerful village lasses raped and their chubby babies impaled on enemy bayonets. It had been less easy to imagine it all in the refined drawing room of Croome Court, difficult to convince the three lords-lieutenant of the reality of the threat to their lands, their lives and all that England stood for. Lord Clive even dared to suggest that the government's urgent call for new volunteer regiments to complement the regular militia, the ostensible reason for the meeting at Croome, was an over-reaction. Wilden had got to his feet angrily and recited the evidence. His companions knew of the great radical convention in Edinburgh the previous December and all the incendiary speeches that had been made at it, but Bateman in particular dismissed all this as nothing more than yet another case of the Scots becoming over-excited. Wilden disabused him. Pikes had recently been discovered in the house of a blacksmith and a wine merchant in the North British city. The men had been charged with treason, but they were not alone. Other favourers of the so-called cause of liberty had been arrested, charged with sedition and transported to England's convenient new penal colony at Botany Bay on the far side of the world. And if Wilden's noble colleagues were not convinced, had they forgotten the riot and massacre in Bristol in the previous year? Did they not know that even now, there were riots in London centred on the crimp houses? Sedition was everywhere, revolutionary poison seeping into every sinew of English life, while across the Channel – and here Wilden hinted at secret intelligence to which he, as a lord of the Admiralty, was privy – Robespierre and his minions were assembling a great army of fanatical and murderous Frenchmen to invade England. It was not true, for not even Wilden possessed such intelligence, but there was little doubt that the French harboured such an ambition. They wanted to bring down all kings and lords the world over. If they were given the chance they would send King George to the guillotine, along with all those meeting in that comfortable drawing room.

And this (it was a strange and unlooked-for thought, to come into his head at that very moment) – and this was the course Cousin Philippe had elected to follow when the choice was offered, the path he had taken, rather than accepting his obvious and natural destiny to serve England. He had made his choice and thrown in his lot with the murderers, the atheists, the regicides. It was inexplicable.

Wilden was not a man commonly given to displays of fervour or emotion. But the complacency of those meeting at Croome Court and the seriousness of the apparent threat to the ancient English constitution and way of life represented by the clear stirrings of Jacobin revolution throughout the land had fired the heart of Edward, Lord Wilden, and inspired him to rare heights of rhetoric. Why, after all, did they think the government had recently suspended *habeas corpus*? Would they have taken such a step if there was no threat? No. The only guarantee of English liberties was to take away the most ancient and fundamental liberty of all. A strictly temporary and regret-table necessity, of course, but if the cure was that drastic, how could they believe there was no disease? How could they doubt the need for new volunteer units when every man in England needed to be in arms to preserve their beloved country from the deadly plague of French Jacobinism and its malevolent toy, the guillotine? To set an example, he announced in this moment of uncharacteristic enthusiasm, he was offering to raise a troop of horsemen from among his tenants and neighbours. The upshot of it all was that the notably unmartial Edward, Lord Wilden, found himself provisionally commissioned as the captain and acting commanding officer of the Alveley Volunteer Cavalry within the Shropshire Volunteers.

When he told the old coachman, Jenkins was greatly amused by it all. He always said that Ned Pardew had been the one little boy in England who preferred nearly anything to playing with toy soldiers.

–

Hartlebury Common was a wild, empty place of poor soil where no crops would grow and no animals would graze on the rough bushes and bare gorse. On Lord Wilden's instruction, though, Jenkins steered the coach down the rough lane that crossed the common. The route enabled Wilden to avoid the main road and the otherwise inevitable courtesy call on the Bishop of Worcester at Hartlebury Castle. Bishop Hurd was a good man, sound of doctrine and political principle, but he was somewhat too other-worldly for Wilden's liking. Despite being a favourite of the king, the man had turned down the Archiepiscopate of Canterbury because its responsibilities would divert him too much from prayer, contemplation and the pastoral care of his flock. Or so he said.

Perfectly unaccountable.

Stourport, their destination, was a new town, built only twenty or thirty years before. It stood where the much-vaunted new canals, bearing goods from the manufactories in Birmingham and the Black Country, reached the new basins and wharves where they could be transferred to the craft that could take them down to Gloucester and even Bristol for onward transhipment. Lord Wilden was suspicious of the place. He disliked industry in all its forms and branches. He detested the iron foundries and the like that had sprung up along the Severn, especially upstream from Alveley Hall at Ironbridge. But he knew that his family, the Pardews, had once been no more than charcoal burners in the Wyre Forest, and that these ancestors had made their money from iron and other industries. So he did not condemn those, including some of his neighbours, who gained their incomes from manufacture. Even so, he intensely disliked the manifestations of that money-making, the dirt, the smoke, the ugly buildings, the noise, above all the smells.

Stourport had all of these. On this particular day, though, it had something else too. As they came into the town, going uphill from a bridge over the principal canal, Jenkins reined in.

'What is it, Jenkins?'

But as Lord Wilden leaned out of the coach window to ask the question, he heard the noises that had alerted his coachman.

'Sounds to me like a riot of some sort, my lord.'

'A riot? Here?'

But the sounds reaching the coach allowed no other inter-pretation. There were shouts and jeers, drunken songs, the unmistakeable sound of windows being broken, a drum being beaten. They could make out a few individual shouts and chants.

'To hell with all lords!'

'*Vive la France!*'

'A fair wage for a fair day's work!'

'Pitt to the guillotine!'

'Fuck the king!'

'We should turn back, my lord. Make for the castle in Hartle-bury. That'll be safe until all this blows over.'

Despite its name, Hartlebury Castle, the bishop's country palace, was not a fortress. But it had high walls and stout gates, for the bishops of Worcester had ever been careful of their security.

'But where's the militia, Jenkins? Where's the magistrate to read the Riot Act?'

Wilden was a justice of the peace for Shropshire, but this was Worcestershire. Despite also being a lord of the Admiralty, he had no authority here.

But he knew a man who did.

'Witley Court, Jenkins – we must go there immediately.'

'Lord Foley's estate, my lord? But he's only a boy.'

The previous Lord Foley, christened Lord Balloon by the wits on account of his prodigious girth, had died in the previous year.

'His uncle is there at the moment – he called on me only last week. He's a justice for Worcestershire.'

'But that means crossing Stourport Bridge, my lord. We'd be going through the body of the rioters. Much better to make for Hartlebury and seek sanctuary with the bishop.'

'The Lord Bishop isn't a justice, Jenkins. He could send for one, but it will take longer than getting Mister Foley to come from Witley. Give the horses their head, Jenkins, we'll scatter any damn Jacobins who stand in our way or else crush 'em under the hooves or the coach wheels. It'll be their choice whether they stand fast or get out of our way. Drive for the bridge!'

'But, my lord—'

'My pistols are primed, man. Any rioter who so much as touches the paintwork of my coach gets a ball in his chest for his pains. None of them will dare. They'll come apart like the opening of the Red Sea for Moses. So drive, Jenkins, drive as though all the furies of Hell are at our backs!'

He tried to sound as confident as possible, but he knew it had been his confidence, nothing else, that had brought them to this pass. Over-confidence, indeed. In normal circumstances Lord Wilden and his coachman would be accompanied by Dysart cradling a blunderbuss on the box seat next to Jenkins and acting as relief driver when needed, but the lad was sickly and, in any case, as Wilden had said, there had been no highwaymen on the roads of Worcestershire for generations. If Jenkins required some respite then Wilden could take the reins himself, as he loved to do ever since he was first taught the handling of a team of horses by the veteran coachman. There would usually also be two footmen riding at the back, but Wilden knew the Earl of Coventry's hospitality of old and thus knew that these would be entirely redundant at Croome Court. Besides, there were more important tasks for them to attend to at Alveley Hall.

Add to that already potent brew his conceit, for it was nothing else, for deciding to make for Stourport solely to save himself an uncomfortable hour or two on the road north from Kidderminster. Folly. Utter, unadulterated folly.

With hindsight, Lord Wilden realised just how insanely foolish he had been.

Reluctantly, Jenkins took up the reins. The coach moved forward, turning left onto the long street that ran down to the bridge. Wilden, still looking out of the coach window, saw the mob a few hundred yards away. There were more than he had thought, but Jenkins had more than enough room to get the team up to a good speed before they drove into the heart of the riot. The coachman had been a veritable Phaeton in his younger days, and although he was much more cautious now, Wilden had no doubt that the dear old man could pull it off and save him from the consequences of his own lunacy.

Not all the people in the town were rioters. He could see men, women and children on either side of the street, watching the disorder but playing no part. There was one boy in particular, a gangling lad of twelve or thirteen with dirty black hair, who was trying to attract his father's attention to the coach. Perhaps he was taken by the coat of arms on the door, knew that it signified the coach of an aristocrat, and was telling his father to attack it.

Or was he simply an honest lad intrigued by the sight of a heraldic blazon?

Damn suspicion, damn doubt, damn them both to Hell.

'*Drive!*' cried Wilden.

Jenkins cracked the whip by the heads of the leaders. The horses snorted but moved forward, accelerating with every yard, their hooves making a frantic drumbeat on the cobbles. A few people, realising what was happening, screamed warnings to the first lines of the mob. Wilden saw the faces of a few rioters, the ones standing where the road began to slope down toward the river, turn to stare at the oncoming coach. Some began to throw themselves out of the way of the terrifying prospect hurtling toward them.

The first screams went up. Wilden pushed himself away from the window in case a chance blow from a cudgel struck him. It was surely inconceivable that any of the rioters had a gun, but he nestled his own pistols against his chest waiting to shoot any man impudent enough to attack the coach.

Shots struck the sides of the coach—

Not shots. A stone came through the window and struck the cushion a few inches to his left. The rioters did not need guns – a fusillade of stones would be enough—

He heard a shout of pain, felt the impact as Jenkins tumbled to his right and off the box seat, saw the coachman fall past the window, glimpsed the hands of rioters reaching out to grab the loyal old man—

But the coach was still moving through the mob, the uncontrolled team of horses still obeying their driver's last command. Wilden glimpsed the large inn at the bottom of the hill, just before the canal basin to the left and the bridge dead ahead. He had to get up to the driver's seat, get control of the team – Jenkins had showed him how – *oh God, Jenkins!*

He swung the door open. There were no rioters down here. Then they were onto the bridge, all the sounds of tumult behind them. All he had to do was haul himself around to the box seat, get control, drive on to Witley Court—

87

One of the leaders, free of Jenkins' persuasion, decided to try and follow its own course, bucking and pulling sharply to the left. Lord Wilden made a desperate grab for the box seat, but the sudden movement left him clutching at air. He was too far out of the door to get back. He was flying out over the parapet of the bridge. As he fell he caught a glimpse of the stern of a trow, sailing upstream toward Bewdley or even beyond.

This is the end. This is death.

Then he plunged into the waters of the Severn.

CHAPTER TEN

The land of Corsica surprised Philippe. He had expected a low island, something akin to a larger version of Sainte-Marguerite, not the towering, jagged mountain peaks that rose from a coastal plain and foothills thick with wild, dense shrub. It had the look and smell of an ancient and singular land, a part of Europe and yet detached, different, indifferent to the eternal squabbles of the continental nations. It had a sense of the otherworldly about it, of a land somehow adrift from the time it was set in. This was the land that had formed General Ercule Leandri, the man Philippe was ordered to win for the Republic, and his enigmatic daughter. He felt unsettled, the same feeling he had known the first time his father took him out into the Virginia backwoods and into the hills where his Powhatan friends had warned him the spirits of the dead roamed abroad for all eternity.

Giordano landed Philippe and the young woman he had now to think of as *la generalissima* on the north-west coast fairly near Calvi, a few miles south-west of the besieged town. A narrow shingle beach gave way to low but steep granite cliffs, then the shrub or *maquis* that stretched the relatively short distance to the foot of the mountains. There was no sign of a village, nor of any sort of habitation other than a couple of ruined shepherds' huts. At one of these, tethered horses awaited the schooner's passengers. These were seemingly guarded only by one old man, a peasant by his dress, but as Giordano, who had landed with his passengers, went over to speak with him, a cloud of dust and the pounding hooves of galloping horses signalled the arrival of some two score riders. For certain, it was no British patrol. Like the old man at the cottage, the horsemen wore peasant attire of short coats of coarse cloth, their heads crowned with black bonnets. Unlike the old man, they were laden with enough swords, pistols, stilettos and muskets to arm a small regiment of the army Philippe had seen at Le Muy.

The leader of the party reined in before them. He was a very tall man, his skin so dark he might have been taken for a moor, but the most striking thing about him was that he had only one hand, the right arm ending in a foreshortened stump.

Carla Leandri stepped forward to greet him.

'It's good to see you, Jacobo,' she said.

The tall man nodded. 'Cousin. I rejoice in your return to Corsica. Paris has been kind to you, I see.'

'Not in the way that some intended. And you, Jacobo? How many children now?'

'Six left. Giovanni died last year, as did Rosa.'

'I heard of it in a letter from my father. I prayed for you, cousin, and for the souls of your wife and son. I prayed that the Squadra d'Arrozza would visit your door no more.'

Jacobo nodded his thanks. With his one remaining hand he waved a stiff and wary greeting to Giordano, then his eyes finally settled on Philippe.

'You're the Republic's envoy, then?'

Jacobo Leandri's tone was at once suspicious and contemptuous.

'No envoy, simply the man ordered to escort your cousin home. Otherwise, a mere captain of the Marine Nationale.'

Jacobo Leandri snorted.

'Ah, that. The invisible navy. All we see off our coast is the other one – the one with the flag that looks like a child trying to draw a crushed spider. You happy to leave your precious tub in the bay there, Giordano, with the English like a plague of locusts on our coast?'

Luc Giordano scowled.

'Leave matters of the sea to those who know about them, Leandri,' he said. 'The English only care about taking Calvi, and they know there's no point patrolling this coast. No French fleet with a relief army is turning up any time soon – that not so, Captain Kermorvant?'

Philippe could only nod at the humiliating but inescapable truth.

Carla Leandri, ignoring the tension between the men, was choosing her horse, finally settling on an alert-looking brown-black stallion.

'The talk can wait,' she said. 'Where's my father?'

'Ghineparu,' said her cousin.

'Good,' she said, 'I've missed it.'

She swung herself effortlessly into the saddle and sat astride her mount, demonstrating once again that the demure creature from the inn at Le Muy had been no more than an illusion, an act staged for the benefit of both Philippe and the young general. Among the dozens of rough, vicious-looking men who surrounded her, Carla Leandri did not look out of place. Instead, the men deferred to her and looked on her with respect and love. It was she, not her cousin Jacobo, who gave the order to ride and took her place at the head of the little regiment, her kinsman, Giordano and Philippe all falling in behind her. Here, in her own land and among her own people, she was *la generalissima* indeed.

–

The road into the mountains was hardly worthy of the name. It was a rough path, used (or so Giordano said) principally as a track for shepherds and their flocks to travel between their summer and winter pastures. It skirted the northern side of a steep valley, the lower slopes thick with oak and chestnut trees, bare granite peaks towering far above. There was no prospect of encountering British patrols, Giordano told Philippe. While they had overwhelming force at sea, as Philippe had seen with his own eyes, the Englishmen had little more than a thousand troops on Corsica and they were all committed to the siege of

Calvi. The only force they were likely to encounter was a unit of General Paoli's militia, but they would present no difficulty. Paoli may have thrown in his lot with the English but Leandri was still neutral, at least in name, and that was why the little army was riding along the precarious mountain track toward the strangely named village of Ghineparu. That, it seemed, was where the two veteran generals, Paoli and Leandri, were meeting in conference, with Paoli hoping to win over his old friend, then enemy, then neutral, to the idea of Corsica as one of the kingdoms of King George the Third.

The party rested overnight at a ruin in the lee of one of the less prominent peaks. Most of the men slept on the bare ground, but blankets were produced for Carla and a few of the men, including Philippe. Fires were lit, cuts of lamb were roasted, flasks and bottles were produced from saddlebags, and after they had feasted the Corsicans sang songs of their homeland.

The summer night was warm and sleep elusive. The Corsicans instituted a rota of watches for those assigned to picket duty, but Philippe's instincts told him it would be a perfect place for a hostile force to execute an ambush. He had ridden and hunted enough with the Powhatan as a boy to have acquired something of their instincts, and all the way through the foothills and into the mountains he had an uncomfortable sense that their party was being watched from somewhere within the cover provided by the trees and undergrowth. He raised his concerns with Giordano, questioning the lighting of tell-tale fires and the party's cacophonous singing, but the schooner captain, who was more than a little drunk, merely laughed. This was Corsica, he said. It was Leandri land, they were Corsicans, Leandris and the friends and followers of the Leandris. The reassurances failed to assuage Philippe's doubts. He slept little, but when he awoke a little before the rest of the camp he saw that the night had passed without incident.

They set off again early in the morning, and a few miles up the track Carla Leandri indicated that Philippe should come forward to ride alongside her, a gesture that amused Luc Giordano but seemed greatly to irritate her cousin Jacobo.

'So, Captain,' said the young woman. 'What are your impressions of Corsica?'

'It is a mighty country, *madem* – citizeness – what should I call you?'

The question greatly amused her.

'Anything but *generalissima*,' she said, smiling. 'My father bestowed the title on me as a conceit when I was very little, because I ordered his men around as if I, not he, was commanding his army. Over time the men took it up and treated me as if I really was a general. Then my only brother died, so I was taught all the things he had been learning – how to ride and shoot, how to wield a sword. Not the usual attributes of a Corsican woman, but I had a talent for all of it.'

'Yet you displayed none of those attributes when I first met you.'

The smile broadened.

'Men tend to be wary of women who can shoot them dead from fifty paces, Captain. But my father sent me to Paris to learn refinement and the ways of a French lady. I've never doubted that he had a view to making me a better prospect in marriage, but his timing was unfortunate. It was three years ago, when all seemed calm in France – before all the madness began and the king was executed, all the rest of it. Then, last year, Paoli broke with the National Convention in Paris to pursue his old dream of an independent Corsica. Citizen Robespierre sought to use my father as a counterweight, so I became a hostage in all but name and was kept in Paris. When the news came that Paoli was planning to offer Corsica to the English, I went to Robespierre and persuaded him that I could convince my father to declare for France.'

'And the general you were with at Le Muy?'

She laughed.

'Poor man, he's always thought himself so clever. We knew each other as children, as I told you. He always had such grand schemes, such wild strategies, such an overwhelming belief in his own rightness. In his destiny, if you like. So I knew that if I played the part of his submissive agent, a humble tool of the France he idolises above his native land, he would serve my purpose. Which purpose, of course, was to go home.'

Philippe glanced across at the extraordinary creature riding alongside him. He had encountered only one other woman who talked in such a way, who bent men to her will and dictated their actions as if they were pieces on a chessboard. But that other woman had been forty years older than Carla Leandri, and she had also been the empress of Russia.

'And what is my part in your purpose, citizeness?'

'Now that, Captain, is no more than what you have been told. You, the son of Verité, will help me to convince my father to declare for France.'

'I am not your prisoner, then?'

She laughed once more.

'Not unless Paoli has convinced my father to go in with him and declare for England. In that case, Captain, I think I will be as much a prisoner as you.'

CHAPTER ELEVEN

Lord Wilden's head broke the surface of the river.

The current had already carried him through the middle of the three stone arches of Stourport Bridge. Turning his head to the left, he saw the locks leading to and from the canal basins. Candles were already lit in the large modern inn that towered over them. There were still sounds of riot in the town, but they were far away. There was no one on the riverbank to even notice his predicament, let alone make an effort to extricate him from the waters. Wilden pulled off his dress coat – expensive, damn it, but it would only drag him under – and struck out for the shore, settling into the rhythm of his strong front crawl.

Peers of the realm did not swim, said his older and eternally insufferable sister, Perdita. But their mother, who had lost her father to a drowning accident and her husband to a fall while riding, took another view. When he was still a baby, Lord Wilden had been taught by Jenkins to swim, and when he was old enough, Jenkins taught him to ride. All through his childhood the boy swam several times a week in the lake at Alveley Hall. At Oxford he swam in the Cherwell and even the noble Isis itself. In London he swam in the Serpentine. His peers thought him an unfathomable oddity, but Jenkins always told him that one day, being able to swim might save his life.

This was the day.

He reached the bank, hauled himself ashore and coughed violently. For some time, perhaps as long as a few minutes, he lay exhausted, gulping in the beautiful late afternoon English air. Then he became aware that he was not alone.

He pulled himself up and found himself staring at the man and the boy who had been standing at the top of the main street in Stourport. It had been for nothing. They would have alerted the mob. They would already be on their way, the rioters, the revolutionaries, the republicans, the scum of the earth who would probably throw him back into the river and ensure that this time, he stayed there until he drowned. They would—

Jenkins.

What had happened to Jenkins?

'My coachman,' he stammered, his teeth chattering. The man took off his rough woollen jacket and placed it over Lord Wilden's shoulders. 'What happened to my coachman?'

'Can't rightly tell ye, Lord Wilden,' said the father, a strongly built fellow of forty or thereabouts with a stubbled jaw and a cropped head.

'You know who I am?'

The man patted his son's shoulder.

'My Ned, here, recognised your coat of arms on the door of your coach-and-four.'

'*What?* How?'

The idea would have been beyond credulity even if Wilden had not been dripping wet, cold, and in shock. A boy from the lower orders who knew heraldry? It was inconceivable.

'Curate at Mitton Chapel lets me look at his books, my lord,' said the lad proudly. He had an open, cheerful demeanour about him. 'I can read, y'see. I know history. I know the peerage. Wilden of Alveley Hall in the county of Shropshire. Show me the arms of any peer in the middle counties of England and I'll name 'em for you.'

'Then you're not with the mob?'

Ned shook his head as if the suggestion was utterly repugnant.

'Hotheads, the lot of 'em,' said the father, his expression no less hostile. 'Craven fools who've taken too much gin and beer. Too ready to listen to a couple of rabble-rousers who've come down the canal from Brummagem. All for revolution today, but once a magistrate comes with a troop of militia to read the Riot Act, they'll shutter their windows fast as you like and cry out how much they love the king.'

'A magistrate – yes! We must get a message immediately to Mister Foley at Witley Court.'

The father looked at Wilden and smiled.

'A couple of good honest lads already went for him when the whole business started and the first few windows got smashed – this is a loyal town, my lord, despite the clowns and ding coves and sots up there on the High Street. But I've heard tell since that it would be faster to go to Hartlebury for a magistrate. Mister Ingram of Ribbesford is paying a call upon the lord bishop. He's a justice too, so I've heard.'

'That he is, Mister—'

'Drew. Will Drew of Mitton. This is my boy, Ned.'

'Well, Ned Drew, do you reckon you can run to the bishop's palace and summon Mister Ingram?'

The boy grinned.

'Happen.'

'There'll be a sixpence for you.'

'And a guinea for my da?'

'A *guinea*?'

Will Drew clipped his son's ear.

'Be off with ye, boy, do as Lord Wilden says. Meantime, my lord, I've got a new sailing barge just come out of the basin through the locks. I need to take it for a proving voyage. Usually head downstream, but I reckon you'd prefer me to go upstream. Alveley Wharf suit ye, my lord?'

'You're a bargebuilder, Mister Drew?' Will Drew nodded. 'Then yes, it would suit me very well. But first I need to find my coachman.'

Father and son glanced at each other, the boy's expression telling Wilden everything.

'Didn't rightly tell ye the whole truth 'bout him just now, my lord,' said Will Drew. 'Ned, you run to Hartlebury now, then go back to your ma and see young Tom's not getting up to any mischief. Tell her what I'm about and tell her I'll be back the day after tomorrow, depending on the river. Meantime Lord Wilden and I have business.'

An hour later, just as Ned Drew was seeking admission to Hartlebury Castle, his father and Edward Pardew, Lord Wilden, stood before the body of Augustus Jenkins. The old man was laid out on a table in the small, simple chapel of Mitton, which predated the canal that lay at the foot of its graveyard. The coachman's right temple had been lacerated by a stone that left a deep cut and a large, black pool of congealed blood. It might have been the fatal blow; Wilden hoped that it was, and that the dear man had not died from the countless bruises from kicks and punches that disfigured his body.

'I'll leave ye alone with him, my lord,' said Drew. 'Five minutes, then we'll go down the towpath for the river. Shouldn't be anyone from the mob down that way yet, but soon as the Riot Act's read and the militia flash their bayonets you'll have scores of folk trying to sneak back to their homes that way.'

Drew went to the back of the chapel, went through the door and closed it behind him. Left alone, Wilden looked down at the man who had been like a father to him. He wanted to speak to him, to say things that had never been spoken. Instead, he did two things that were almost entirely beyond his compass.

First, he wept. He bent almost double as the tears flowed.

Second, he was overwhelmed with rage. He roared aloud. He beat his fists on the table until they were red and painful. He looked at the cross upon the altar, and up to the heavens, but he did not pray for the soul of Augustus Jenkins. He prayed for vengeance.

He would be avenged on all those responsible for the cold, broken, lifeless body of the man before him. He would be avenged on the Stourport rioters. He would offer rewards, he would send his own Alveley men down river to search out the ringleaders, he would see the man who had thrown the fatal stone dangle from the gallows. He would be avenged on those in King George's realms who sought the overthrow of monarchy and religion, who cried out for a republic, who demanded a warped, perverted vision of liberty.

Above all, he would be avenged on the source of all those monstrous notions. All that falsity. All that sheer evil. And that source was one word, one alone.

France.

He already hated the French Republic with every breath in his body and every beat of his heart. He already worked night and day to undermine and overthrow the satanic wickedness of Robespierre and all the Jacobin devils. But now he would redouble his efforts. France would pay for the death of Augustus Jenkins. In a way, the murder of the old man before him and the meeting he had attended at Croome Court were two sides of the same coin. The new volunteer regiments, including the one in which he was now commissioned, would keep England safe from the republican hydra. There would have been no riot in Stourport, and Augustus Jenkins would still live and breathe, if instead of having to wait for a magistrate and the militia to arrive, a unit of volunteer cavalry had been stationed nearby, able to level their swords and charge into the heart of the mob before it got out of hand.

But then he had to strike at the origin of the plague, at the root of its tree of sedition.

His cousin Philippe came to mind again. Philippe had rejected his offer and chosen the side of evil, the side taken by the murderers of Augustus Jenkins, the side of revolutionary France. So be it.

Wilden vowed that he would work even more indefatigably toward the defeat of the diabolical national enemy and the cancer it had spawned in England. Although he did not know how, he felt a powerful sense that Cousin Philippe had some part to play in this titanic final struggle, the Armageddon of the Book of Revelation.

CHAPTER TWELVE

The village of Ghineparu seemed to cling warily and precariously to the lower slopes of a colossal grey peak. Consisting chiefly of very plain high-walled, small-windowed houses redolent of a bygone era, it gave the impression of still standing on guard against the invaders of those times long past: the likes of the Moors, the Aragonese and, yes, the French too. In fact, it was another set of invaders, the Genoese, who had built the fort on a large rock outcrop above the village, a middling-sized square tower within a defended enclosure surrounded by a more recent addition, a rudimentary star rampart. The one building that stood out in the village itself was a square and lofty church with whitewashed walls and a spindly campanile, an edifice that appeared far too large for the number of houses that surrounded it. This, according to Jacobo Leandri, was the place where the meeting between the veteran leaders was being held.

The choice found little favour with Luc Giordano, who was now riding alongside Philippe.

'Ghineparu,' he said. 'Stupid place. Nothing there. But the same would be true of any of these pigsties in the mountains. Too far from the sea, all of them.'

'Yet you say the sea is full of the English,' said Philippe, who thought he now had the measure of the man.

'I'd still say have the conference on *Lucrezia*. Fast enough to outrun any frigate, safe from any ambush or a stray English patrol, not like up here. But getting the noble General Paoli afloat? I'd like to meet the man who could manage that. None of these great ones want to get their feet wet. Look at the old king, for instance.'

Such a debatably sympathetic remark about the guillotined King Louis the Sixteenth would place Giordano in danger of his own life if the wrong ears heard it.

'You mean Louis Capet?' asked Philippe.

'No, the one before the one before that. Louis *le Grand*. The Fourteenth. They say he only saw the sea three times in his life, and he ruled seventy-two years. Ever since then, no man of rank chooses to go to sea if he can help it. So instead, they get the rest of us traipsing up mountains to shitholes like Ghineparu.'

The party of riders was sighted long before the track climbed high enough to reach the first house in the village. A small army advanced to the edge of the village in front of them, blocking the road. There were at least a hundred men, all as irregularly dressed but as formidably armed as the men Philippe rode with. Although they were all on foot, an engagement against the smaller number of Leandri horsemen would probably be a close-run thing. The front ranks were levelling their muskets. Philippe smiled to himself. Verité had no truck with the notion of fate, but how fateful it would be if the great thinker's son, who had survived war in America, Russia, Turkey and on the high seas against the English Royal Navy, were to perish in the dust of a rough track on an obscure hillside in Corsica, just as his father had died in a skirmish almost too small to be worthy of the name.

Without a hint of trepidation, Carla Leandri rode forward toward the armed barrier, her cousin coming up to ride alongside her. She studied the ranks ahead of her, the men in which were clearly startled by the sight of a woman at the head of an armed force.

'Vincent Oggiano,' she called. 'I see you, Vincent, and I know there's a state of truce between your general and my father.'

A stout, jowly fellow with a cleft lip pushed his way through to the front of the men controlling the road into the village.

'Carla Leandri and her pet dog, Jacobo,' said the fat man in a deep growl. 'Giordano the pirate too. Well, well. Heard tell you were still in Paris, Carla. Heard tell you were Robespierre's whore.'

The Paolist troops, although they scarcely merited the word, laughed, but Jacobo Leandri turned puce and stabbed a finger at Oggiano.

'Vendettas have been sworn for lesser words than those, Oggiano!'

'That is true,' said a new, loud, confident voice from behind Oggiano's men. 'Stand down, Captain.'

'But, General—'

'*Stand down!*'

Without another word, Oggiano and his men separated to create a corridor for Philippe, the Leandris and their men to ride into the town.

Carla reined in before the man who had been addressed as General. He was old, probably seventy or thereabouts, and Philippe thought he bore a vague resemblance to another general, George Washington, whose Virginia plantation had bordered Philippe's mother's. A shock of white hair crowned a distinguished visage. He was a tall man, although now slightly stooped by age, and his physique still suggested the strength he must have possessed in his youth. Unlike the roughly attired peasant army around him, he wore an elegant costume of green and gold that would not have been out of place in any court in Europe.

Carla dismounted and kissed the general on both cheeks.

'It is good to see you again after so many years, General Paoli.'

'Not so many when you are my age, Carla. But you do not want to waste time on a reunion with me, a pleasure though it is. Your father will be in the church—'

'Not quite, Pasquale,' said a new voice from behind Paoli.

Philippe had watched the other party of armed men, only a little smaller than Paoli's, move silently into place on and at

103

the sides of the steps into the church. They had not announced their presence as brazenly as Paoli's men, but by taking their positions where they did they would have rained fire into the other force from behind if Oggiano had given the order to open fire on the horsemen. The Paolists would have been trapped in a pincer between the men at the church and Carla Leandri's mounted contingent. It would have been a massacre.

The leader of the new force stepped forward. Paoli turned, evidently disquieted by what had happened and what could have happened. Carla, though, gave out a sudden scream and ran forward without any thought for maidenly dignity or decorum. She flung herself into the outstretched, welcoming arms of her father.

In all ways but one, General Ercule Leandri cut a less impressive figure than Pasquale Paoli, the leader of Corsica. He looked even older, was considerably more stooped and much shorter, and had lank, thinning hair. He had a pronounced limp, favouring his left leg. But he wore a rough green uniform that Philippe had never seen before. Judging by the faded dye and threadbare cloth, this could only be the same uniform in which General Ercule Leandri had fought against the Genoese and then the French some three or four decades before.

Jacobo Leandri, too, dismounted and went to greet his uncle, although the sobbing Carla was reluctant to break off from her embrace. Giordano also went across to receive General Leandri's thanks for conveying his daughter safely back to her homeland. Then it was Philippe's turn, although he dismounted and began his walk across the village square with considerable trepidation. Paoli's men were allies of the English. It was only months since Philippe had been on a prison hulk in Portsmouth harbour. With more men now drifting into the square from all sides, it was clear that Paoli's forces were significantly larger than Leandri's. What could prevent Paoli ordering his arrest, then handing him over to whichever British general was commanding the siege operations against Calvi?

'Father,' said Carla, 'I present Philippe Kermorvant, captain in the Marine Nationale of the French Republic.'

There were loud murmurs among both sets of irregular troops, and not a few angry expressions on the faces of Paoli's men. The general's expression could not have been more furious if Robespierre himself was standing there, beside the stone water trough in the village square of Ghineparu. But Ercule Leandri was beaming, and the old man came forward to give Philippe an enthusiastic *bise* and to shake his hand vigorously.

'You look like him! Doesn't he look like him, Pasquale?'

'You've lost your wits, Ercule. Who is it he's meant to look like?'

'Verité, you fool. His father. He can call himself Kermorvant all he likes, but this is the Vicomte de Saint-Victor, the son of Verité. And as such, he is under my safe conduct and protection for the whole time he is on Corsica.'

Pasquale Paoli frowned, then nodded.

'In that case, he is also under mine.' The great statesman stepped forward and put out his hand, which Philippe took. He did not offer any more intimate salutation. 'And you're right, Ercule. He does look like his father.'

—

The interior of the church of Saint Devota was wholly at odds with its plain exterior appearance. For certain, the official atheism of the French Republic had made no impact high in the mountains of the Corsican interior. Crude but colourful murals adorned the walls and pillars. Images of the saints abounded, illuminated by the hosts of the candles that proliferated in every corner of the building. A grand reredos filled the wall behind the altar. Today, though, the church was not the setting for any of the sacraments of baptism, marriage and burial. The two sides, the Paolists and the Leandrists, sat on stools facing each other across the nave. Philippe had been watching for two hours and the argument seemed to have become wholly circular, with both Paoli and Ercule Leandri repeating points they had already made. He now knew why Luc Giordano had refused to attend, preferring to return to the coast and the sleek *Lucrezia*.

'Too far from the sea,' said the gruff piratical skipper. 'I get lightheaded this far up in the mountains. Besides, I've fulfilled my side of the contract and had my payment for getting you and *la generalissima* over here and into the safekeeping of the Leandris. Anyhow, I don't have any patience with all the fine politicians and all their talk. So I'm for the tavern, then for *Lucrezia* once I sober up tomorrow and remember where I am. No, I wish you well of it, Captain Kermorvant. When you're ready to leave, and assuming the English or the bandits or the vengeful spirits of the dead don't get you, then *Lucrezia* will be waiting for you. And I'll be waiting for my second instalment.'

Philippe was alongside Carla Leandri in an uncomfortably small space behind the side wall of the nave, watching the proceedings in the main body of the church through a squint apparently installed centuries ago so Franciscan nuns could observe the elevation of the Host and other such superstitions without being sullied by the immediate presence of men. Carla had initially expressed outrage at her father's suggestion that she should hide herself away there when her cousin Jacobo and a brace of other remotely related but male Leandris sat alongside the old general for the main business of the day.

'I am better than any of them,' she hissed as she and Philippe took their places. 'Look at old Jean-Marc, there. Not a thought in his head that isn't concerned with sheep.'

Philippe said nothing. Carla had a point, but not even in the white heat of republican freedom in Paris were women admitted to the councils of the State and discussions of great affairs. He had heard from Frank Parmentier that many women had risen and protested, demanding a place in politics, even marching on and occupying the Palace of Versailles in the very early days of the revolution. Eventually the rulers of the

Republic suppressed them with considerable fervour, insisting that women remain in their traditional roles as mothers and makers of households.

There was certainly a marked contrast between the two parties. Whereas Ercule Leandri alone spoke for his side, Paoli said very little. Instead most of the arguments for the pro-English party were presented by a much younger fellow, probably around Philippe's own age and elegantly dressed, who possessed a long, thin, pale face and sad eyes that might have belonged to a much older man.

'Carlo-Andrea Pozzo di Borgo,' whispered Carla. 'Paoli's factotum. In name, the head of the civil government. The prime minister, if you like.'

Pozzo di Borgo had been speaking for some minutes, reiterating once again the supposed advantages of Corsica entering into a monarchical union with Great Britain, repeating an argument he had already deployed an hour before and, by the sounds of it, several times on previous days, too.

Pozzo di Borgo's discourse clearly tested the patience of the veteran general, for Philippe could see the back of Ercule Leandri's head shaking slowly.

'No, no, no,' said Carla's father impatiently. 'As I have said time and again, the English will be as bad as the French, perhaps worse. They want Corsica only to give them a naval base now they've lost Toulon, just as they only wanted Toulon because they'd lost Minorca in the American war. You know that as well as I do, Pasquale. And do you really think King George and William Pitt will make you viceroy? They'll put in one of their own – that Scot Elliot, I expect – and where will your precious constitution stand then, Pasquale? A constitution that gives far too much power to the King of England and his viceroy, as I have told you countless times before? The viceroy can veto any laws. He can dissolve our parliament. Suffrage will be restricted to voters with over six thousand *lire* of property, not a birthright of every man. This is not the constitution we devised and followed in Corsica over thirty years ago, Pasquale. This is not freedom.'

Pozzo di Borgo rose to counter the argument, but Ercule Leandri ignored him and pressed on.

'And will our new masters really treat Corsica as an equal of England? As a brother kingdom, standing proud alongside them? You lived there for all those years, Pasquale, while I've only read about it in books, but am I wrong when I say that England is an elephant to Corsica's mouse? We will be nothing to them. They will barter us away when we cease to be of use to them, just as the Genoese did, and who do you think they'll sell us to then, hmm? The Austrians? The Russians? The Turks? Do you want the Sultan to rule over Corsica, Pasquale?'

Pozzo di Borgo seemed amused by the thought, but his older companion's face was cold. At last, Pasquale Paoli stood and spoke for himself.

'Mere hypotheses, Ercule, as you know them to be. My concern is with the here and now, and the cause of Corsican independence that you and I have fought for these forty years can only be achieved by allying with one of France or Britain. We have experienced France. We know the sort of people who rule there now. Atheists, men of no faith and no conscience, among them apostates from our own cause – who prefer a criminal government that cuts the head off its king to honest Corsican virtue and religion. Do you really want to place us under the rule of Robespierre, Ercule? Do you want to bring the guillotine into Corte and Ajaccio and Calvi and Bastia? Do you want our old friend Carlo's brats to come back and lord it over us?' The leader of the Corsican nation took a deep breath. 'And I say this to you, Ercule, as an old friend and comrade-in-arms. The *consulta* of the whole nation, representing all the *pieves*, has given its verdict. You were in the minority, as you know. The throne of Corsica has been offered to King George, and accepted on his behalf by Sir Gilbert Elliot. We are now in a union of the crowns with Great Britain. I have been lenient to you for old times' sake, Ercule, but enough is enough, man! If you continue to hold out, if you continue to toy with declaring for France, then you are a rebel and traitor to Corsica. You, all your kin and your people will be proclaimed as such. My troops and English soldiers will come back here, we will hunt you all down and destroy you. It will be the vendetta of all vendettas, and it will have only one ending.'

Ercule Leandri began to rise from his stool. In the cell behind the wall, his daughter tensed. Philippe, pressed up against her so both could see the debates in the nave, could feel her muscles tighten and saw her fists clench.

Then Jean-Marc Leandri gave out a very loud and very long fart. There was a moment of astonished silence in the church, then Pozzo di Borgo and the three others in the Paolist delegation broke down in uncontrollable laughter. Ercule Leandri turned to stare at his cousin, but his face had broken into a wide smile. Finally, Pasquale Paoli, too, smiled thinly.

'That, I think, is a cue for us to adjourn until tomorrow. A chance for wise heads to think upon what has been said here today. Do you concur, Ercule?'

General Leandri nodded tersely.

CHAPTER THIRTEEN

Most esteemed, worthy and gallant father,

I am grateful for receipt of your recent letter. I rejoice that you are well, and that our campaign on the northern front continues to prosper. I am grateful for the news of my mother and sisters, and will not fail to write to them by the next post from Cannes.

As for the fleet in which your unworthy son serves, we sit at anchor here in the Bay of Gourjean, shamefully blockaded by the English who parade arrogantly up and down off the coast. We are kept busy with drills and exercises ordered by Rear-Admiral Fidelin, a vigorous and impressive man, and by our acting captain, Lieutenant Malhuret. Our true captain, the Vicomte de Saint-Victor, went ashore some days ago and has not been seen or heard of since. There is some talk among the men that he has been arrested as an English spy, sent to Paris and despatched on the guillotine. One of the cooper's mates says he has it on good authority that the captain's mother was English. I do not know if it is true or not, but if it is then I fail to understand how such a man could be entrusted with command by the authorities in Paris. But that is not a matter a mere aspirant should consider, and there are others among the men who tell a different story. One of the Marines says that when he was last ashore with the crew that was sent to obtain fresh water barrels, he encountered an old messmate now stationed on the flagship who said he had been on guard outside our admiral's cabin and heard our captain being given orders to undertake a confidential mission for the Republic. I would not usually give credence to such a breach of confidence, of course, and it is surely even more unlikely that a man with the captain's history should be entrusted with such an important task. I expect the truth of it all will emerge in time. Perhaps though, Father, you may wish to write to those you know in the Ministry of War and the Committee of Public Safety to make enquiry into all of these matters. The safety of France surely cannot be entrusted to those whose loyalty to the Republic might be questionable.

I thank you for restating your injunction to me to seek every opportunity to demonstrate my courage and do justice and bring glory to our revered family name. I regret to inform you that there is little or no opportunity for this while the fleet remains at anchor. We are not a fleet, we are no more than driftwood floating in this accursed bay. I trust, though, that the day will soon come when we are able to venture out and I will finally have a chance to prove to you, Father, that I am worthy of the name of de la Porte.

I am well. Vive la République!
Your dutiful and obedient son,
T de la Porte

Philippe, Carla and her father were at supper in the house of another Leandri, a vast, shambolic woman named Claudia who was the widow of the general's only brother. This, it transpired, was Ercule Leandri's temporary abode while he generously permitted Paoli and the rest of his delegation to occupy the watch tower higher up the mountain. Carla's return had been celebrated in jubilant fashion, with cousins and neighbours calling throughout the evening to pay their respects, but now, with Claudia Leandri having retired to her outhouse to tend her animals, it was only father and daughter across the table from Philippe in the sparsely furnished upper room. They were eating *bruccio*, apparently a favourite dish of the Corsicans but which seemed to consist only of baked cream cheese, washed down with a sweet white island wine.

Carla Leandri outlined France's offer of the remains of Columbus, her father nodding occasionally, but Philippe found the whole conversation odd. If this really was the one remaining ambition in life for General Ercule Leandri, the fulfilment of a question and a passion many decades old, he displayed remarkably little excitement about it. But neither did he ask the questions Philippe thought he should ask, about Carla's and Philippe's assessments of the sincerity of those making the offer, of the likelihood that the French would be able to deliver on their promise. Nor did either father or daughter consider the French offer in the light of Pasquale Paoli's outburst in the village church. Both the old man and the young woman seemed to be deliberately avoiding the truth of what they had heard spoken that afternoon. It was as though the entire discussion between father and daughter was a play in the theatre, the actors reading from a script that Philippe Kermorvant did not possess. He had been to plays where the actors all too evidently had no enthusiasm for the words they were speaking, and it seemed to him that both Ercule and Carla Leandri were cast in such parts on the stage they now occupied, the low-roofed room in a ramshackle house clinging to a hillside in the mountains of Corsica.

Finally, though, Philippe knew he had to speak out. The matter of the bones of Columbus seemed an irrelevance, a mere obstacle in the way of the more urgent conversation that all three people in the room should surely be having.

'General, how will you answer what General Paoli said to you today? The threat of being charged with treason?'

Carla interrupted before her father could answer.

'He *dares* to declare Ercule Leandri a traitor,' she said, her cheeks flushed with anger. '*Ercule Leandri!* A man who has fought for Corsica for half a century? A man who fought at Ponte-Nuovo in 1768 when the French destroyed our army and our independence – and where was Paoli that day, the great general, the leader of the country, who had ordered our men to fight there? Not with the army, unlike my father, and every Corsican knows that. So Paoli's own people won't allow it, Captain. No Corsican would dare arrest my father. Paoli could order Ercule Leandri shot to death, but no Corsican would ever pull the trigger.'

The general seemed greatly amused by the exchange.

'And he would never pull the trigger himself, of course,' he said, 'although I think Pozzo di Borgo would, and gladly. No, you're quite right, dear daughter. Pasquale Paoli has made threats against me every so often throughout all the years he and I have known each other. He gives himself the airs of an enlightened man – a Roman patrician, if you like, who stands above the rage and violence of the common herd. But scratch dear Pasquale hard enough and the true Corsican comes out. I have heard him say things that would make the bandits who lurk in the shadows of Monte Cinto blush. I have said the same or worse back to him, of course. So pay no heed to our great general's bluster.'

Philippe was reluctant to intervene in the dialogue between father and daughter. They both knew Pasquale Paoli of old, Ercule Leandri for a lifetime. Yet one thing seemed obvious to Philippe Kermorvant, and neither of the Leandris was speaking it aloud.

'Sir, I cannot know what passed between you and General Paoli in the past. But surely there's a difference now? Corsica is allied to England. In a sense, it has just become almost a part of England, and England is at war with France. Even if you're right, General Leandri, and Paoli himself is bluffing and blustering, his new friends won't be. I've fought against the British, in this very year I've been in their country as their prisoner. They see this war as the Armageddon foretold in the Bible, the final battle between good and evil. They are a powerful country, sir, they have troops and ships here in Corsica, and they will now undoubtedly see General Paoli as being on the side of the righteous.'

'Which means they will see my father as being on the side of evil if he declares for France,' said Carla.

Still Ercule Leandri seemed unwilling to accept the reality of his situation.

'At my next confession, I must ask Father Colonna if he thinks me a convincing Antichrist,' he said. 'But I thank you for your concern, daughter, Captain Kermorvant. Please understand me, I realise what Paoli's new kingdom is, and I don't underestimate the change that the presence of the English brings to Corsica. I shall think upon it, I promise. Yes, I shall think upon it. But now, Captain, let us talk of your father. Tell me, how did he die? In battle during the American war, wasn't it? A hero's death, the kind we all pray for.'

Philippe described Verité's death in a minor skirmish during the Siege of Savannah and related a few anecdotes of his father's last years in America. Ercule Leandri seemed more comfortable and interested in talking to Philippe about Verité than about his attitude to the new situation in Corsica or even the French offer to return Christopher Columbus's remains at Calvi. Now at last the old man's eyes gleamed with real enthusiasm for his subject.

'He was one of the most prominent men in France to praise the constitution Paoli and I put into effect nearly forty years ago. We were the first in the world – *in the world*, Captain, mark that – the very first to proclaim the sovereignty of the people as the foundation of government, the first to declare the inalienable right to happiness, the first to give a vote to all men without distinction of wealth or birth... Ah, Captain, there was nothing like it in Europe at the time, not anywhere, and there still isn't. As your father wrote, it was a shining beacon to the world of what true democracy might look like. We invited him to Corsica, and he came – this was in sixty-two or sixty-three, just after he'd been sent into exile by Louis *Quinze*. I met him, as did Paoli. We talked to him for many hours over many days. Such nobility of mind. Such clarity of thought. It was an honour to meet him, and when I knew his son was with the Toulon fleet – that France would grant me nearly anything I asked for to secure my support against Paoli and the English – well, I could not resist the conceit of inviting you here, d'you see.'

'It was not couched as an invitation, General. More of an order, if anything.'

'Yes, it would be. That boy never had any manners, and now he's a general, you say? Incredible. Is France really so desperate?'

'He'll come to nothing,' said Carla. 'He was so convinced that I was a poor little retiring mouse, eager to serve the republic he so venerates...'

'You convinced me, citizeness,' said Philippe, amused. She blushed at the compliment.

'Your father had an interest in Columbus, of course,' said Ercule Leandri, 'and this was long before he went to America. He listened intently when I explained why the body should be brought back to Calvi. He was sympathetic to my argument, all those years ago.'

That rang true to Philippe. For all his much-vaunted reputation as a rationalist and free-thinker, Verité revered the myths of King Arthur and Merlin. His attempt to prove that the grave of the sorcerer lay on the Brechelean estate – to Verité's mind, the legendary Forest of Broceliande – consumed an inordinate amount of time before the search was abruptly curtailed by the king's order for the Vicomte de Saint-Victor to leave French territory and never return. Philippe remembered his father once telling him that his greatest regret about being exiled from his homeland was that he would never now find the bones of Merlin. In that light, his sympathy for a seemingly quixotic quest to repatriate the bones of Christopher Columbus to Corsica was perfectly explicable.

'You cannot decide your allegiance based on a promise to deliver you a set of old bones, Father,' said Carla. 'Who's to say that Robespierre and his henchmen, like our old friends from Ajaccio, won't try to fob you off with the skeleton of some tramp found in a Parisian gutter? Or the remains of some old nag found on a battlefield?'

'I will know,' said Leandri with confidence. 'I will sense it. And if I do not, there are many on Corsica with the second sight, those with a foot in the other world, those who walk with the dead. I shall assemble them, a *consulta* of seers and *mazzeri* and *signadori*, and they will judge whether the bones are truly those of Columbus or not.'

Carla shook her head but did not reply to her father. Privately Philippe agreed with her scepticism. They were living in the time that was known by the old calendar as the last decade of the eighteenth century, yet here was a rational man, a devotee of the writings of Verité, talking of communing with the dead and the second sight. Publicly, though, and as an agent acting on behalf of the French Republic, Philippe had his orders and could only obey them, which meant humouring General Ercule Leandri. Even so, he could not dismiss the feeling that this whole project was a trick, an illusion, a simple ruse intended to win the loyalty of a man who the smug Parisian elite would no doubt dismiss as a backward rustic, easily deluded and bought at no great cost to the state. But if he was to somehow convince Ercule Leandri of that without being seen to disobey his orders, he needed to know more about the general's obsession.

'But sir,' said Philippe, 'what is the evidence for Columbus being from Corsica – from Calvi? Surely mankind knows him as a Genoese.'

'And Genoa ruled Corsica for centuries,' said Leandri patiently. 'In my own lifetime, I can plainly remember the red cross on white of Saint George, the flag of the Genoese Republic, flying from the tower above this village. My tower, now, but it was not so when I was a young man. You ask for evidence, though. Very good, very good. Your father was never as inquisitive on the subject. Evidence, then. Well, for one thing there is no record that Columbus was born in Genoa itself, in the city that is. A child born in any place that Genoa ruled could grow up to be a citizen of the Genoese Republic. That was what Columbus was, but it cannot take away the truth that he was still a Corsican. What's more, Genoa can show you no house associated with Columbus, no birthplace. We can. It is in Calvi. And our traditions state it proudly. We Corsicans, for many centuries our history has been passed down by word of mouth, not by means of dusty manuscripts that are often found to be forgeries. Your father knew this, Captain. He understood it.'

Philippe nodded. As well as according perfectly with his memories of his father, Leandri's explanation reminded him of the Powhatan Indians, whose history was also passed down orally from one generation to the next. The colonists of Virginia, drowning in an ocean of paper records, assumed that the absence of writing and a dependence on the spoken word rendered the Indians somehow inferior and savage. But as a boy, Philippe Kermorvant had sat by campfires and listened to the song-like recitations of the tribal storytellers, understanding perhaps one word in ten but entranced by the rhythm and the utter certainty of both speakers and listeners that these were word for word the same tales that their ancestors a thousand years before had recited and listened to.

For several hours until well after the bell in the campanile of Saint Devota chimed the midnight hour, Ercule Leandri lectured Philippe on the supposed evidence for Columbus being Corsican. The great seaman's father, it seemed, was a Calvi man who had followed many trades in his lifetime – weaver, innkeeper, cheese merchant, a half-dozen others. There were stories of the young Columbus serving as a privateer for the king of France, sailing to Iceland long before his famous voyage to the Americas, and taking a Corsican Franciscan with him to the New World. Leandri digressed for a half hour and more on the names Columbus gave to the islands he discovered. Santa Maria de la Conception was, it seemed, the patron saint of Calvi, San Teramo the patron saint of Corsican sailors. Haiti was supposedly named after Aiti, a village in the Corsican mountains. There was much more, but it all seemed to Philippe to be wholly circumstantial, the result of mixing large doses of coincidence and wishful thinking. Worse, the general had a habit of digressing into obscure tales from Corsican history that seemed to have no relevance to Columbus nor to the question of Leandri's allegiance. There was much talk of men named Sampiero and Rinuccio, who fought the Genoese some two centuries earlier and whom Leandri clearly regarded as great heroes, and a discourse on another Corsican warrior chief called Sambucuccio, another two centuries before that. The general was more ambivalent about him, for it seemed that Sambucuccio had fought *for* Genoa. Leandri talked almost as though these long-dead men had been personal friends, their brave deeds occurring only yesterday. For him, past and present seemed to be as one, the dead always somewhere nearby. The general was unfailingly polite, regularly recharging Philippe's cup of sweet local wine, but he was infuriatingly indirect. Philippe was hardly surprised when Carla, who must have heard her father's monologues and digressions many times before, yawned theatrically, pleaded extreme tiredness and retired to her bed. But despite his age and the fact that he had to resume the conference with Paoli and Pozzo di Borgo in the morning, Ercule Leandri showed no sign of flagging, while Philippe, tired from spending the previous night on hard ground beneath the stars but constrained by the straitjacket of propriety, felt he could not cut off his host and retire to his own bed.

'Now,' said Leandri, 'as I once explained to your father, Columbus was known formally as Columbus de Terra-Rubra, which is Spanish for Terra Rossa. There is no Terra Rossa in mainland Genoa. Take my word for it, Captain, for I have employed agents to search the archives of that republic. But there is a Terra Rossa in Corsica, not too far from Calvi—'

Whatever the demands of propriety, Philippe's patience was not limitless.

'Forgive me, General, but the hour is late. I must know what answer to convey to France. Tell me frankly, sir – will you accept the offer of the remains of Columbus and declare for the Republic and the union of France and Corsica? Will you declare rebellion against General Paoli and the rule of Corsica by Britain, even if that means being declared a traitor to your country?'

Leandri took a sip of his wine and studied Philippe's face.

'You are more direct than your father,' he said. 'I like that. Direct men deserve direct answers. So tell me, Captain Kermorvant, or Monsieur le Vicomte, if you prefer – what do you think my direct answer will be?'

CHAPTER FOURTEEN

It was anything but a direct answer, and an utterly impossible question. But during the course of the day, Philippe had formed an opinion of General Ercule Leandri. He had also thought much about the elusive relationships between Leandri, Pasquale Paoli and the family of the young Corsican general from Le Muy. There were many years of history between those families, multiple antagonisms and jealousies that he could only guess at. He also recalled that his father had known Leandri. Verité had been a complex man, a bundle of enigmas and contradictions in one restless frame, and Philippe suspected that he would never know more than the tiniest fraction of the different elements that shaped Edouard Kermorvant, Vicomte de Saint-Victor. Even so, he remembered how his father invariably preferred the company of men like him, complicated men, with whom nothing was what it seemed and where satisfaction was to be obtained from peeling back the layers to discover the real person beneath all the facades of dissimulation and misdirection. Paoli was clearly one such, a man who was all for democracy and the liberty of mankind just as long as he, Pasquale Paoli, was the unchallenged ruler of the state and could decide exactly what democracy and liberty meant. Ercule Leandri was another cast from the same mould. But what lay beneath all the facades he had carefully erected around himself?

When it came to him, the answer was startlingly obvious.

'I think you have played a game with them all,' said Philippe slowly, weighing his words very carefully. 'You needed to see how far the leaders of the Republic would go to win your loyalty. A lesser man would have demanded gold and power, but you wanted something very different to that. So you devised a demand for something at once so simple and yet so difficult as the return of Columbus's bones, a demand that accorded precisely with what the young general and his superiors in Paris knew of you. You knew they would probably create some elaborate sham, some fake body in an ancient coffin from some other grave, believing that they were duping some poor unsophisticated provincial bandit chieftain – my apologies if that causes you offence, General.'

Leandri's ancient face broke into a broad grin.

'I have been called worse, Captain.'

'So you asked for something so strange, so unexpected, that it blinded them to what you really wanted, the true prize you were pursuing.'

'And what was that, Captain?'

'The return of your daughter.'

That which any father would want above all else.

'Ah,' said Leandri, lifting his goblet of wine to his lips but taking no more than a small sip. 'Yes, I see why you would think that, of course.'

'You never had any intention of declaring for France.' Philippe felt emboldened and poured out the thoughts that had been forming in his mind since the meeting at Le Muy, the thoughts that had been reinforced many times over since he met and talked with Ercule Leandri. 'You and Paoli may have had disagreements, but you are old friends and you are both Corsicans. Besides, you know that for now, the British are far more powerful than the French in the Mediterranean, and simple prudence demands that you throw in your lot with them. That is the real reason why I'm here, isn't it, General? I am the living proof that France is too weak to relieve Calvi and drive the British out of Corsica, because if it had that power then I would be at sea aboard my command, not here with you. Am I right, sir?'

The smile was still fixed on Ercule Leandri's face, but there was a new emotion apparent in his eyes.

'Your father taught you well,' said the old man, very quietly.

There was a sound at the back of the room, behind Philippe, and as he turned to face it he saw that Ercule Leandri's face had fallen. There, framed in the doorway, stood Carla, a loose gown barely concealing a thin shift, her face a deathly white.

'I dreamt I hunted with the *mazzeri*,' she said, her voice trembling. 'I was out in the mountains with them, hunting a mighty wolf. I helped to kill it. I witnessed its death agonies as I plunged my stiletto into its belly and dipped my hands in its blood.'

'You are not a *mazzera*,' said her father, calmly but with a tension in his voice. 'They are low born, not of our rank.'

'My mother was. Claudia is. You and your uncle alike married women who were not of our rank, Father.'

Carla's aunt appeared behind her, tears staining her cheeks, and the two of them, the two *mazzeri*, came fully into the room. Philippe stood like a statue, gripped by a coldness that defied all rational explanation. It was as if he stood in the presence of inhabitants of another world, a world where the living and the dead understood and communed with each other. An older, stranger world.

'I did not have the dream,' whispered Claudia Leandri. 'I cannot fathom why she should have it and not me. Have you ever had one before, child?'

Carla shook her head, her eyes full of tears. 'Never. It frightens me, aunt.'

'You were taken away from us, taken to Paris where your gift would not reveal itself,' said Claudia. 'It is late for someone to develop the gift, but not unheard of. I shall train you, niece.'

'But what of my dream? What of the wolf?'

Claudia looked helplessly at her brother-in-law. Ercule Leandri's expression was grim, his lips pressed so tightly together that Philippe wondered if the old man was having an apoplexy. Finally, he looked at his guest and spoke.

'The *mazzeri* are those who are able to foretell an imminent death,' he said, 'and in many cases, the telling of their dream brings it. They hunt at night. Rational men, men like your father, say that they hunt only in their dreams, but others will tell you that they have gone bodily to a different reality, to the dark borderland between this world and the next, where past, present and future, dreams and what we call truth, become one.'

'You believe this?'

'Enough of me believes it. Enough of the Corsicans believe it.'

'But what could such a dream mean?' Philippe demanded.

'One of you will die,' said Carla, her face white and her voice terrified of her own words. 'You will die very soon, and you will die violently. I sensed it. I knew the wolf was one of you, but I could not tell which.'

Her composure deserted her. She ran across the room and flung herself into her father's arms, weeping and sobbing as urgently as a mother grieving the loss of her child.

–

Philippe was given a pallet bed in the corner of the room where he and the Leandris had dined. Before the extraordinary events of the evening unfolded, Claudia Leandri had proclaimed this to be a great honour and an even greater luxury, beds apparently being a rarity in ordinary Corsican homes. The bed had been occupied by the general, but he insisted on giving it up to his guest, contenting himself with a mattress on the floor of an upper room. Philippe suspected that the elegant Pasquale Paoli and Pozzo di Borgo, who were housed with his retinue in the old Genoese fort above the village, would not have demeaned themselves by accepting such lowly accommodation.

As he lay on the bed, listening to the distant and unfamiliar animal noises and the tolling of the church bell, he thought about the peculiar scene he had witnessed. Carla Leandri had struck him as a very modern woman, level-headed and rational, yet it seemed that even she was infected with the plague of ancient superstitions that seemed to be rife in Corsica. Her aunt Claudia had taken her immediately to the church to spend the night in prayer, to confess to Father Colonna, the village priest, and, so General Leandri alleged, to begin her instruction in the life of the *mazzeri*. He, too, a man who had once exchanged philosophical precepts with Philippe's father, seemed to revert to an older sensibility, awed by his daughter's prophecy and the realisation of what she was.

No, Philippe chided himself, *the realisation that she, too, has swallowed the primitive and ludicrous superstitions of this place.*

Perhaps Carla's return to Corsica after so long, and her reunion with her father, had momentarily unhinged her. The alternative explanation was unthinkable, and Philippe needed to put it out of his mind. The simple word of one person, predicting or even willing the death of another, could have no such power. He was the son of Verité, one of the greatest champions of rationalism. He was an officer of a republic that claimed to be in the vanguard of modernity. So whatever Carla Leandri, her father and her aunt believed, he, Philippe Kermorvant, would have no truck with such primitive delusions.

And yet.

What if …

The heavier his eyes became, the more elusive sleep proved to be. He had known shamans among the Indians of Virginia who were universally believed to be able to foretell the future. In a village close to the Chateau de Brechelean, in the ancient forest said to contain the last resting place of Merlin the sorcerer, lived an old man who had predicted the revolution and the execution of the king twenty years before it happened. Verité himself was always open to the notion that there might be knowledge as yet unknown to mankind as a whole that a few favoured individuals already possessed. But if all that was true and Carla Leandri really had foreseen the future, then who would soon suffer a violent death – her father or Philippe?

Surely not Ercule Leandri here in his own village, among his own people. But Philippe Kermorvant was a stranger here, both a representative of a nation whose beliefs and actions were anathema to most of the Corsicans and an enemy of Paoli's allies the British. Would safe conducts from Paoli and Leandri really be enough to protect him from a devout Catholic enraged by the atheism of the Republic and Philippe himself, or from a patriot determined to strike at the hated French who had eradicated Corsican independence once and now sought to do so again?

He tossed and turned. He was not afraid of death, having faced it countless times, but a foretelling of death was a different case. He could not entirely banish from his thoughts the sight of Carla's pale, horrified expression, nor the words she had uttered.

He forced himself to think instead of his exchanges with the infuriating Ercule Leandri. Was the old man really as vague as he seemed? Was Philippe's interpretation of his position correct, or far wide of the mark? Would the general have given him a clear, unambiguous answer but for the startling intervention of his daughter? The next day, and no matter what effort it took, he would obtain a definitive response. Then, perhaps, he could leave this den of primitive superstitions and vicious jealousies. He longed to be back on the quarterdeck of *Le Torrington*, and imagined her riding a gentle swell, a fresh breeze stirring her sails, the water lapping the hull…

He was being shaken awake. Surely he could not have been asleep at all? Unwillingly he opened his eyes.

He was looking down the barrel of a pistol.

One of you will die. You will die very soon, and you will die violently. The curse of the *mazzera*.

The face of Jacobo Leandri, who held it, was flushed and furious, the cheeks stained with new tears.

'Murderer,' he snarled.

Philippe tried to get up, but the pistol was pressed hard against his forehead.

'He gave you his hospitality,' said Jacobo Leandri. 'Yet you killed him.'

Jacobo's mother, Claudia, wracked with hysterical sobs, came into the room.

'Poor Ercule,' she muttered. 'Oh, poor, poor Ercule.'

Finally Philippe understood. General Ercule Leandri was dead, murdered, and his nephew was accusing Philippe of the killing. The *mazzeri* had their sacrifice.

CHAPTER FIFTEEN

A baying mob of villagers followed as Philippe, his hands bound behind his back and Jacobo Leandri's pistol still pointing at his head, was led up the steep track that wound its way to the ancient watch tower. Philippe had faced the guillotine and the guns of half-a-dozen enemies, but death had never seemed closer than it did on that early summer's morning, with the sun barely risen above the jagged peaks of the Corsican interior. Jacobo Leandri was in no mood to listen to argument and the mob at his back clearly wanted nothing more than to string up the Vicomte de Saint-Victor from the nearest chestnut tree. Of Carla Leandri there was no sign. Instead, a substantial party stood before the crumbling Genoese structure that lay ahead, the other men who had formed the Paolist force in the village square spread out across the mountainside next to the tents they had just vacated. Paoli and Pozzo di Borgo were front and centre of those waiting in front of the tower, standing at the foot of the staircase that rose to the entrance door on the first floor. Philippe also recognised a couple of other men who had been on the Paolist side in the church the previous day, and a little way behind was the foul-mouthed so-called captain, Vincent Oggiano. Philippe could have anticipated the presence of all these hostile Corsican faces, the one exception being the stunned and sympathetic features of Luc Giordano, still seemingly the worse for wear from his evening's debauch in the village tavern. Yes, these were all expected. But Philippe was alarmed by the sight of two previously unseen men who stood on the other side of Paoli from Pozzo di Borgo. One wore the red uniform and epaulettes of a colonel in the British Army, the other the very familiar dark blue uniform of a post-captain in King George the Third's Royal Navy. This man was notable for his remarkably small frame and the bandage that covered his right eye.

It made sense, of course. The British were hardly likely to trust in the potential outcomes of a clandestine meeting in the mountains between two old men with decades-old reputations for rebellion and opposition to every successive power that sought to hold sway over Corsica. They had been willing to concede the illusion of independence by allowing the Paolists to attend the conference in the church without them, but their presence in this ruined eyrie high above the village would surely have weighed on the minds of both sides debating in the church of Saint Devota.

It was Pozzo di Borgo, the nominal civilian head of the Corsican government, who took the lead.

'Is this how your French Republic repays the hospitality of your hosts, Captain? By slaughtering a helpless old man? By snuffing out the life of one of the greatest heroes of Corsican freedom?'

'I didn't kill him! Why would I?'

'You deluded him with a mad tale that only he believed, and pretended to be the son of a man he had once known and respected! But in truth you were no more than a spy and an assassin, sent by that notorious turncoat, that traitor to Corsica, that second son of a family of vipers, General—'

'He is the son of Verité,' said Paoli quietly.

Pozzo di Borgo, clearly irritated at being interrupted and contradicted even by the man he served, conceded the point with bad grace.

'Even if so, General, any man's son may be a murderer. But if not this man, then who? The village is full of Leandris, the blood of the dead man. The only others staying at the house were the two women, Claudia and Carla Leandri, and they spent the night at prayer in the church. Would you offer up either of them as an alternative to yourself, Captain?'

Carla had not been in the house when her father was killed. He remembered that now. He remembered, too, the troubling curse of the *mazzera*, so swiftly fulfilled.

But where was Carla now?

'Hang him,' shouted Oggiano to the loud approbation of the villagers and the Paolist troops. 'Here and now! Nothing to be gained by waiting.'

Philippe was doomed. He could see it, but it was far too late. No man present would listen to a word he said, except perhaps for Luc Giordano who could say or do nothing. He had no motive for killing Ercule Leandri, but most of those surrounding him and baying for his blood certainty did. They all knew that just the previous day, Ercule Leandri had been denounced as a traitor by the leader of the Corsican nation, Pasquale Paoli. One of those on the Paolist side – perhaps the brutal Oggiano himself? – might have decided to ignore the time-consuming formality of a treason trial and taken immediate action.

Pozzo di Borgo leaned over to Paoli and whispered something that the older man seemed to agree to. *What if Paoli, or more likely the serpentine Pozzo di Borgo, had ordered the murder of General Ercule Leandri and then accused the all-too-convenient scapegoat presented by Philippe Kermorvant, Vicomte de Saint-Victor?*

'I tend to concur,' said Pozzo di Borgo. 'As *procureur-général-syndic* of the Kingdom of Corsica, I—'

'*Attendez!*' snapped the British colonel, raising his hand.

'Colonel Moore?' said Paoli in English, his expression quizzical.

'With respect, General,' said Colonel Moore, continuing in respectable French, 'if this man is truly a commissioned officer of France then he should be tried under military law. I propose, sir, that you turn over the prisoner to us, as the representatives of your sovereign, King George the Third.'

'This is a Corsican matter, Colonel Moore, and a Corsican matter alone.'

But was it? thought Philippe. It would surely suit the purpose of the British military commanders in Corsica to remove the only significant threat to their unchallenged possession of King George's new kingdom. What if the blade that killed Ercule Leandri had been held in an English hand?

The little British naval officer coughed to clear his throat, then spoke out. For such a small man he had a surprising presence about him, as well as the actor's and statesman's knack of scanning his audience so that every person in it thought the speaker was looking directly at them.

'Not necessarily so – if you will forgive my impertinence, General, Colonel.' For all his rhetorical ability his French was abominable, and clearly a source of amusement to the Corsicans who understood the language. 'My understanding is that this man escaped from the *Agincourt* hulk in Portsmouth at the start of the year. I'm no lawyer, gentlemen, but it seems to me there may be a case for saying he remains under the jurisdiction of the Admiralty in Whitehall.'

'Nonsense,' said Colonel Moore, who all too obviously had little time for his companion. 'But in any case, I think this man should be surrendered into British custody and placed before General Stuart for his decision in the matter.'

'And Admiral Lord Hood,' said the naval officer emphatically.

'Of course,' said Moore, conceding with bad grace.

'Enough of all your laws and jurisdictions!' cried Jacobo Leandri, waving his pistol. 'We have an older law here on Corsica. A better law.'

'You cannot vow vendetta against an outsider, a foreigner, Leandri,' said Pozzo di Borgo.

'Can I not? Didn't our ancestors swear vendettas against the Genoese, and the Aragonese, and the Romans? How do we know *they didn't*, Count? And you, General Paoli? Are all you fine gentlemen really so sure?'

'I have read that your vendettas embrace the entire family of he who has offended you,' said the doggedly persistent one-eyed English sea-captain. 'Would you then, Monsieur Leandri, seek to kill all of this man's relatives? If you do, then I believe you would have to go after some of them in faraway America. You would also have to murder one of my superiors, a Lord of the Admiralty, and as I understand it, our king and our prime minister take umbrage at such affronts. Indeed, I would be forced to take action to pre-empt such an occurrence. But there's another matter, of course. My understanding is that this man travelled here under safe conduct from the late General Leandri and also from yourself, General Paoli. I'll admit that reneging on such a grant of safe conduct is not comparable in any way to murder, but surely summarily hanging from a tree a man whose safety you had guaranteed, without even a pretence of a trial, is hardly an auspicious precedent for His Majesty's Kingdom of Corsica.'

Despite the precariousness of his position, Philippe could not restrain a very slight smile. If the little captain was this formidable when arguing points of law on a dusty rock ledge in Corsica, he would very much like to witness how he fought at sea – just as long as it was not his ship that the determined Englishman was engaging.

The captain's intervention caused chaos. Paoli and Pozzo di Borgo turned away and began what was clearly a ferocious argument in low voices. Colonel Moore similarly began an animated but inaudible dialogue with his naval colleague. Only Jacobo Leandri remained entirely focused on Philippe, who could almost read his captor's thoughts. Leandri was weighing raising his pistol while all the leaders were distracted, exacting justice for his uncle with one bullet, and taking whatever consequences might follow.

'You've made a fool of yourself again, Jacobo.'

The new and very familiar voice came from behind the hanging party, from the road that wound up the hillside from the village. Jacobo turned, Paoli, Pozzo di Borgo and the British officers fell silent, and Carla Leandri strode through the crowd. Behind her shambled the odiferous figure of her cousin Jean-Marc.

'You should be with the other women, mourning your father,' said Jacobo Leandri, his voice quivering.

'Oh, don't be ridiculous, cousin. While you men have been arguing over who has the right to execute an innocent man, cousin Jean-Marc and I have established who really murdered my father.'

'*Him?* But we have the murderer here—'

Jacobo pointed angrily at Philippe.

'Tell them, Jean-Marc,' said Carla.

The old shepherd was awed by being in the presence of such august men and mumbled his first words so softly that both Philippe and his would-be judges had difficulty making it out.

'Would have been between four and five. Well before sunup, anyhow, but there was just enough light in the sky to make things out. I was down in the valley, but I could hear a rider up on the road making for the village. He dismounted a good way short, though, as if he wanted not to be heard. So I went a bit higher up to take a look. He couldn't have seen me where I was, not with the light as it was and all the cover I had, but I could see him. Strange, I think. Stranger still a little while later when I see him running out of the village then riding back down the road, only this time he's galloping as if he had the devil himself on his tail. I knew straight away he can't have been doing any good, not with all that went before. So when I came up and heard from Claudia that Ercule, the general that is, had been killed – well, it was easy to see what had happened. So I was on my way up here when Mademoiselle Carla, here, caught up with me.'

'Who did you see, old man?'

'Maestracci.'

There were shouts and cat calls from the villagers. The name was known, even if it meant nothing to Philippe, Paoli and Pozzo di Borgo.

'Pierre-Paul Maestracci,' said Carla for their benefit. 'His family and ours have been in vendetta against each other for generations.'

Jacobo, who was no longer pointing his pistol at Philippe, stared at his cousin.

'The Maestraccis were all for the king. Pierre-Paul left the island the summer before last, hasn't been seen since. What would bring him back? Just to seek revenge on our general? They were never liked by any of the families – the ones who favoured the Republic and the ones who want a free Corsica with you, General.' He inclined his head to Paoli, who nodded in return. 'Who would shelter him? Who would give him refuge?'

The answer came from an unexpected party.

'I fear I have your answer, Senor Leandri,' said Colonel Moore. 'Captain Pierre-Paul Maestracci serves in the Royal Louis Regiment, one of the units laying siege to Calvi. Captain Maestracci is an officer in His Britannic Majesty's Army.'

CHAPTER SIXTEEN

The funeral of General Ercule Leandri took place on the following day. The haste surprised Philippe, but Carla assured him it was not unusual in her family or the region. In her father's case, holding the ceremony so soon meant that Paoli and Pozzo di Borgo, the nominal rulers of free Corsica, could attend before returning to the mountain capital of Corte to finalise their alliance with Great Britain. The British officers had discreetly left for the siegeworks before Calvi, leaving the Corsicans to bury their own.

The body of the general had been taken the evening before to the ancient Genoese fortress above the village. At noon, the single bell in the campanile tolled, and the coffin emerged into the grey drizzle and murk of a day that reminded Philippe more of November in Virginia than the height of summer in the Mediterranean. At Carla's request he was one of the mourning party that followed the coffin, walking behind Father Colonna and the principal mourner, Carla herself. The priest had protested against such a prominent place being assigned to an irreligious republican, the son of one of the most notorious atheists of the age, but *la generalissima* gave him short shrift and the priest could find no fresh argument to counter her. Perhaps Colonna, like Philippe, was unsettled by the extraordinary sight that stood before them. Veiled and clad from head to toe in black, Carla Leandri resembled one of the unquiet wraiths from the old Breton folk tales that Verité dismissed with laughter, but which had terrified his young son.

The other mourners around Philippe were chiefly Leandris. He was a few places behind Jacobo and close to Jean-Marc, the witness whose testimony had saved him from summary execution. Next behind Carla walked Pozzo di Borgo and Pasquale Paoli, now dressed in a faded red general's uniform that must have dated from the campaigns of the 1760s and which now barely fitted him. The track from the fort to the village was lined on both sides by the irregular troops of the Leandrists and Paolists, standing in single ranks and making at least a sketchy effort to stand at attention and present arms like an elite regiment. The unique white-and-black flag of Corsica, adorned by a defiant Moorish head, flew from banners held high, dipping in salute as the coffin passed. In silence but for the tolling of the bell, the shuffling of the mourners' feet and the psalms recited by Colonna, the coffin, borne by six of Ercule Leandri's old comrades-in-arms, was borne into the village. The army that had been lining the road fell in behind it, and as the coffin was carried into the church the men began to sing the song General Leandri had described to Philippe, '*Dio vi salvi Regina*', the haunting, mournful, unsettling battle hymn of the Corsicans.

As the service began, Philippe realised with a shock that he, who had been nominally brought up as a Catholic despite having an atheist father and an Anglican mother, had never attended a requiem mass before. There had been too few Catholics in America to form congregations or build churches, and although he had visited Catholic lands since, attendance at mass had never been important to him. He attended Orthodox services in Russia, largely at his beloved Tasha's instigation, but by the time he went to his native France the power of the Church had been broken by the tidal wave of scepticism that his father, Verité, had done so much to unleash. Yet here, in Corsica, it was as if the revolution and even the Protestant Reformation of earlier centuries had not taken place at all. Incense burned, dense clouds of its sweet, cloying smell filling the church. '*Requiem Aeternam*' was sung, Father Colonna, clad in a purple chasuble over a white robe, recited the ancient Latin prayers over the coffin of Ercule Leandri, and the congregants crossed themselves passionately. Philippe glanced across at Paoli, who had been as much a stalwart of the Enlightenment as his own father, and thought the general looked deeply uncomfortable.

Philippe made the responses, spoke the words that he still somehow recalled from his childhood, and listened to the polyphonic *lamentu* sung by the men of the congregation, but his thoughts were elsewhere. With Ercule Leandri dead, his mission to Corsica had ended in failure. He was now certain the outcome would have been the same if the veteran general still lived and breathed. Philippe Kermorvant, Vicomte de Saint-Victor, and the general at Le Muy, and Robespierre, and the entire Committee of Public Safety, had all been outwitted by a wily old fox who was far more cunning than any of them. By the fox's cub, too, who proved that man's eternal folly, ever since Adam and Eve, was underestimating a woman.

As the Lacrimosa wound its eternal path forward, Philippe's thoughts turned to his ship. He had been away from her for too long. This had been a fool's errand, a consequence of his being the son of a famous father and bearing the name he bore. He longed to be gone from Corsica before the two British officers from Ghineparu had a chance to reconsider their tacit acceptance of Philippe's safe conduct. He desired only to be present on the quarterdeck of *Le Torrington* on that glorious day when Admiral Martin would finally hoist the signal for the fleet to weigh and leave the Bay of Gourjean. Perhaps he would even do battle one day with the peculiar little English captain with the damaged eye who had intervened to try and save his life. He knew he would never again receive any charity from that man, but nonetheless, he offered up a silent prayer of thanks for what he had done.

The service concluded. The dead general's coffin was borne out of the church to the grave, freshly dug in the rudimentary cemetery on the lower slopes of the mountain. The grim-faced, austere Colonna's timeless Latin prayers provided a solemn accompaniment to the sombre procession. At the graveside, Philippe recalled another place and another open grave, the hole dug with much difficulty in the frozen ground of Kronstadt where his slaughtered wife and son were laid to their eternal rest. The committal of General Ercule Leandri would be brief and perfunctory, as had been the last rites for those he loved. The crowd would disperse, and the memory of the dead would immediately begin to fade.

But that was not what happened in the burying place of Ghineparu.

Carla Leandri stepped forward to the graveside, lifted her veil and began to sing. It was not like any song Philippe had ever heard before. It had elements of the bass dirges of the Russians, the wailing of the Arabs and the hysterical melodrama of the Paris opera, but it was all and none of these things. Philippe could make out none of the words, which had to be in the Corsican tongue, but the spectacle of the general's daughter singing them elicited a remarkable reaction from the congregation. Father Colonna's features drained of blood and he crossed himself vigorously. The Leandri kin looked at each other with startled, even frightened expressions. Claudia Leandri, who had been moving toward the graveside when Carla began, now stood stock still, tears staining her cheeks as she watched and listened to her niece.

Carla had been singing for two or three minutes. There were many verses to the lament, almost all in Corsican, some in the Tuscan dialect of Italian. Then, finally, she stared directly at Philippe and sang a verse in French.

He is gone, our lion, our general,
There are no sons to avenge him.
I will be all your sons, the avenger of Leandri.
I will take my gun, take my stiletto,

I will hunt down the killer of our hero.
The slaughterer will become the slaughtered.

—

After the funeral was concluded, Philippe sought out Carla. She was sheltering from the relentless drizzle in the lee of the church, where she was engaged in a low, urgent conversation with Paoli and Pozzo di Borgo. Her cousin Jacobo was also hovering nearby, craving her attention. But after the two statesmen parted from her, kissing her hand and bowing extravagantly as they did so, it was Philippe whom she approached, greatly to Jacobo Leandri's annoyance.

'My condolences once again, citizeness.'

'I'm grateful to you for them, Captain, although condolences are not really the Corsican way.'

'But your song was.'

Carla Leandri blushed.

'I don't know what drove me to do it. I felt… I felt as if some other force, some force unseen, was compelling me. But they all say that, all those who sing the *voceru* for the dead. Some say it comes from the spirits of all those who have gone before compelling the singer to improvise verses in honour of the newly departed. I never felt such a compulsion before, Captain – not when we buried my mother, nor my brothers. There are those who make it their living, going from one funeral to another, singing the verses they are inspired to sing and receiving payment. My aunt Claudia is one, as well as having the gift – or the curse – of the *mazzera*. Perhaps that way lies next for me, to become one of those who can foretell death and bring it to the doomed.'

They were astonishing words from the lips of such a young, well-educated and beautiful woman, and Philippe could think of no response. Instead, he changed the subject and informed

138

her that with his mission concluded in failure, he wished to return to the mainland immediately.

At once the newly fledged *mazzera*, the singer of *voceru*, the dweller on the narrow margin between the living and the dead, gave way to the practical, confident *generalissima*.

'You won't reach the coast before nightfall, and there's no certainty Giordano will still be there in any case.' Philippe realised he had not seen Giordano at the funeral, so the captain of *Lucrezia* must have returned to her. 'You shall stay here for tonight, Captain. We are feasting and honouring my father in the castle.'

'I am grateful for the offer, citizeness, but for all we know the English officers have gone back to Calvi and ordered a troop to come and arrest me. I've seen enough of English captivity for one lifetime.'

'The English will not spare men from the siege of Calvi,' she said with finality. 'And even if they do, how will they make their way here, through mountains they don't know and past men who will resist them?'

'Paoli and his men are allied to the English.'

'Paoli is a Corsican. Whatever passed between them recently, and despite the words he spoke in the church, he and my father were friends for most of their lives. Paoli also gave his word of honour to you, Captain Kermorvant, just as that English captain said. To the Corsican the word of honour is a blood-oath, more precious than life itself. He will not betray you to the English. He will not dishonour his old friend's memory. Even if he is bowing the knee to their King George, he will ensure that his men defend you from the English king's soldiers for as long as you are on Corsica. No. Tonight you are a Corsican, the respected guest of the late General Ercule Leandri and his daughter, and tonight you sleep in the tower of the Leandris.'

CHAPTER SEVENTEEN

The feast in honour of Ercule Leandri was long over. Philippe
lay on his bed in the tower room that had been occupied by
Pasquale Paoli himself for the preceding four nights. The meal,
in a spacious hall filled with old furniture and with walls hung
with ancient armour, had been an uncomfortable, strained business. Carla Leandri insisted on seating him next to her in the
place of honour to her right, to the obvious fury of Jacobo,
who was placed at the furthest end of the table. The seat to
Philippe's right was occupied by the eldest and most revered
member of the Leandri family, the youngest brother of the dead
general's father, who was well over eighty and could clearly
remember the strange episode nearly sixty years before when
a German adventurer had fetched up in Corsica, proclaimed
himself King Theodore the First, and reigned for a few months
until the Genoese and the Corsicans themselves had grown tired
of the ridiculousness of it all and sent him packing. The old
man's deafness and inability to remain awake for more than a
few minutes at a time meant that Philippe talked principally
to Carla, who was both inquisitive and a good listener. She
drew out of him his memories of his father, of growing up in
America and the war for independence against the British, of
Russia and the Empress Catherine, of the battles he had fought
for her against the Swedes and the Turks. Inevitably, she asked
him if he had a wife and children, and he spilled out the story
of Natasha, his son, and their brutal fate at the hands of Tasha's
brother, Count Bulgakov.

'And this Bulgakov still lives? You have not pursued him? You have not declared vendetta against his entire kin?'

'That may be the Corsican way, but it is not mine. Not that of the French, nor the English, nor the Bretons. Besides, Bulgakov is in Russia, a very long way away.'

Philippe knew that this was not necessarily true. He knew that Bulgakov, seeking to repair his relations with the Tsarevich Paul that had been damaged by his murder of Philippe's wife and son, had been putting his name forward for diplomatic postings. There had been rumours that he was in Berlin or Dresden, but both of those cities were still a very long way from Corsica or Toulon.

'That was what I found strange about Paris,' said Carla. 'All those poor souls who went to the guillotine – if all their kinsmen had sworn vendetta against Robespierre and the rest of the tyrants, they would soon have done for them all. But no, I heard the same excuses there. Paris was too far, the enemy was too well guarded, the French were too civilised, and so on. Feeble.'

The words were entirely at odds with Carla Leandri's appearance, an elegant black silk mourning dress making *la generalissima* seem once again the very image of a sophisticated French lady. Yet Philippe had never known a woman speak so readily of killing and cold-blooded revenge. She intrigued and astonished him in equal measure.

'But blood for blood enduring for years, centuries even? Why the vendetta against this Captain Maestracci, for instance?'

'Oh, the feud between Leandri and Maestracci has gone on for generations. No one now remembers how it began, which party wronged the other first. Perhaps a killing, perhaps a stolen cow, perhaps no more than a badly chosen insult. But in living memory, my father killed Maestracci's grandfather, so I suppose this death is revenge for that in his eyes. And I'll give him his due, he did it in the true Corsican way. Show no fear, ride right into the heart of your enemy's territory, kill your enemy when he is in the midst of his own people. Little good it will do him. Next, of course, I will kill Maestracci.'

She said it so casually that she might have been asking for the salt.

'*You*, Carla?' Forgetting himself, Philippe called her by her name. 'I know you sang of it at the funeral, but surely it is not your place to seek revenge – not *to kill a man*. I have killed men. It is not to be taken lightly.'

She looked angrily at him. He could not fail to notice her bosom heaving with fury.

'Look at my family,' she said, waving her hand around the room. 'There's not one real man among them. Jacobo fancies himself as one, of course, and as the new head of the family, especially after he's married me. So he thinks. I would rather marry the Ottoman sultan, and not because Jacobo has only one arm. I think whatever brains he had were in the one he lost.'

'I don't doubt you're capable of it, citizeness. But Maestracci is an officer in the British Army. He will be in an armed camp, surrounded by soldiers, and he will be expecting a Leandri to come after him.'

'He will be expecting a man,' she said, 'and he has not seen me since I was a child.'

Philippe could think of no adequate response. Carla's determination was obvious, her purpose undeniable.

'But tell me more of the Indians of the Americas, Captain,' she said, her expression softening. 'What are their favoured ways of killing their enemies?'

–

Much later, Philippe lay awake upon the bed in the uppermost room of the ancient tower. This was a special mark of honour, Carla told him. On the previous nights, the room and the bed had been occupied by none other than General Pasquale Paoli himself.

Carla Leandri's vendetta was not his affair, he told himself. The next day he would set out for the coast. It did not matter whether or not Giordano's ship was still there. He would wait if he had to, or else he would seek to buy another captain and crew willing to carry him back to France. That was fraught with risk, though. Giordano was a known quantity, and as far as he could judge he was ferociously loyal to Carla. There was no guarantee that an unknown captain would not betray him to the English. But the longer he remained with the Leandris, the greater the risk that, safe conduct or no, some man or other might be tempted by a purse of William Pitt's gold.

Sleep would not come. Instead the choices waged a civil war in his thoughts, the arguments swinging this way and that. As the minutes passed, though, his ability to concentrate on them faltered. No matter which way he turned, the face of Carla Leandri somehow intruded into his thoughts. He had suffered similarly before, notably on the *Agincourt* prison hulk when the features of his sister-in-law, Leonore, often appeared uninvited in his mind in the moments between waking and sleep. He thought then that no one could ever usurp Leonore's place in his conscious or unconscious mind. Yet there was the image and memory of Carla Leandri, planted in his thoughts and immovable.

At last, though, Philippe's limbs relaxed and he felt himself begin to slip from the waking world.

The noise of his door latch being raised brought him fully awake, and instinct made him reach at once for the pistol at his bedside.

The shape in the doorway was not that of a murderer. It was that of Carla Leandri, wearing a loose gown over a white shift. She slipped into the room, quietly closing the door behind her.

'Citizeness,' said Philippe uncertainly, 'you should not be here.'

'Why, Captain? Because my father is newly dead and buried, and I should be grieving for him like a good daughter and a good submissive Corsican woman? That I should be clad in black and locking myself away for a year or the rest of my life, as Jacobo and the old-thinking ones would have me do? Or is it because I am an unmarried woman, and my being here is scandalous? Or do you not like me, Captain Kermorvant? I've heard the tales of sailors preferring boys.'

She moved toward him and sat on the side of his bed. He felt confusion and uncertainty, emotions that had been absent when he and Frank Parmentier visited the girls at Madame Sarron's. But none of them had been like Carla Leandri.

'I like you, citizeness – Carla. You are a beautiful woman. But it is not appropriate—'

No, it was not. But he had a sudden memory of a *soirée* in the Peter and Paul fortress in honour of Admiral John Paul Jones and in the presence of the Empress Catherine herself, where he had been approached by a very beautiful but also remarkably forward young woman who gave her name as Natasha Bulgakov.

'Perhaps you think I'm a maiden,' said Carla. 'My father thought I remained so through all my time in Paris. I even had *two* chaperones, dry old crones who he sent with me to keep my virtue intact. But who cannot discover love in Paris, Philippe, whatever obstacles might lie in the way? So I am not... inexperienced, if that is your concern.'

'You barely know me, Carla.'

'You are not Corsican,' she said, smiling ruefully. 'If my fate is to marry Jacobo or some other foul-smelling pig-brained cousin, then I will have this one last night where I have the freedom to lie with a man of my choosing.' She placed a finger on his lips. 'Remember, Philippe, that I am *la generalissima*.'

She took off the gown and let the slip shift from her shoulders, then lay down by his side. Philippe placed his hands on her bare flesh and drew her to him. Their first kisses were tentative, then swiftly more passionate. Philippe forgot that he was in the tower of the Leandris, still full of those like Jacobo who would gleefully snatch at any excuse to kill him. At *this* excuse. At an act they would consider almost as heinous as the slaying of their chief.

They came together. Philippe was lost in memories of other women, then of only one other, then of no woman at all but the astonishingly responsive, practised and eager creature beneath him. They moved in harmony, no words passing between them, their gasps becoming more frequent and more urgent.

–

Dawn was breaking, its light through the tower room's single unshuttered window illuminating the exhausted lovers. Carla lay in Philippe's arms, stroking his chest.

'I must go before one of the women finds I'm not in my room,' she said. 'Then I must leave to find and kill Maestracci.'

She made to get up, but Philippe restrained her.

'Wait,' he said. 'Wait, Carla. I thought upon this in the night, when we were not engaged in other ways. How did Maestracci know? How did he know that your father was in your aunt's house with little protection, not up here in the tower – in this very room?'

She thought on it for some moments.

'The British knew the conference was taking place. That was why the colonel and the captain were here. Maestracci might have learned of it from that Colonel Moore.'

'Why would Moore tell such a thing to a junior officer? How would he even know that the Maestraccis and the Leandris had been at feud for years? No, Carla, there's only one way he could have found out. Who knew that your father had moved from the tower to your aunt's house?'

'Paoli, Pozzo di Borgo, the rest of their party. The offer of the rooms in the tower was a gesture of goodwill toward them.'

'But although they'd fallen out over the alliance with Britain, your father and Paoli were not in a vendetta. Paoli wanted your father's support, not his death.'

She understood. He could see the realisation in her eyes.

'It could not be one of us,' she said. 'It could not be a Leandri. But none of my cousins would even think of such a betrayal of their name, of their blood. No Leandri would even think of killing their patriarch and general.'

'So who else? Who else knew where your father slept?'

'No more than four or five men, all of them trusted by my father for many years. Another would be the priest. But Father Colonna baptised me and married my parents. He has taken our family's confessions and kept our confidences for generations.'

'Then we must learn who the traitor is before we pursue Maestracci,' said Philippe.

'"We", Captain Kermorvant? I thought you wished to leave for the coast immediately.'

'The ones I loved who were violently killed – they have not been avenged. Perhaps they never will be. I'd spare you that feeling, Carla. That knowledge. That failure. I'll do all I can to help you conclude the vendetta. I'll help you to kill Maestracci.'

CHAPTER EIGHTEEN

The ceremony was conducted in the middle of the morning, and it took place in the church of Saint Devota. The village priest, Father Colonna, and indeed the Catholic Church as a whole, officially condemned vendetta, considering it to be a vicious, unchristian relic of pagan times. But Father Colonna was a Corsican, and as they entered the nave Carla whispered to Philippe that he would be there, behind the squint, taking in everything that was said, perhaps even offering up a prayer to bless her mission.

The party gathered in the church was a dozen strong. Jacobo Leandri was there, as was Jean-Marc, the ancient fellow who had sat to Philippe's left at the feast, and a few other cousins whom Philippe vaguely remembered from that occasion. There were four or five men who did not share the Leandri surname, sergeants who had commanded contingents during the funeral procession.

Jacobo's face darkened at the sight of Philippe:

'Why have you brought him here, cousin? He is an outsider. A foreigner. This is no business of his.'

'Jacobo Leandri, you sought to hang Captain Kermorvant for a crime he did not commit. Don't you think that gives him a natural interest in seeing justice brought against the true murderer?'

'I'm the head of the family now, Carla. I decide who avenges your father. When, where, how – all of it.'

'Really, Jacobo? Head of the family? *Really?* Then speak, cousin. Who will avenge my father? You? Maestracci is a few miles north of here, in the camp before Calvi. The English colonel has told us exactly which regiment he serves in, and we know exactly where that regiment is. The avenger of my father can be there and back in a day. So, will you be the man who kills him, Jacobo Leandri? And how will you do it? We're all waiting for the self-proclaimed new head of the family to speak, cousin.'

Jacobo looked at the statue of the Virgin above the altar, as though seeking her intervention and guidance. But that day Mary the Mother of God provided him with no inspiration or enlightenment. His reply was less confident than his initial bluster.

'It is difficult,' he said. 'We need to lure Maestracci out of the English camp. But there are many troops, and all the approaches to the siegeworks are well guarded. We must think of a ruse.'

'Did my father waste time trying to think of ruses? You fought under him, cousin. He made his plans rapidly, he executed them immediately and decisively, he always attacked, and he always won. That is what our people expect of the head of the Leandris.'

'I – I am thinking about it.'

'Think too long and the Squadra d'Arrozza will be at all our doors, bidding us to join their legion of the dead. Maestracci will be a doddering old man. You'll be too feeble to wield even a stiletto. Enough of your thinking, Jacobo Leandri. I am the general's daughter, his *heir*, and I demand action. I demand revenge. I demand blood. And I will draw it myself.'

There were shouts of protest from the others gathered behind Jacobo.

'Women do not engage in vendetta,' said an old man with a shattered face that had once been ravaged by smallpox. 'Vengeance is a business for men, only men. The women remain at home. You should be clad in black and locked away in your house, Carla Leandri. None of us should see your face outside for a year and more.'

'Would you have said that to me if my father was still alive, Antonio? No, I thought not. And women *have* engaged in vendetta, even within our own family, even within living memory. Isn't that so, Nicolas?'

Philippe's neighbour from the meal, the old man who remembered the brief reign of King Theodore, nodded.

'It has happened throughout our history,' he said. 'Throughout Corsica and, yes, in the annals of the name of Leandri too. If the men do not act, or if there are no men left, then the blade may be wielded by a woman. When I was a very tiny boy, I personally witnessed my aunt Letizia cut the throat of Giovanni Maestracci in 1730 or thereabouts.'

'There,' said Carla triumphantly. 'So does any other man deny my right to avenge my father?' There was silence in the church. Jacobo Leandri nearly spoke up, but instead he looked down to the floor. 'No? Then bring me the Bible from the lectern. And, aunt, if you please.'

Claudia Leandri, who had been standing in the doorway, brought forward the bloodstained shirt of her brother-in-law, General Ercule Leandri. Carla touched it with reverence, and all the men bowed their heads. Jacobo was scarlet-faced with fury, but he could sense, as could Philippe, that his support had drained away among his own kin. Another cousin went to the lectern and brought the Bible, upon which Carla laid her hands. She offered up a prayer in Latin that Philippe did not recognise, then uttered a long speech in Corsican that might have been some sort of poem or vow. Finally, she spoke in French for Philippe's benefit.

'I shall seek out Pierre-Paul Maestracci tonight, in the English camp. I will ride out in an hour to reconnoitre it. I will find a way of avoiding the English guards. I will kill him in his tent. I will avenge my father and enhance the honour of the Leandri name. This I swear by the Virgin, all the saints and all my ancestors to the beginning of the world.'

There was utter silence in the church. Then the priest, watching from the squint, sneezed, and the moment was gone.

Carla and Philippe returned to the tower as if to prepare for Carla to fulfil her promise to ride to Calvi. Instead they climbed to the platform at the very top, which provided spectacular views for many miles around. A golden eagle circled lazily, then flew off to see if there were any more interesting prospects on the other side of the mountain. Occasionally barely audible sounds in the far distance demonstrated that the British bombardment of Calvi continued in its intermittent, indecisive fashion.

'You might be wrong,' said Carla.

Philippe studied the village below as if he was assessing an enemy warship, scanning first one way, then the other, methodically and repeatedly.

'A message had to go to Maestracci to trigger your father's killing,' he said, 'and a message has to go to him now, to let him know you're coming at the hour you announced in the church. Whoever the traitor is dare not wait. He, or his messenger, must reach Maestracci before you do, and he'll think you're going to set out in less than an hour from now.'

'People are coming and going all the time.'

'If I'm right, none of them will be in such a hurry.'

For long minutes there was nothing suspicious. Two heavily laden carts came up the road that Philippe and Carla had taken to the village, a group of widows went down to the stream to wash clothes, a dozen or so ragged-looking boys played a riotous game of their own devising in the dust of the village square. Philippe began to doubt his own judgement. Perhaps there was no traitor in the Leandri camp. Perhaps sheer luck had directed Maestracci to Ercule Leandri.

There was movement at the edge of the village. A man mounted on a grey mare rode out at a brisk canter on the road that led north, toward Calvi.

'No,' gasped Carla.

Philippe shared her disbelief. The rider was the village priest, Father Colonna.

'No!' she repeated, nearly shouting the word.

Philippe and Carla sprinted down the spiral staircase of the tower and mounted the two tethered horses awaiting them in the courtyard. They set off in the opposite direction to the village, taking a tortuous shepherd's path around the eastern and northern slopes of the mountain. They would have to ride more slowly than the priest, said Carla as they rode out, for the path was precarious in places. But it was a short cut that would bring them back down onto the Calvi road ahead of Father Colonna.

Philippe considered himself a competent horseman, having been taught to ride both by his father and rather less formally by his childhood friends among the Powhatan of Virginia, whose equine skills were more unconventional but often more effective than those of a French nobleman born to the saddle. But the narrow mountain track tested his abilities, and several times he found himself deliberately looking away from the steep slopes that fell away sharply to his right, down into the valley and the dense forest far below. A goat, startled by the sight of intruders in its domain, bolted and made Philippe's horse whinny in fright, but somehow he kept control. Carla, riding confidently ahead, must have known this track and the entire mountain since her early days, and showed no sign of any trepidation.

They descended the north-western slope, coming out onto the Calvi road only a few miles from Ghineparu. No more than a minute or two passed before Philippe heard the sound of an approaching horse. He drew his pistol, levelling it at the astonished face of Father Colonna as the priest came round the blind corner formed by a rock outcrop.

'Why, Father?' asked Carla.

Colonna looked around, perhaps hoping to see some way of escape or some miraculous intervention to save him from what now confronted him. Perhaps he was trying to think of a plausible lie, some tale that would convince Carla Leandri and her foreign lover. But there on an empty mountain road in Corsica, he realised that the only course left to him was to tell the truth.

'Maestracci is a true son of the Church,' said the priest, slowly and nervously at first. 'A loyal follower of the lawful king of France. Your father was an atheist, Carla Leandri, as was this man's father, one of the high priests of atheism.' He gestured toward Philippe, then looked again at Carla. There was anger in his eyes, but also something that might have been sorrow. 'The Corsica your father wanted would have been an abomination, a cesspit of slaughter and ungodliness, just like the tyrant Robespierre's so-called French Republic. Had Maestracci not taken him from this world, your father would have made an alliance with a force worse than the Antichrist.'

He would not, thought Philippe. He knew now that Ercule Leandri never intended to declare for France, that his threats to do so were a bluff. But Colonna had not known that — Carla's father cannot have revealed his true motives even in the confessional — so the priest, deceived by a lie, had colluded in the general's death for no reason.

'You are a priest,' growled Carla, 'bound by the vows of the Church. Bound by the holy sacraments. Yet you sanction murder? And now you seek to betray me, *me*, Father, the child you baptised — you seek to betray me to my enemy?'

'There are things I regret... I have prayed, I have confessed to the bishop, I have struggled with my conscience for so very many years. But my grandmother was a Maestracci. When I heard that Pierre-Paul had returned to Corsica, that he was with the royal troops at Calvi — it was surely a sign. Blood will out, Carla Leandri, even if a man wears a cassock.'

'You lived among us for all those years! You were respected. You were *loved*.'

'And I will answer for it all before the throne of Heaven. Not to you, Carla Leandri. Not to an unnatural creature who dresses like a man, shuns an honest Corsican marriage and whores with this foreigner, this son of one of the most notorious deniers of Christian truth—'

'I spoke *in confession* – do you betray that sacrament too?'

'I serve God as I believe He would wish to be served,' said Colonna. 'And I die for Him willingly.'

He cracked the reins, spurred his horse's sides, and galloped directly at Philippe and Carla. Philippe waited for point blank, then pulled the trigger. Father Colonna took the shot in his chest. The impact flung him backward and to the side, and his movement pulled his horse with him. Man and beast both plunged over the edge of the road and smashed into the slope, the horse's legs flailing hopelessly as they fell into the gorge and down to the raging, rock-strewn stream far below.

Philippe went to Carla, who was sobbing loudly and weeping tears of shock and regret. He reached over and held her tightly to him.

'I thought him a good man,' she murmured.

'There are no wholly good men,' said Philippe, softly.

'Who will baptise the children? Who will bury the dead? I must write to the bishop, I must arrange for a priest to come from another village.'

'Carla, you can't worry yourself with such things. Not now. Grieve for your father, grieve for your priest if you must. Other matters can wait.'

'One matter cannot,' she said, swallowing her sorrow and resuming the mantle of *la generalissima*. 'Maestracci.'

'Not now,' said Philippe. 'Not today, Carla. You need a plan.'

'I have the plan,' she said sharply, 'I just need the moment. And I need you to help me, Captain Kermorvant.'

CHAPTER NINETEEN

Three days later, Carla Leandri and Philippe Kermorvant went to Calvi to kill Captain Pierre-Paul Maestracci of the Royal Louis Regiment, nominally in the service of the Most Christian King Louis the Seventeenth of France but actually in that of His Britannic Majesty King George the Third. The intervening time saw the burial of Father Colonna, the entire village and Leandri clan finding his betrayal shocking and unaccountable. Carla held meetings with her cousins, firmly establishing herself as the new head of the family and quelling the masculine outrage from the likes of Jacobo. At night, she and Philippe made love with the desperation of those who know they have only a very short time in each other's company, after which they will probably never meet again on this earth. Then, at last, they took the road that Father Colonna had been taking when he met his death.

They went with Jean-Marc Leandri, who knew the tracks and byways of the country better than anyone else. A few miles outside Calvi he advised that they dismount and proceed the rest of the way on foot. There were occasional and desultory Paolist patrols, he said. They may not encounter one, for no one in the besieging army seriously expected any threat from behind, meaning that security beyond the immediate perimeter of the siege camp was lax, but three travellers on horseback, one of them a woman, would be bound to attract attention. So they tethered the horses by a stream in a clearing that they could easily locate again, then made their way on foot along one of the narrow, almost imperceptible paths that led through the thick bushes of the maquis.

As they walked, the sound of intermittent cannon fire became louder. Philippe even caught the familiar but faint smell of powder-smoke on the brisk northerly breeze. When they finally emerged from the dense maquis, Philippe stifled a gasp. He was overlooking a vast tableau, a table-top war of tiny armies and navies, his distance from them lending an unreal quality to the spectacle. Their position gave an uninterrupted view of the entire Bay of Calvi, with the town itself at the very centre upon a towering promontory that formed a narrow peninsula jutting out into the bay and protected from assault by colossal ranks of redoubts, bastions and glacis. Many, but not all, of the defensive fortifications seemed to be of considerable age. To the west, the bay was sheltered by a long rocky peninsula that Carla named as Cape Revellata. Mountains reared up to the north and east, leaving only a small coastal plain divided into tiny fields between the British positions in the foothills fronting the town. From the citadel of Calvi, a large *Tricolore* billowed defiantly. It was the only flag of the French Republic in sight. The batteries on the plain in front of the town, the platoons and regiments moving to and fro across the bare fields, and the ships anchored in the bay, almost all flew the blue-and-red-and-white jumble of crosses that made up the colours of the kingdom of Great Britain. Almost all, but not quite. Here and there a very different flag flew at the head of small columns of roughly dressed, poorly drilled irregular troops: the flag that Philippe had seen for the first time at Ercule Leandri's funeral, a black Moor's head on a white ground, the emblem of independent Corsica, now flying at the head of General Pasquale Paoli's pro-British militia.

The enemy's position was all too evidently exceptionally powerful. Out in the bay lay half a dozen men-of-war, the largest of them, at anchor almost due north of Calvi, unmistakeably HMS *Victory*, flying the flag of Lord Hood. Close to her lay a Forty that looked to be of recent French design, probably one of the many prizes that had been captured since the start of the war and taken into King George's Royal Navy. A Seventy-Four lay between these and the shore, a tender alongside her unloading its cargo of water barrels, the ship's boats moving with impunity into the bay to bring ashore a large party of seamen and Marines. A Thirty-Two lay off to the northeast, close inshore, while another frigate was visible in the far distance, cruising to deter and intercept any vessel attempting to bring relief to the trapped garrison. Right under the citadel itself, moored within easy range of the small part of the town that lay on the plain, beneath and outside the walls, lay another Forty, just inshore of another Thirty-Two. The French guns in the citadel could not possibly be trained low enough to hit these ships, which, by contrast, could blast the lower part of the town with impunity if any resistance was offered from it. But there had been no Frenchmen in that area for some time, judging by the newly ruinous, charred state of the buildings. Carla said that the British possessed the best harbour on the coast, the Bay of Fiorenzo to the north-east, so they could easily rotate which ships were on station off Calvi and those which could rest their crews and replenish their stores. It was an enviable advantage.

If the array of British power at sea was impressive, that apparent on land was overwhelming. An old star-shaped redoubt with a keep-like central tower, probably a legacy of Genoese rule like the tower at Ghineparu, lay on the plain, defending the road up to the town. The Union flag flew from this, and Philippe counted twenty guns of different calibres, all presumably at maximum elevation to bring within range the walls of the citadel of Calvi. Further out stood a smaller round tower that had been converted into a mortar battery. Between the two older fortifications lay two newly improvised batteries, one with a dozen large guns, which Philippe reckoned were probably eighteen-pounders by the English way of calculating calibre. West of this, right on the coast, was a small battery with just two guns, albeit much larger ones. With the two frigates anchored to the east of the peninsula providing fire from that side if necessary, the enemy could mount a devastating crossfire against any troops trying to sally forth from the citadel. Closer to Philippe's position, to the east of the positions covering the road up to the town, were two more enemy batteries: a redoubt which, so Jean-Marc said, a party that slipped out of the citadel had tried and failed to mine; and a battery with three large guns, probably twenty-four or twenty-six pounders, mounted on higher ground than the other besieging ordnance so that despite being further away, the enemy would be able to strike some of the higher positions. A different flag, albeit a very familiar one, flew over this battery and the white-uniformed soldiers who served it, alongside the ubiquitous Union flag. Fleur-de-lis on a white ground, the old royal colours of the Bourbon kings, flew over what Jean-Marc named as the Royal Louis battery, the station of the eponymous regiment of diehard royalists in exile who fought with the English and Corsicans against their native country. That was where Captain Pierre-Paul Maestracci would be.

There was no prospect of relief by land, for the entire island was in the hands of Paoli and the British. As Philippe knew from his own experience, no French fleet could possibly break through against the overwhelming enemy superiority at sea. Calvi was doomed. Both attackers and defenders alike would know it, but the unwritten laws of war insisted that the siege would continue until just enough men had died in an utterly pointless cause for the honour of all sides finally to be satisfied.

A gun fired from the star battery down on the plain, and Philippe saw the impact in the wall close to the city gate. But no other shots followed it to try and create a breach. The whole business on the plain between Philippe and the walls of Calvi had an air of ennui about it. There was no urgency anywhere. The British seemed to fire a gun from time to time only because they supposed that was what they were expected to do. Platoons and regiments marched hither and thither, but at a slow, almost funereal pace. It was as though both sides knew that Calvi was doomed to fall sooner rather than later, and there was simply no point in expending powder, effort and men's lives in expediting the process.

During their days and nights together in Ghineparu, Carla had been silent about her plan to seek out and kill Maestracci. Now she was scanning the battlefield as keenly as Philippe, but with an entirely different purpose in mind.

'There are camp followers,' she said. 'See? There, down by the lower road.'

'They will wait there until dark, then make their way into the siege camp.' Philippe turned to her. 'I know what you're thinking, Carla, and if the camp was new then it would be a sound plan. But these women will probably have been here for weeks, they'll know each other, a stranger in their midst would be obvious at once. Besides, they'll be for the common soldiers. The officers will be apart – see those tents over there? And officers share their tents, maybe four to each in ones that size. You won't just have to get to Maestracci, you'll have to get past whoever shares his quarters. Then you have to get out of the camp again – I assume you do want to live?'

She made no reply, and Philippe saw the anguish in her face. Her plan lay in ruins. Her dream to avenge her father was dying in her eyes.

'I will find a way,' she said.

They found a deserted and ruinous house nearer to the shore, seemingly just beyond the perimeter patrolled by the British and Corsican sentries. It would make a suitable base until Carla achieved her goal or finally accepted that it was impossible. Philippe was convinced that this was the case – he had seen enough siege camps in America and at Izmail in the war between Russia and Ottoman Turkey to know the difficulty of penetrating one

– and that he had to persuade Carla of this. If she persisted, it was certain to bring about her own death.

'You're set on murdering him in cold blood,' he said as they shared a loaf of bread. 'That's not an easy course, Carla. To look a man in the eyes as you kill him… that takes a special kind of courage. It takes utter ruthlessness. Are you certain you have that?'

She looked at him with what might have been pity.

'He will suffer the same fate as the one he bestowed on my father. It is the way of the vendetta, the way it has always been. He knows that way as well as I do. If I see that understanding in his eyes and then see those eyes go blank, I will have redeemed the honour of the Leandris.'

'But then it will go on, won't it? Another of his name will hunt you down, and Jacobo or one of the others will seek to avenge you, and so it will continue. Where is the law in all this, Carla? Where is the justice?'

She blinked at the words law and justice as though they were entirely new to her, and words that were entirely inapplicable in Corsica.

'He is the last Maestracci. The last male. There were others, but they all went to France two or three generations past. They'll consider themselves modern Frenchmen, civilised men, loyal citizens of the Republic. They'll regard themselves as pillars of the law and justice you extol, Philippe Kermorvant. I met one of them in Paris – a fop, uninterested in the history between our families. Uninterested in *me*.'

'But there'll be more distant relatives, like Father Colonna.'

She shrugged. 'It is a risk Corsicans take, the way of the vendetta. We learn that from the cradle. Yet you lecture me about law, Philippe Kermorvant? You lecture me about justice? I saw French law and justice in Paris. I saw dozens of poor souls go to the guillotine, some of them women and children, often on the flimsiest of charges. Please tell me, Captain, how exactly is that somehow more noble than vendetta? More just than my killing Maestracci? And what would you do if Count Bulgakov was just a few miles from you now? Would you challenge him to a duel as a man of honour? Would you have him arrested? By whom, exactly? Or would you hunt him down yourself, and avenge your wife and son as you long to?'

Philippe was in no position to argue with her. He got up, went outside and looked out to sea while occasional fire from the guns besieging Calvi kept up a pale, desultory imitation of a bombardment. Carla was right. He had often dreamed of what he would do if Bulgakov ever came within his orbit again. He had convinced himself it would never happen, but if it did – if, by some unfathomable miracle, it did – what would he do? Honour demanded a fair challenge, the justice of a duel, the judgement of God. But his father, Verité, had insisted there was no God, and God or no, Bulgakov had hacked to death his own sister and nephew. There was no doubt of it. There were witnesses. The case against Count Vladimir Kyrilovich Bulgakov was undoubtedly even stronger than that against Captain Pierre-Paul Maestracci. Philippe Kermorvant, Vicomte de Saint-Victor, had as much reason to swear an oath of vendetta as did Carla Leandri—

He did not hear her come up beside him. She was grinning.

'I have thought of a way,' she said.

CHAPTER TWENTY

On Sundays, the war in Corsica ceased.

With any sense of urgency over the taking of Calvi having long disappeared, the usual and rightful respects could be paid to the Eternal Father. The men of the British Army, assembled next to their batteries on the plain before the fortress-town, heard sermons from their tedious Anglican chaplains and took drumhead Communion. No equivalent rites were performed in the besieged town itself, the republican army under the native Corsican General Raphael, comte de Casabianca, adhering firmly to the revolutionary principles that categorically rejected the errors and superstitions of the past.

The one group of warriors who worshipped differently, who sought the solace of the eternal Mother Church, were the proudly and ferociously Catholic officers and men of the Royal Louis Regiment. The common soldiers of the regiment went to a couple of barn-like and unremarkable village churches close to their camp, but the officers made a longer pilgrimage. This took them south and west of the besieged town and up the steep path that led to the chapel of Notre Dame de la Serra. This stood on a hill with an unobstructed view of Calvi, its bay, and all the land round about. It was a place of breathtaking beauty, and it seemed to Captain Pierre-Paul Maestracci as though it was close to the Notre Dame herself, to the presence of the Blessed Virgin Mother. He relished attending mass in the chapel, partly because it was a place of such beauty and divinely inspired serenity, partly because it brought back memories of his childhood in Calvi, of his parents, his brothers, sisters and aunts, all now gone to be with the Virgin and her son. Until that glorious day when the atheistical scum in the town finally surrendered, the men of the Royal Louis marched through the gates chanting 'Montjoie Saint Denis!' and Pierre-Paul could once again see the Host elevated at the altar of the cathedral in Calvi, the chapel on the hill was as close as he could get to God and his long-lost childhood.

He and his fellow officers walked toward the chapel in quiet solemnity, very different to the profanities and raucous laughter that characterised their weekdays. They were all aware of their responsibilities, no more so than when peasants, shepherds and washerwomen watched them as they passed, took note of their white uniforms – so different to the blood-red of their allies – and knew them for who they were. They were the soldiers of the true France, of royal France, warriors in the service of the rightful King Louis the Seventeenth. They revered the memory of the king's father and mother, both murdered on the guillotine by the craven madmen who ruled the godless abomination that was the so-called French Republic. They prayed every Sunday that their young king might be liberated from the Temple prison to ride in glory at the head of a white-clad army through the streets of Paris. They prayed that the people of France might return to the true way, the godly way, the royal way. They prayed that the Tricolore might be torn down from every flagpole and trampled underfoot, its place taken by the ancient and glorious white standard bearing the fleur-de-lys emblem that was once borne into battle by Saint Joan of Arc.

Admittedly, it was unfortunate that for the time being the agency necessary to achieve all these goals could only be that of England, France's eternal enemy, the same foe against whom Saint Joan had led her righteous crusade. The English were Protestants and therefore heretics, but they believed at least nominally in the same God, and they were a kingdom ruled by an anointed king. So if the only way to liberate Calvi, and ultimately the whole of France, was to rely on the English, then so be it. God did, after all, move in mysterious ways.

Pierre-Paul Maestracci stood upon the soil of his homeland, outside the walls of his hometown, and felt an even stronger sense of mission. Poor Corsica, presented with a devil's choice between King George and King Guillotine by the would-be messiah, General Pasquale Paoli. Corsica should have no truck with any of them. The Corsicans were a straightforward people who had been led astray by demagogues and scoundrels. Only the return of the true king would make them content again. That was Pierre-Paul Maestracci's mission. That was why he had given up the comforts of Barcelona when he heard that Toulon had declared for the king. That was why he abandoned his beautiful Jacqueline and made a dangerous journey across the sea. That was his thought, his compulsion, when the Royal Louis Regiment formed and trained at Toulon, when it was the last unit to be evacuated from the town before it fell to the republicans, and above all when it was ordered to Corsica. If it took the vile so-called free-thinker Paoli and the English to free Corsica from Robespierre and his hyenas, so be it. But then he heard the talk that another of the self-proclaimed leaders of the Corsican people, Ercule Leandri, was prevaricating and might even seek to put Corsica back under the rule of the demonic republic. What his colleagues in his regiment and the wider British Army did not know was that Pierre-Paul Maestracci knew the name of Ercule Leandri for quite another reason.

That Sunday he had another prayer to make, another candle to light. He had to beg God's forgiveness for his killing of General Ercule Leandri. Of course, it would undoubtedly be forthcoming, even if only after significant penance. It was a matter of faith in Corsica that God always forgave the righteous in a vendetta, no matter what the priests said. Pierre-Paul had redeemed the honour of his grandfather, slaughtered fifty years before by Leandri's father. When Pierre-Paul had learned that the Royal Louis Regiment was to be posted to Corsica, he took it as a sign of God's blessing upon him. He could return to his native soil and drive from it the last vestiges of the vile republican poison, and at the same time he and his blood ancestors for generations past could be avenged on the head of the Leandris. By doing so, he would also remove the most immediate threat to the liberation of his homeland in the name of King George and King Louis. Surely there could be no clearer proof of God making His purpose apparent to His unworthy servant.

At his last confession the priest, who was a Corsican and who therefore understood such matters, warned him that the killing he was then contemplating might bring Leandri vengeance against him in turn. He had been dismissive of the suggestion. Jacobo Leandri and the other men of his name were feeble creatures, products of too many centuries of in-breeding up in the mountains. Besides, none of them knew he was even on the island, none of them knew of his fortuitous connection with Father Colonna, and certainly none had seen him making his way to and from the general's temporary quarters in the village. Even if they did know what he had done and where he was, he was quartered in the heart of General Stuart's army. By day, he was on duty at the heart of the siege operations, by night, he slept in a camp guarded by countless sentries, patrols and defensive positions. No, Pierre-Paul Maestracci had no fear of the Leandris. The death of their general cut off their head, and as on the guillotine, without the head the rest of the body could not survive.

He was on the lower part of the track up to the chapel, talking quietly with two of his colleagues-in-arms, when he saw a solitary nun. Her habit marked her as an Augustinian. There was nothing unusual in this, for although monasteries, nunneries and the like throughout France had been declared state property by the atheists in Paris, the holy orders themselves survived, especially in remoter places like Corsica and especially now that the island was again almost entirely under the control of those like Paoli who may not have been notably religious themselves but were at least tolerant of the older ways.

'Captain Maestracci.'

Her addressing him by name was a surprise. It startled his companions, but he raised a hand to them as he began to approach her, indicating that they should continue on their way and that he would rejoin them shortly. It was, after all, only a nun.

'Sister? How do you know me?'

'You have been pointed out to me. May I speak to you briefly, Captain? Never fear, I won't detain you from mass.'

'It is always humbling and a profound privilege to speak with a bride of Christ, Sister.'

The nun turned and began to walk away from the path, Maestracci falling in beside her. Out of the corner of his eye he saw his friends enter the chapel.

'So, Sister, how may I assist you?'

'I come on behalf of my Mother Superior, who in turn has been in conference with the Bishop of Sagona. There is property of our Order in Calvi, Captain, and both His Excellency and the Reverend Mother are keen to ensure its preservation when the garrison surrenders and the army you serve enters the city.'

The sound of a sung *Kyrie* indicated that the mass was beginning. Keen as he was to respect Holy Church and all those who selflessly devoted their lives to it, Maestracci wished the sister would get to the point.

'I still do not see how this concerns me, Sister.'

'There is concern that the English, being heretics, will not respect what is rightfully the property of the Holy Church, no matter what the atheists in Paris say. A good man, a reliable man, an officer in the victorious army, is needed to ensure the preservation of all that belongs to the Church, especially that of the Order I serve.'

Maestracci noticed a man watching them from the side of a thick bush, a little way away. He seemed familiar—

Maestracci recognised him. It was the stranger who had been asleep on the lower floor of Ercule Leandri's lodging when he went to kill the old general. The stranger who he was certain would wake and challenge him, who might even frustrate Maestracci's pursuit of the vendetta. He had offered up a prayer of gratitude to the Virgin when the man did not stir, yet now here he was watching him and the nun at his side.

'What is this?' he demanded.

Maestracci went to draw his sword, but by doing so he missed the glint of the stiletto in the nun's hand. She plunged it into his ribcage.

'Don't recognise me, Pierre-Paul? Well, I recognised you. Know that you die at the hand of Carla Leandri, in revenge for the death of my father.'

But Pierre-Paul Maestracci was dead before she finished the sentence.

PART THREE

CHAPTER TWENTY-ONE

Albion was launched.

The gates of the double dry dock were open and the colossal new ship was afloat. Warping lines were edging her slowly out into the tideway that lapped the foreshore of Deptford Dockyard. The ensign staff and the three temporary pole masts flew the flags that proclaimed her to be part of King George's Royal Navy: the red ensign at the stern, the Union flag at the mizzen, the royal standard at the main, the Lord High Admiral's anchor flag at the fore. The volunteer band mangled what had to be its eleventh or twelfth renditions of 'Rule, Britannia' and 'God Save the King'. The spectators and dockyard workers lining the sides of the dock, and the wealthier gawpers in the fleet of boats, yawls and skiffs lying just off the dockyard, sang along and roared success to the *Albion* in increasingly drunken tones.

Lord Wilden hated it all and withdrew as soon as it was polite to do so to the stern cabin of the Admiralty yacht. Rather sooner than was polite, if he was being honest with himself. He should have gone with the other members of the Board to the no doubt sumptuous repast laid on in the Master Shipwright's house, where there would be platters of beef and pork, trenchers of ale and brimming punchbowls. It had been enough of an ordeal to be present with his colleagues on the platform specially erected for the launch, sheer purgatory to be informed by the First Lord that he, Wilden, was expected to christen the ship. But the First Lord, the Earl of Chatham, was the prime minister's brother, and it did not do to get on the wrong side of the Pitts. Wilden had thrown himself into his work even more than usual following the murder of Augustus Jenkins, but his definition of work entailed burying himself amid mountains of paper in his dimly candlelit office. Chatham had upbraided him for this, reminding him that an Admiralty Lord had a public role too – arguing the navy's case in the House of Lords, undertaking tours of inspection, attending launches and naming new ships. So he was persuaded against his better judgement to take centre stage at the launch of the new Second Rate building at Deptford. Wilden had tried (and failed, for he was no orator) to raise his voice so that more than those immediately adjacent to him might hear him name the new eighty-gunner *Albion*, and to call down the blessing of God upon her endeavours. That part, at least, Wilden felt comfortable with, for those endeavours would consist chiefly of blasting to glory any French ships she happened to encounter. Every French ship sunk, every Frenchman killed, was one small act of revenge for the death of Augustus Jenkins.

His duty done, not even Chatham could quibble when Wilden pleaded a headache and retired to the Admiralty yacht, anchored just offshore, where he had the entire great cabin at the stern to himself. There he could resume the activity from which he had been reluctantly diverted, namely working systematically through the most recent and urgent correspond-ence selected by his reliable principal clerk, Bristow, who knew his master's inclinations almost better than Wilden did himself.

The intelligence was still dominated by the stunning news from Paris, where Robespierre and his clique had been suddenly overthrown on the day the revolutionaries called 9 Thermidor II, but which good Christians and sane men every-where called 27 July. The tyrant was denounced in the National Convention he had dominated for so long, and although forces loyal to him within the city of Paris attempted to stage a counter-coup, it petered out. On the following day, Robe-spierre went to the guillotine, the fate to which he and his lapdogs had consigned so many poor innocent souls. Paris was in turmoil, which meant that France was in turmoil, and a France in turmoil was a thing of boundless joy to Edward, Lord Wilden. It was unclear what form of government would emerge from the chaos and who might dominate it. This new upheaval had been triggered by hatred of Robespierre alone, and it was very evident from the reports in front of him that those who led the coup had no coherent plan to replace the fallen tyrant, no new dictator nor even a figurehead to put in his place. Suddenly, the many exiled French royalists in London were strutting around more confidently than ever before, believing the day of their triumphant return to their motherland could not be long delayed. Several of them had been at the launch of *Albion* proclaiming that the great ship would not be needed because England and France would soon both be brother kingdoms again, the war against the bastard republic over. Wilden knew his history well enough, knew how very often England and France had warred with each other when they both had monarchs safely seated on their thrones, and was glad that the reassuring bulk of the new *Albion* sat proudly in the tideway of the Thames.

Outwardly, he concurred with the French royalists and all those Englishmen, the vast majority, who fervently wished for the war to end as quickly as possible. In his heart, though, Lord Wilden prayed that the war went on and on, forever if necessary, until the corrupting seed of Jacobinism was extirpated from the world once and for all. Only then would Augustus Jenkins, and all the others like him who had perished because of the evil France had embraced, finally be avenged.

It was difficult to tear himself away from the breathless reports from Paris, but it was one of those times when his agents had almost too much to report and he had almost too much to digest. The French had been duly subdued at sea following Lord Howe's victory a few weeks before – the songwriters and scribblers of bad poetry were calling it the Glorious First of June – so the reports out of Brest and France's other Atlantic dockyards were unenlightening. On land, though, it was a very different matter. The republican army somehow continued to sweep all before it, its latest victory at Fleurus allowing it to wholly overrun the Austrian Netherlands, the southern half of the Low Countries. This brought France to the borders of the United Provinces, one of Britain's most important allies in the war, where a strong Dutch opposition party, the so-called Patriots, agitated loudly for the French cause. If the northern Netherlands were to be overrun it would place a hostile army and navy on the shore directly facing the mouth of the Thames and London, potentially exposing the nation's beating heart to the risk of invasion. Britain undoubtedly needed its finest general in Flanders to battle the revolutionary tide. Instead, the man it had commanding in the theatre was the Duke of York, the king's utterly mediocre second son. Even Lord Wilden's loyal and steadfastly patriotic heart wept at the thought.

So to Corsica, now, remarkably, the latest of King George's kingdoms. The union of the two crowns had been proclaimed, the allegiance of the Corsican leader, Paoli, cemented, and Sir Gilbert Elliot installed as the first viceroy. There were several letters relating to the interminable siege operations against Calvi. He hoped the length of the siege, and indeed the acquisition of this whole new kingdom, would prove to be worth it, and that the assurances of the generals and admirals about the utility of Corsica as a base for operations against the south of France would prove to be justified. It was the one thing they seemed to agree upon, Lord Hood and General Stuart both being hell-bent on demonstrating that the sole reason for the inordinate length of the campaign was the other one of them. Well, time alone would tell. But there was another matter relating to Corsica, seemingly trivial, that piqued Lord Wilden's interest. He read and re-read the letter, now several weeks old, from the captain of *Agamemnon*, that odd little fellow with a grating Norfolk accent and a remarkably high opinion of himself. That the captain had been suborned by the commanders of the army in Corsica, General Stuart and Colonel Moore, was one thing; the excuse of mountain air to relieve the discomfort from a wound to the eye, sustained during siege operations ashore, was frankly feeble. But it had become a fortunate coincidence, for it enabled the captain to have an unexpected encounter with Philippe Kermorvant, Vicomte de Saint-Victor, Wilden's cousin. Quite why Philippe was in Corsica was a mystery, but there had been talk for some time of French efforts to suborn General Ercule Leandri, one of Paoli's old gang from many years before. Somehow, Philippe had been accused of the murder of Leandri, only to be saved from the noose by the intervention of the general's daughter, who was evidently an out-and-out harpy. An odd business, by the sounds of it, and surely of no concern to Wilden. But it was intriguing that Cousin Philippe now seemed to be employed by France as an agent – perhaps an aptitude for intelligence ran in the family – and that he was clearly involved in some way in the business of Corsica, or at least he had been when *Agamemnon*'s commander penned his letter. Wasn't there something else about Corsica in one of the other despatches, too? Yes, he believed there was. He searched the leather case once again and found it. A copy of a letter to Dundas, the very newly minted secretary for war, containing a brief and passing mention of the unexplained murder in the siege camp at Calvi of one Captain Maestracci, a native Corsican and an officer in the Royal Louis Regiment, one of the French royalist units serving in King George's army. Philippe is accused of a murder and then this Maestracci is murdered. Or was it the other way round? He checked the dates of the letters. No, that was the correct sequence.

Very intriguing indeed.

Lord Wilden still nursed hopes that his cousin would one day see sense, forsake the murderous and erroneous cause of the French Republic, and give his loyalty to his exiled king and that monarch's ally, Great Britain. That he had rejected freedom in favour of confinement in a prison hulk, only to escape back to France, suggested that cause was lost. In the immediate aftermath of Jenkins' death, Wilden's impotent rage had briefly found a target in his cousin Philippe, the personification in his mind of all the murderous wickedness of the French Jacobins. It took him a few days, and the long journey back to London with young Dysart now driving his coach, for his rage to subside and his thoughts to become clearer.

It would be too easy to kill Philippe Kermorvant. Although Toulon had fallen to the republicans and most of her royalists had been evacuated, there were still many secret sympathisers in the town. Wilden's agent in the French fleet could undoubtedly find a man willing to slit Philippe's throat in an alleyway after his ship next came into port. But for all his grief and anger, Lord Wilden could not bring himself to sanction the cold-blooded murder of his own kin. As Jenkins always said, especially often in the days when the child owner of Alveley Hall got into yet another scrape with the village roughs, 'Blood is all, my lord, and blood will out.'

Wilden, despite the austere and detached figure he cut in society, was at heart a hopeless optimist. The prospect of a reunion with his mother, long thought by Philippe Kermorvant to be dead, had not been enough to persuade him to come over to the side of the *soi-disant* French king and his ally, the king of Great Britain. Wilden had assumed too much, reckoning that there would be a loving bond between long-lost mother and errant son when in fact there was none. But there was one other thing that Wilden knew Cousin Philippe wanted far more, one emotion, one ambition, one *compulsion*, that impelled him more powerfully, one other carrot that he, Lord Wilden, could perhaps dangle in front of his cousin. The difficulty lay in locating the carrot.

The drunken singers had moved on to 'Heart of Oak', which at least offered a little variety to the usual diet. Lord Wilden chided himself for allowing himself to be distracted once again by thoughts of Philippe Kermorvant. He should not waste any official time on a purely personal matter. He should certainly not waste the time of others. Philippe was one man, the captain of a middling man-of-war, not one of those who normally occupied Wilden's concerns – monarchs, influential statesmen, successful generals and the like. Bringing him over to the royalist side, to Britain's side, would make not one jot of difference to the outcome of the war. And yet...

And yet. During his most recent sojourn in Alveley Hall, he had made a rare appearance in the parish church, his principal purpose being to pray for the soul of Augustus Jenkins and give thanks for the dear man's life. The minister, a dull Cambridge man whom he regretted putting into the living some years earlier, delivered an unmemorable sermon, but it centred on a text that had always struck a chord with Wilden; more so for some reason since he had first met his cousin Philippe some months before.

Luke Chapter 15, Verse 7: *joy shall be in heaven over one sinner that repenteth, more than over ninety and nine just persons, which need no repentance.*

The passage dominated Wilden's thoughts throughout the rest of the service and during his walk back to his house. He barely heard and did not acknowledge the respectful bows and greetings of his tenants and staff. For some unaccountable reason, the words of Luke put him in mind of a name he had seen in a book in his library. When he got home, he went directly to the bookcase and took down his well-thumbed *Almanach de Gotha*, flicking through the pages until he found the particular listing of diplomatic personnel he sought.

Yes, he was right, but then his memory never failed him. There was the name he remembered, the name he sought.

He stood, went to the stern windows of the yacht and looked out at the towering hull of HMS *Albion*. He did not regard himself as a particularly religious man, certainly not an evangelist. But in this one particular case, he would continue to make every effort to bring this one sinner, his cousin Philippe, to repentance. Perhaps that was the way in which he could give purpose to the death of Augustus Jenkins.

Edward, Lord Wilden, sat down again at the captain's table in the great cabin of the yacht and began to pen a note paying his respects to Count Vorontsov, the amiable Russian ambassador to the Court of Saint James, and enquiring whether His Excellency might be at home to a social call on the following day.

Lord Wilden allowed himself a rare smile. Such, he reflected, was the nature of diplomacy.

CHAPTER TWENTY-TWO

Honoured father,

I thank you for your last, delivered by the agency of the ship Chevalier Roland bound from Marseilles for Ragusa. I note your suggestion that it is still not impossible for me to request a move to the army, that you have friends in Paris who could expedite this, and that I could then follow in the footsteps of all the countless generations of de la Portes before me. You tell me that if I consent to this course, I may still have the honour of fighting alongside you in battle. We have talked of this matter many times, Father, and you know my reasons for following my own path. But I must confess to you that these last weeks have tested my resolve. It is very true that being at sea is better than dishonourably swinging at anchor, but all we have done since sailing from Toulon is to hail one mean trading vessel after another, seizing those found to belong to enemy nations or carrying cargoes for enemy ports. Our captain lectures us that these captures are important for the triumph of the fatherland. He says that each hull taken means less money in the coffers of France's enemies. The men cheer and toast their good fortune. But I cannot say it is active or distinguished work. These are not fights that test a man's mettle or his courage. Usually they are not fights at all, just a token pursuit until the enemy sees he cannot get away and then he hauls down his colours. I have commanded a couple of boat crews sent across to take possession of some of these vessels, but their crews have been dirty, craven men who seek nothing more than to surrender as quickly as possible. I have hoped that the captain would give me command of one of these prizes and orders to take her back to France, but he has preferred to entrust such commands to mere mates and suchlike unworthy fellows.

There is still much talk about where the captain was for all those weeks he was away from the ship. Vidos tried to get the valet to the captain and lieutenants, one Courtois, drunk in the hope he would reveal confidences. But the miserable creature said nothing, and I suspect he knows nothing. Captain Kermorvant is a close man, and some say he has many secrets in his past. One of the Bretons, who was at Brest last year when our captain was given his first command, says there was some talk of a wife in Russia, and that she was viciously murdered. Some in his mess took this as meaning that the captain killed her and then fled Russia to evade justice, offering his services to the Republic as a means of escape. It is all a mystery, and if you will excuse my frankness, Father, I much preferred it when Lieutenant Malhuret, an honest straightforward Frenchman, commanded us.

I do not know if you have had occasion to write to Paris about our captain, as I requested in my last. I am sure that if good cause is found to remove him from command, Lieutenant Malhuret will prove worthy of promotion.

I am well. Vive la République!
Your dutiful son,
T de la Porte

The chase tacked again, desperately trying to outrun the pursuing *Torrington*.

Philippe saw the expectation on the faces of Malhuret, Grignon, Doucet, the mates, and Rampillon of the *aspirants*. He looked up once more at the tension of the sails, then again at the enemy merchantman a couple of miles ahead. The weather braces and sheets, the lee tacks and bow-lines – everything was ready. Then, when Philippe judged the right moment had come, he gave the time-honoured command.

'*Voyez à-lee!*' Helm's a-lee.

He nodded to Malhuret, who continued the stream of orders.

'Let go foresheet, foretop bowline, jib and staysail sheets!'

The commands were repeated, but there was barely any need. The men were expecting the manoeuvre – were, indeed, transparently eager for the order to be given – and they were now practised enough to anticipate the commands that were about to come and to execute them swiftly and seamlessly. The bow of *Le Torrington* came round onto the new tack, the ship made stays, and the pursuit continued on the new course. She might be *La Tortue Anglaise*, but she could surely still outsail a heavily laden Levanter in a brisk westerly. Word of the chase's identity had got round among the crew, and men were eager with anticipation of a rich prize. Such an argosy as this, fully laden and westbound for distant England, was likely to be full to the gunwales with lucrative cargoes from the Levant and even further east, a rich haul for any crew that took her. *Le Torrington* had been lucky on this cruise, and this new prize would be the eighth she had taken since sailing from Toulon. Most of the others had been small Sicilian and Sardinian traders, hardly worth the trouble of chasing and delegating prize crews, but a big English Levanter was a very different matter.

Philippe had finally rejoined his command a few days after leaving Corsica. The bulk of the fleet under Martin and Fidelin was still in the Bay of Gourjean, but Martin – or rather

Fidelin, whose idea it was – had sought to test the rigour and attentiveness of the blockading English by sending a couple of frigates by night through the inshore passage between Île Sainte-Marguerite and the Bay of Cannes. *Le Torrington* and Parmentier's *Forbin* were chosen for the mission, the attempt having to await a storm that the admirals hoped would drive the enemy ships off their station. Despite an alarm when *Forbin* came under fire from the westernmost of the British ships, still stubbornly holding her position despite the raging elements, the two frigates made it safely back to Toulon. Malhuret, in acting command of *Le Torrington*, had apparently acquitted himself well. Philippe returned to the port a few days after his ship. He expected a summons to the general who had sent him on the failed mission to Corsica, but none came. The coalition of enemy powers had taken advantage of the turmoil in Paris that saw the overthrow and execution of Robespierre by launching a new offensive on the Italian front, so it was no surprise that all of France's generals in the theatre were entirely focused on that. Rather than reporting to him, Philippe wrote to Admiral Martin to report his return and received a reply within three days, confirming his formal reinstatement to command and enclosing orders for *Le Torrington*, in company with two other frigates, including *Forbin*, to cruise in the Sicilian and Tyrrhenian Seas to intercept enemy merchant shipping. Thus far, the voyage had been an unqualified success. Many merchants and skippers had evidently assumed that France could send out no ships at all in the Mediterranean, her fleet being either still trapped in Gourjean or at the bottom of Toulon harbour, so they sailed as complacently as if it were the height of peacetime. *Le Torrington* had done well, but Frank Parmentier in the newer, faster *Forbin* had done even better, taking seventeen enemy hulls at the last count.

The cruise enabled Philippe to restore the discipline and fighting efficiency of his crew. It was certainly not Malhuret's fault that these had slipped during their long sojourn in the Bay of Gourjean, for as Philippe knew well, sailors in harbour swiftly became bored, lazy, and too susceptible to the attractions of the shore. Courtois, as well as expressing obvious delight and relief at his captain's return, told Philippe that Admiral Martin had to greatly curtail shore leave after the arrival in the villages around the bay of the denizens of several whorehouses from Toulon and Nice led to an epidemic of syphilis, or as Courtois, like most Frenchmen, called it, 'the Neapolitan disease'. (It was curious, Philippe thought, that the British and Italians named the same condition 'the French disease'.) So as soon as *Le Torrington* was clear of Toulon, Philippe ordered frequent exercises of the main armament and some unnecessarily complex evolutions. He moved constantly about the decks, sometimes upbraiding and reprimanding, more often encouraging and praising. Slowly the men's efficiency returned, bolstered by the success in taking prizes that raised their spirits and made them remember their profession, their duty, and their pride in both. Several of those who had sailed from Toulon as *matelots d'eau douce*, complete lubbers, were now highly competent hands, well up the invisible ladder that led to promotion through the three classes of *matelot*, then to mate or helmsman, then, if fortune favoured them, eventually to warrant offices or even higher. The crew's renaissance was crowned by their good fortune in taking prizes. Now, pursuing what promised to be the most lucrative of them all, men grinned and laughed as they competed to obey orders faster and better than their fellows. The age-old seamen's songs and the newer hymns to the Republic were sung with renewed lustiness as *Le Torrington* closed the Levant prize, the Basque veteran Zabala leading the choruses in his strong tenor voice.

'A warning shot, sir?' asked Malhuret.

'No need, Lieutenant,' said Philippe. 'He can see as plain as day that we heavily outgun him. Bring her up on his starboard beam, our larboard battery fully run out, and mass the men on deck, armed as if for boarding, Marines forming the front rank. I'd say a man entrusted with the command of a ship like that will prefer to live a prisoner than die a hero, so I hope a voice trumpet will be the only weapon we need.'

Le Torrington drew alongside the Levant ship. Philippe and every man on the upper deck of the frigate could see the grim expressions of the Englishmen, who would be contemplating either the certain suicide of attempting to fire first on the much more heavily armed Frenchman or the almost equally unappealing alternative of long, grim years in a prison camp somewhere in France. Philippe, who had no wish to repeat his experience of the *Agincourt* hulk, sympathised with their plight, but as he and they knew, there were far worse plights in war.

'English captain!' he called in the man's own language, his words carrying easily across the water. 'I am Philippe Kermorvant, captain of the frigate *Le Torrington*. In the name of the French Republic, one and indivisible, I call upon you to haul down your colours and heave to!'

There was a pause of what might have been an entire minute, then a large crop-haired man raised a voice trumpet and shouted his reply.

'*Torrington*? That's the old *Torrington*? Damn my eyes, I served on her at Manila back in sixty-two. Taken by one of my old ships, and one with a Devon name to boot. Where's the justice in that?'

Philippe had a good ear for accents, and the times he had gone into Carrick Roads and Falmouth in Gask ships made it easy for him to identify the man's voice as Cornish. He thought the garrulous skipper might try to argue the case until he would have to be silenced by a French broadside, but after a few moments more of staring at the ship he had once called home, the Englishman turned, gave an order, and the colours came down.

The prize was named the *Earl of Carbery*, and she was bound from Smyrna to London with a cargo every bit as lucrative as Philippe had hoped for, silks from far beyond Aleppo, peppers, indigo and raisins in abundance. But she was in a bad way, holed beneath the waterline by a stray shot from *Le Torrington* that had exacerbated a leak which, according to her captain, a blunt Cornishman called Trevanion, had been getting worse ever since she left Smyrna, to the point where the pumps were barely able to cope. He had hoped to be able to reach the British-held anchorage at Gibraltar, confident that all of France's warships were still bottled up in the Bay of Gourjean, and the encounter with *Le Torrington* came as an unwelcome surprise. Trevanion protested that his ship needed proper repair and attention from experienced shipwrights, and the carpenter of *Le Torrington* confirmed the assessment. Reluctantly, Philippe studied his charts. The coast of Provence and thus mainland France was too far, the Balearic Islands and Sicily enemy territory, the entire shore of North Africa the domain of the ferocious and avaricious Barbary corsairs. Greece was also too distant and its overlord, the Ottoman sultan, hostile to republican France in any case. That left one territory, one harbour alone, that was at least nominally neutral and might provide a sanctuary where the damage to the Levanter could be repaired, or at least repaired sufficiently to enable her to reach Toulon.

With Malhuret and Doucet alongside him at the table in his cabin, Philippe plotted a course for Malta.

–

His parting from Carla Leandri had been bittersweet.

Philippe left Corsica three days after her killing of Pierre-Paul Maestracci. The surrender of Calvi was imminent, with General Casabianca known to have requested terms from General Stuart, so for the time being the fate of Corsica was settled. With the British in full control of the island, the powerful protection of General Ercule Leandri removed and regardless of any safe conduct from Pasquale Paoli, Philippe's position was becoming more precarious by the hour.

Luc Giordano's schooner came into a cove a little way south of where he had first landed them, at once a few short weeks and an eternity before. Carla came down to the beach to say farewell to him. There was a strong escort in attendance so it was a stiff, formal business, giving no suggestion of any feelings between them. Their true parting had come earlier that morning, when she left his bed in the ancient watch tower of Ghineparu.

'What will you do?' he asked as she dressed.

'Will I marry Jacobo or one of the others, do you mean? No. A hundred thousand times no. Aunt Claudia takes my side – God, how she hated all those years of being shackled to my uncle – and no Leandri will dare cross her lest they bring forth the death-curse of the *mazzera*. Perhaps if it becomes common knowledge that I, too, possess that art, then men will not want my hand in marriage in any case.'

'Then what?'

'With no man, you mean? No husband?' She smiled. 'You met the Empress Catherine, Philippe. She has had no husband for over thirty years.'

But countless lovers, thought Philippe. Would that be Carla Leandri's fate? To be feted and fawned upon by many smitten men like him? To take men for her pleasure for a few nights, perhaps a few years, and then discard them as easily as the pips in a grape?

'What will the Leandris do about their allegiance? France or England? What will *you* do, Carla?'

She paused before replying.

'Only my father could have held a different line to Paoli. Only he could have convinced enough Corsicans to go with him. Besides, things were different while the matter was in the balance – while Calvi held out. But now we have no real choice in the matter. Raising the *Tricolore* in the name of Leandri and France would be suicide. So I will go to Corte, see Paoli, and if the need dictates it, I will swear an oath to King George. It will be worthless in any case. The English will not be in Corsica for long – they have more important battles to fight. When I was in Paris, there was talk that Robespierre and his gang were planning an invasion of England. Do you think there'll be one Englishman left on Corsican soil if their own island is under threat?'

Philippe acknowledged the point as he got out of bed and reached for his shirt. They both dressed in silence for a minute or so, then Carla looked at him mischievously.

'And you, Philippe? What will you do now? I don't mean going back to your ship. Will you go back to Leonore?'

'*Leonore*? How can you know? I've never mentioned her name!'

Carla grinned.

'You talk in your sleep. In that state, you say her name almost as often as your Natasha's.'

Philippe made to reply, but he knew his cheeks were burning.

'I would have to be in Brittany, and there's no prospect of that unless I get a command at Brest.'

'A pity. Then it seems we are both fated to be alone, Captain Kermorvant.'

He went to her and took her in his arms.

'Fate is a fickle master,' he said. 'I think I know that better than most.'

She kissed him.

'Then perhaps fate will bring us together again one day, Philippe.'

He held her face in his hands.

'Be safe, Carla Leandri. I shall hold you in my prayers.'

'The son of Verité prays,' she said mockingly. 'The revolution is surely doomed.'

They kissed longer and harder, their arms holding each other tight, their embrace desperate in its finality. Three hours later he had his last sight of her from the deck of *Lucrezia*, standing rigid on Corsica's shore like a statue of the Virgin. Neither waved, and Philippe did not hear the *voceru* she sang under her breath, her hymn of farewell to one who had died in her heart.

CHAPTER TWENTY-THREE

As the dawn's haze began to dissipate, Philippe got his first proper sight of Malta. Illuminated by the bright morning sun, its golden ramparts and turrets gave it the appearance of a celestial city. The prospect before him should have been crowned with a halo and attended by angelic choruses singing Alleluias. The moment of fancy was no more than that, though. As *Le Torrington* and her prize edged slowly toward the harbour mouth in light breezes, Philippe could see that what lay before him was very far from being an unearthly vision. The fortifications seemed endless, encircling a harbour seemingly as large as any Philippe had ever seen and thronged with dozens, perhaps hundreds, of masts. Two mighty forts lay on either side of the harbour mouth. This was the fabled island fortress that had resisted the entire might of the invincible Ottoman Empire and saved Christian Europe by withstanding one of the most epic sieges in history. This was the impregnable bastion of the Knights of Malta, the legendary military Order that had defended Christendom for centuries.

But as *Le Torrington* drew level with the first of the forts, off to starboard, Philippe saw that while Malta might once have deserved its almost mythical reputation, the reality before him was very different. Whole sections of rampart, even entire bastions, were crumbling away. Many of the cannon lining the fortifications looked to be ancient, and some were stained green. More than one of the red-and-white flags of the knights flying over the ramparts were faded, torn, or simply reduced to nothing more than tattered rags by too long an exposure to sun and wind. Malta was an illusion. It was like the ancient suit of armour in the hall of the Chateau de Brechelean, Philippe's family home in Brittany. From a distance it looked formidable, even frightening. But standing close to it revealed the many years' accumulation of dust. The joints no longer worked, the metal was stained with rust donated by the infinitely generous Breton damp. The armour was ancient, and it was empty.

Even so, the proper courtesies had to be observed. Philippe gave the orders for a salute to the flag of the knights. Two of the twelve-pounders in the fo'c's'le rendered the appropriate honours as *Le Torrington* entered the Grand Harbour.

'No other men-of-war, sir,' said Malhuret, 'other than the Order's own.'

'Fortunate,' said Philippe. 'Let's trust it remains so for as long as the repairs take.'

'Let's hope they permit us to make the repairs at all, Citizen Captain,' said Bertin. 'Even if they do, they'll charge a king's ransom. I docked here six, seven years ago. They almost bankrupted my ship's owners.'

Malta was neutral, and in name it was. But it was obvious that an Order which bore the name of Saint John and had been for centuries the elite military arm of the Catholic Church was hardly going to be sympathetic to the revolutionary principles of the French Republic.

A boat came out to *Le Torrington*, disgorging a fat, surly pilot who demanded his fee in advance before conning the ship to an anchorage far up the harbour, beyond the creek where a single decaying warship of the knights was laid up. The Levanter limped her way to anchor astern of *Le Torrington*. There were several British merchantmen at anchor in the harbour, and their crews watched nervously as the warship flying the feared *Tricolore* made her way past them.

An entire navy of the curiously shaped harbour boats, with their high bows and sterns, appeared around the two ships. Tanned, grinning boatmen shouted up in broken French, offering the officers and men of *Le Torrington* and her prize tobacco, drink and women, all at the most reasonable prices in the whole of the Mediterranean. One boat, however, had a different purpose, and the boatman brought her in deftly under the port quarter of the frigate. As Philippe watched from the quarterdeck, the boat's small, wiry, bespectacled passenger stood up tentatively, as though he expected to lose his balance and fall into the Grand Harbour.

'*Le Torrington*!' the fellow shouted in an amusingly high voice. 'I am Citizen Paul-Baptiste Allard, consul of the Republic here in Malta. Your permission to come aboard, Citizen Captain?'

Philippe saw Malhuret's smirk and suppressed one of his own.

'Granted, Citizen Allard,' cried Philippe.

A few minutes later, in Philippe's cabin, Paul-Baptiste Allard was holding forth about how difficult *Le Torrington*'s arrival with an English prize would make things for him.

'I shall do my best to procure the services of a shipyard willing to make the repairs, Captain, but I can make no guarantees. They are not sympathetic to us. Besides, their charges would be extortionate even if we were not French – this is the only commodious neutral harbour for many hundreds of miles, so they exploit their monopoly. And the truth is the English and even the Russians have more influence here than we do. Grand Master de Rohan is a Frenchman, of course, but you won't be surprised to hear, my dear captain, that he favours the royalist party. So, yes, it will be very difficult. Very difficult indeed.'

'Then, Consul, can you at least secure us a quiet corner of the harbour, or some other berth elsewhere in Malta, where my carpenter and his crew can make the repairs themselves? It will take longer, but if necessity demands it—'

'Alas, Citizen Captain, that, too, will be very difficult. Let me tell you why...'

After another two hours of Citizen Paul-Baptiste Allard, Philippe felt as though the lifeblood had been drained out of him and his brain had begun to decompose. As the consul finally disembarked, though, he said one thing that raised Philippe's spirits a little. There would be no problem if the Citizen Captain or any of his officers wished to go ashore. It was probably inadvisable to give leave to the men, for the taverns of Valletta and the smaller towns that fringed the harbour tended to be full of Englishmen and the niceties of the laws of neutrality tended to be forgotten when men from the two warring protagonists encountered each other, especially when they were in the presence of strong drink. Previous visits by French warships had led to fatalities, even to pitched battles in the streets, so it was best not to take any risks, if the citizen captain took his meaning.

The citizen captain did.

–

The next morning, Philippe decided to take advantage of the proffered leave and went ashore with the three *aspirants*. They toured the fortified city as if they were Grand Tourists gawping at the remains of ancient Rome or Athens, but Rampillon and Vidos were quickly bored and made unsubtle comments about how cool and pleasant some of the taverns looked. De la Porte, though, fancied himself as something of a student of history and chattered away animatedly about the Great Siege of 1566 and the history of the Knights of Malta. They viewed the Sacra Infermeria, the vast hospital erected by the Order two centuries earlier, the lavish *palazzos* of the senior officers, the palace of the grand master himself. Compared to other cities Philippe had known, Paris and London and Saint Petersburg, Valletta was tiny. In some respects, it reminded him of Calvi, a promontory cut off and defended by powerful fortifications, the buildings of the town packed in tightly behind the ramparts. Valletta was also quiet. There were the carts and stalls on the streets, but the cries of the hawkers and traders seemed somehow half-hearted.

So they came at last to the Cathedral of Saint John. The exterior was modest but the interior was a riot of baroque extravagance, the sort of gaudy superstitious display that had outraged Verité and the leaders of the Republic, leading to the destruction of such wanton idolatry through the length and breadth of France. The most striking feature of the cathedral, though, was the colourful memorial floor tablets to long-dead knights, all of them crowned by the now familiar cross of the Order.

'So many French names, sir,' said de la Porte.

'My understanding is that to this day, the majority of knights are French.'

'Then they won't favour the Republic, will they, Citizen Captain.'

'As you say, *aspirant*. I think Malta will be poor soil for the seeds of liberty, equality and fraternity.'

Rampillon and Vidos, still seemingly wishing they were in one of the nearby taverns, moved away to study other corners of the cathedral, but de la Porte continued to read the tombstones.

'Look here, sir!' he cried, a little too loudly for the liking of a pair of nuns reciting their rosaries. 'Isn't this a coincidence?'

Philippe looked down at the memorial slab de la Porte was indicating, registered the surname of the dead knight, and agreed with his young companion that it was indeed a remarkable coincidence, the name being not particularly common and the grave, dating from 1786, being relatively recent among all the tablets commemorating men who had been dead for one or two centuries. It probably meant nothing, but as the little party from *Le Torrington* emerged from the cool darkness of the cathedral into bright sunlight, the sight of the familiar name emblazoned on cold marble troubled Philippe for a reason he could not quite grasp.

The three *aspirants* were young and naïve, and none of them seemed to share the growing sense of unease that Philippe felt as they walked further through the streets of Valletta. The native Maltese fell silent as they passed, but the expressions on their faces were unmistakeably hostile. A group of nuns, turning a corner and seeing the Frenchmen before them, hastily turned and went the other way. A young curate in the cathedral stared at them, his expression growing more hostile with every moment that passed. Finally, he made to move toward de la Porte, who was gazing intently at a particularly interesting tomb, but a senior priest grabbed hold of the curate's arm and pulled him into a side chapel. Philippe immediately ordered the *aspirants* out of the cathedral, much to de la Porte's annoyance. They would make one final excursion toward the harbour mouth, Philippe decided, and then return to the ship. Consul Allard had been right. The French, or at least the republican French, were not well regarded in Malta.

They made their way past the other side of the palace of the grand master toward Saint Elmo, the fort at the harbour's mouth that *Le Torrington* had saluted the previous day. The streets finally opened onto a broad terrace overlooking the lower batteries, which were as decayed as Philippe had assessed them to be from his quarterdeck. From their position they had an uninterrupted view over the Grand Harbour and out to the sea beyond. A British merchantman was making its way out of harbour, perhaps wanting to be elsewhere as quickly as possible before the French warship was able to put to sea and pursue them. Out at sea to the east Philippe could make out the distant sails of five ships, all inbound.

'The one there, sir,' said Vidos, who seemed to have particularly keen eyesight. 'The one on the horizon, east-north-east two points.'

Philippe screwed up his eyes to study the far distant sail. Vidos was right. The nearer ships were innocuous merchantmen, inbound to trade or to take in water and victuals. But the furthest ship was a different matter. Philippe wished he had his telescope with him, but after a few minutes the naked eye was sufficient to tell him that the pattern of sails was not that of some innocent trader. The approaching vessel was a man-of-war, and a big one.

'Should we return to the ship, sir?' said Rampillon. 'Should we at least send a message to her – to Lieutenant Malhuret?'

'To what effect, Aspirant? The ship could never get ready for sea before that vessel, whatever it might be, enters the harbour. Besides, Malta is neutral, remember? Even if it's HMS *Victory* herself, there can be no hostilities in the waters of the Knights of Malta. And how do we know it's not one of ours, eh, citizens?'

The three *aspirants* and their captain watched for some time as the approaching ship slowly grew larger.

'Sixty guns, give or take, sir,' said Vidos. 'Maybe fifty-eight, maybe sixty-two.'

'Can you make out the flag yet?'

'Not quite, sir. If the wind can just blow it out a little further – it's tangled in the mizzen shrouds – no, there it is. White ground bearing a coat of arms surmounted by a crown. You know it, Citizen Captain?'

'Only from the signal books,' said Philippe. 'The colours of the Kingdom of Naples. An enemy of France. We are at war with Naples.'

'Then, sir...'

'Yes. Now we return to the ship.'

CHAPTER TWENTY-FOUR

The street leading back down to the wharves was particularly narrow, with high-fronted houses on either side, but no residents were to be seen. Windows were shuttered despite it being a relatively cool day. A feral cat wandered from door to door, as proud as the grand master, looking for an opening that would lead it to food. But at the far end of the street stood two men in long black cloaks bearing white stars, the unmistakeable uniform of the Knights of Malta.

'Well, what have we here?' said the taller of them. The two knights were relatively young, perhaps around Philippe's own age, and they were advancing slowly up the street.

'I smell the stench of atheism,' said the other. Both of the knights were French. 'The rotten stink of republicanism, too.'

'My brother died on the guillotine,' said the taller knight.

'Yet these men walk the sacred soil of Malta with impunity.'

'Why does the grand master permit it, Brother?'

'All reverence to the grand master, but justice must be taken when it presents itself.'

'That it must. Justice for all those slaughtered by the guillotine. Justice for my brother. Justice and vengeance, both. Damnation to the Republic!'

The two men drew back their cloaks, revealing the hilts of their swords.

'Honoured knights,' said Philippe, spreading his hands in the ancient gesture of peace. '*Messieurs.* We mean no offence. We are merely visiting your splendid city – your *neutral* city.'

'Now that's the thing,' said the shorter knight. 'Can there be neutral in the war between right and wrong? Between Christianity and atheism? Between good and evil?'

The two men continued to advance. The *aspirants*, thoroughly alarmed, looked to Philippe for guidance or an order. De la Porte had gone very pale and appeared to be shivering.

'You will have to answer to the grand master for what you do,' de la Porte shouted.

'One of the children speaks,' said the shorter knight, smirking. 'Run away, little boy. Run while you still can.'

'You think the grand master will spill tears over acolytes of the cause that cut off the heads of the king and queen of France, God rest their souls in glorious immortality?' demanded the taller.

'It's broad daylight,' said Philippe. 'There are witnesses. Kill us, and whatever your grand master may say or do, you can be certain of the wrath of the French Republic—'

Both of the advancing knights laughed.

'The French Republic couldn't save Corsica!' cried the taller knight. 'So what can it do to Malta, Captain? What can it do to *us*?'

The two knights drew their swords. Somewhere further up the street, a woman screamed.

Philippe drew his own sword, and two of the three *aspirants* followed suit. The exception was de la Porte, the offspring of a great French military dynasty. His face was white, his eyes wide and distant. He swayed, and despite Vidos grabbing hold of his arm he fell heavily to the cobbles. De la Porte brought up his knees as if trying to make himself into a ball, pressing his head into his raised arms. He began to sob violently.

'Is that what your precious Republic sends out to fight for it nowadays, Captain?' said the shorter knight. 'Poor little maidens who faint at the first sight of a blade?'

Vidos stopped tending to his friend, got up, drew his sword and, screaming with rage, he ran headlong for the two knights.

The speed and ferocity of the boy's onslaught startled them, but Vidos's attack was crude and desperate. The taller knight sidestepped and the *aspirant*'s diagonal slash with his cutlass sliced through nothing but air. Vidos ran several paces beyond the knights before he was able to halt his momentum and turn. Philippe and Rampillon, their own swords drawn, took up defensive postures. The shorter knight lunged at Philippe, but he parried and their blades slewed together as they clashed. The taller engaged both Rampillon and Vidos, easily fighting off their attacks. He was toying with them, Philippe realised. With his reach and experience, the tall knight could easily despatch the *aspirants* whenever he chose. Instead, *he was toying with them*.

Philippe's own opponent was a different matter. Fleet-footed and skilful, the knight of Malta cleverly moved a little further uphill with each attack, separating Philippe from the *aspirants* and slowly gaining the advantage of the slope. Their blades clashed time and again, but neither had clear superiority. There was a yelp of pain, and Philippe saw Vidos recoil as a vicious slash on his left arm began to bleed heavily. A few paces downhill, de la Porte was slowly coming to his sense and trying to stand, but he still looked terrified beyond all measure and was making no attempt to draw his sword and join the affray. There was no sign of anybody raising an alarm coming to the Frenchmen's aid. The doors and windows on both sides of the street remained firmly closed.

'Stop this!'

The command, loud, categorical and delivered in accented French, came from the top of the street. The combatants disengaged, and Philippe turned to see an unexpected sight. The man coming down the hill toward him was portly and elegant, bewigged and with delicate hands and features. His expression was angry, his cheeks flushed with rage. He wore no cloak but was attired instead in an ordinary uniform coat, not unlike Philippe's own save for its colour, a brilliant red. On his breast, though, he wore a miniature version of the white cross that adorned the two knights' cloaks.

'You two,' sighed the man. 'Of course it would be you two. Who else?'

'We are doing our duty to Holy Church, Turcopilier!' protested the taller knight.

'Your *duty*? Slaughtering guests of Malta, of the Order, in the open street is doing some sort of duty, is it? And it isn't the first time, not by any means. Hotheads, the two of you, and unworthy of serving the Cross of Malta. But for this affront, you will answer before the grand master himself!'

'But, Turcopilier—'

'Or would you prefer me to summon the common police and have you treated the same as any thieving peasant or pick-pocket? Yes, I think a spell in the dungeons of Saint Elmo might allow you to consider where your duty really lies. Your swords.'

Shamefaced, the two knights reversed their swords and presented them hilts first to the man called the turcopilier, whatever office or rank that might be.

'Go to the cathedral,' he commanded. 'Prostrate yourselves. Pray for forgiveness. Light candles. Make your confessions. I will expect to find you there, on your knees, within the hour.'

The two knights looked at each other, at their superior and at Philippe. In the France of revolutionary liberty, a man of any rank might well baulk at being ordered in such a way. Even on *Le Zephyr*, his first command in the Marine Nationale, Philippe had known many instances of men challenging or simply disobeying orders they did not like. Here, though, the two errant Knights of Malta slunk away uphill.

The turcopilier watched them go, then turned to Philippe.

'On behalf of the grand master and the Sovereign Council of the Order, I must apologise for their conduct, Captain. They are young, hot-heated and bitter, like so many of the new French knights who have come here since your revolution. But forgive me, I am remiss. I am Johann, Baron von Flachslanden, Turcopilier of the Order.'

Philippe bowed his head.

'Philippe Kermorvant, captain of *Le Torrington* in the service of the French Republic, one and indivisible. These are the ship's *aspirants*, officers under training.'

De la Porte, now steady on his feet again but still deathly pale, had rejoined his companions, brushing off all their attempts to express their concern for him.

'Then, Captain, I will accompany you down to the harbour. My presence should serve to prevent any further incidents and affronts to the worthy seamen of France.'

Once the anger left him, Baron von Flachslanden proved to be an amiable, talkative fellow, although Philippe was none the wiser as to what duties a turcopilier might fulfil. The rank had to be a high one, for all the native Maltese they passed bowed their heads and showed the sort of deference that Philippe had witnessed when Russian peasants witnessed the passing of a grand duke. Von Flachslanden was plainly as much of a royalist as the two knights who had attacked Philippe and the *aspirants*, but he was more of a pragmatist. He talked pleasantly of the nature of the Order, its history and constitution. He discoursed with regret on the passing of the Order's naval strength. As a boy in America, Philippe had read of the halcyon days when the galleys of Malta roved across the Mediterranean, feared by some but respected by all. Those days were long gone, as the turcopilier freely admitted, and the remaining navy of the Order was largely laid up and unworthy of the name.

While von Flachslanden spoke, Philippe glanced occasionally at de la Porte. The *aspirant* had something of his old colour back, but he refused to engage in any way with Vidos and Rampillon, let alone with his captain and the turcopilier of Malta. Instead he walked briskly, looking only ahead, his features expressionless. It was impossible to tell what was going through his mind. Shame? Embarrassment? Dread? Philippe vowed to go out of his way to reassure and encourage the young man in the coming days.

Yet there was a concern more pressing even than the abject failure of Aspirant Thibaud de la Porte. All the while,

Philippe's eyes turned to the topmasts of the incoming Neapolitan warship, occasionally glimpsed over rooftops and at the bottom of alleyways. The turcopilier noticed this concern.

'The *San Giacomo*,' he said. 'She's been in and out of here for months now. I gather that her captain, Guidici, has taken a liking to a certain widow in Birgu, or so I'm told. I expect he'll claim he's come in to replenish his water barrels, again. Remarkable how much water his crew seems to get through. Almost as much as the wine.'

'It doesn't trouble you that France is at war with Naples, yet you'll have ships of the two countries in your harbour?'

Von Flachslanden smiled.

'Captain, if two ships from warring countries were tempted to fire on each other in the Grand Harbour, it would of course be the most heinous breach of Malta's neutrality and would undoubtedly provoke the most serious diplomatic consequences. Not that it would be of any concern to you or Captain Guidici, of course, as you would both most certainly be dead.'

The turcopilier waved his hand vaguely, but Philippe knew he was indicating the batteries. They stretched along virtually the entire frontage of Valletta and the opposite site of the harbour, in the towns that he now knew were called Birgu and Senglea. The fortifications that had once repelled the entire might of the Ottoman Empire were indeed ancient and in disrepair, as he had observed from seaward, but the guns lining them would still be more than sufficient to blow out of the water any ships of the combatant nations that decided to bring the war to Maltese waters.

At the quayside *Le Torrington*'s longboat awaited, her crew watching intently as the hull of the Neapolitan warship edged slowly past them and anchored at the old watering place on the north side of the Grand Harbour. As he embarked, and during the journey across the harbour to the ship, he did what every captain of a man-of-war did when faced at close quarters with a potential army. He assessed her trim, the state of her rigging, the smartness of her paintwork, the look of her men. It was impossible to tell which, if any, of them was the captain, assuming he was on deck at all. *San Giacomo* was an old but well-found ship. She was a two-decker of sixty-four guns, twenty-four pounders on the gundecks and what looked to be twelves on the quarterdeck and fo'c'sle. He knew the French tended to mock the Italians as sailors – Frank Parmentier was brutally scatological on the subject – but the vessel before him defied expectations. What she would be like on the open seas, and how tough an opponent in battle, remained to be seen. Philippe Kermorvant knew it was likely that not too many days would pass before he found the answer.

CHAPTER TWENTY-FIVE

Sir,

We lie in the famous harbour of Malta while our best and largest prize is repaired. This is a fascinating place, though it is much declined from its former glory. You will know that it held off the invincible legions of the sultan, just as you now defend France against today's forces of darkness. You and the other heroes alongside you uphold and outdo the glories of the past. I think of all the warrior de la Portes who have come before us, how they have all been worthy of the name as you are now. I am yet to be favoured with that opportunity, and I do not see that I will on this ship and with this captain.

I have undertaken a tour of the principal town of Malta with the captain and Rampillon and Vidos, of whom I have written before. I observed the ramparts, churches and palaces of the ancient Order of knights, now also much decayed. This could be made a strong and useful place by our vigorous republic. It could be made a powerful place again. There are still knights here and it is said many of them are French and favourers of the Capets. We did not encounter any of them. This was as well for I am sure I would not have been able to restrain myself from challenging them in the name of the Republic. We met one of the senior officers of the Order. He is a German who bears the strange name of a turcopilier. He was kind and respectful to us.

*An enemy ship has come into the harbour and now
lies at anchor opposite us. She flies the flag of the
Kingdom of Naples. This kingdom is of course a much
less formidable foe than those against whom you battle
with your brave companions in the Army of the North.
But their ship seems well founded and carries many more
guns than we do. I have no doubt that we will fight
this ship. I trust I will be recovered in time to serve the
Republic and do honour to my name. I have had a slight
sickness which has kept me below decks and prevented
me from attending to my duties. I assure you, Father, it
is nothing serious. I will be ready when the time comes.*

*I apologise for the brevity of this letter. I try to think
of more words I can say to you, but none will come.*

*Your son,
Thibaud de la Porte*

For three days, an uneasy peace reigned in the Grand Harbour.
Le Torrington and *San Giacomo* were moored within sight of
each other. Philippe's crew had never holystoned the decks
so vigorously, nor painted the beakhead so enthusiastically. As
Tremoulet, the frigate's veteran gunner quipped, if Frenchmen
and Italians were unable to kill each other they would instead
bend every sinew to looking more beautiful than the enemy.
In the quiet times, though, when the noise from the docks
and the other ships in the harbour diminished so that the two
ships were within earshot of each other, the two crews fired
broadsides of abuse across the Grand Harbour. Few on either
ship could speak or comprehend each other's language, but
there was a universal language of the sea, a colourful patois that
borrowed from several dozen tongues and was known the world
over. So the men of *San Giacomo* undoubtedly knew that their
counterparts on *Le Torrington* were calling them bandits and

monkey-men who fucked their sisters, while the Frenchmen were denounced as nun-murdering atheists, the offspring of unnatural unions between whores and donkeys.

Such exchanges were, of course, beneath the dignity of a captain. Philippe's attention was fixed firmly on the repairs to the *Earl of Carbery*, which were proceeding far more slowly than he would have desired. As Consul Allard had predicted the Maltese, good Catholics all, were singularly reluctant to assist the republican French in any way, and Philippe was becoming increasingly convinced that it would be better to abandon the Levanter and take *Le Torrington* out of harbour before the grand master's patience became exhausted and he impounded the frigate on some trumped-up pretence. The Order of Malta's sympathies were certain to lie with the crew of *San Giacomo*, their co-religionists.

It was with such considerations in mind that Philippe strengthened the harbour watches. By night a particularly strong presence of Marines was arrayed along the sides and in the tops to deter any attack from the Neapolitan crew, perhaps using the small boats that criss-crossed the Grand Harbour at every hour of the day and night and might be crewed by Maltese sympathisers.

At midnight on the third night, Philippe was on deck with Bertin, Launay and Vidos. The bells of the cathedral and the countless other churches ringing over the harbour tolled the hour. Philippe's officers were apprehensive. The towns and fortifications that ringed the harbour seemed unusually quiet.

'They'll come tonight,' said Grignon, ever the pessimist.

'Perhaps,' said Philippe, 'but breaking neutrality is no little thing, Lieutenant. The grand master will want to blame us for any breach, I'm sure – the perfidious atheists who respect no law, and all such lies. So we give them no excuse, citizens. We offer no provocation, we only fire if under attack from enemies we're certain come from the *San Giacomo*.'

'And how can we be certain of that, sir, with all these boats milling around even at this hour?' demanded Grignon.

'We keep our eyes and ears wide open, Lieutenant. And our pistols primed, naturally.'

Philippe looked at the dark outline of the fortifications of Valletta on the other side of the harbour, then at the silhouette of the Neapolitan ship. Was the enemy captain having similar conversations with his own officers? Were his men silently descending into boats on the hidden far side of the hull? Had the Neapolitans come to an arrangement with the grand master by which an attack on the hated atheist French would be condoned? Philippe tried to imagine himself in his opposite number's place. Would he be overseeing the arming of his boarding party? Would he be giving an impassioned speech to his men, inciting them to slaughter the murderous French scum who had executed their king and queen, closed the churches and outlawed God?

There was a sound from the enemy ship. A single man's voice, but not a voice giving commands or ordering men into battle. The fellow, whoever he was, was singing. His voice was a strong bass that carried easily over the water to the confused men on the deck of *Le Torrington*. Philippe's officers and the Marines looked at each other.

'What in God's name is that, sir?' murmured Vidos, briefly forgetting that loyal republican Frenchmen no longer invoked the name of God.

'That, Aspirant, is an aria. That is opera.'

CHAPTER TWENTY-SIX

No attack came that night. By dawn it was clear that the weather had changed, a breeze from the north-east steadily strengthening and making the waters of the Grand Harbour choppy. The bright blue skies of the previous few days gave way to heavy grey clouds that were more reminiscent of Brittany. Philippe was in his cabin, writing formal letters to Paris, to Toulon and to Admiral Martin, presumed still to be in the Bay of Gourjean. He also wrote less formally to Leonore at the Chateau de Brechelean, albeit with little expectation of an answer, and to Frank Parmentier, who had surely returned by now to Toulon with his haul of prizes, requesting an unusual favour of him. A small Venetian merchantman was due to sail imminently for Marseilles, and her captain, perhaps mindful of the French armies campaigning in northern Italy, uncomfortably close to the borders of the Serene Republic, was willing, even eager, to curry favour with the authorities in France by agreeing to Philippe's request to carry the mail from *Le Torrington*. Philippe had just completed his last letter when Rampillon knocked, entered and delivered a brief note from the turcopilier, Baron von Flachslanden, inviting Philippe to dine with him in an hour. The invitation puzzled Philippe, for what cause could there possibly be for it? But it would not do to snub one's hosts, so he donned his best uniform and had the longboat take him across to Valletta.

The turcopilier's house was a substantial building of three stories on a busy street close to the grand master's palace. A well-mannered servant who spoke passable French admitted Philippe and showed him to von Flachslanden's opulent dining room, where the turcopilier was in conversation with a stout, flamboyantly moustachioed fellow in a gold-fringed, red-collared uniform of very dark blue.

'Ah, Captain Kermorvant,' said the turcopilier, 'welcome to the humble residence of a mere foot soldier for Christ and his cause upon earth, which is to say the cause of peace. In that spirit, Captain, I have the honour to present Captain Salvatore Guidici of the ship *San Giacomo* in the service of His Majesty the King of Naples and Sicily.'

Guidici inclined his head in a slight bow, and Philippe reciprocated.

'Ah, *Capitano*,' said Guidici effusively and without a hint of hostility, 'it is an honour to meet you.'

'Likewise, Captain,' said Philippe.

Were it not for the neutrality of their host and the soil on which they both stood, Philippe knew that he and the Italian would already have their swords unsheathed and poised to clash, each intent on killing the other. Philippe could not stop himself estimating the man's reach and the likely qualities of the blade that hung at his side. But the crosses of Saint John adorning the turcopilier's breast, the livery of his servants and the ceiling of the opulent dining room provided ample reminders that in that house and in that moment, there was no war.

'I have invited you here so that there may be an understanding between us,' said von Flachslanden. 'In violent times, it is so important for men of honour – men of intellect, should I say? – to talk rationally. To know each other's thoughts and aspirations, if you take my meaning. That is what I hope for during our meal.'

'A noble sentiment, my lord,' said Guidici.

'Noble indeed,' said Philippe, 'although we represent countries that have declared war on each other. Surely, my lord Turcopilier, Captain Guidici, our thoughts and aspirations focus on how one may kill the other?'

Guidici laughed. All of the man's words and deeds seemed to be extravagant, and his laugh was perhaps the loudest Philippe had ever heard.

'If that is truly so,' said the Italian, 'then may we at least try to kill each other after dinner is concluded? I have sampled the turcopilier's fare before and can vouch for its exquisiteness. You will miss a delight if I kill you before we eat, Captain Kermorvant.'

Guidici was grinning, but Philippe had little doubt that the Italian would have relished nothing more than the opportunity to do exactly that.

Von Flachslanden took the head of the table with Philippe and Guidici facing each other on either side. Any awkwardness was swiftly dispelled. The turcopilier was an amiable and attentive host, his servants were capable and discreet, and Guidici was an easy, even garrulous conversationalist. It swiftly became apparent, though, that the Neapolitan had one topic of conversation above all other, and it did not relate in any way to their ships or the war.

'You know the opera, Captain Kermorvant? You'll have frequented the Paris opera, I expect. Is that still open, or has it gone the way of religion?'

It was not a question Philippe expected to be asked by an adversary, least of all at the dinner table of one of the highest officers of the Order of Malta, but von Flachslanden's glazed expression suggested that it was not the first time he had heard Guidici hold forth on the subject.

'I only visited Paris for the first time in my life a few months ago,' said Philippe to the evident astonishment of his companions. 'I regret that I could not find the time to attend the opera, but the newspapers I saw while I was there indicated that it flourishes. I believe Gossec and Méhul are the composers in vogue.'

Guidici's expression was shocked by Philippe's admission that he had never attended the opera in Paris, but he nodded at the mention of the two composers.

'Ah, Gossec. I know his work, I heard his *Nitocris* when it was staged at San Carlo in Napoli. Haven't heard of the other fellow. So you don't know opera *at all*, Captain?'

'There was none in America when I grew up there. But I served in Russia for some years, and had the privilege to attend some operas at Kammenïy in Saint Petersburg. Sarti, mostly.'

The gregarious Dmitri Kharabadze, the first officer to befriend him when he joined the naval service of the Empress of Russia, was a great lover of the opera and insisted that Philippe accompany him several times. It was evident at once that Kharabadze's interest was less in the music and the often laughably convoluted plots than in the plunging necklines of the court ladies in the audience and the female singers on the stage.

'Sarti!' cried Guidici, his eyes lighting up. 'I saw his *Alessando nell'Indie* in Palermo. An interesting composer. Not to be compared to Mozart or Paisiello, of course, but interesting. Paisiello also worked in Russia for a while, I believe, before he saw sense and came back to Napoli. I've met him, you know. Paisiello, I mean. A splendid fellow.'

It was easy to forget that the enthusiastic, entertaining Captain Guidici was Philippe's enemy, a man he was honour bound to kill as soon as an opportunity arose. But then and there, in the comfort of von Flachslanden's house and with a splendid repast before them, the war between France and Naples seemed very far away.

'I take it your singing was what I could hear from my quarterdeck last night, Captain Guidici?' said Philippe.

The Italian beamed.

'My poor voice carried that far? I must remember to tell my wife that. She will be so very proud. Yes, Captain, when I was young I wanted nothing more than to tread the boards of San Carlo, but I was then a tenor and all the choirmasters told me my voice was too reedy. As I got older and my waist grew larger, I became a bass. But by then it was too late, I was already a lieutenant in the navy.'

Von Flachslanden, who must have had heard the Neapolitan's story before, clearly wished to move Guidici away from the subject of opera.

'You said that you grew up in America and served in Russia, Captain Kermorvant?' the turcopilier asked. 'Strange experiences for a Frenchman of your birth, surely?'

Philippe put down his fork and gave a heavily edited account of his life: his father's exile, the plantation in Virginia, his service at sea in the American war for independence, his campaigns under the ensign of the Empress Catherine, his arrival in France, the homeland he had never known. He omitted much, notably the shocking murder of his wife and son by her brother Bulgakov, and his narrow escapes from the guillotine during the previous year. Naturally, he made no mention at all of Corsica and Carla Leandri. Throughout it all, the Turcopilier of Malta seemed enthralled and the Italian captain unimpressed.

'Your life would make a good opera, Captain Kermorvant,' said Guidici at last. 'A first draft of a libretto, at any rate. Oh, this is capital pork, my lord Turcopilier. Your kitchen has excelled once again.'

'I am merely a humble citizen of the Republic, Captain Guidici,' said Philippe. 'My life would be unworthy of a sentence in a book, let alone an opera.'

'Oh, sir,' said Guidici, 'opera contains all of life and more, much better than any book you could ever read. These last few years I have sometimes thought that we are living in an opera, that we have been set on an invisible stage and play out our parts from an unseen libretto. Such a monumental plot! The deaths upon a scaffold of a king and queen, the murder of thousands of innocents, the eternal battle of good and evil – what a story, but what composer could possibly be worthy of setting it?'

'And where is God in your opera, Captain?' said von Flachslanden.

'God is there, sir, of course He is there! He sees all, and in the final act He judges the outcome between good and evil.'

Philippe smiled indulgently. He had no doubt of the sides in that final battle that Salvatore Guidici imagined the two of them representing.

'I prefer my entertainment to be more diverting, Captain,' said Philippe. 'In other words, to actually entertain me. When I go to the theatre, I don't want to have to think upon such weighty matters as the meaning of life and death. My father devoted far too much time to such questions, and I was very young when I vowed never to do the same as him.'

'But opera can both divert and entertain us *and* present us with great subjects, all in one performance! A great composer can take any story and make it a pleasant few hours' entertainment on one level of understanding, but if you care to explore the other levels you find eternal stories and eternal truths. For instance, do you know Mozart? Ah, your life is so much the poorer, Captain Kermorvant – or rather, *Il Visconte di Saint-Victor*, is it not?'

Philippe nodded an acknowledgement of his title but did not reply. If Guidici had not already known his antecedents, von Flachslanden would certainly have told him in their time together before Philippe arrived at the house.

'I chanced to be in Vienna five or six years ago and attended the premiere of *Don Giovanni*, with Mozart himself present. One of the greatest occasions of my life, Captain, after my marriage and the births of all my children, of course. I have eight of them, sir, *eight*! My dearest wish is that they all grow into singers, then I can direct them in *Don Giovanni* with myself singing Leporello!' He began to sing. '*Madamina, il catalogo è questo...*' Von Flachslanden raised his eyebrows. 'And you say you don't know it, Captain Kermorvant? Astonishing. Probably the greatest opera I have ever heard, and I have heard very many, believe me. But do you know what drives the story, Captain, what lies at its heart? A challenge. A duel. The sad but inevitable death of one of the protagonists.' Guidici paused, and his broad, disingenuous smile froze into a rictus. 'And that is our situation now. We are here, in this moment, and just as fate compels Don Giovanni to duel with the Commendatore, so it compels us to duel, you and I, and one of us must die.'

Von Flachslanden sniffed. 'There will be no duel on the soil of Malta,' he said, calmly but emphatically.

Guidici inclined his head. His expression was serious now, the opera-obsessed buffoon exiled to a very far distant place.

'Of course not, my lord. My king has always respected the rule and rights of your esteemed Order, as I hope you agree, and I treasure your hospitality too much to take advantage of it. No, I propose a duel at sea. Your ship against my ship, Captain Kermorvant, outside the waters claimed by the knights. What do you say?'

It was ridiculous. Duels were of the past; had not the great Cardinal Richelieu tried to ban them in France over a century and a half before? And duels at sea flew in the face of every instinct in every bone of every sailor, with the exception, it seemed, of Captain Salvatore Guidici. One ship against another in an arranged combat, to take place at a given time and in a given place… That was not how combats at sea happened.

Even if he agreed to it, *San Giacomo* was by far the larger ship. *Le Torrington* still lacked the guns that had been taken out of her in the Bay of Gourjean, so the Neapolitan broadside would hold close to a two to one advantage. Philippe also presumed that Guidici's complement would not have been weakened by detaching men to form prize crews.

Yet as Philippe looked at Guidici's determined expression and at the tense, expectant features of Baron von Flachslanden, he knew it was not such a strange notion. One of *San Giacomo* or *Le Torrington* would have to sail from the Grand Harbour first, and whichever that was would undoubtedly wait for the other just beyond the limit of the territorial waters of the Order of Malta. Agreeing a time and rules of engagement in the presence of a neutral adjudicator like the turcopilier might diminish the potential advantage the ship leaving harbour first should possess, the ability to take the weather gage which so often determined the course of engagements at sea. Moreover, the wind was strong, unpredictable and threatening to strengthen further, conditions that might help even the odds. In heavy seas Philippe would trust his officers, the seamanship of his men and the seaworthiness of his command, built as she was for the perpetual gales in the seas around Britain.

No, not a strange notion at all.

'Very well, Captain,' said Philippe. 'A duel it shall be. Perhaps that will make a worthy libretto for an opera.'

'Tomorrow morning, then,' said von Flachslanden, who was naturally eager to get one or, preferably, both of the combatants out of Malta as soon as possible. 'The tide will be on the ebb, which will help you as much as the wind will hinder if it stays in this quarter and at this strength. Captain Guidici, you are moored nearer to the harbour mouth so you will take *San Giacomo* out first. Captain Kermorvant, you will weigh exactly an hour later. Neither to fire on the other until you are beyond the range of any gun on the island.'

So reasonable, yet the turcopilier was handing the advantage in the fight to the Italian, and he would have known it. Guidici could take the advantage of the wind, choose his line of attack, engage *Le Torrington* while she was still beating up against the wind to be out of range of the guns on Forts Ricasoli and Saint Elmo, the two fortresses of the Order on either side of the harbour mouth. But Philippe had agreed to it, and his consent had been witnessed by one of the most senior officers of the knightly Order of Saint John.

Philippe raised his glass and toasted Guidici and von Flachslanden.

'To tomorrow, gentlemen.'

'To honour and glory,' responded Guidici. 'May one of us obtain those garlands in fair and honest combat.'

'May God grant victory to the just,' said the turcopilier, raising his own glass in salute to the two combatants.

CHAPTER TWENTY-SEVEN

At dawn on the following day, Philippe stood impassively on his quarterdeck as he watched *San Giacomo* weigh anchor. Initially towed by her boats, the Neapolitan man-of-war began to edge out into the main channel of the Grand Harbour, her bow slowly turning north-east. He consulted his watch. Fifty minutes until the allotted hour when *Le Torrington*, in turn, could begin her passage out to sea. Philippe paced the deck impatiently, attracting the curious stares of his men. They were already at their stations, even though it was long before their captain would begin to issue the commands to weigh and follow *San Giacomo*. For a fleeting moment Philippe considered ignoring the turcopilier's injunction, but one glance at the batteries on the point of Senglea told him that the batteries of the knights were fully manned. Any movement from *Le Torrington* until the exact moment specified by von Flachslanden and the devout Maltese gunners would doubtless relish the excuse to blow the Frenchmen into their imaginary next world.

Philippe looked across to *San Giacomo* and saw the large and unmistakeable shape of Salvatore Guidici on his quarterdeck, his hat raised in salute to his adversary. Philippe returned the gesture but did not attempt to emulate the other element of the Italian's salute, an aria that Philippe vaguely recognised – Gluck, perhaps? – which was just audible from *Le Torrington* in the moments when the brisk and rapidly strengthening breeze eased a little.

'Will the prize be safe, sir?' asked Aspirant Vidos, his eyes on the wharf on the other side of the harbour where the Levanter lay.

'Mornay is a good man,' said Philippe, 'and he has good men with him. They'll be waiting for us when we return after our victory. Perhaps proof that atheist republicans can fight will finally make the Maltese work harder, eh, Aspirant?'

Jacques Mornay was indeed a good man, one of the best of the master's mates, but Philippe had only been able to spare him half-a-dozen men as a shipkeeping crew to mount a nominal defence of the prize. If the Maltese decided to storm her, Mornay and his crew would stand no chance. Philippe calculated that they would only attempt such an outrage if *Le Torrington* lost her forthcoming battle, and if that was the case the status of the prize would be academic. He had given Mornay confidential orders to that effect. If the Maltese stormed her, the young master's mate was to surrender immediately. Mornay, an ardent republican and firm patriot, resented the command but promised to obey.

The hands of the watch moved toward the appointed hour.

The ship's boats were in position, the tow ropes secured but, for now, slack. Men were already out on the yards, even though it would be some time before *Le Torrington* was clear of the harbour and able to make sail. The gun crews on the upper deck were grim-faced and determined. Philippe's officers were at their posts, all of them glancing at their captain to see if he could somehow make time accelerate.

The hands continued to move too slowly. Impossibly slowly.

Over in Valletta, a single bell began to toll. Philippe's watch told him there were still two minutes remaining, but perhaps the turcopilier was being unexpectedly generous.

'*Lever l'ancre!*'

Weigh anchor.

The men of *Le Torrington* came to life like mannequins suddenly infused with a life force. The capstans turned, the boat crews took up the slack, and the frigate began to move out into Grand Harbour. The ever-freshening breeze caught the *Tricolore* at the stern, which billowed out proudly.

Both sides of the harbour, and the points of the peninsulas that protruded into it, were packed with curious, silent Maltese. Some women were praying, perhaps imploring their God to punish the atheist regicides. Philippe doubted very much whether any were praying for the victory of *Le Torrington*.

The same turn to the north-east that *San Giacomo* had made, into the teeth of what threatened to become a fully fledged gale. The wind was blowing almost directly into the mouth of the harbour, giving *Le Torrington* no leeway to make sail. The boat crews struggled to make headway, and Philippe pitied the men at the oars. He gave an order for every one of them to have a double ration of wine when they returned to the ship and upon conclusion of the forthcoming battle.

The progress toward the harbour mouth seemed almost as interminable as the wait for the moment to weigh anchor. Philippe raised his telescope to study the batteries on either side of the narrow channel and had a premonition of a hellish crossfire from the Maltese guns reducing *Le Torrington* to matchwood long before she could confront *San Giacomo*. But the neutrality of the knights yet held firm. As they came level with the walls of Fort Saint Elmo, Philippe saw a small party of grandly attired men standing on one of the ramparts, silently watching the French warship proceed to sea. One of them he recognised as the turcopilier, Baron von Flachslanden. The older and even more elaborately dressed man alongside him could only be the grand master himself, His Most Eminent Highness Emmanuel de Rohan, Prince and Grand Master of the Order of Saint John of Jerusalem, Rhodes and Malta. A Frenchman watching his countrymen sail forth to do battle with an enemy of France, but Philippe had no doubt that all de Rohan's sympathies would be with Guidici and *San Giacomo*.

Then they were clear of the Grand Harbour, and Philippe could see *San Giacomo* off to the north-north-east, beating up against the wind. The pilot sent to *Le Torrington* by the turcopilier, a cheerful and surprisingly young man named Caruana, expressed some surprise that Guidici had elected to beat into the teeth of a *gregale*, the cold wind which blew from that quarter, especially as it was an unusually strong blow for the summer, as strong as any Caruana had ever known.

'Deadly coast this, in an easterly,' Caruana had said as he showed Philippe a detailed chart before *Le Torrington* weighed anchor. 'Rocks here and all along here, shoals there and there. Expect you've forgotten the Bible, Captain? Not approved in your republic?'

Philippe smiled. He remembered the Bible well enough thanks to all the long hours when his father, the atheist Verité, forced him to study it.

'I remember it.'

'The Acts of the Apostles, Book Twenty-Seven. Saint Paul was shipwrecked on Malta. This –' Caruana pointed to a rock-studded bay to the north-west of Valletta '– this is the very bay where his ship was wrecked. A captain underestimates this coast and the winds of the Mediterranean at his peril.'

Caruana's words made Philippe see the sense in what his Neapolitan enemy was doing. He had the weather gage, so he was likely to try and force *Le Torrington* onto the deadly lee shore of Malta. Conversely, he could easily bear away if the battle went badly for him. Bearing away would carry *San Giacomo* to the nearby coast of Sicily, no more than five or six hours away and the territory of the King of Naples. A friendly shore for Salvatore Guidici, an implacably hostile one for Philippe Kermorvant.

Philippe weighed Caruana's information and advice against his instinct to make his move.

'*Perroquets, huniers, civadière!*' he cried, the decision made. 'Hands to make sail, topsails and spritsail only! Helm, larboard five points!'

San Giacomo, her advantage and ample searoom secured, was coming round to sail back toward *Le Torrington*. Philippe had briefly considered steering almost due east, trying to seize the weather gage from Guidici. Perhaps the Neapolitan would fall for the feint and assume the French were running, scared of his larger ship and seeking to escape instead into the broad waters of the eastern Mediterranean. If Philippe was in Guidici's position he would anticipate such a move and could easily intercept it, especially as *Le Torrington* would need to tack at least once. Instead, Philippe would rise to the challenge immediately.

As *Le Torrington* rose and fell on the lively sea, crashing through the angry waters, the topsails fell and the helmsmen turned the ship directly for the enemy.

CHAPTER TWENTY-EIGHT

San Giacomo, off to the north-east, was coming down fast upon the increasingly ferocious wind with the advantage of the weather gage.

'We'll make a pass on the opposite tack,' said Philippe to Malhuret and Vidos, the most senior officers alongside him on the quarterdeck, 'then try to come round and rake him.'

'*Commande*, Citizen Captain!' cried Vidos.

Philippe beckoned Launay and the gunner to join him on the windward side of the quarterdeck.

'Well, Citizen Tremoulet,' said Philippe, 'what do you think?'

'Difficult water for full broadsides, sir. Better for each gun to fire as she bears, I'd say. Even then aiming will be difficult if the weather stays like this.'

'I concur. Pass the order to the starboard guns – it'll be a good while before we'll need larboard. And ready the bow chasers, we'll try a shot or two as soon as we're in range.'

'Aye, aye, Citizen Captain!'

The ever-strengthening wind made it difficult for *Le Torrington* to make significant headway. The courses were now reefed. The ideal course to steer was too close to the wind, but *San Giacomo* could easily adjust her own course to ensure that she stayed to windward of the French ship. It would also be easier for Guidici, when the moment came, to manoeuvre into a position where he could rake *Le Torrington*, rather than vice-versa. But Philippe thought that the Neapolitan captain was overconfident. He had too much canvas aloft, certainly more than Philippe had ordered. Guidici was gambling on a quick victory.

The gap between the two ships seemed never to lessen. As a sudden rain squall lashed the quarterdeck of *Le Torrington*, Philippe watched the bow of *San Giacomo*, and the waves breaking over it, for what felt like an eternity. With the wind filling his sails so amply, Guidici should surely be able to make more speed. If *Le Torrington* was an English tortoise then *San Giacomo* had to be an even slower creature, an Italian snail perhaps.

The force of the wind and the vicious movement of the sea, now supplemented by intermittent but vicious rain, made it increasingly difficult for Philippe and the others to stand unsupported, so he lashed a rope around his waist and secured it with a hitch knot. He was aware of his officers shouting orders through their voice trumpets, but all of his attention was fixed on his opponent. He was aware of the ominously black clouds looming above and astern of the *San Giacomo*, filthy weather indeed for the Mediterranean in summer, but he had no control over that. The guns of *Le Torrington* were a different matter, and the bow chasers were surely almost in range.

A little further… a little further…

An eternity of a few minutes passed.

Now!

'Fire *Vengeur*!'

The men's nickname for their weapon was more easily understood than an order to fire the starboard bow chase gun.

The order was relayed almost instantaneously. Even at the other end of the ship, Philippe felt the recoil of the twelve-pounder. He saw the smoke, but the wind dispersed it before it reached his position and he caught only the faintest whiff of the familiar smell of gunfire. The sound of the firing came to him as an insignificant pop carried upon and away by the breeze.

The shot fell short, although not too far short. Philippe knew his gun crew would be reloading for their next attempt—

He saw the smoke from the corresponding gun on *San Giacomo*. This, too, fell short, albeit close enough to *Le*

Torrington's bow to bring up a spout of water that broke over the beakhead.

'*Pour la France!*' he cried into the wind. '*Pour la liberté! Pour la gloire de la République!*'

Even if not everyone heard the words, Philippe's meaning was clear. The men cheered. Philippe drew his sword, and his lieutenants followed his example. Grignon would probably have much preferred to fight the English and avenge his dead brother, but he was a valiant man, if a dour one, and that day an Italian opponent would do just as well for him. Philippe wished he had the second lieutenant's certainty. The simple fact was that the oncoming enemy was by far the larger ship, able to fire a much heavier weight of shot from her broadside. If Guidici did not make a catastrophic error, and unless fate intervened, he ought to obtain the victory and return to the Grand Harbour in triumph.

The French drummers beat out an insistent rhythm. The two ships reared like bucking stallions as the range closed, the hulls rising and falling, pitched and yawed. The men manning the starboard battery of *Le Torrington* tensed for the command, even though those for'ard on the upper deck were drenched by the foaming spray thrown up as the ship ploughed through the waves.

'*Now!*'

Gunner Tremoulet, up for'ard, echoed the command. The first two guns in the starboard battery fired. One fired too high, but Philippe saw part of the starboard rail of *San Giacomo*'s fo'c'sle shatter into a thousand splinters. The Italian's reply came almost immediately, two guns firing on the downroll. Philippe felt the impact of the iron balls striking the hull, felt the old timbers of *Le Torrington* shudder. But the English had always built their ships to take such punishment, planking them with the stoutest oak and constructing them with heavier scantlings than the French custom. She was no greyhound of the seas like Frank Parmentier's *Forbin* or Philippe's former command,

Le Zephyr, but he would wager that no ship in the Marine Nationale could take punishment as well as the old English tortoise.

'*Fire!*' cried Philippe.

The next guns engaged, this time striking the enemy's hull. Philippe heard a man scream, but otherwise there was no obvious damage to *San Giacomo*. The Neapolitans fired again, this time a ragged volley from three or four guns at once. Their aim was higher this time, severing a few shrouds but otherwise causing no damage that Philippe could see. The enemy ship was well within small arms range, so he lifted his pistol, but it was impossible to aim steadily and he lowered it again. His own Marines, at the rail and in the tops, were letting off the occasional shot, but they had all seen enough service to know that accurate fire was impossible. The Italians were not of the same mind and were shooting indiscriminately. One man in a midships gun crew was struck by a ball in the shoulder and fell to the deck, but he got up immediately and, after a cursory inspection from Tremoulet, he was sent below to be bandaged in the surgeon's cockpit.

He was the sole casualty of the first pass. *Le Torrington* took two more hits, *San Giacomo* perhaps three or four, but neither bothered to engage with their stern chasers. They drew apart on opposite tacks, Guidici aiming to keep the wind by making a turn to the west then turning sharply back to go onto a north-north-westerly course, seemingly aiming to get back to his original position.

'So much for any chance of raking her,' said Philippe to Malhuret.

'Your orders, Citizen Captain?'

'We'll wear ship, Malhuret, bring her round then come down on the opposite tack to the enemy. Let's see if we have better fortune if we have the wind on the larboard beam.'

'Aye aye, sir. And the outlying shoal that the pilot pointed out?'

'Saint George's Rock. I am mindful of it, Lieutenant, but if we turn smartly enough we'll have ample searoom to steer clear of it.'

The crew responded briskly to the commands, hauling to bring the jibs and staysails around and take the ship onto the opposite tack. Philippe saw more than one of them looking apprehensively at the clouds, which were getting darker and angrier by the minute. Philippe could feel the wind blowing ever more viciously into his face. He had encountered such conditions in the Atlantic in winter but would never have expected to encounter them off the north-east coast of Malta in a Mediterranean summer.

Philippe saw *San Giacomo* off to the south-south-east, slowly working its way back, now with the wind on its starboard beam. Guidici had reefed his courses but still had topsails set, which seemed excessive to Philippe. But then, the Neapolitan was bound to have better knowledge of Mediterranean conditions and the capabilities of his own vessel. He also still had the advantage of both the wind and power of broadside.

The two ships closed each other once more for a second pass, again on the opposite tacks. Then, in a single instant, the battle was transformed.

'Sir!' cried Malhuret, shouting himself almost hoarse to make himself heard above the wind and the seething waves. 'The Italian, sir! He's closed—'

Philippe wiped spray from his eyes.

'I see it, Lieutenant. I see it.'

The gunports for the lower tier of *San Giacomo*'s guns had indeed been closed. The Italian must have been shipping water at an alarming rate, and Guidici must have believed there was a real danger of his ship being swamped. It was the only plausible explanation, for no captain willingly deprived himself of nearly half his main armament.

An unlikely memory came to Philippe. Once, when he was a boy in Virginia, his friend Opechancanough took him to see a wrestling contest between two Powhatan warriors, the champions of their respective tribes, who had defeated all comers for countless years and were now, finally, matched with each other. Philippe was excited by the prospect, but when he reached the camp and joined the hundreds of spectators who formed a circle around the combatants, he felt only profound disappointment. The two men before him were old and fat. They spent most of their time merely circling each other, growling insults as they struggled to get their breath back. They were both soaked with sweat. Every so often one would attack the other and they would grapple for perhaps a minute or two, drawing cheers and gasps from the crowd, but the contact between them never lasted for very long. That, too, was the combat between *Le Torrington* and *San Giacomo*, he realised. Two old, sluggish ships, both of which would struggle against younger, faster vessels, which were unable to manoeuvre quickly, which could not land a decisive blow on each other. *San Giacomo* should have had the advantage of size and weight of ordnance, and Guidici can only have ordered the closing of the lower gunports with the greatest reluctance. The two ships were nearly equal now, as the two old Indians had been. As on that day in Virginia, the victor would not be the more skilful of the fighters but the one that could endure longer.

The second pass was even less decisive than the first. The roaring, swelling, surging sea made accurate fire very nearly impossible for both ships. *Le Torrington* made no more than half a dozen hits, *San Giacomo* perhaps one or two fewer. There was no apparent damage to either ship. This time, though, Philippe ordered a rapid turn to starboard the moment *Le Torrington* was clear of the Italian. As rapid as the circumstances permitted, at any rate. Guidici would surely make the equivalent turn to keep the advantage of the wind—

No. To the astonishment of Philippe, his officers and all the men on the upper deck of *Le Torrington*, the bow of the Neapolitan ship came round to port. Guidici was going to risk both losing the weather gage and the proximity of the deadly shoals, gambling everything on delivering a raking broadside into the stern of his French opponent.

The two rearmost guns on *Le Torrington*'s larboard quarter managed to bear and fire before the Italian crossed the stern and fired his larboard battery. In the moments before *San Giacomo* engaged, Philippe caught a glimpse of Guidici on his quarter-deck. His mouth was opening too often to be giving the only short, simple orders that were necessary. *Damn the man, even now he was singing.*

The Italian had fired on the downroll. Philippe felt the impact as several solid iron shots smashed into the stern of *Le Torrington*. He heard glass shattering and knew his stern cabin would be wrecked. He hoped Courtois was elsewhere, anywhere, as long as he was far from the stern. He knew, though, that if the Neapolitan gun crews had fired on the uproll, it was likely that Philippe Kermorvant and most of the officers of the French frigate would have perished amid a maelstrom of iron cannonballs and lethal timber splinters. As it was, Philippe, Malhuret and the others lived. Timbers could be replaced, a cabin repaired, but in the heat of battle those in command were irreplaceable.

The gamble might have worked if Guidici had been able to open his lower ports. A full broadside of twenty-four pounders from the sixty-gun Neapolitan warship might have proved fatal to *Le Torrington*. As it was, Guidici had lost the weather gage and was now closer to the deadly lee shore of Malta than the French ship.

Le Torrington plunged into a deep trough in the sea, walls of water rearing up on all sides, and for a moment it seemed she must continue her momentum downward, ever downward, to the watery graveyard that awaited hubristic captains and their crews. But as the next wave swept in, drenching those on the upper deck of the frigate, the ship's bow rose again. Thank God, thought Philippe, for the English shipwrights who had built the old ship to survive all that Poseidon and his aquatic legions could throw at her.

He wiped the stinging salt water from his eyes and looked across to *San Giacomo*. Even in such a wild sea, her hull sat at an unnatural angle. *Had Guidici run onto a submerged rock or shoal?* Had he struck Saint George's?

The Italian's rig had changed, too—

The maintopmast was broken, snapped like a twig on a winter's day. Instinctively, Philippe looked up to his own topmasts. They were groaning their forlorn protests, as were the yards, but they were holding.

Objectively, though, and assuming he had not grounded, the loss of the topmast should not present Guidici with too much difficulty. It would slow him, but speed was an irrelevance upon that turbulent sea—

There was a new sound, one that eclipsed even the shriek of the wind. Philippe watched aghast as the foremast of the Neapolitan ship, perhaps hit by one of the last shots on the uproll from *Le Torrington,* perhaps weakened further by the relentless storm, perhaps finished off by the impact of striking an unseen rock, broke apart about halfway between the deck and the mainyard. The mast remained upright for a moment, then began to fall to port. Its descent was halted by the rigging, even though several shrouds and stays were snapping under the intolerable new strain on them. But the impact also had to be pulling the mainmast forward and sideways, threatening to bring it down also. In the fleeting moments afforded by the tumultuous seas when Philippe could see the Italian ship, he could just make out parties of men trying frantically to hack at the rigging. But it was clear that *San Giacomo* could not steer, could not make any headway at all. She had to have moved far enough to have come away from any subterranean obstacle, but that no longer mattered to her prospects. *Le Torrington* still had ample searoom and could hold her own against the storm, beating further out to sea if needed, but both Philippe and

Malhuret could see that Salvatore Guidici and his men were doomed.

The men on the upper deck of *Le Torrington* watched, utterly helpless, as the worst nightmare of every seafarer played out before their eyes. The Neapolitan ship, a proud and noble man-of-war until mere minutes before, became nothing more than a cork, utterly at the mercy of the implacable waters. There were only fleeting glimpses when the violent waves and their own desperate endeavours to keep *Le Torrington* on course permitted, but they were enough to bring home the unfolding horror. The hull of *San Giacomo* was driven inexorably toward the cliffs as if being hauled in by invisible ropes. The Frenchmen were all imagining how it would be for the Italians: the realisation that none of their frantic efforts were having any effect, the sense of utter hopelessness, the certainty that death was inevitable and imminent. In Naples, Palermo and all the other ports under the rule of King Ferdinand, hundreds of widows and orphans were about to be made. As he barked orders and encouragement, Philippe remembered Salvatore Guidici talking fondly of his wife and eight children, whom he would never now direct in *Don Giovanni*. Perhaps he was thinking of them now, in his last moments, as he prayed to God to preserve and protect them all their days. Perhaps the last song Salvatore Guidici would ever sing was the *Ave Maria*.

Philippe saw the moment of impact as the port beam of *San Giacomo* struck the cliff. The bow rose abruptly as the ship was flung violently onto its starboard side, the masts tipping toward *Le Torrington* in what looked like a final salute to a victorious adversary. Then Philippe's ship plunged into another deep trough in the waves and the Neapolitan warship was lost to view. When the hull rose again and the waves and rain permitted a glimpse of the shore, Philippe saw a sight that would stay with him to his dying day.

San Giacomo was gone. At the end there was only the sight of timbers, canvas, rigging and what had been entire sections of the ship being smashed against the rocks by ferocious waves. The only sound was that of the murderous wind, howling over the hundreds of corpses that were either being tossed on the surface or already lying beneath the waves. Mighty rollers broke against the cliffs, smashing the remnants of ship and men to oblivion. But just before Philippe lost sight of the wreck for the last time, he thought he heard another sound upon the wind. It could be nothing more than a trick of the conditions or his imagination, for the wreck was too far away for any sound from it to reach *Le Torrington*. But for all that, just for a moment, Philippe thought he heard the faint, distant, fleeting, impossible sound of a bass voice singing a few notes of an aria.

PART FOUR

CHAPTER TWENTY-NINE

Thibaud de la Porte's life was over. He still breathed and walked and talked. He stood his watches and carried out his orders. He dutifully maintained his journal and his navigational workbook. He continued to write regularly to his father, as Colonel de la Porte demanded. But it was all an illusion. He was seventeen years old, but he felt as if he were in his grave.

The men knew. Oh yes, they knew. He was sure they knew. He was certain they were murmuring about him behind his back. Out of the corner of his eye, he saw them glancing at him. Some smirked, he was sure of it. The eyes of others were contemptuous, others pitying. No man said anything to his face. Calling an *aspirant* a coward was a sure road to a flogging. But they knew.

He had disgraced his name. For centuries, generations of de la Portes had drawn their swords for France. They had defended impossible positions, led charges, commanded great armies, died covered in immortal glory. All of them, without exception, had been brave men.

Until him.

He remembered how, when he was a child, he was told endlessly of the brave deeds of previous de la Portes. Every relative he encountered told him what a great warrior he would be, how worthy of the name he bore. He was an only son, and as such the reputation of the family depended on him. At first the tales of his ancestors' courage thrilled him. He longed to pick up a sword, to prove himself a true de la Porte. But when he was perhaps ten or eleven, a couple of younger boys mocked him in the street, laughing at his birthmark, calling him names and throwing stones at him. Thibaud de la Porte knew he should stand up to them. His blood and his family's honour demanded it. He was bigger than them. He should walk calmly toward them as his father had told him. He should slap them or punch them or do whatever was necessary to teach them that nobody, *nobody*, insulted a de la Porte. Instead he felt his legs buckle. His bowels seemed to turn to water, threatening to humiliate him beyond measure. His eyes filled with tears. He turned and ran.

That was the moment when he knew he was a coward.

He hoped he would learn courage as he got older. But every time he encountered even the mildest, most fleeting danger, the familiar tightness in his chest began to close its malignant claws around his heart. His limbs felt as though they were made of lead. He would often begin to sweat.

This was why he chose to join the navy, to the astonishment of his father and uncles who were all soldiers, like all their forebears. But the navy fought at a distance, broadside against broadside, and in any case when he first went to sea in the summer of 1791 the king and queen still had their heads on their shoulders and France was still at peace. Only during that first cruise did he realise the awful mistake he had made. If war broke out there would be boarding actions, hand-to-hand fighting as vicious as any that could be expected in a land battle. Above all there was the constant enemy, the ever-present foe that was the sea itself. Thibaud de la Porte realised at once that the simple act of venturing out upon the ocean demanded far more courage than merely shouldering a musket and marching.

He had persevered. He learned how to suppress his fear so that he showed only imperturbability when cannon fired during exercises or when he had to wield a cutlass during small arms drill. He proved to have a good stomach for the waves and was hardly ever seasick. He had an aptitude for mathematics, so the complexities of navigation, the technicalities of ballistics and all the other elements that baffled so many of his messmates came easily to him. He found that command, the giving of orders and the gaining of respect from his superiors, equals and inferiors, also came naturally. But for all that, he knew the fear was still buried deep inside him. The fear of cold steel, the fear of death. He prayed to a god he did not believe in to give him courage when the day came.

He had not needed it at the battle of Neerwinden. His father ensured that he stayed well behind the lines, a mere observer and not a participant. But what he saw that day horrified him. The slaughter of General Miranda's brave men, hacked down by the relentless charges of Archduke Charles's cavalry – how did men stand and fight amid such a vision of hell, amid the blood, the dismembered limbs, the shattered remnants of what until mere moments before had been living, breathing, thinking men? Even in the safety of the command position, overlooking the battlefield, he could feel his legs shake, his palms begin to sweat and his bowels ache, just like that shameful first time against the younger boys. Yet men like his father and countless de la Portes before him made this their trade, their life's business. He knew he was not like them. He was a coward, too much of a coward even to stand up to his father and family and declare his intention to enter a different occupation, perhaps as a lawyer or a teacher or a librarian. He had a rare sense of self-awareness for a de la Porte, and knew that any of those trades would suit him far better than that which had been ordained for him.

He had not expected the fateful occasion, the moment when he would be tested in public and found wanting, to occur on a mean street in Valletta. Not when the odds should have been in favour of him and his three companions, one of them the captain, a veteran warrior and an undoubtedly fearless man. It was ignominy beyond all measure, and now he was certain that every man in the crew of *Le Torrington* knew. The world knew.

He hoped he would redeem himself in the fight with the Neapolitan warship, but there was no real opportunity. He was at his station on the gun deck, bawling encouragement at the men manning his allocation of guns. The broadsides, the first in anger he had ever experienced, nearly deafened him, and he saw men almost within touching distance perish as huge splinters struck them. Once again, he felt the compulsion to run or curl himself into a little ball, praying the horror all around would somehow pass over him and not touch him. But somehow he found the will to maintain his dignity, to fulfil his duties, to play the part assigned to him. The ship's movement was too violent to think about much more than keeping his feet and not spewing in front of the men. The passing broadsides were brief, while the main damage sustained on *Le Torrington*, that caused by the Italian's final raking broadside, was at the other end of the ship. He felt fear, but he knew it was chiefly fear of the elements and that every man in his proximity shared the feeling, which made it easier to accept. Then the enemy ship was overwhelmed by the violence of the storm and the battle abruptly ended. De la Porte, like all the men aboard, now had more urgent concerns, securing the ship and ensuring it rode out the tempest.

No, he was sure he had not shown cowardice during the battle. And yet *the men knew*. He was sure of it.

Only three individuals had witnessed his shame in Malta, so one of them must have spread the poisonous story of his cowardice. Two were his messmates, Rampillon and Vidos. Their behaviour toward him was outwardly unchanged. In the hours and days immediately after his craven failure in Malta, the two youths who proclaimed themselves his friends were sympathetic and supportive. They did not mention what had happened. But *they knew*. They were there. They had witnessed his shame. *They knew.*

He took a cursory bearing on a distant and receding hull, a Venetian bound for Alicante whom they had stopped to inspect the cargo manifest a couple of hours earlier. His heart was no longer in it. His heart was no longer in anything.

It had to be one of them. Vidos or Rampillon.

Thibaud de la Porte's thoughts raced, the demons whispering into his ear. If it was not one of his two fellow *aspirants*, then his nemesis had to be the third witness to his ignominious humiliation in Valletta.

The captain of *Le Torrington*, Philippe Kermorvant.

–

After the wrecking of *San Giacomo* Philippe kept his command well out to sea and away from the fatal lee shore of Malta until the following morning, by which time the rare summer storm had blown itself out. By then he had the butcher's bill. Only nine men had perished in the fight with *San Giacomo* with another fifteen wounded, most of them recovering under the diligent care of the surgeon, Antoine Saint-Cloud. A couple of them, *matelots d'eau douce* who were less accustomed to the movement of the sea, had knocked their heads from losing their footing as the ship bucked, swayed and rolled. The casualty list was brief, but the violent *gregale* and the murderous sea it whipped up dictated that it was a battle of intermittent passing fire alone, not a full-scale engagement with the combatants laid alongside each other, shattering each other with broadsides or one boarding the other.

So *Le Torrington* returned victorious to the Grand Harbour, to the evident delight of Consul Allard and the even more evident discomfort of the turcopilier. Despite this, von Flachslanden congratulated Philippe through gritted teeth and assured him that a large number of shipwrights, carpenters and labourers were now available to assist with the repairs, their work on other ships having terminated suddenly and conveniently. The Levanter was ready to sail within three days, and *Le Torrington* duly returned to sea with the prize in her wake before parting company – the *Earl of Carbery* bound for Toulon with a prize crew commanded by Aspirant Vidos, *Le Torrington* returning to her original orders from Admiral Martin to cruise independently in the Tyrrhenian and Ionian seas, and in the

Mediterranean as far west as Minorca, returning to Toulon no later than the last day of Vendémiaire.

Three days out of Malta, with the course north-north-westerly for the waters off Cape Tolare at the southern tip of the enemy kingdom of Sardinia, Philippe entertained his officers to dinner. On the turcopilier's order, the victuallers of Malta had proved markedly generous to the victorious French frigate. Although the stores taken on at Toulon were by no means exhausted, the fresh meat, bread and wine supplied by the Maltese made a welcome change from what had become tedious, unchanging fare. Philippe decided to take advantage of their good fortune while also taking an opportunity to celebrate their victory over *San Giacomo*. As they sat down to eat, the officers were largely in good humour. The exceptions were Grignon, long-faced as ever, and de la Porte, who seemed to be wallowing in some inner misery of his own. Philippe had considered seating the young man next to himself to reassure him of his continued confidence despite his brazen cowardice in Valletta, but one look at the *aspirant*'s face caused Philippe to favour Rampillon instead. Malhuret sat at the other end of the table.

For once the cook did not overcook the meat, and the fresh lamb taken aboard in the Grand Harbour could hardly have been equalled in Paris. Rampillon was an easy conversationalist, his Breton roots giving him something in common with his captain. They talked of the dangers of the Breton coast, of Brest, of Rampillon's first voyage at sea when he was only nine, although this went no further from his hometown of Vannes than Belle-Île where he was put ashore. The ship owned by his father sailed on to Africa to gather a cargo of slaves for the onward voyage to the Americas.

'It depends how long the war lasts, sir,' said Rampillon in reply to a question from Philippe about his ambitions. 'If it goes on long enough for me to become a captain, all well and good, but I think *lieutenant de vaisseau* would be sufficient to qualify me for command of one of my father's ships. It may be that even my current rank will be sufficient qualification. And in the fullness of time, well, I expect I'll succeed my father in the business. None of my brothers show any aptitude for the sea or trade.'

'You're sure that's your favoured path?'

Philippe weighed his words carefully. Conditions on the slave ships, like those owned by Rampillon *père*, were said to be hellish, while Philippe's father, the renowned Verité, had been outspoken on the evils of the trade and the very institution itself. The great thinker's son had learned to be more circumspect, but growing up on a plantation in Virginia, counting one of the slave boys as a friend, had given him his own opinions on the subject.

'As I say, sir, it all rather depends on the war,' said Rampillon with the airiness of the young. 'Ten years would be ideal. Anything longer and I would be happy to remain in the navy and settle for becoming an admiral.'

'An admiral? Your ambition is commendable, Aspirant.'

'But the war won't last ten years, will it? Two, perhaps. The triumph of the Republic is inevitable – that's what my father says.'

Philippe envied the youth and his father their confidence. Perhaps the lesser foes like Naples, Sardinia and the Dutch would be defeated in two years. But Philippe thought of the powerful armies of Austria and Prussia, of Russia especially if the empress finally decided to play her part in seeking to destroy the regicidal French Republic. Above all he thought of the countless British warships on the world's oceans, of Lord Hood's ships off Gourjean and Corsica, of what he had seen of Portsmouth dockyard during his captivity there. He remembered the size and wealth of London when he called there aboard a Gask ship almost ten years earlier. Would men like William Pitt, his own cousin Edward, Lord Wilden, the monied men of London and that strange little English sea captain whom he had encountered at Ghineparu, really be brought low by France in two years?

'Sir?'

'Sorry, *Aspirant*, I was lost in my own thoughts. If you do rise to a captain's rank, you need to learn that a captain cannot desert his own table for a minute, not even to indulge his own flights of fancy.'

'Sir.'

'But tell me, Rampillon – your messmate, there, Aspirant de la Porte. How has he been since that day in Malta?'

He could see de la Porte at the far end of the table, either ignoring Malhuret's questions and comments or responding to them in monosyllables.

Rampillon seemed to struggle to find the correct words.

'Different, sir. Withdrawn into himself. I have gone out of my way to be friendly to him and not to mention what happened. Vidos did the same before he went off in the Levanter – we agreed that was what we should do. He does his duty, as you know. He stands his watches. But his eyes seem to be glazed. It's as though something in him has died.'

No man knew how he would react in his first fight, in his first taste of battle. De la Porte was luckier than most of those who faltered, for his shame had been witnessed only by his captain and his friends, none of whom would trumpet the tale to the world – certainly not to the self-contained little world that constituted the ship's company of *Le Torrington*. True, the renegade knights of Malta, the turcopilier and those Maltese who peeped out from behind shutters or watched from their doors and windows could bear witness to de la Porte's cowardice, but how would their witness spread further, spread back to France, especially when they could not possibly know the *aspirant*'s name?

Philippe vowed to pay the young man more attention for the remainder of their cruise. If he could, he would find ways to reassure him, perhaps by placing him in a situation where he could command and display valour.

As he glanced again at de la Porte, whose expression was miserable and who clearly longed to be somewhere else, Philippe vowed to himself that, yes, he would somehow find a way for the *aspirant* to redeem himself.

CHAPTER THIRTY

Father,

I now know what duty I must fulfil.

~~*You wished me to be a warrior. You will hear that I have struck such a blow for France* –~~

~~*Philippe Kermorvant. Who is he? What is he?*~~

~~*I cannot be what you wished me* –~~

Rousseau tells us that Le monde de la réalité a ses limites; le monde de l'imagination est sans frontières. ~~*I think much on that.*~~

~~*Rousseau. Voltaire. Verité.*~~

~~*Kermorvant.*~~

~~*The men whisper. Vidos and Rampillon whisper. I hear them*~~

Father, whatever may become of me and whatever you may hear, I ask that you convey my deepest love to my very dear mother and sisters.

Your unworthy son,
Thibaud

–

'Sails ho! Off the larboard bow, four points!'

The lookout's call brought Philippe to the quarterdeck, where Bertin had the watch. Raising his telescope, Philippe saw at once why the lookout had used the plural rather than the singular. There were two ships off to the west, both sailing close-hauled upon a fresh south-westerly breeze. One was clearly pursuing the other, the chase trying to outrun her pursuer. The chase looked to be a large deep-hulled merchantman, her tormentor a warship of some sort. For a moment Philippe hoped it might be Frank Parmentier's *Forbin* chasing a rich Englishman. The two ships were certainly sailing a fair course for Livorno, the great *entrepôt* for Tuscany and the whole of northern Italy, the destination of choice for many of the richest hulls that sailed the Mediterranean. But the pursuing ship was too small, no larger than a corvette, so perhaps it was an enemy, maybe a Neapolitan or Sardinian chasing a French hull making for Marseilles – but if so, surely her course would have been more northerly? – or else for one of the harbours held by the French east of the Bay of Gourjean, perhaps carrying important supplies for the army. He judged that the pursuing vessel was unlikely to be British, for at that size the Royal Navy favoured brigs and the ship visible through his telescope was certainly not a brig. Still he could not make out the colours of the pursuer, so he had ample cause to sail closer, investigate what business was afoot, and take the side of pursued or pursuer depending on their identities.

With the wind on her port beam, *Le Torrington* steadily closed the gap to the two ships. Both would have seen the frigate by now, but neither showed any sign of changing course either toward or away from her.

Philippe turned to Bertin, who was studying the pursuer through his telescope.

'Well, Lieutenant? What do you make of her?'

'I've seen her like before, Captain. When I was on a merchant voyage from Marseilles to Lisbon before the war, we were stopped by one of her kind to inspect our passport. All was in order, thanks be to – ah, and up go his colours. He must have waited until he was sure what we were. See, sir? Blue, green and red stripes. The colours of Algiers.'

Philippe levelled his own telescope again, and saw the ominous ensign at the stern of the corvette. In name, Algiers was a regency of the Ottoman Empire that sprawled from the Straits of Gibraltar to the borders of Persia, and against which Philippe had fought for the Russian Empress a few years before. In reality, though, Algiers and the other North African regencies, Tripoli and Tunis, had been effectively independent for centuries, and during that time their low, fast craft and supremely capable but ferocious crews had earned a fearsome reputation. They were the Barbary Corsairs, preying on the shipping of all Christian nations and carrying many thousands of men, women and children into lifelong slavery. After many wars and bombardments of their port cities, the regencies had finally agreed treaties with the most powerful nations of Europe, including France, and thereafter largely left their ships alone.

Not all countries of the world had treaties with the corsairs, though, and they included the homeland of the ship being pursued. Philippe could see her colours now, and felt a sudden chill upon his heart. It was the flag under which he had grown to manhood, the flag for which he had fought his first battles and killed his first enemies.

Thirteen stars, white upon a blue ground. Thirteen horizontal stripes, red alternating with white. The colours of the United States of America.

—

The corsair vessel opened fire with her larboard bow chaser, throwing up a waterspout a little way off the American ship's larboard quarter. The merchantman made no reply. Philippe estimated her armament at no more than twelve guns, perhaps half the complement of the battery on the corsair. He could imagine the debate that must be going on at that moment aboard the American ship: resist or surrender? One would mean certain death, the other the interminable living death of captivity in Algiers.

Le Torrington could tip the balance. The men on the merchantman would once have been countrymen of his. He might have sailed and fought alongside one or two of them. He longed to call his crew to action, to hear the sound of the decks being cleared and the cannon being run out. His heart screamed at him to do it. He now wore the uniform of France and had pledged undying allegiance to the Republic, but he had once worn another uniform and made a different pledge to a different land. He, and he alone, could save those on the American ship from whatever fate the corsairs – heathen, alien, different-skinned men with a name for brutality – had in store for them.

His heart screamed it, but his head kept him inert on his quarterdeck, his mouth sealed. France had a century-old treaty with Algiers. French ships sailed the Mediterranean unhindered by the corsairs. The Ottoman Sultan Selim, the nominal over-lord of Algiers and all the corsairs, had friendly relations with the Republic. If Philippe raised one finger to prevent the corsair vessel seizing her quarry, he might trigger a war at a time when France was already at war with most of Europe.

The United States, still not twenty years old as a sovereign nation, had no treaty with Algiers. Before the rift with Britain, American ships upon the oceans of the world sailed safe and unmolested under the protection of British warships. But inde-pendence, that dream for which his father and some of his closest friends had bled and died, was not entirely an unqual-ified blessing. With no cloak to protect them, American ships were now desperately vulnerable. Above all, those that risked the valuable Mediterranean trades knew they ran the risk of encountering the corsairs. He had heard that Congress, which had dissolved the old Continental Navy, in which Philippe had served, as quickly as possible after the end of the war to save money, was finally compelled by the protests of shipowners and Christian congregations to allocate funds for a new, albeit tiny, navy of powerful frigates. Six in all was the word from across the Atlantic, a force barely worthy of the name of a navy but perhaps a beginning, the foundation of something grander. In the darkest days during the previous year when he had doubted the leaders, the policies and the very morality of the French Republic, Philippe sometimes wondered whether this new navy might give him a final berth, the third and last allegiance of his life. Perhaps his life would turn full circle and he would end where he had begun. But his captivity on the *Agincourt* prison hulk in Portsmouth harbour had given him ample time to think, and he knew that for good or ill, his fortunes were now inextricably intertwined with those of the French Republic.

He could still issue the order. There was still time, and *Le Torrington* was on an ideal course to intercept the corsair corvette. The French ship easily outgunned the Arab vessel and would fire a far greater weight of shot. Yes, he could still issue the order. But would his men go with him? Would Malhuret, newly arrived on the quarterdeck? Malhuret who did things by the book, who knew the state of France's international alliances and enmities as well as Philippe did and had amply demonstrated that he was fit to command *Le Torrington* while Philippe was in Corsica – would Malhuret or, indeed, any of the other officers concur if their captain gave the order to engage the corsair and save the American merchantman?

'Your orders, Citizen Captain?' said Bertin.

Philippe looked through his telescope once again. He could see individuals on deck now, the Americans running about and climbing the shrouds in what was clearly a frantic and hopeless effort to find another scrap of canvas, to somehow conjure up the miracle of another knot or two of speed. On the corsair, though, everything seemed calm, men's movements unhurried, as though they had no concern at all either for the ship they were chasing or the French frigate that still approached but remained a very long way beyond firing range. A frigate flying the colours of a nation that had no quarrel at all with the Dey of Algiers and Sultan Selim.

He lowered the telescope and turned to Bertin.

'Bear away, Lieutenant. Six points to larboard. If the Algerine salutes, we return the dignity with appropriate honours.'

'*Commande!*' cried Bertin.

The decision was made, the orders transmitted, the helm was put over, the bows began to turn onto the new course, and *Le Torrington* began to bear away from the protagonists.

De la Porte, who had been seemingly lost in his thoughts on the leeward side of the quarterdeck, stepped in front of Philippe. His cheeks were flushed, his birthmark seemingly ablaze, his eyes darting from one side to another and avoiding his captain's steady gaze.

'Sir,' he said. 'Citizen Captain. Surely we must save them.'

'My orders have been given, Aspirant.'

'But, sir, they are people like us. People who look like us. People who think like us. You knew people like that, didn't you? You sailed with people like that. They were your countrymen, sir. If we don't save them, they'll face a life of hell – a harem for the women, if there are women aboard—'

He could not give the young man the slightest inkling that he felt exactly as he did. He did not need reminding that those on the American ship had been his countrymen once. His chest was pounding, his stomach churning.

'I'm well aware of what they might face, Aspirant. But the order has been given, Citizen de la Porte. The French Republic is at peace with Algiers, and it is not for us to imperil that – just as it is not for an *aspirant* to question his captain's orders. I will put your impertinence down to natural and commendable eagerness to save your fellow human beings, Aspirant de la Porte, otherwise you would face a flogging at the very least.'

De la Porte looked around wildly as if seeking allies. But the expressions of Malhuret, Bertin, Doucet and Launay displayed only pity, while the helmsmen, mates, Marines and seamen within earshot looked at de la Porte with a combination of astonishment and contempt. The *aspirant* seemed to shrink before all their eyes. He saluted Philippe in a perfunctory manner, then went below.

'It's still his watch, sir,' said Bertin.

'Only for another ten minutes or so,' said Philippe as quietly as he could, not wanting to exacerbate the situation. 'In the circumstances, I shall overlook the misdemeanour.'

Whatever his thoughts about de la Porte's indiscipline, Philippe remembered another young man of the same age, a long time ago, boldly and brazenly arguing with a captain who had decided not to attack a British warship three times their size.

He had a memory of his first captain, the inscrutable and intrepid Ben Fairfax, smiling indulgently at the young Philippe Kermorvant.

'Always remember this, lad,' Fairfax had said, 'the hottest heads make for the coldest corpses.'

Some force, some terrible whisper from the darkest corner of his mind, compelled Philippe to watch through his telescope as the so-familiar colours came down on the American ship, the corsair vessel came up alongside her, and dozens of robed and turbaned men clambered onto and swarmed all over their new prize. Philippe Kermorvant handed the ship to Malhuret, went below to his cabin and went into his privy, where he vomited long and hard.

CHAPTER THIRTY-ONE

After the encounter with the corsair and her doomed prey, *Le Torrington* cruised for eight more days in the seas bounded on three sides by Sardinia, the Balearics and the coast of North Africa. There were three sightings of distant sails and Philippe ordered a pursuit of one of them, but this was abandoned after an hour when it became clear that the chase was faster and would comfortably reach the safety of Port Mahon on Minorca. Perhaps word of a Barbary corsair operating in those waters was keeping many cargoes in port until the threat had passed. Perhaps the depredations of Frank Parmentier's *Forbin* and Philippe's own command were achieving the same end. In any event, there was no opportunity to secure another prize, so Philippe was unable to pursue his notion of displaying his confidence in de la Porte by putting the young man in charge of a prize crew and giving him his first command. He made a point on several occasions of talking to de la Porte, both when the *aspirant* was on watch and at dinner. But questions were met with responses of one sentence at most, and praise for de la Porte's record-keeping in his journal was greeted with a blank, almost hostile expression. It was probably academic, Philippe thought. They would soon return to Toulon, where he would ensure the lad got some leave. A bout between a whore's thighs, or else several bottles of wine in a quayside tavern, should set him to rights. There might even be time for him to visit his family, who hailed from Avignon – not that great a journey from Toulon.

Three bells of the morning watch were rung. Philippe was in his cabin finishing a light *petit déjeuner* of eggs and coffee, writing up his own journal and signing off various manifests presented to him by Loison, the urbane steward of *Le Torrington*. Malhuret had the watch. It promised to be a beautiful day, a moderate and steady south-westerly breeze bearing the ship toward Toulon. Perhaps they would find the fleet there if Admiral Martin had finally got it out of the Bay of Gourjean. If so, and if the reinforcements that had been fitting out in Toulon were finally ready, perhaps they could venture out in full strength at last, give battle to the British, defeat them and liberate Corsica. In that case, perhaps there would be an opportunity for him to go ashore, to return to Ghineparu, to reunite with Carla Leandri.

He chided himself. It was all fantasy, the notion that they could defeat Lord Hood's dread sea-legion, that France could retake Corsica, that he would ever see Carla again. Pure fantasy—

There was a faint knock on his cabin door.

'Come.'

The door opened slowly. It was de la Porte, his face even paler than usual. His eyes were wide and staring, but he avoided Philippe's gaze.

'Aspirant. Do you have a report? What is it you wish to say?'

'Malta,' said de la Porte. 'About Malta.'

No coming to attention to address his captain, no salute, no 'sir', no 'Citizen Captain', no mark of respect at all. But the lad was clearly disturbed in some way. Philippe would let it pass for now.

'What about Malta, Aspirant?'

'What happened in Malta. What I did. What I didn't do. What you saw.'

De la Porte was speaking much more rapidly than usual, the words spilling out of him. Still he did not look directly at his captain.'

'I consider the matter closed, Citizen de la Porte. I considered it closed the moment after it happened. Every man makes mistakes. Every man should have a chance to make amends.'

This time, the youth did not reply.

'Is that what has been concerning you, Aspirant? Is that what—'

'Liar.'

The word was spoken under de la Porte's breath, so quietly and indistinctly that Philippe barely made it out.

'*What?* What did you say to me, Aspirant? What did you call me?'

De la Porte changed. His cheeks coloured, his lips tightened into a snarl of contempt.

'I said you are a liar. You're the one – the one who started the whispering among the men. The one who told them all what I did. How I failed. That I'm a coward. *You.*'

De la Porte drew a knife. Philippe glanced around for his pistols and sword, but they lay out of reach on his sea-bed. He could call out, but de la Porte would have the knife at his throat or through his heart before any help could come.

He tried to keep his voice low and calm.

'I did not, Thibaud. No man did. No others on the ship know what happened that day.'

'*More lies!* I see them. I see their eyes. I see their contempt. They know, all of them know, that I am a coward. The first coward among the de la Portes! And it's because of you! *You!*'

'We all falter in battle, Thibaud. When I was at the siege of Charleston—'

'Spare me stories from your past, Kermorvant! America? Russia? Are you French at all? How can you – *you* – be commanding a ship for the Republic?' He jabbed the knife toward Philippe, waving it threateningly before his captain's eyes. 'That's it! That's the truth! That's why you told on me! You're an enemy of France! I'll redeem myself by killing a traitor. I'll be a hero of the Republic despite Malta! I'll be worthy of the name de la Porte despite all!'

'Thibaud, I—'

'Good morning, Citizen Captain, I trust—'

The door opposite Philippe and behind de la Porte was open, and Courtois stood framed in it, as still as a statue as his eyes tried to make sense of the impossible spectacle before him.

'Sir?'

De la Porte cried out then turned and charged at Courtois, stabbing him in the chest before running through the door and out into the deck beyond. Philippe ran to his fallen servant, but de la Porte's knife still protruded from his heart and it was immediately obvious that the eager, attentive, good-natured young man who had been Henri Courtois was dead.

Philippe snatched for his sword and ran through the empty great cabin, then out onto the main gundeck, where the nearest men were stock still and silent, disbelieving of what they were seeing.

'Seize Aspirant de la Porte!' Philippe shouted. 'He's a murderer! Arrest him!'

A man pointed upward. Philippe jumped onto the companionway, striking his head on a beam but reaching the upper deck in three strides. Malhuret and Rampillon looked at him in astonishment.

'Sir, what—'

Philippe did not hear his first lieutenant complete the question, for he could see de la Porte. The murderous *aspirant* was midships, his foot already on the lowest ratline of the mainmast shrouds.

There were plenty of men on deck, including several of the nimblest topmen. But Philippe did not call out to them, did not give them an order to secure de la Porte and bring him back on deck. Instead, he left his sword with Rampillon and took hold of the ratlines himself, hauling himself outboard and then upward.

De la Porte had a head start and was well above him. But with Philippe below him and the astonished lookouts in the maintop above, he had nowhere to go. Launay already had two of his best Marine sharpshooters at the quarterdeck rail, taking aim at the deranged *aspirant* and awaiting the command to shoot from Philippe or Malhuret.

Philippe gave no order. De la Porte would have killed him if the unfortunate Courtois had not entered the cabin when he did, so it was the duty of the captain, and him alone, to bring the desperate episode to a conclusion.

De la Porte, clearly aware of the men above him, had reached the foot of the futtock shrouds. Philippe had only ever seen him get onto the top by way of the lubber's hole, but now the young man swung himself out and upward as confidently as any veteran *gabier* or *loup de mer*. No, Philippe realised – he was not aiming for the top but for the mainyard. Shunning the footrope, de la Porte inched his way outward along the yard itself, his captain following him. Philippe had always felt confident on the yards, shrouds and tops, immune from the aversion to heights that plagued some he had sailed with. It was a glorious day, the sea at its most radiant in the morning sunshine, the empty horizon visible all around *Le Torrington*, but Philippe's one focus was on the youth ahead of him. A youth – no, a killer – who had nowhere to go, no way out.

'Come down, Thibaud,' said Philippe as calmly as he could.

'To what? There'd only be a firing squad or the guillotine for me.'

Tears were soaking the youth's cheeks.

'Perhaps not. I'd testify you were gripped by a madness—'

'*Madness?* The only madness was my parents begetting me – my being born into a family with the name I bear when I've proved to be so unworthy of it. And now I'm a coward and a murderer. That's the only testimony you can give, Captain, isn't it? The only testimony. The only truth. The truth that will destroy my family. My poor sisters – my poor mother—'

Philippe could make no meaningful reply. He looked down and saw the men, seeming so very tiny, standing on the deck. They were all looking upward, their heavy silence broken only by the occasional murmur, the movement of the sails and shrouds in the wind, the gentle sea breaking over the bow. Launay's Marines still had their muskets trained on the yard, awaiting the order. All of the officers of *Le Torrington* were on the quarterdeck now, regardless of whether they were on watch or not. Even the young ship's surgeon, Saint-Cloud, was there, probably anticipating a body plunging from the yard to the deck.

Philippe leaned forward and stretched out his arm.

'Take my hand, Thibaud. Come down. All can be managed. All can be made better.'

'Another lie, Lord Vicomte. There is only one way this ends.' De la Porte looked down at the deck and at the sea far below him. 'Tell my family I faced death as a brave man would.'

He released his grip on the mainyard and sat upright. For a moment he remained stationary as though somehow fastened to the timber. Then he toppled to his left. Philippe made one last lunge to try and grab hold of his hand but almost lost his own grip on the yard, felt himself losing balance, and instinctively hugged the yard like a lover. As he did so he saw Thibaud de la Porte fall, strike and shatter the starboard rail, then plummet into the sea.

Even if he had survived the impact with the ship's side, the young *aspirant*'s back was surely broken. Even if it was not, Philippe recalled from *Le Torrington*'s long days at anchor in the balmy Bay of Gourjean that Thibaud de la Porte could not swim.

It was over.

CHAPTER THIRTY-TWO

Le Torrington returned to Toulon in triumph. She came into the outer Rade, the commodious outer harbour, from the southeast, saluting Fort Balaguier to port and the so-called Great Tower, the former Tour Royale, to starboard. Men aboard the ships at anchor in the outer and inner harbours, including Frank Parmentier's *Forbin*, manned the sides and cheered enthusiastically. A band ashore played endless verses of '*La Marseillaise*'. Word of Philippe's victory over *San Giacomo* had reached Toulon several days before, thanks to a meeting with a Marseille sloop that agreed to carry *Le Torrington*'s despatches back to France. The presence in the harbour of the Levant prize, the *Earl of Carbery*, provided even more proof of the success of *Le Torrington*'s cruise. Thus far in the war the men of France's Marine Nationale had precious few victories to celebrate, so Philippe and his crew were feted with an enthusiasm out of all proportion to their achievements.

Toulon, France's naval depot on the Mediterranean, had all the characteristics of dockyards the world over: quays, building slips, cranes, storehouses, magazines, a ropery, offices, boats, and vessels in every state of construction, repair and disrepair. The sounds, too, were familiar, with sawing, hammering, shouting ever present from dawn to dusk. Within the inner Rade, Toulon possessed two small artificial harbours formed by breakwaters, the Old Harbour to the east with the Hotel de Ville front and centre of the buildings that fronted the sea, and the New Harbour to the west. Behind the town to the north-east, hills rose to an impressive height. The town stood upon the eastern arm of the inner Rade, most of which, along with most of the ships, lay to the west. It resembled Brest, which Philippe had come to know well in the previous year, in that it had all the paraphernalia of a dockyard but differed markedly from it in other ways. The Rade of Brest was larger, more difficult of navigation but more easily defended, than the inner and outer Rades at Toulon. But Brest lay at the western tip of Brittany, a poor hinterland with little timber and desperately long and precarious roads for naval supplies to traverse, meaning that Brest relied overwhelmingly on supply by sea. Toulon, though, lay on the coast of Provence, considerably more prosperous than poor Brittany and with easy communications to some of France's greatest cities – Lyon, Montpelier, and above all Marseille, one of the Republic's mightiest and wealthiest ports, no more than a day's ride away on a decent horse.

For all that, there was one marked difference between Brest and Toulon at the end of Year II of the Republic, the season that the enemies of France would have called the late summer of 1794. As *Le Torrington* moved toward her anchorage in the inner Rade, almost due west of the town and dockyard, Philippe could once again see clearly the evidence of the previous year's extraordinary events, especially the terrible siege when the armies of the Republic retook Toulon from the royalists who had controlled it for much of the year, inviting in the British and Spanish to support their cause. There were still dozens of roofless buildings, mere shells with scorched walls, forts with ramparts pockmarked by cannonballs, ruinous batteries and the remains of the siegeworks that had ringed the town. It was a sobering sight, a reminder of how close the Republic had come to destruction and of the fragility of its hold over France.

Le Torrington took in sail and dropped anchor. Philippe gave orders for the longboat to be readied to carry him ashore, where he expected to report to the senior official of the dockyard. But before the boat was in the water, Vidos pointed out a pinnace threading its way between the ships at anchor. It was making directly for Philippe's ship, and its passenger was a very familiar and welcome sight.

It was Frank Parmentier.

The captain of the *Forbin* was piped aboard. Philippe led his friend down to his cabin, where they embraced and raised a glass to celebrate their respective triumphs. But Philippe noticed that Frank was more reserved than usual.

'You're not to report ashore,' said Parmentier with a pained expression. 'You're to report to *Forbin*.'

'Your ship? Why? Are you an admiral now, Frank?'

'No, but I'm a flag captain, would you believe it? There are Seventy-Fours and Sixties in the Rades, but no, he has to hoist his flag in *Forbin*. Fidelin, that is. Martin sent him overland to take command of the squadron at Toulon, now there are so many more ships here that are ready for sea. No idea why, considering the Committee of Safety sent down a *représentant en mission* to oversee all naval matters in Toulon. You're to meet both of them, Phil – Fidelin and this *représentant*, who hadn't come aboard yet when I disembarked to come here. But Fidelin gave orders that you were to report at once to *Forbin*. I could have sent a lieutenant or an *aspirant* with the message, but I wanted a chance to toast your success.'

Fidelin, of all men! A *représentant en mission*, too. Philippe had encountered two of them in the previous year when his first French command, *Le Zephyr*, was involved in operations off Brittany and the western shores of France. Members of the National Convention and the Committee of Public Safety, *représentants en mission* were sent out into the far-flung regions of France to enforce the will of the Republic, a task that translated primarily as repressing dissent and royalist rebellion. They were feared, often hated, and their rule could be brutal and arbitrary. Philippe had witnessed one of the most extreme manifestations of their methods at Nantes, when he watched adherents of the old, proscribed religion – monks, nuns, priests and the like – suffer the justice of the Republic in mass drownings in the River

Loire. 'Revolutionary marriages' in 'the national bathtub', the *représentant* responsible for the display had called the *noyades*. Philippe thought it mass murder, pure and simple, a mockery of the ideals he thought he was fighting for and for which his father had suffered long years of exile.

Philippe followed Frank Parmentier down into *Forbin*'s longboat with a mounting sense of trepidation.

Forbin lay just off the old harbour, the command flag of Rear-Admiral Sebastien Fidelin flying from the mizzen. Philippe and Frank Parmentier were piped aboard and went down at once to what was normally Frank's cabin. Now, though, and despite being less roomy than Philippe's quarters on *Le Torrington*, it had been commandeered by Fidelin and three clerks, whom the rear-admiral dismissed as the two *capitaines de frégate* entered.

'Parmentier. Kermorvant. Good. About time.' They saluted. Fidelin did not beckon them to sit. 'Not that you're the last. We still await the presence of the high envoy of the Republic, the *représentant en mission* himself. But your lookout, Captain Parmentier, informs me that the eminent personage was seen just now embarking into a pinnace in the new harbour.'

Fidelin fell silent, turning his attention to a paper on his table – Frank Parmentier's table, of course, but the admiral showed no sign of vacating it. For perhaps three or four minutes, the three men waited in awkward silence. Then they heard the familiar sound of a *sifflet* piping a salute to a dignitary coming aboard. Loud steps on the companionway heralded the descent of the dignitary from the upper deck. A Marine guard opened the cabin door and brought his musket crisply to attention.

'Sorry, Admiral, I was detailed at the arsenal,' said the *représentant*. 'Ordnance. Fucking nightmare, every time. You'll be Parmentier. Good command, this. Trim. Good crew, too, by the looks of them. And so many prizes, eh! You're a lucky bugger, Captain Parmentier. Ah, Kermorvant. Must be the first time I've seen you in sunshine. Makes a change from all that fucking Breton rain up in Brest, eh?'

The *représentant* pulled up a chair on the same side of the table as Fidelin, who was forced to move slightly to the right. The fastidious admiral seemed startled at the coarseness and levity of his guest, but he did his utmost to appear unfazed. The envoy of the National Convention exuded an air of blunt jollity that Philippe knew to be deceptive. For unlike Admiral Fidelin and Frank Parmentier, Philippe knew Jeanbon Saint-André of old. They had encountered each other in the previous year at Brest during one of the *représentant*'s earlier postings. It was largely due to this man that Philippe Kermorvant, a man with such a unique history, a member of a class that the leaders of the Republic despised and guillotined in their thousands, a man whom some regarded as not even a true Frenchman – how Philippe Kermorvant had obtained a commission as a *capitaine de frégate* in the Marine Nationale of the French Republic.

'Right, let's get down to business, shall we?' said Jeanbon Saint-André.

CHAPTER THIRTY-THREE

Saint-André was the man in command, despite being in the same cabin as the captain of *Forbin* and the man who flew his admiral's flag from her. But like Fidelin, the *représentant en mission* did not beckon the two captains to sit.

'So, Captain Kermorvant,' said Saint-André, 'we await your journal, of course, and the journals of your other officers. But based on your letters, there are matters that clearly demand investigation.'

'I am prepared to answer whatever questions you have, citizen. And yours, Admiral Fidelin.'

'You'd better be, Citizen Captain,' said Fidelin. 'Now, this Neapolitan ship you took on. A duel? Really? Under the noses of the Knights of Malta? Do you know how many letters of protest they've had in Paris from the grand master?'

'My crew and I respected Maltese neutrality at all times, citizen. So, to be fair to him, did Captain Guidici of the *San Giacomo*. That was why we fought outside the waters claimed by the knights. Besides, the whole matter was arranged in the house and under the auspices of one of the most senior officers of the Order, Baron von Flachslanden, the turcopilier. So I imagine any protests from the grand master will merely be ploys to save face with the King of Naples, who has lost one of his few large ships.'

'Expert on the motives of princes are we now, Kermorvant?' snapped Saint-André. 'Damn me, well there's a thing.'

'Why were you in Malta at all, Captain?' demanded Fidelin levelly.

'I explained in my letters, sir. It was the nearest port where we could expect to be able to repair our prize—'

'So you risked an incident with a neutral power out of simple avarice, Captain. Your wish to preserve your prize.'

'With respect, Admiral – yes, it was a valuable prize. I did not have my own gain in mind but that of the Republic. An English Levanter, sir. My understanding is that very few of them have been taken since the beginning of the war simply because there are very few of them actually trading. Like all nations, England prefers to send valuable cargoes in neutral hulls with papers that are often false. To come across one flying her real colours was an opportunity that had to be taken.'

'I'm well aware of how all nations twist the laws of neutrality, Captain Kermorvant.'

'Our own included,' said Saint-André, smirking to himself. Fidelin ignored the remark.

'The grand master demands punishment for you, Captain Kermorvant. Preferably the guillotine, but failing that I think the Most Eminent and Supreme Grand Master will accept your dismissal from the Marine Nationale.'

Philippe felt himself sway. For a moment, the cabin and the faces before him seemed to spin crazily. He saw Frank Parmentier's look of horror and pity.

Execution? Dismissal? But what had he done wrong?

'Admiral,' he said, 'if I may—'

'Enough of this fucking farce,' snarled Saint-André, leaning forward and putting his arms on the table. 'No disrespect intended, Fidelin, but *seriously*? Kermorvant won a battle. He destroyed one of Naples' biggest warships. And you're proposing we kick him out of the navy or even cut off his head because of a protest from the *Knights of fucking Malta*? "Most Eminent and Supreme Grand Master", my arse. De Rohan's as French as any of us in this cabin, but he's a foaming-at-the-mouth swivel-eyed royalist, like all the French knights out there. Gather you encountered a brace of them, eh, Kermorvant? You should have had a portable guillotine on your ship and lopped the heads off the whole fucking lot.'

Fidelin's face was contorted with conflicting emotions. It was obvious that he wanted to argue the point with Saint-André, but the rear-admiral was too capable and intelligent a man to perish in a lost cause. He knew, just as Frank Parmentier and Philippe Kermorvant did, that at that moment in the cabin of the frigate *Forbin* in the inner Rade of Toulon, the *représentant en mission* of the National Convention and the Committee of Public Safety held a monopoly of power. In that place and in that moment he was more of an absolute monarch than any of the Bourbon kings had ever been.

'As you wish, citizen,' said Fidelin with bad grace.

'But then there's the other matter, Kermorvant,' said Saint-André. 'De la Porte. Your letters are rather vague on the subject. An accidental fall from the mainyard? Just why would an *aspirant* be out on the mainyard, Captain?'

This was uncomfortable ground, but Philippe tried to keep his voice level.

'Citizen de la Porte was an eager young man who wished to experience every aspect of the seaman's trade at first hand, citizen.'

'So, he has his first stab at hauling himself along a yardarm weeks into your voyage? Don't know about any of you three fine officers, but it was one of the first things I did when I first went to sea, and I'd have been half de la Porte's age at the time.' Philippe recalled that Saint-André had spent many years in the merchant service, rising to command ships, and it was this experience that had qualified him to become the Committee of Public Safety's expert on all maritime matters. This was said to be no great accolade, for it was widely believed that most of those who served on the Committee had never seen the sea. It was even said that one or two had no idea what a ship looked like. 'No, it won't hold, Captain. Colonel de la Porte is berating Minister Dalbarade – it seems the news has

258

sent the boy's mother half mad, but the minister reckons the esteemed colonel is more concerned that his precious son just fell off the fucking yardarm and didn't die gloriously in battle, as all the de la Portes are meant to.' Saint-André sighed. 'So all this, Captain, means it's only a matter of time before Minister Dalbarade berates me, so I might as well berate you now and save myself time later. Y'see, Kermorvant, yours wasn't the only letter that came home on the *Acanthe*.'

Philippe had been foolish to believe that the literate men of *Le Torrington*, a small minority but one that comprised almost all the officers, would all report de la Porte's death as an accident. He could hardly order them to do so, although he had suggested discretion in a meeting of the ship's *équipage* convened hastily after the *aspirant*'s death. Somehow, one of the more accurate and explicit accounts must have reached the *représentant en mission*.

'We are waiting for your account, Citizen Captain,' said Fidelin. 'Your true account.'

Philippe swallowed and clenched his fists. He knew he was not at fault for de la Porte's death. Indeed, but for the timely but unfortunate arrival of Courtois it was likely that Philippe himself would have died at de la Porte's hands. It might incur the rage of Colonel de la Porte, but the truth had to be told. The true account as Fidelin demanded, then.

'He was a coward, citizen. If his mother is mad now, then perhaps madness runs in the family. He turned and ran from a fight ashore in Malta where the odds might otherwise have been in our favour. I witnessed it, and he got it into his head that I told the entire crew what he had done. He tried to kill me, but we were disturbed by my servant, who he killed instead. Then he went up to the mainyard and flung himself from it. So a coward, a murderer and a suicide, citizen.'

Fidelin raised an eyebrow, but Saint-André said neutrally, 'So I'm supposed to tell that to Colonel de la Porte, am I?'

'It is the truth, citizen.'

'I don't doubt it.' Saint-André shook his head. 'Very well, Captain, I will somehow mollify Minister Dalbarade who will then somehow have to mollify Colonel de la Porte and his wife. So with that, citizens, are we done here? I have a hundred things to do, and must be back ashore by the end of First Dog.'

'Wait,' said Fidelin. 'You said there was a fight ashore in Malta? A fight not mentioned in your account of your doings there, Captain Kermorvant. Surely, Citizen Saint-André, we must investigate if this, too, endangered the neutrality of the knights and France's diplomacy with them?'

'Really, Admiral?' Saint-André was clearly exasperated.

'Surely, Admiral, you don't want us talking of Malta?' said Frank Parmentier with equal measures of exasperation, devilment and aggression.

Fidelin said nothing, but Saint-André was intrigued. 'And why wouldn't Admiral Fidelin want us to talk about Malta, Captain Parmentier?'

'It's nothing, citizens,' said Philippe, who knew what was in Frank's mind but thought it an inappropriate occasion to raise the matter. 'As was the fight involving Aspirant de la Porte. I had taken the three *aspirants* ashore to learn something of the city. We were attacked by two of the younger Knights of Malta – two Frenchmen. Men of a violent royalist temper. When de la Porte ran, the other two *aspirants* and I defended ourselves. It lasted no more than a minute or two, then it was halted by the arrival of one of the senior officers of the Order, the turcopilier whom I named previously.'

'Trivial indeed,' said Saint-André. 'Enough.'

He rose from his chair, but Frank Parmentier straightened.

'Forgive me, Citizen Saint-André, but I must make a denunciation.'

'*No*, Frank!' whispered Philippe urgently, but the captain of *Forbin* was set on his course.

'You'll know, citizen, that for months now there's been talk that the English have an agent in our fleet.'

'Only one?' asked Saint-André mischievously.

Fidelin shifted in his chair. 'I have had my suspicions,' he said. 'I discussed them with Admiral Martin, but he took the matter no further.'

'Your suspect, Admiral?'

'Captain Philippe Kermorvant, here. The Vicomte de Saint-Victor. Son of an English mother. Cousin to a known English spymaster, Lord Wilden. Brother of a condemned and executed traitor to the Republic.'

'Also the son of Verité,' said Saint-André. 'A man who chose to offer his services to the Republic at a time when he knew a man with his birth, title and connections might be sending himself to the guillotine. A man who spent weeks on an English prison hulk, escaped, had another opportunity to go anywhere else in the world, but chose once again to return to France to serve the cause of liberty.'

'But surely, citizen, this man's birth – he is an *aristo*, a foreigner, half-English—'

'Forgive me, Admiral,' said Saint-André, 'but I don't think the armigerous family of Fidelin were exactly peasants, were they? Not *sans-culottes*, that's for certain.'

Philippe coughed.

'Quite so, Citizen Saint-André. And yes, Admiral, my mother was English, and she taught me many English expressions that have no equivalent in French. One of them was "those who live in glass houses shouldn't throw stones".'

'Stones? Glass houses?' snorted Fidelin. 'What lunacy is this, other than proof that the English and their damn incomprehensible language are far beyond the understanding of all decent civilised men?'

'If I may, citizens?' said Frank Parmentier with a politeness belied by his angry expression.

'Speak, Captain,' said Saint-André.

'Citizen, Captain Kermorvant and I believe we know the identity of the English spy in the fleet. In the name of the Republic, one and indivisible, I denounce Rear-Admiral Sebastien Fidelin.'

CHAPTER THIRTY-FOUR

There was a moment, one single moment, of utter silence in the captain's cabin of *Forbin*. The constant sounds of the men on deck and on the boats in the harbour, of the hull, of the waves, of the wind and the seabirds – for all four men, there was nothing but the silence of the tomb.

'That,' said Rear-Admiral Fidelin at last, his usually impassive features taut with fury, 'is absurd. Indeed, it is mutiny. It is treason! Marines!' Looking bewildered, the two guards from the other side of the door entered the cabin in response to the admiral's cry. 'Arrest Captains Parmentier and Kermorvant! Confine them—'

'No,' said Jeanbon Saint-André.

The Marines looked at the *représentant en mission*, then back to the admiral, then back to Saint-André once again.

'I command at sea,' said Fidelin, his voice rising. 'I command this squadron, citizen, and this is a matter of naval discipline.'

'Fuck that,' said Saint-André. 'You can argue respective jurisdictions all the way to the Committee of Public Safety and back, Admiral, by which time we'll all be white haired and only able to eat through straws. Pointless anyway, because they'll take my side and you know it. Stand down, Marines.'

Open-mouthed, Fidelin gaped at Saint-André. But he made no reply other than to give a slight nod to the guards, who returned to their previous station.

'All right then, Captain Parmentier,' said Saint-André, 'let's hear it. Let's hear your evidence that Admiral Fidelin, here, is an English spy. And it had better be good, else I'll second the charge of mutiny and call the guards back in.'

'Citizen,' said Parmentier with a breezy confidence that belied his situation, 'it is Captain Kermorvant who should give you the first piece of the puzzle. He was the man who discovered it. I only became aware of his suspicions when he wrote to me from Malta, where his ship then was.'

'Come on then, Kermorvant, speak up!'

Philippe felt even more uncomfortable than he had done on the disastrous occasion when he was reprimanded by the formidable Empress Catherine herself. Still, Frank Parmentier had committed the two of them to the charge, and there was nothing for it but to gallop headlong for the enemy guns and face certain death.

'Citizen Saint-André, I have in my cabin sworn depositions from my three *aspirants* aboard *Le Torrington*, including the deceased Aspirant de la Porte, as well as from Citizen Paul-Baptiste Allard, consul of the Republic on the island of Malta, that the cathedral of Saint John in the city of Valletta on that island contains the grave of one Joseph Fidelin, a Knight of Malta, deceased in December 1786. We saw it with our own eyes, citizen, as may any man who visits that place. So yes, I mentioned this to Captain Parmentier in a letter I wrote before we sailed. He is a man of the Pas-de-Calais, as are you, Citizen Admiral, are you not? Further enquiries by both Captain Parmentier and myself have established that the Joseph Fidelin buried on Malta was your older brother, and a Knight of the Order of Saint John. His devotion to the Roman faith and the old monarchy was a byword in Malta and Saint-Omer, your hometown. Is that not the case, Citizen Admiral?'

'This is preposterous, Citizen Saint-André!' blustered Fidelin. 'I protest! This is against all justice!'

Republican justice has sent many Frenchmen and women to the guillotine on less evidence, thought Philippe, but he held his tongue.

264

'Really, Admiral?' said Saint-André. 'Well, I'll be the judge of that, shall I? For now, I'd like to hear more about your relationship with your brother. Close, were you? Held beliefs in common, did you?'

'What was it the book of the old superstition said?' snapped Fidelin. '"Am I my brother's keeper?"'

Fidelin was furious, but Saint-André remained calm and even a little amused.

'As I recall the passage, Admiral, Cain did not deny having a brother at all.'

'I have not denied it! I have never denied it! But Joseph and I fell out many years ago – he joined the Knights of Saint John, and I didn't see him for twenty years before his death! He was always attracted to the old idolatry. We had nothing in common. Surely, citizen, you can see that this is nothing but the desperation of that man, Kermorvant, the bearer of a noble title, half English, the cousin of a known English spymaster!'

Saint-André drummed his fingers on the table.

'So, let me see if I understand the case,' said the *représentant en mission*. 'You, Admiral Fidelin, deny the accusation of Captains Kermorvant and Parmentier, which it seems to me is based on nothing firmer than suspicions born of knowing who your brother was and what he believed. Whereas your denunciation of Captain Kermorvant is based on the infinitely stronger evidence of the identities of his mother and cousin and what *they* believe. You're right of course, Admiral, none of us are our brother's keepers, but neither are we our mother's nor our cousin's.'

'But, citizen—'

Saint-André raised his hand impatiently.

'The matter is closed, Admiral Fidelin.' He turned to the two frigate captains. 'Thank you, citizens, that will be all.'

Philippe and Frank Parmentier came to attention, turned, and left the cabin, glancing at each other in astonishment as they did so. Thus they did not hear Citizen Jeanbon Saint-André, *représentant en mission*, cite the authority of the people of France as manifested in the National Convention and the Committee of Public Safety as his justification for relieving Rear-Admiral Sebastien Fidelin of his command. Nor did they hear Saint-André go on to say that, while giving no credence whatsoever to the accusation brought against him by the two captains, in his opinion Fidelin would be much better suited to the command of a proposed expedition to the Caribbean, where it would aim to retake Martinique and bolster the defences of Guadeloupe. This, with its ample opportunities to garner victories and glory, would be a much worthier posting for him than remaining admiral of a squadron that would remain harbour-bound for the foreseeable future and which he, Jeanbon Saint-André, could order perfectly well while it was.

Saint-André did not give voice to his thoughts that the Caribbean was too remote and strategically insignificant for it to matter if an admiral was secretly in the pay of the enemy, while it was also a notoriously sickly station where admirals had an unfortunate habit of dying after only a few months from a bewildering variety of fevers.

–

Shepherds pursued nymphs across fields strewn with gold in a delightful Arcadian utopia. A string quartet played a delicate, heavenly harmony.

Then, somehow, the sky darkened and when Lord Wilden and his companion looked down again, the entire scene had changed. The shepherds had caught the nymphs and were rutting them energetically. The string quartet had vanished, its place taken by cloven-hooved bagpipers who belched forth a discordant rendition of 'God Save the King'.

No, he cried. No. *No* –

His companion faded away –

A sharp dig in the ribs from his neighbour to the left, Lord Eskdalemuir, woke Wilden.

'Damn it, Ned, you're starting to snore!'

Wilden murmured an apology, then tried to make sense of the scene around him. He was in an ancient oblong chamber, the walls covered in thick and heavy tapestries illustrating England's defeat of the Spanish Armada. At one end stood an elegant chair beneath a canopy of crimson velvet, and on this, clad in his robes of black and gold, sat the refined but remarkably dull and pompous figure of the Lord Chancellor of Great Britain. He, too, seemed bored beyond measure with the seemingly interminable speech of the peer whose tedious rhetoric had pushed Wilden into the world of dreams. His Grace, the Duke of Bedford, seemed no nearer his conclusion, and Wilden stifled a yawn. To deliver such a dull speech upon any subject was unforgivable, but Bedford was moving a resolution in favour of ending the war with France. The motion was rightly doomed to an embarrassingly heavy defeat, but a little more passion from its promoter in the Lords might have swayed one or two of the weaker-minded or more senile peers. Bedford, a black-haired fellow of about Wilden's own age, showed rather more enthusiasm on the racecourse – the infernal man's horses had won the Derby three times, after all – and in the bedchamber, where his own grandmother had arranged for him a *ménage à trois* with Lord and Lady Maynard. Strange family, the Russells of Bedford, mused Wilden, strangest of all because they were staunch Whigs. He found it incomprehensible that any family of noble birth and ancient title should throw in their lot with Charles James Fox and his guillotine-envious acolytes, but the Russells had been contrary for countless generations. Whenever a false prophet arose shitting forth the usual manure about 'the people' and 'freedom', a Russell would be found alongside him. In Wilden's day the false prophet was undoubtedly the diabolical Charles James Fox, the Whig leader, and true to his bloodline there was His Grace of Bedford, the puppy sniffing the arse of the leader of the pack.

Wilden would not speak in the debate; he almost never spoke in the House. The government had any number of far more proficient orators, although the speeches of several of them were founded upon briefing notes provided by Wilden. It also had perfectly capable spokesmen in the House, notably the foreign secretary, Lord Grenville, who could clearly barely restrain his eagerness to rise and eviscerate Bedford's fatuous arguments in favour of that nonsensical notion, immediate peace with France. But it was good for Wilden to put in an appearance in the House from time to time, if only to remind others of his continuing existence. Johnny Eskdalemuir, an old acquaintance from his schooldays, was relieved to see with his own eyes proof that Ned Wilden was not dead, this rumour reportedly being rife in the more outlying parts of the kingdom.

Bedford droned on. Peace with France, indeed. Wilden was seeking the same end, albeit rather more purposefully than His Grace. There would only be peace when the republican atheistical regime in Paris was brought down, the ringleaders executed on their own infernal beheading machine and the rightful king of France restored. Wilden was working on several promising schemes to that end. He talked regularly with those who could aid him in achieving his objective, and his conversations with Vorontsov, the Russian ambassador, were particularly productive in that respect. Only weeks before, Wilden had been standing on the deck of Admiral Duncan's flagship *Venerable*, the slight lord of the Admiralty alongside the towering white-haired commander-in-chief of the North Sea Fleet as they watched a squadron of warships enter the Thames, saluting *Venerable* as she lay at anchor at the Buoy of the Nore. The incoming ships flew a saltire with a diagonal blue cross on a white ground, an inverted mirror image of the flag of Duncan's native Scotland. This, at last, was the Russian squadron sent by the Empress Catherine to supplement King George's Royal Navy. Duncan had commented caustically on the general filthiness and slovenly sailing of the Russian ships, but none of that mattered a jot to Wilden. Their presence in British waters was proof that Wilden's vision of peace with France was more realistic and attainable than the happy but unachievable fantasy being peddled by the likes of the Duke of Bedford.

The arrival of the Russians was not the only consequence of Wilden's amiable conversations with Count Vorontsov. For instance, there was also the matter of interest to Wilden in Corsica, where again Vorontsov had been true to his word. What the upshot would be Wilden could not know, but in the dream of the nymphs and the shepherds the man standing alongside him had been Philippe Kermorvant, finally loyal to his mother's British homeland rather than his father's atheistic, regicidal republic, bound in eternal gratitude to his cousin, the Lord of the Admiralty.

Wilden had played his part. Now Philippe had to grasp the opportunity being presented to him.

–

Frank Parmentier remained on *Forbin* to oversee the disembarkation of the admiral, his retinue and his luggage. Philippe considered returning to *Le Torrington* but knew there would be little point in his being aboard her. He had reported to the senior authority in the dockyard, namely Saint-André, his paperwork was complete and in order, his lieutenants had the tedious business of managing the ship's transition from sea to harbour well in hand even before Philippe left for *Forbin*. He needed to clear his head after the troubling confrontation with Fidelin, so he got the boat crew to take him to one of the flights of stairs set into the quays of the inner harbour, then ordering the boat to return to *Le Torrington* to deliver a verbal message to Malhuret informing the lieutenant of his captain's movements.

From the harbour Philippe made his way past the old Minimes' monastery, recently taken over by the navy, to the Porte d'Italie, the eastern gate through the defences of Toulon. This had been hammered by the guns of the Republic and was undergoing repairs. Philippe walked down to the River

Eygoutier, where he sat on a large stone by the water's edge, looked out toward the ships at anchor in the harbour.

Philippe thought on all that had happened that day and in the previous weeks. He was uncomfortably aware that it could all have ended so very differently. Only the sheer chance of seeing a familiar name in an unexpected place, on a grave-slab in a church in a different land, had probably saved Philippe from a charge of spying for the English. If it had not been brought by Fidelin this time, though, there was every chance that it would be at some other time in the future. Philippe had narrowly escaped the guillotine more than once since coming to France, but he knew there would always be men who would suspect him, who would murmur about him not being a true Frenchman. His being the son of Verité would not always be a mark in his favour. The fall of Robespierre signalled the decline of the Jacobins, who had drawn so much of their inspiration from the writings of the previous Vicomte de Saint-Victor, and their replacement by men of less radical opinions. His mother's nationality could not be denied, nor could the profession of his cousin, who had directly offered Philippe the chance to change sides and take the part of Britain and its French royalist puppets, men like Maestracci, who he had seen die at the hands of Carla Leandri. Saint-André and his colleagues and superiors in Paris did not know that and there was no proof of the offer; unless, that is, Edward, Lord Wilden, that enigma who was so utterly unlike him despite their shared blood, decided it suited his purpose to throw his cousin to the wolves. Philippe was sure he would never betray his country, the republican ideal that his father had believed in so passionately and which he, Philippe, had elected to serve at a time when sane men, and men of his rank above all, were fleeing France in their hundreds every minute of every day. But no matter how strongly he felt all of that, no matter how successful he was in commands like *Le Torrington*, there would always be whispers.

Philippe Kermorvant always seemed to be arriving at cross-roads, the right direction to take never perfectly clear at any of them. Here he was again with no sign to show the way.

After a few more minutes of fruitless contemplation, he stood and made his way back into the fortified town. He would return to his ship shortly, but before he did so he decided to pay a brief visit to the lodging house where he had taken a room for the duration of his time in Toulon and with *Le Torrington*. He had spent barely a handful of nights there, but he needed to check that his landlady had not slyly let it to another, that she knew he had returned and would be using the room again, and to check whether any mail had come for him. It was unlikely as he had given the address to virtually no one, the principal exception being his erstwhile sister-in-law, Leonore, far away in Brittany. As he approached the nondescript tenement in one of the less war-scarred parts of the town, he hoped there might be a letter or two from her. But there was none. Disappointed but not surprised, he went up to his room, unlocked it, and found it exactly as he had left it. The shutters had probably not been opened since he went to sea. The bedding and his civilian clothes smelled musty. There was a shallow layer of dust on every surface.

A letter lay on the small, rickety table by the fireplace. Its presence was baffling. The landlady, a large woman with a wobbling gait, placed any mail for her lodgers on a small table in the entrance hall, three floors below, and that was where he had looked for any letters from his faraway home, the Chateau de Brechelean. How and why this one envelope had found its way into his room was a mystery.

Philippe picked it up. The wax seal was tight, with no obvious sign of having been opened. He opened the envelope, took out the note within, and recognised the handwriting at once. It was Carla's, no more than a brief note.

Captain. Lord Vicomte. Philippe.

I hope you still remember your old friend.

I send my congratulations on your great victory over the Neapolitan warship, the news of which has reached even the most obscure mountain fastnesses of Corsica. But this is not the reason why I write. Instead, I convey to you an item of news that you might find of interest, and leave it to you to decide whether or not you wish to take any notice of it.

The English lord it over Corsica, their redcoats strutting around Corte and Calvi, Paoli and Pozzo di Borgo their puppets, and my country acquires all the trappings of a kingdom. One proof of this is that diplomatic missions from other countries, none of them friendly to France, flock to present their credentials to King George's viceroy, the Scot Elliot. We have an ambassador from the Spanish and the Dutch and the Swedes, and now one has arrived very recently from Catherine, the Russian empress. The names of most of those in the mission will mean nothing to you, but I heard one name spoken, that of the envoy himself, and it is that intelligence which, I believe, will be of interest to you. The envoy's name is one Count V. Bulgakov.

CL

EPILOGUE

Vladimir Kyrilovich Bulgakov loved the smell of the Corsican forests. They had an aroma utterly unlike that of the endless legions of pine trees around his country estate in Siberia. Oak and chestnut rose above a carpet of fragrant bushes in temperatures that the churlish would say were merely warm but that Bulgakov, accustomed to a much colder northern climate, considered to be indisputably hot, even now as autumn began to give way to winter. In such conditions, he refused to be cooped up in the tiny house in Corte that had been allocated to him. Corte, a miniscule mountain village surrounded by ancient ramparts, pretending to be a capital city! How feeble its pretensions were to a man who knew every inch of Saint Petersburg, its salons and the grandeur of its palaces. Even Dresden was greater by far than Corte. Dear Mother of Heaven, it made even little Coburg seem metropolitan, even stately. But he would humour his hosts, for Bulgakov was desperate for those he now encountered every day to speak well of him. If they did then perhaps they would record a high opinion of him in letters back to their masters, and from them the reports of his good conduct might reach the banks of the Neva and the ears of the empress herself.

Even so, there were limits. Vladimir Kyrilovich considered himself an active man who enjoyed long, vigorous walks and rides. Here in a very different setting, where the climate was so temperate and the scenery so memorable, he saw ample reason to maintain his usual routine. So at least twice a week he set off from Corte shortly after dawn and went out onto the mountain paths, breathing the clear air, savouring the aroma of myrtle, drinking from sparkling streams, and returning invigorated around dusk.

King George's viceroy, Sir Gilbert Elliot, had advised Bulgakov against wandering out into the Corsican countryside. There were bandits everywhere in the hills, he explained. Bulgakov scoffed at the advice, which seemed womanly. He could ride for hundreds of miles through the Russian empire and not fear a soul, for no Russian peasant, no matter how desperate, would dare affront a man who by his dress and bearing was quite clearly a noble. Wild beasts were a different matter, of course, but Vladimir Kyrilovich had killed countless deer, wolves and wild boar in Russia and had no doubt he could do the same in Corsica. Reluctantly, though, he accepted Elliot's offer of two soldiers to guard him during his excursions. He understood. Elliot would not want to have to explain to William Pitt and the Empress Catherine how he had allowed the Russian ambassador to be slaughtered on some godforsaken mountainside in the arse end of a remote, poor and barren island.

The Imperial Russian ambassador to the viceregal court of His Britannic Majesty's Kingdom of Corsica.

How strange his title still sounded to Vladimir Kyrilovich Bulgakov. How unreal that he should be here on this great lump of barren rock in the Mediterranean and holding such a worthy office, albeit in a small insignificant backwater.

After all that had happened.

After all that he had done.

It had all been triggered by that unfortunate business with his sister and her child, the Frenchman's bastard. He had warned her, of course. As head of the family he had prohibited her sham marriage, forbidden her to see and fornicate with the Frenchman. Bulgakov insisted she should instead proceed with the marriage he had arranged for her with a much-respected, if admittedly much older, colonel of the Preobrazhensky Regiment. She had ignored him, found a tame priest to conduct

274

the wedding, and then continued to defy him by living in open whoredom with the Frenchman in Kronstadt and Petersburg. His good friend the Tsarevich Paul had urged him to let it pass, to shun her, to forget it as if his sister was dead; and for a time, the imperial heir's admonishments restrained him. But then the day came when he saw her on the Nevsky Prospect and followed her home. There had been vodka, too much vodka, and there had been his sword, too readily drawn.

He regretted what he did. He looked down at her corpse, at the body of the boy, his nephew, at his own bloodstained hands and clothes. He realised at once that his reputation was gone, that if he did not act quickly his life would be gone too. He went at once to the Tsarevich at the Pavlovsky Palace in Tsarskoye Selo and prostrated himself, abjectly begging forgiveness. He asked the prince to intercede for him with his mother, the empress, who was sure to be outraged. He escaped the city and went far to the east, beyond the Urals, back to his estate, where he had to explain his crime to his ancient mother and suffered her tears, rage and scorn for his murder of her daughter and grandson. He prayed much and spoke often with his chaplain, Father Grigori. He did penance for his mighty sin before the entire congregation in his village church, debasing himself before all those pungent peasants. He gave alms on a more generous scale than ever before in his life. He thought of entering a monastery, but that would have made matters awkward for his sons. Despite it all, Vladimir Kyrilovich Bulgakov remained convinced that he was damned for all eternity.

As it did unfailingly, time provided his path to redemption. His friends wrote from the imperial capital to tell him that the horror of his deed was no longer the talk of the salons at the Winter Palace. Word of new and ever more terrible evils came every day from France, and not even the all-seeing, all-remembering empress now mentioned Bulgakov or his unspeakable act. Proof of her indifference was the failure of troops bearing an arrest warrant to arrive at the gates of his estate. Instead, a letter came from the tsarevich, suggesting that Bulgakov could further redeem himself, perhaps even earn a return to court one day, by serving Russia in a foreign embassy. Diplomacy and exile from the motherland had never appealed, although several of his friends had taken that path in previous years and were now distinguished envoys of the empress in foreign courts. So he jumped at the proffered and unexpected opportunity and had found himself in Dresden, presenting his credentials to the elector, Frederick Augustus the Third. Dresden was a relative backwater and none there seemed to take the slightest notice of the Russian envoy, nor to enquire about his troubled history. He suspected the same would not have been true in Berlin, certainly not in Vienna where gossip was akin to a religion. So Vladimir Kyrilovich Bulgakov spent over a year in quiet and obscure exile, diligently reporting the uninteresting and utterly unimportant doings of the electoral court of Saxony to the empress's foreign minister, Count Osterman.

The one potential threat to his redemption – to his very life – was Philippe Kermorvant, his sister's so-called husband. He had heard from a naval friend that Kermorvant was swearing revenge, was vowing to hunt Bulgakov down and show him as little mercy as had been shown to Natasha and whatever their bastard was called. Vladimir Kyrilovich understood this. It was a natural sentiment, in so many ways a Russian sentiment. As he had sat by his fireside in Siberia, he wondered whether the next knock on the door would herald the troops come to arrest him or the avenging wrath of the Vicomte de Saint-Victor, the son of a notorious atheist and enemy of the natural ordering of humanity. But then he learned that Kermorvant had left Russia to return home to France. The death of his wife and son had plainly unhinged him, for what man with a noble title, even one defined and defiled by the enormous sins of his father, would go to France of his own free will? The cursed country had beheaded its divinely anointed king and would do the same to its queen. It was summarily executing dozens, sometimes hundreds, of those of Kermorvant's rank, each and every day. To all intents and purposes, it had abolished God. To Bulgakov, the only rational explanation was that his erstwhile brother-in-law, tormented by the deaths of his wife and child, had gone mad and chosen to commit suicide by the agency of *Madame Guillotine*.

He had thought more than twice when Foreign Minister Osterman wrote to him unexpectedly to offer him the embassy to Corsica. Even more unexpected was the fact that Bulgakov's name had been recommended for the position not only by the Tsarevich Paul but also by Count Vorontsov, the ambassador in London, whom Bulgakov could not recall ever meeting. But the means no longer mattered. The end was all, and that end was Corsica. In name at least, the island had been a part of France until the English took it, and it was uncomfortably close to the shore of Philippe Kermorvant's country. But even if Kermorvant was somehow not dead, he was a Breton and so was likely to be at the opposite extremity of France if he was not at sea, commanding a ship on some far distant ocean. Besides, how would Kermorvant possibly learn that he, Vladimir Kyrilovich Bulgakov, was in Corsica? And Corsica was an armed camp, full of enemies of the bastard French Republic, so a single Frenchman had no hope of reaching him. Besides, the posting to Corsica was undoubtedly a promotion, even if it was a kingdom only in name and, in truth, a mere puppet of England. Surely the empress could not live much longer, so all Bulgakov had to do was to fulfil his minimal duties in Corsica quietly and efficiently, awaiting the accession of the soon-to-be Emperor Paul who would surely summon him back to Saint Petersburg and complete his rehabilitation.

All in all, Corsica was even more of a backwater than Dresden, albeit with the benefit of better weather.

'Vladimir Kyrilovich.'

His name came from nowhere, from somewhere in the thick-scented *maquis* all around. He turned and saw that his two escorts, red-uniformed British soldiers, had been captured and disarmed without a sound by half-a-dozen roughly dressed peasants who seemed to have emerged silently out of nowhere. Their leader was a black-clad man with a bushy beard of the same colour, a fashion Bulgakov had not seen since leaving Russia.

'Vladimir Kyrilovich.'

Perhaps it was one of the spirits of the dead that every Corsican claimed to see and hear—

Philippe Kermorvant emerged from the tangle of bushes. Just behind him was a woman, dressed in the unseemly garb of boots, trousers, shirt and tunic, exactly like the men who held Bulgakov's escorts prisoner.

'Kill him, Philippe,' said the woman.

The Vicomte de Saint-Victor drew out a pistol, raised it and straightened his arm, aiming directly for Bulgakov's eyes.

—

'*Kill him*,' insisted Carla Leandri with greater urgency. 'This is the vengeance you've sought for so long, Philippe. This is where your vendetta ends. You have the right. Kill him.'

Philippe was grim-faced, his expression the hardest she had ever seen. Yet there was hesitation. The gun remained fixed on the Russian, but he did not pull the trigger.

'Philippe?' she said.

He blinked. Then he bent his elbow and raised the pistol skyward.

'Swords,' he said.

'*What?* You want a duel? You want to give him a chance? Did he give Tasha and Ivan a chance? Kill him, Philippe, or else let me do it!'

'No. It is not honourable. It's not what men like us do.'

Bulgakov's eyes darted from one to the other.

'Men like you?' Carla was incredulous. 'Men like *him* are nothing but wild animals. Put an end to him, Philippe! Avenge your wife and son, as a Corsican would!'

'No,' said Philippe Kermorvant. 'Swords, and to the death. You agree, Bulgakov?'

The Russian's expression bore equal measures of confusion and relief. Suddenly he could see a way out of his seemingly impossible situation.

'To the death. As you say, Vicomte.'

He inclined his head to his erstwhile brother-in-law and smiled.

Carla Leandri took an instant dislike to Count Bulgakov. Even setting aside her knowledge of the horror he had committed, she studied his ridiculous moustache, his womanly hands, his slight build and his insistence on wearing the height of fashion – dainty buckled shoes, no less! – on a mountain walk during the Corsican autumn. He spoke perfect French, as did every diplomat the world over, but his voice was harsh and unpleasant. Even if she had not known any of the previous history of the combatants, nor enjoyed the sins of the flesh with Philippe Kermorvant, she knew which of the two duellists she would favour. She also knew that Bulgakov would never have given Philippe the chance he was now being offered.

Beneath a nearby bush was a small cache of weapons, muskets, pistols and several swords. Philippe picked up his, the cutlass of an officer of the Marine Nationale. Bulgakov's sword already hung at his side, and he drew it. The weapon was a slender, elegant rapier that looked pristine.

'You can be the judge of the contest, Carla,' said Philippe.

'Judgement is already passed,' she said emphatically. 'If you fall, I kill him. Whatever happens in your little show of noble chivalry, you die in this place, Russian.'

'And if you don't kill him, *Generalissima*, rest assured that I will,' said Luc Giordano, standing by the Russian ambassador's British guards.

'You are like no Corsican woman I have met, mademoiselle,' said Bulgakov. 'I have met very few of your kind in any nation.'

'The worse for humanity,' said Carla.

'When I win, I will appeal to your mercy.'

'And will receive none. Corsica is a land where mercy has never been much in vogue, especially not to men who kill their own flesh and blood.'

Vladimir Kyrilovich Bulgakov nodded in silent salute to the woman who would kill him, he now knew, if Philippe Kermorvant did not. There would be no escape after all.

The two duellists took their positions and adopted their stances.

'*En garde*,' said Carla.

She dropped her hand as the signal to begin. The blades clashed, the echo ringing off the granite cliffsides, and the two men engaged.

Carla saw at once that the styles were entirely different. Philippe relied on diagonal cuts and slashes, the stroke that best suited the cutlass. His technique was crude and brutal, fashioned in engagements on sea and land since he was a boy. Bulgakov, though, was the epitome of elegant thrusting and parrying, of little feints and bluffs learned in the fencing schools of Saint Petersburg, of nimble footwork and rapid adjustment. The blades clashed constantly, but neither man seemed able to gain an advantage. They circled each other, looking for an opening.

At first, Bulgakov was the more aggressive, pressing forward with quick and threatening thrusts. Philippe parried each attack competently, but his own attacks lacked finesse and were easily evaded by Bulgakov. The blades clashed time and again, the clash of steel ringing around the hillsides and down into the valley below. Surely the noise would be noticed. Surely it would attract the attention of a British patrol, or a detachment of Paoli's militia. But apart from Carla, Giordano, their fellow Corsicans, their British prisoners and the two antagonists, the only other living creatures in sight were a straggling herd of goats, high on the slope above them and utterly uninterested in the deadly proceedings below.

Philippe feinted left, then swung at Bulgakov's side. But the Russian had anticipated such a move and daintily shifted his weight to avoid the attack, then responded with a rapid and skilful counter-thrust of his own. This time, the blade struck home.

Philippe was hit, and Carla suppressed a scream. But it was only a scratch, the arm of his shirt torn and a little blood drawn. The vigorous slashing movements of Philippe's cutlass were slowly wearing down the Russian's defence, each blow to the raised rapier threatening to break the elegant blade in two. There was complete silence from Carla's men and their captives, the two British soldiers. The protagonists circled and circled again, neither gaining the upper hand. Philippe made a savage onslaught, cutting hard for Bulgakov's head, but the Russian weaved out of the way. Philippe's attack had been too vigorous – he had left his flank exposed – Bulgakov thrust for the gap, for the terrible old wound made by a Turk's scimitar, the still-savage line of which Carla had traced with her fingers—

Philippe yelped as the point of Bulgakov's blade scraped his side, drawing fresh blood from the old wound. He lost his balance and staggered a pace backward. Bulgakov pressed forward for the kill. Carla screamed, and the sudden sound distracted the Russian. It was only for a moment, but it was enough time for Philippe to recover his balance and parry Bulgakov's next savage thrust.

The two duellists circled each other. Philippe was in pain and trying to adopt a stance that protected his open wound, but it was clear to him and to Carla that Bulgakov was tiring rapidly. An elegant courtier and diplomat lacked the endurance of a seaman, and Bulgakov's breathing was getting more laboured by the moment. He attempted another attack, but Philippe parried it, then made a fresh onslaught of his own which drove

Bulgakov back and nearly penetrated his guard. The envoy backed away, parrying every fresh assault from his erstwhile brother-in-law. But Vladimir Kyrilovich Bulgakov was dressed for a court reception in Saint Petersburg, not for rough Corsican mountain paths. He made to step back once more, but his elegant shoe caught a loose rock. Bulgakov lost balance and stumbled backward, instinctively putting out his free arm to break his fall. Philippe saw his opening and swept his cutlass upward, knocking the Russian's sword from his hand. Bulgakov fell heavily to the dusty soil, looked around desperately and tried to stretch out for his weapon. But Carla kicked it away, out of the envoy's reach, and Bulgakov looked up to see Philippe Kermorvant standing over him, the cutlass pointing toward his heart.

'*Szhal'sya!*' Bulgakov raised his right arm, presenting the flat of his hand raised in the age-old gesture of surrender. 'Show pity, Philippe! Have mercy, brother!'

'And did Tasha cry *Szhal'sya* too? Did she beg you, her true brother, for mercy before you cut her and your nephew to pieces? Is that what happened that day, Bulgakov?'

The envoy had no answer. His eyes reddened but he kept his hand raised as though his palm alone could repel the final, fatal blow when it came. Vladimir Kyrilovich Bulgakov began to murmur the words of the fifty-first psalm, the *Miserere*, in his native tongue.

'*Have mercy upon me, O God, after thy great goodness; according to the multitude of thy mercies do away mine offences. Wash me thoroughly from my wickedness, and cleanse me from my sin. For I acknowledge my faults, and my sin is ever before me...*'

—

Philippe recognised the words, even though his command of Bulgakov's and Tasha's language was rudimentary.

He readied his sword arm for the final, fatal thrust. Nearly every day in the years since the man on the ground before him had killed his wife and son, Philippe had dreamed of the moment when Vladimir Kyrilovich Bulgakov was defeated and at his mercy. He would avenge Tasha and Ivan by taking the life of the man who had slaughtered them, destroying Philippe Kermorvant's only two loves by doing so. He had imagined countless ways by which Bulgakov would die at his hand. Now the reality lay before him.

He had killed many men. He had thrust swords into their hearts and bellies, heard the gurgling of the death-blood in their throats, watched their eyes glaze over as they left this world and their mortal husk. Bulgakov was just one more man he had defeated and would be one more victim of his sword. Philippe had more reason to kill him than any of the others he had despatched. One sword thrust and it would be over at last.

'*Deliver me from blood-guiltiness, O God,*' mumbled Bulgakov, '*thou that art the God of my health; and my tongue shall sing of thy righteousness. Thou shalt open my lips, O Lord, and my mouth shall show thy praise. For thou desirest no sacrifice—*'

No sacrifice.

Philippe had sought Vladimir Kyrilovich Bulgakov's death with every breath and every thought. But he could not do it. Would not do it. The death of their murderer would not bring back Tasha and Ivan, nor the fleeting months of happiness they had known in Russia. Bulgakov would be just one more death among the countless thousands that had taken place in France and on the battlefields of Europe. What purpose would his killing serve?

Philippe raised his sword. Bulgakov stared up at him, uncomprehending. Philippe seemed to be about to speak, then changed his mind and began to turn away. Bulgakov reached down to snatch at the newly purchased Corsican stiletto concealed within his tunic jacket.

The shot sent the birds of the mountainside screaming skyward. The bullet blew away Vladimir Kyrilovich Bulgakov's right temple. Philippe turned back to see the shattered head of the dead Russian envoy strike the Corsican earth and the stiletto fall from his hand into the dust. Philippe looked to his left and saw Carla standing stock still, the pistol that had killed Bulgakov still smoking in her hand. Luc Giordano was staring at her in astonishment.

'It wasn't honourable,' Philippe whispered. 'He had surrendered.'

She lowered the fatal pistol.

'And reneged on his surrender. He would have killed you with that stiletto, even though he knew Luc and I would have killed him anyway moments later.' She looked down at the corpse of Vladimir Kyrilovich Bulgakov. 'But your vendetta is done now, Philippe. The souls of Tasha and Ivan can be at peace for all eternity. It's over.'

Philippe staggered and Carla rushed forward to support him, then insisted on attending to the wound in his side.

'It needs a surgeon,' she said as she staunched the bleeding. 'I know one who'll come out from Corte. He won't ask questions about how a lone Frenchman comes to have a duelling wound out here.'

She turned and nodded to Giordano, who made an almost imperceptible gesture to the men under his command. Wordlessly they cut the throats of the two British soldiers.

'No witnesses,' said Carla Leandri coldly. 'The viceroy and everyone else need to think that the Russian ambassador foolishly went out for a walk in the hills and that he and his guards were killed by bandits. Such a pity that none of their bodies will ever be found. Unfortunate, but such things happen here.'

Philippe grimaced as another stab of pain washed over him.

'I was the one who should have decided his fate, Carla,' he said between gasps. 'That was the rule. That was the honourable course.'

She smiled.

'But, Monsieur le Vicomte,' she said, 'you made me the judge. *Pe far lato vendetta,*

Sta sigur, vasta anche ella, as our old song puts it. In your tongue, "But, be assured, even she is competent to wreak thy vengeance". So I judged. I wreaked vengeance in the name of my lost sister Natasha. Judgement was given, and the sentence executed. Is that not the rock upon which justice stands?'

A little way away and without needing orders, Carla's and Giordano's men were already digging three shallow graves. That was the way of things in Corsica. That was the way of the vendetta.

HISTORICAL NOTE

The Anglo-Corsican kingdom of 1794–6, and the military campaign that enabled it to come into being, is now almost wholly unknown in Britain. It was not so much a road not taken of history as a pointless wrong turning into a dead end. The essential course of events, and the *raison d'être* for one of the oddest international unions in history, is essentially as outlined in the story: the Corsican leader, Pasquale Paoli, horrified by the revolutionary excesses in France, sought to re-establish the independent Corsica that he had briefly led in the 1750s and 1760s, while Britain sought a naval base in the Mediterranean from which to conduct operations against Toulon, the dockyard and town retaken by the French republicans in December 1793, this being the first major success for a young and previously unknown artillery officer called Napoleon Bonaparte. The Crown of Corsica was duly offered to King George the Third and Sir Gilbert Elliot was installed as viceroy, much to Paoli's chagrin as the native leader undoubtedly had unrealistic expectations of securing the post for himself. This began a rapid rift between the two parties, the British largely indifferent to Corsican aspirations and the Corsicans, in turn, increasingly disillusioned with their foreign rulers. The situation worsened in 1795 when Spain changed sides and joined the war on the French side, rendering all the British footholds in the Mediterranean desperately vulnerable. In October 1796, the British evacuated the island, leaving it open to reoccupation and political integration by France. For narrative purposes I have taken some slight liberties with the sequence of events in Corsica in June and July 1794, and also with the events outlined in the final chapter, where I have pushed back the debates upon the doomed Whig peace motion by six months and brought forward the arrival of the Russian squadron to join Admiral Adam Duncan's command by a few months more.

Some might raise eyebrows at the presumption of any author who dares to include both Napoleon and Nelson in the same story, even if he has tried to preserve a little mystery by anonymising them. Yet Philippe Kermorvant, or a real contemporary figure, actually could have met both men in the space of a few weeks in June and July 1794, when they were geographically the nearest to each other that they would ever be. Both men are so famous that their movements can be and have been chronicled day by day for most of their adult lives. At the time when most of the action in *Tyranny's Bloody Standard* is set, Nelson was in command of HMS *Agamemnon* off Corsica and played a prominent part in the siege of Calvi, where he famously lost the sight in his right eye (although it is unlikely that this ever needed to be bandaged). At the same time, Napoleon was less than two hundred miles away, moving back and forth between Marseille and Nice – a journey that would potentially have taken him through the village of Le Muy, which is a real place now bypassed by the A8 autoroute through the hills of Provence. He came from a family that had always been hugely prominent in Corsican politics, and he had been on the island as recently as May 1793. He had once idolised Pascal Paoli, although they had fallen out over the course the French Revolution was taking; the Bonaparte family as a whole was ordered into exile by Paoli in 1793.

By one of those odd quirks of history, another renowned figure of the Napoleonic age happened to be in Corsica in the summer of 1794 and would certainly have known Horatio Nelson there. The 'Colonel Moore' who appears as a character in Chapter Fifteen would ultimately die as General Sir John Moore, victor of the Battle of Corunna in 1809 and who, like

Nelson, fell in battle knowing that his victory was assured. He was immortalised in the poem (much beloved of the Victorians) 'The Burial of Sir John Moore after Corunna' by Charles Wolfe:

Not a drum was heard, not a funeral note,
As his corse to the rampart we hurried;
Not a soldier discharged his farewell shot
O'er the grave where our hero we buried.

We buried him darkly at dead of night,
The sods with our bayonets turning;
By the struggling moonbeam's misty light
And the lantern dimly burning.

No useless coffin enclosed his breast,
Nor in sheet nor in shroud we wound him,
But he lay like a warrior taking his rest
With his martial cloak around him...

Of all the major Corsican characters in this book, only the Leandris are fictitious. Pasquale Paoli, of course, was very much a real personage, one of the most famous men of the age. His two periods of exile in Britain, the first lasting nearly a quarter of a century, brought him into contact with many of the leading men of the Georgian era from King George the Third downward. He knew the likes of David Garrick, Edmund Burke, Horace Walpole, Fanny Burney and Sir Joshua Reynolds. He was lionised by James Boswell, who thought him a noble, selfless classical hero set down in a different age, and wrote a pen portrait of the Corsican that bordered on hagiography. The constitution that Paoli devised and implemented in the fleetingly free state of Corsica in 1755, inspired by the works of Rousseau and Montesquieu, was far and away the most advanced democratic system of its time, containing such radical provisions as the proclamation of the sovereignty of the people and universal male suffrage with no property qualification. The much-vaunted French Republic of 'liberty, equality and fraternity' proclaimed in 1792 was nothing like as democratic; nor, it must be said, was the Constitution of the United States of America, which had come into effect three years earlier.

Pozzo di Borgo had perhaps one of the most extraordinary careers of the Napoleonic era (quite some bragging right). After serving as the *de facto* prime minister of Corsica during the Anglo-Corsican kingdom he spent several years in exile, wandering between different European courts, before ending up in Russia, where his considerable political and diplomatic skills were recognised and his vehement hatred of the Bonapartes was a useful asset. During an interlude in London he had an affair with Emily Lamb, Countess Cowper, sister to one future prime minister of the United Kingdom (Lord Melbourne) and wife to another (Lord Palmerston). Returning to Russia, the tsar employed him to convince the *de facto* ruler of Sweden, the Frenchman Marshal Bernadotte, to enter the war against Napoleon. Pozzo di Borgo was at the Battle of Waterloo, was one of the Russian delegates to the Congress of Vienna, and subsequently served for many years as Russia's ambassador to the restored French monarchy. Transferred to London, he had a markedly difficult relationship with the foreign secretary, Lord Palmerston, who knew full well that Pozzo di Borgo had once been his wife's lover. Pozzo di Borgo is one of those historical characters who demands to have a novel written about him and a film to be made of the novel, but his career was so multinational, his status in any individual nation probably not quite notable or heroic enough, that it is unlikely ever to happen.

As for my irreverent mistreatment of the bones of Christopher Columbus: to this day the people of Corsica claim the great navigator as one of their sons, and proudly advertise a ruin in Rue Del-Filo, Calvi, as the house where he was born, the son of a local fisherman. Some of the arguments that have been put forward over the years to support this claim are advanced by Ercule Leandri in Chapter Twelve. Some of these, it has to be said, are rather tenuous and often rely on coincidence and wishful thinking. For example, why would Columbus name Haiti after the obscure Corsican village of Aiti, some forty miles from his supposed birthplace of Calvi, when he could have chosen from countless more notable Corsican place names? Having said that, there is a considerable amount of uncertainty about Columbus's actual burial place. He died in Valladolid and was first buried there, but in 1537 his bones were moved to the new cathedral of Santa Domingo, now in the Dominican Republic, according with his wish to be buried in the Americas. During the fighting between France and Spain on the island in 1794–5, alluded to in the text, the bones were moved to Havana for safety, and were supposedly later moved to Seville in 1898 when Spain was again at war in the region, this time with the United States. However, in 1877 workmen in Santo Domingo cathedral had discovered a leaden box with an inscription declaring that the box contained the mortal remains of Columbus. This generated a theory that the wrong remains had been taken to Havana and then Seville. The remains in Seville have been DNA tested and are an exceptionally close match to those of Columbus's son. Perhaps unsurprisingly, Santo Domingo refuses DNA testing of the remains it holds. Given this extraordinary saga, perhaps the idea of Columbus's remains being used as a bargaining chip to sway a Corsican rebel leader in 1794 is not too fanciful after all!

For those who are interested in such things, Philippe's command, *Le Torrington*, is based loosely on the Minerva-class frigates built for the Royal Navy from 1778 onward. As Lord Wilden mentions in Chapter Four, and unlikely though it may seem, the prime minister of Naples during this period was a Shropshire baronet, Sir John Acton, whose branch of the family had long been domiciled in Italy. Curiously, Acton was also a seaman and had risen to the rank of admiral; he was well known to Sir William and Emma, Lady Hamilton.

My description of the siege dispositions around Calvi is based on the contemporary drawings of the scene made from the exact position where I have placed Philippe, now preserved as MPK1/12/1 and 2 at the National Archives. The Royal Louis Regiment, a unit of French royalist exiles serving as part of the British Army, was indeed there during 1794. Unlikely though it may sound, Johann, Baron von Flachslanden, was a real person, and he held the real position of turcopilier of the Military Order of the Knights of Saint John of Malta. Rear-Admiral Sebastien Fidelin is my invention, but Jeanbon Saint-André was a very real person (although I have no doubt that he was rather less potty-mouthed than I have made him out to be). After reorganising the fleet and dockyard at Brest in 1793, which was where and when Philippe Kermorvant encountered him in *Sailor of Liberty*, he returned to Paris, promulgated the strict new disciplinary code alluded to during this book, and then went to Toulon in the summer of 1794, the timing of his move there being remarkably convenient for the chronology of my story. Being able legitimately to place Saint-André in both Brest and then Toulon a year later was one of those rare occasions for an author when a coincidence that would seem completely outrageous if it was invented (a bit like the fanciful meetings between Queen Elizabeth I and Mary Queen of Scots in every film ever made about the latter) actually happened in real life.

Malta prides itself on 'three hundred days of sunshine', but the weather that destroys Salvatore Guidici and his ship, *San Giacomo*, is by no means an implausible plot device. The *gregale* brings severe storms and flooding to the islands even in summer (as in August 2022) while in September 1555 Valletta was devastated by a cyclone that killed some six hundred people.

Like many writers on Corsica I owe a huge debt to the books of Dorothy Carrington, whose eye for detail was extraordinary, whose insights were always perceptive, and whose deep empathy for the land and its people shines through every sentence. My depictions of the *mazzeri*, the *voceru* and other Corsican customs, as well as of the country itself, owe a great deal to her. The other indispensable source for the island, certainly for the period I have written about, is James Boswell's *Account of Corsica*, based on a visit he paid in the 1760s. To this was appended a detailed eyewitness description of Pasquale Paoli with an account of Boswell's conversations with him. I have drawn much of my own pen picture of Paoli from Boswell.

The drinking song quoted in the Prologue, 'To Anacreon in Heaven', was contemporary to the time, although it was originally sung by rather more refined company as the song of the aristocratic Anacreonitic Society. Its tune is rather better known these days as that of 'The Star-Spangled Banner', the national anthem of the United States of America.

There was no recorded riot in Stourport-on-Severn in 1794, although the first incarnation of the town's bridge, the one over which Jenkins and Lord Wilden attempted to drive, did collapse in that year. However, the population of the fledgling canal port at that time did contain two residents named William and Edward Drew, father and thirteen-year-old son. William was a bargebuilder, a trade followed in later years by his son. Edward and William Drew were, respectively, my four- and five-times great-grandfather.

By a bizarre coincidence, I began sketching out the ideas for *Tyranny's Bloody Standard* in the week when France's President Macron tentatively offered autonomy to Corsica in a bid to defuse growing nationalist discontent and violence, many strands of which can be traced back directly to the events referred to in this book. The striking and unique flag bearing the Moor's head, black upon white, still flies in Pasquale Paoli's erstwhile nation.

ACKNOWLEDGEMENTS

Thanks as always to Kit Nevile and the wonderful team at Canelo for their support and hard work on behalf of *Tyranny's Bloody Standard*, and thanks once again to my ever-supportive agent, Peter Buckman. Yet another big thank you, too, to Wendy, 'beta reader one', for her indispensable critical eye, editorial input, cups of tea and cakes.

The main ideas for this book were sketched out during a stay at a Landmark Trust property in March 2022. Over the years, Landmark has provided me with many tranquil and pleasurable opportunities for 'brainstorming' as well as simple 'R and R', so I thought it was high time I acknowledged the important contribution to my work of their wonderful properties. Finally, a big and long overdue 'thank you' to you, my readers. Perhaps you've read most or even all of my books since the early days of 'the journals of Matthew Quinton' (in which case you probably deserve a medal, or at the very least for me to buy you a drink!), or maybe this is the first title of mine that you've come across. Whether you're a seasoned *loup de mer* or a *matelot d'eau douce*, you're my reason for typing 'Chapter One' at the top of a page when every new book gets under way!

David Davies
Bedfordshire, May 2023